THE GANGLAND SAGAS OF BIG NOSE SERRANO

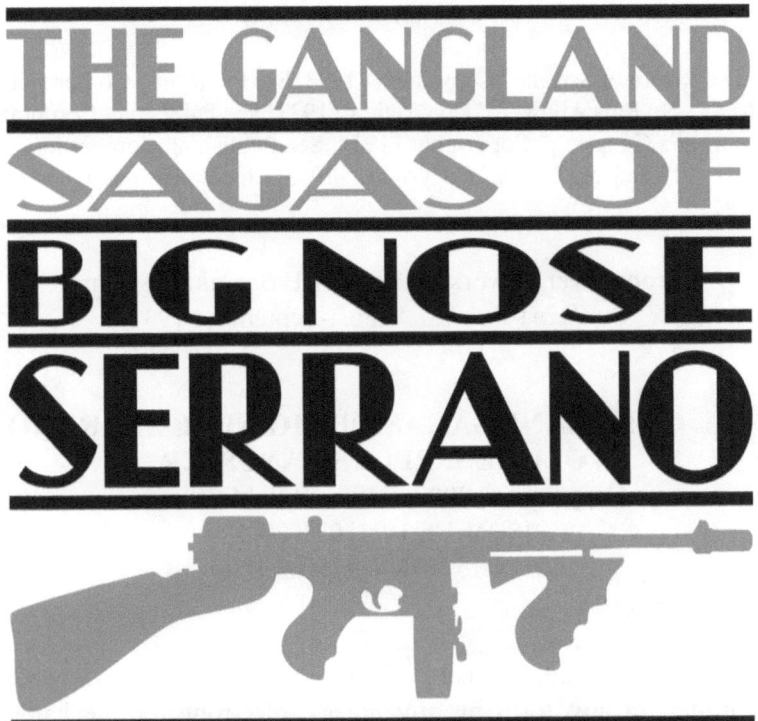

VOLUME 3: HELL'S GANGSTER

Off-Trail Publications

Elkhorn, California

Thanks to John Gunnison for all the help.

Front cover artwork by Walter M. Baumhofer from
Speakeasy Stories, August-September 1931

**THE GANGLAND SAGAS OF BIG NOSE SERRANO
VOLUME 3: HELL'S GANGSTER**
Copyright © 2009, Off-Trail Publications
ISBN-10: 1-935031-07-4
ISBN-13: 978-1-935031-07-9

OFF-TRAIL PUBLICATIONS
Castroville, CA 95012
offtrail@redshift.com

Printed in the United States of America
First printing: February 2009

CONTENTS

Of my broad felt made lighter,
I cast my mantle broad,
And stand, poet and fighter,
To do and to record.
I bow, I draw my sword.
En garde! with steel and wit
I play you at first abord . . .
At the last line, I hit!

—CYRANO DE BERGERAC

Robin Hoodlum
By Will Murray

AND SO WE COME AT LAST, with an abiding sadness, to the final volume of the riotous saga of Big Nose Serrano.

These are the declining days of the Sheik of the Stockyards. Felled, not by gangster or police bullets, but a combination of Repeal, blue-nosed censors, and the formidable-nosed Shadow. After three entire magazines were shot out from under him, Big Nose finally succumbed. Pulp magazine readers were on a brand new tear. It read: Crime Does Not Pay.

In keeping with the literature of kings of all eras, the saga of Big Nose Serrano partakes of tragedy. Here his sad fall from power is recorded.

Who is Big Nose Serrano, you ask?

Imagine a cross between Jimmy Durante and Conan the Barbarian.

You say your head hurts? Let's try again.

Imagine a cross between Cyrano de Bergerac and Jimmy Durante. Now *that* picture is clear. Both have big noses and outsized personalities to match.

Now cross Cyrano with Conan. That almost works. Hold that thought.

Next take your Cyrano-Conan hybrid and cross him with the Cyrano-Durante concoction. It begins to jell, does it not?

Finally, fold into this mélange Al "Scarface" Capone, then drop him in Prohibition Chicago. Throw in a dash of Robin Hood, add a seasoning of Don Quixote. Simmer with bootleg booze.

And you have the immortal Big Nose Serrano, bandit-chieftain of old Chicago.

Let me begin by quashing the ridiculous rumor that Big Nose Serrano was nothing more than an alias of The Shadow during that mysterious period between the Great War and his emergence in a magazine of his own early in 1931.

True, the similarities are striking: Intimidating nose, gargantuan laugh, gigantic automatics, doom to gangsters, etc. True also, Big Nose wore a derby as often as he affected a slouch hat, but that is a mere bagatelle of detail. One sang, the other laughed. They were two different men. Case closed.

The undeniable fact that both were illustrated by Tom Lovell is just one of those things.

But for the record, Shadow creator Walter Gibson never mentioned Big Nose Serrano to me. And Street & Smith would never have this lug. Hell, even *Black Mask* wouldn't dare print him! Damon Runyon would have been terrified of him.

Now, to address another rumor, I don't know what pulp magazines Robert

E. Howard was reading in the period leading up to his creation of Conan the Cimmerian in 1932. But my money is on *Gangster Stories*.

Consider the parallels:

Both rose from humble banditry beginnings to oversee a vast, sprawling empire, having earned their bones as bruising barroom brawlers.

Neither one, while tactically gifted and demon-possessed in battle, were very bright. They preferred to slug and slay their way out of trouble.

Both warriors possessed an uncanny sixth sense in battle, but not otherwise.

Both drank and wenched like nobody's business.

Serrano, when challenged, pounded his chest like a gorilla. Well, that was technically Tarzan of the Apes. But the Ape Man and Conan were practically cousins, so we'll count it anyway.

Both were, despite doubtful ethics and low morals, unquestionably on the side of the underdog.

Finally, both anti-heroes were the kings of their respective sub-genres, never to be equaled.

Big Nose Serrano was born in 1930 when a failed playwright improbably named Anatole France Feldman converted Edmond Rostand's classic play *Cyrano de Bergerac* into a pulp novel, *Serrano of the Stockyards*, for publisher Harold Hersey's *Gangster Stories*. The big guy went over big, no doubt thanks to the huge happy helping of schmaltz Feldman schmeared over his creation.

Introduced as a special agent who infiltrates the underworld in order to undermine it, Big Nose either succumbed to the wine, women and wealth that went with his cover, or author Feldman clean forgot the premise. More likely, that premise was concocted to avoid charges of glorifying gangsters— and conveniently forgotten as Feldman's gargantuan hero took the Windy City by storm.

A true force of nature, the Beaked Berserker stormed through the pages of *Gangster Stories* all through 1930-32, until the worsening Depression and soaring crime rates caused the celebrity hoodlum to fall out of public favor like a Republican office-holder.

At the end of 1932, *Gangster Stories* collapsed under these twin weights. But the very next year, Hersey revived it as *Greater Gangster Stories*. For ten long months, it was as if Big Nose slept, a lily clutched in his hammy paws. That glorious summer, under pressure of popular acclaim, *Greater Gangster's* star writer produced *The Return of Serrano*. Cue the fanfare and trumpets.

It was a resurrection worthy of a Sun God. Having slaughtered the sinister Spider in his previous exploit, Big Nose reverts to business as usual. No explanation is ever given as to what happened to his career as assemblyman of Chicago's Bloody Tenth Ward. But it's not hard to guess the reasons: Politics was doubtless too much like going straight for the big galoot. When, in *The Return of Serrano*, he refers to having "served time" in the State Legislature, Big Nose wasn't woofing. Yet according to one later account, he is still operates as a ward boss, so rumors of his impeachment for malfeasance remain unfounded.

As this volume opens, the big boy oversees his own night club, complete with a hot jazz band. But the Great Depression had really begun to bite. And when the downtrodden are being trampled, Big Nose rears up like the Windy City Napoleon that he is, and once again goes Robin Hooding in a saga that while 75 years old, is strangely relevant to today's 21st Century mortgage and bank catastrophe.

In 1933 Franklin D. Roosevelt was the newly-elected President of the United States. Swept into office on his promise to right the foundering ship of state, he promptly initiated the New Deal, beginning with the National Recovery Act, passed by a highly-motivated Congress in June of '33. It allowed the President to regulate banks, as well as set wage and price controls calculated to stabilize the faltering economy.

Ever the patriot, Big Nose hoists his own battle flag for democracy in *N.R.A.—No Rats Allowed*. Perhaps it will come as no surprise to his fans that the erstwhile Serrano of the Stockyards was a prominent if bare-knuckled early New Dealer.

But a final sunset lay in store for the Colossus of Chicago. For Roosevelt had come to power on the strength of quite another promise—one not in keeping with Big Nose's illicit agenda.

Part of the social revolution wrought by the Great Depression was a realization that Prohibition wasn't working. On December 5, 1933, Repeal was enacted. The Volstead Act was dead. Beer again flowed legally. The citizens could drink freely again. Crime Lords went legit, or slithered into other less socially-acceptable venues. Eliot Ness' Untouchables nailed Capone for tax evasion. J. Edgar Hoover's F.B.I. was on the rise. A new reality was taking hold.

The Repeal of the Eighteenth Amendment was to Big Nose and his cohorts, in Durante's immortal phrase, "a catastrastroke." The Napoleon of the Midwest had met his Waterloo.

This tragedy was recorded in *Hell's Gangster*, a rambunctious Irish wake for the speakeasy era in which the Windy City wildman must for the first time in his rollicking life, figure out how to make an honest buck. Inevitably, this new endeavor revolved around battling thugs less savory than he.

Manfully Big Nose soldiered on, his prodigious nose "radiating energy" Rudolph-the-Red-Nosed-Reindeer-style, no more sober, and hardly any wiser than before, on through to the eventual demise of *Greater Gangster Stories*.

Public condemnation had dogged Hersey and *Gangster Stories* from the start. Chased off newsstands in some cities, Hersey persevered through threats, legal action, and unsold-copy returns. His readers loved his salty, frank fare—and imagined they were getting an unvarnished inside look at the real Underworld. Maybe they were.

Unfortunately, a satiated pulp public soon moved on, broke, disillusioned and captivated by a new trend toward crime-busting—mystery men like The Shadow, The Spider and The Phantom Detective.

Did the blue-noses bump off Big Nose? Or did Harold Hersey kill the goose that laid the golden Chicago pineapple by recklessly adding *Gangland Stories*, *Racketeer Stories*, and *Prison Stories*—saturating the market with too much of a good thing?

History is unsure. But a careful search of the contents pages of all those semi-illicit Hersey magazines show that prolific as he was, there just wasn't enough Anatole France Feldman to go around.

Not that he didn't try. He wrote as Anthony Field, A.F. Fields, and probably other names too. Big Nose was merely the tip of his literary iceberg. He was the author of such cockeyed epics as *Sock Exchange*, *The Squeal Widow*, and the unforgettable *Tomorrow We Croak*.

Out of the wreckage of the gangster pulp sub-genre rose Lincoln Hoffman's *The Gang Magazine* in 1935. Big Nose returned yet again for his swan song.

This final outing brought him back to his rough roots, the stockyards of Chicago. *Lead and Lyrics* closed out what future historians may call the Serrano Story Cycle. Serrano ended his days defending the turf from which he had emerged, his final exploit a mere novelette. More were promised, but *The Gang Magazine* expired after three issues—snatching from a disappointed posterity any last Big Nose Serrano story Anatole France Feldman may or may not have penned.

Otherwise we might look forward to even more Big Nose yarns with such fanciful titles as "Broads, Booze and Bullets," and "Song and Slaughter." The Jimmy Durante catchphrase, "Wotta revoltin' development!" perfectly captures the morose sentiments of Serrano aficionados yearning for a fourth volume of *The Gangland Sagas of Big Nose Serrano*.

After The Shadow and his imitators routed the gang pulps, Feldman and his confederates—who included D.L. Champion (writing as "Jack D'Arcy"), Edwin Burkholder ("George Allan Moffatt"), and Feldman's wife, stage dancer turned pulpster Hedwig Langer Feldman (AKA "Beech Allen") switched sides. Three of them were responsible for many of the early exploits of The Phantom Detective, who if he ever went up against

Big Nose Serrano, might have enjoyed a much briefer career. The first years of *The Phantom Detective* coincided with the *Greater Gangster Stories* phase of Serrano's career, possibly explaining the big bruiser's otherwise-unaccountable absence from his usual haunts.

Feldman was the author of the infamous early Phantom novel, *The Tick-Tack-Toe Murders*. Infamous because although it was promised for the February 1934 issue, it was instead replaced by *Death's Diary*. No doubt the great Feldman blew his headline. The catastrophe was so absolute that when it did finally appear along with a lame editorial excuse for its delay, the house name G. Wayman Jones was summarily replaced by another mythical scribe, Robert Wallace. It was the first time in pulp history that a nonexistent author was fired off a series. Only Anatole France Feldman could have engineered such a feat.

Other illustrious alumni of Hersey's gang-magazine chain, George A. MacDonald, Norman A. Daniels, and future Thrilling editor-in-chief, Leo Margulies, also went on to shape the Phantom's pulp destiny.

Still another, one Adrian Lopez, was catapulted to even greater fame. Playing the horses one day, he placed a wad of dough on a nag named Volitant. The 20-to-1 shot came in first and Lopez walked away with a bundle. He promptly founded Volitant Publications, eventually hiring Anatole Feldman as one of his editors. This career stretched clear to the end of the '40s, if not beyond.

Comparatively little biography comes down to us of the life of Feldman. He was born in Cincinnati on April 7, 1896 of Russian parents. His first known publication is a soldier-poem in *The Outlook* in 1918, when only a lowly private stationed at Air Field No. #2 in Garden City, Long Island. He served with the Casual Detachment. Only Feldman could pull such a cushy duty in the midst of the Great War! But before he could achieve his dream of becoming a battle ace, he was unceremoniously mustered out on grounds of fraudulent enlistment. His play *The Red Thirst* was written in 1920. But Broadway appears to have spurned him. Still, he did a stretch as a theatrical manager's secretary, crossed the mighty oceans as a merchant seaman, and once paymastered an oilfield construction gang down Mexico way. Such is the stuff of his legend.

Feldman starts popping up in Harold Hersey pulps like *Ghost Stories* and *Flight* in 1929. He discovered that he could write by accident, while scrounging a living in Chicago. He made a big splash in the bullet-riddled pages of *The Underworld Magazine*, where his rough genius was first recognized by a mesmerized reading public. For four glorious years, Feldman blazed like a sub-literary comet in Hersey's string of gangster-themed magazines, the uncrowned yet undisputed king of gang pulp.

Feldman was briefly editor-publisher of *Far East Adventure Stories*, a short-lived adventure pulp. He may or may not have been identical to Arthur Feldman, who was editing true-crime magazines in the mid-'30s and wrote for Trojan Publications in the '40s. For the record, Anatole had a brother by this name, and he may also have made his mark in the world of letters. With an unerring instinct for bottom-of-the-barrel pulp houses, he pops up in Martin Goodman's *American Sky Devils* near the end of the decade. His credentials were typical for his breed: he once joked that he learned how to write air-war fiction riding up and down office elevators. No doubt he was actually reliving his crushed wartime dream of shooting down the Red Baron. Yet Feldman did manage a solitary sale to *Black Mask* in 1937. His byline wavers schizophrenically between Anthony Field and Anatole Fields.

As the '30s wound down, Feldman seems to have abandoned fiction to write for and edit entertainment and true-crime magazines for Volitant, Hillman and Harrison Publications. In that phase of his life, he was known as Tony Field, sometimes Fields. All through the '40s, he bounced back and forth between these three houses, stopping only to script the random radio programs like *Crime Photographer*, based on the Black Mask hero, Flashgun Casey. In 1943, he was reported to be working on a play. Indeed, the unproduced *Combined Operations* was so-authored by Hedwig that year. *Fire in the Flint* was registered for copyright in 1946. For a short period, he edited comic books for Hillman. But all trace of him seems to fade out circa 1949.

Under the name Anatole Field, he may have been residing in Boonton, New Jersey, where he ascended to his richly-deserved heavenly reward in May of 1972. Assuming this was he.

For the ultimate fate of Feldman remains as unknown as Big Nose Serrano's Christian name. But a century after his birth, his amazing legacy lives on.

Snub-nose revolver in one hand, red-nozzled Tommy-gun in the other, and a savage-snouted automatic in his teeth, this is Big Nose Serrano in his final blaze-of-glory days: Brawling and boozing, singing and slaughtering his way to immortality.

I don't know if the great Jimmy Durante ever came across a Big Nose Serrano story. I suppose he must have. As a former speakeasy owner himself, and one thrown into close contact with the lower denizens of Manhattan, no doubt *Gangster Stories* was unavoidable reading.

I can only imagine his reaction would have been the same as when Al Jolson started crooning a song meant for him in *Show Girl*. Schnozzola lay down on the stage and growled, "Everybody wantsta get into the act!"

ANNOUNCING

The Return of "Big Nose" Serrano

WITH a song on his lips and a gat in his hands "Big Nose" lives again in Anatole Feldman's thrilling story of GREATER GANGSTER'S most popular character. We didn't know how great his popularity was until you readers started flooding our desks with demand letters telling us that "Big Nose" just had to return. So that's what we've titled Feldman's latest yarn—"The Return of Serrano" and if you think his early escapades were breath-taking just wait until you've read this latest and greatest of all Serrano stories. It's got everything that you mean when you say: *"A great gangster story!"*

Don't miss this sensational feature in the September issue of GREATER GANGSTER STORIES—you'll say that this story alone is worth the price of the magazine.

Greater Gangster Stories, August 1933

The Return of Serrano

Oh, Ruby came to Big Nose
Loaded with a gat;
She said, "Give me a thousand dollars,
But I can't pay it back."
From the lyrics of Serrano.

"THE WHITES ARE C'S, THE RED FINIFS AND THE BLUES G'S."

With the usual preamble, Charlie LeBrett shoved the varied assortment of chips around the green baize table. There was Roaring McGinnis there, who had made his pile in a neat and discreet gin-mill up on State Street. Also present was Two-gun Goldstein, who, with the advent of prohibition, had turned from safe-cracking to alcohol-cracking and had made a neat fortune thereby.

And of course, to complete the quartette, there was Big Nose Serrano, his gargantuan nose more flamboyant, more warty, more pugnacious than ever.

Just a friendly little poker game between four of the boys who had graduated from the stockyards and the slaughterhouse to bigger and better things.

The cards were dealt. Big Nose tilted his derby far back over his cauliflower ears, unbuttoned his vest, shifted the wad of cut plug in his mouth and spat expertly at the nearest cuspidor. Above the lisp of cards and the clink of chips came the faint but insidious rhythm of the jazz band knocking out a hot blues number in the night club beyond.

Serrano's night club; Serrano's jazz band. And they both were playing to a packed house of suckers.

Serrano cocked one ear to the beat of the drums and he smiled; he cocked the other to the wails of the saxophone and he pursed his lips in a whistle. But just then a pair of muted trumpets cavorted in a weird falsetto and with an ominous rumble he cleared his throat preparatory to bursting into full song.

Fortunately for the rest of the players LeBrett caught the signs in time. He looked up sharply at Serrano, his dour and saturnine face cracking into an acid smile.

"Listen, Big Nose," he implored patiently, "are you playing poker or are you trying out for the Met? Save the little act for a more appreciative audience! Why in the hell you're a gunman is beyond me. If I had that voice and figure of yours, I'd team up with Fleusy Le Fleu as an adagio team with a duet as a sideline."

Big Nose swallowed at his Adam's apple, glared at LeBrett a moment, then shook his head sadly.

"Running true to form, eh, Charlie? Always crabbing the act. No appreciation of art! No appreciation of genius! And if I had that disposition of yours I'd take six bottles of Pluto Water and get over it."

LeBrett heard him out patiently. Then he reiterated: "Are we playing poker or ain't we?"

The game proceeded.

Some half-hour later came another interruption. The door to Serrano's private room back of his Frivolity Club was softly opened and softly closed again. The four men looked up, casually at first, then their eyes widened and as suddenly narrowed.

Without a word they took in the figure of the girl leaning against the portal. But it was not the fact that Ruby Taylor had entered, uninvited, into Serrano's private sanctum, that made them stare. More than one gilded lily had entered that back room uninvited or otherwise.

No; the thing that held the rapt attention of the men was the businesslike automatic that glinted evilly in the girl's right hand.

Serrano studied both the gun and the girl and, as usual in his amorous career, found the latter the most interesting. There was a suspicious fullness to Ruby's high bosom. Hips that had once been slender and supple had lost their former insinuating grace. As Winchell would have put it, by all the signs and portents, a blessed event was in the offing.

Big Nose gazed at the girl a moment, then cast a swift, accusing glance at the three men around the board. But he discovered no sign of guilty paternity in their sombre faces. He turned back to the girl.

"What is this, Ruby," he called easily, "a shot-gun wedding or a stick-up?"

No one smiled, least of all the girl.

"It's a stick-up, Big Nose," she answered desperately. "I need a grand—and I need it bad."

Serrano's gaze flirted with her oversize waist line, and a faint smile twitched at his lips, but he repressed the obvious crack that rumbled in his throat. With a ponderous hand he reached inside his coat and extracted a heavy wallet. He flicked it open, thumbed over a sheaf of golden-backed bank notes, and extracted a few. He extended them in his hand towards the girl.

"Okay, babe, come and get it."

An eager light sprang up in Ruby's eyes. With tentative hesitant steps she crossed the room towards the table. But so intent was she on securing the little fortune held out to her that she became careless with the automatic. Just as her fingers touched the crisp bills, Serrano's left hand shot out, caught her wrist and as gently as possible (always remembering her condition) twisted the gun from her hand.

Ruby's answer to this was to break into hysterical tears. Serrano dropped the captured gun into his pocket, heaved himself out of his chair and threw an awkwardly tender arm across the girl's shoulders. Gently he pushed the girl into the chair he had vacated.

"Easy, Ruby—easy," he begged. "Turn off the faucet."

At the gentleness in his voice her sobbing checked.

"Now what's it all about? Jeez, babe, you can get a grand from me any time, without coming gunning for it. What's the story?"

"You mean I can have the grand?" incredulously.

"Sure; more if you need it. Why the Jesse James act?"

Ruby clutched the bills with one hand and dabbed at her eyes and nose with the other.

"It's the bank, Big Nose," she began irrelevantly. "The Packers Bank and Trust. It went flooey—closed its doors."

Serrano nodded his head. He was beginning to see the light. Some few months back, Ruby had teamed up with Tommy Taylor. Their union had not only been solemnized by the Sovereign State of Illinois but by the genial Father Ryan of the notorious Stockyards Ward—the Tenth. And from that time on, Ruby and Tommy had gone it on the straight.

And now, from external evidences, it looked as if the state and Father

Ryan would have another function to solemnize.

"The bank goes bust! So what, Ruby?" prompted Serrano.

The girl looked coyly down at the table. "Tommy and I had all our dough in the bank. Now we can't get it. And—and . . ."

"And as you said before—you need it bad—damn bad!"

The girl nodded. Big Nose grinned and patted her hand.

"Well, you got your grand, kid. Let me know when the big event comes off and me and the boys will drive around with a truck load of beer. And if it's a boy . . ."

The proposition that Serrano was about to propound was cut off as Ruby rose in her chair, flung her arms around his neck and implanted a firm, moist kiss on the point of his bulbous nose. Then, with becoming modesty she was gone.

Serrano rubbed a calloused hand reflectively over the tip of his proboscis and for a moment stared blankly at the door through which the girl had retreated.

"Nice kid, Ruby," he commented.

"Yeah," agreed LeBrett. "And a lousy deal that bank gave the Tenth Ward."

"What's the story?"

LeBrett shrugged. "It's the same old story. Every poor sucker working in the yards who saved a cent put it in the Packers Trust. Morton gambled with it, cleaned up a couple of million for himself—then when things got tough let all his depositors hold the bag. It's a rotten deal."

"The rewards of virtue and industry," said Serrano portentously.

"Yeah, for the poor devils slaughtering beef at eighteen per week. Look at Banker P. Jay Morton and you'll call it the rewards of vice and high finance."

"I heard about it, but I didn't know it was as bad as that," said Serrano.

"It's worse than that," put in Goldstein. "The papers did a lot of squawking. The D.A. had Morton up on charges of embezzlement, but he beat the rap. He got clear of the courts today with an apology from the judge for wasting his time."

"Yeah," added McGinnis wryly. "And his pals are giving a big banquet to him tonight down at Webster Hall. I know! The dirty rats bought a dozen cases of Scotch from the Greek's and didn't even give me a tumble!"

"A banquet to Banker Morton, eh?" mused Big Nose.

"Yeah," answered LeBrett, "to celebrate his taking every honest man, woman and child in the Tenth over the hurdles."

"I'll admit that doesn't include us," replied Serrano, "but we're going to do something about it just the same."

"What?"

"We haven't been invited to that banquet, but we're going there nevertheless."

"And I'm going to bring at least one bottle of *good* whisky along," added McGinnis grimly.

"What are you going to do when you get there?" demanded LeBrett the practical.

Serrano turned on him. "How the hell do I know, Charlie? Jeez, I ain't no fortune teller! Ain't it enough that you got an invite to a swell banquet with Banker Morton? Come on, you guys, let's scram."

And as they sallied out of the door into the night club, the musical voice of Serrano drifted back. And these were the words of the lay he sang:

> *Oh, Ruby came to Big Nose*
> *Loaded with a gat;*
> *She said, "Give me a thousand dollars,*
> *But I can't pay it back."*

II

THE CRUSADE

SOME TWENTY MINUTES LATER an ebon sedan rolled to a silent halt before the garishly lit marquee of Webster Hall. Big Nose Serrano eased his massive bulk from behind the wheel, and followed by his three satellites, pounded his way up the flight of stone steps that led to the portal of the banquet hall.

In addition to the official doorman, the outer door was guarded by a low-browed, surly individual who watched the approach of the newcomers with a jaundiced eye.

To the polite request of the flunky for "tickets, please," Serrano planted his hamlike hand, gently but firmly, in that individual's startled face, heaved his shoulder and sent him sprawling down the hall beyond.

At this delicate juncture the second doorman projected himself into the discussion. Manfully he straddled his legs in the open doorway. His eyes narrowed and his bullet head sank down on squat shoulders.

"Say, what the hell's the big idea?" he demanded. "You guys can't crash in here!"

"No? Why not?" flung back Big Nose.

"Where's your tickets? This is by invite only."

"Oh, yeah? I had twenty bucks in Morton's bank. That'll cover the tax for the four of us. Are we going in like gents or are you going out like a bum?"

The guard made the fatal mistake of flashing for his hip. Serrano whooped gleefully: "He's going out like a bum!" His right fist flashed back and then forward with lightning precision. It collided with cataclysmic force flush on the point of the gorilla's chin. The guard forgot all about his gun. His knees buckled, his long arms flung upward in an imploring gesture to heaven and he collapsed into the waiting arms of LeBrett.

"Nailor," grunted LeBrett, as he eased his unconscious burden to the floor. "One of Venizelos' men."

"I should have hit him harder, then," answered Serrano. The battle light was in his eyes as he turned to the others. "I got a hunch this little party is going to turn out better than we planned. There may be fireworks if Venizelos' mob is here. After me, boys, and remember it's for the honor of the Old Tenth!"

With an arrogant swagger and his derby cocked aggressively over one eye he led the way down the long hall towards the double doors at the far end from behind which came the noise of high festivity. LeBrett and the other two crowded hard behind him, but it was a tribute to their good sense that they had already eased the guns in their shoulder holsters.

The distinguished banker of the Bloody Tenth, P. Jay Morton, was in the act of making a few choice remarks anent the achievement of success by not watching the clocks and by doing a little more than the next man, when his philippic was rudely interrupted by the unexpected entrance of Serrano and his cohorts.

"And, my good friends, it is only by an honest integrity, a complete devotion to the interests of . . ."

The door opened and shut with an ominous bang. Four men stepped into the room and ranged themselves against the wall. Their hands bulged in the pockets of their coats with something more menacing than their fists.

Banker Morton hesitated—came to a complete stop. He flushed uncomfortably, ran a nervous tongue over lips suddenly dry. He looked hopefully, pleadingly, appealing towards the far end of the table where Joe Venizelos, leader of the Tenth Ward, sat, surrounded by a handful of his minions.

And Joe Venizelos responded to that mute appeal for help. With an oath, he kicked back his chair and stood up.

"If you guys are looking for trouble . . ."

LeBrett took three long strides across the room. With the back of his hand he swiped Venizelos across the mouth.

"We are! One more crack out of you and you get it plenty. Big Nose is here to say a few words and everybody listens when Serrano talks. You and Morton, both, Venizelos. Sit down!"

Joe Venizelos responded to that curt command for order. With an oath he kicked back his chair and sat down.

• • •

Peace and quiet once more restored, Serrano again took the floor. He turned back to the trembling figure of the banker. "Come on, Morton, finish what you were going to say," he urged. ". . . a complete devotion to the interests of . . ." he prompted. "Spill it." But Morton's glib tongue was strangely silent. Words failed him completely. With fear-widened eyes and ashen face he stared apprehensively at the towering figure of Serrano.

"Okay," growled Serrano. "Then I'll finish it for you." He paused dramatically, looked around the room as if he challenged anyone beforehand, to deny the truth of the statement he was about to make. But no one was foolhardy enough. Only from the corner of the table where Venizelos sat, surrounded, by his men, came a subdued, ominous rumble.

Big Nose ignored it and in his best senatorial manner, launched forth into speech.

"Gents, unaccustomed as I am and all that baloney, I got a mouthful to say. Lend me your ears." He turned swiftly to LeBrett and whispered in a loud aside: "Get that Charlie? A nifty, eh? Shakespeare!" Then back to his audience: "There's lots of ways of piling up a bank-roll. One is by being honest and hoping for the breaks. The other is by being as crooked as a snake"— Serrano had an utter indifference to the way he mixed his metaphors—"and by showing a complete devotion to the interests of yourself.

"And P. Jay Morton got his the last way. P. Jay Morton got his do-re-mi, not by sweating in the stockyards and slaughter house at twenty per? Hell, no. That's a man's job. Morton got his by taking the pennies of the poor boobs who punch a time clock and who put their nickels and dimes in his bank for safe keeping. He sold 'em down the river. He cheated 'em out of their dough. He robbed a flock of poor kids out of their milk. He took the last dollar from a lot of old widows and sent them to the poorhouse."

Big Nose warmed to his theme and waxed eloquent.

"Ladies and gents, I'm here to tell you that P. Jay Morton is a chiseling, shyster sneak-thief, trying to break into the big time." His enormous forefinger shot out accusingly and stabbed in the direction of the flustered gentlemen on either side of Morton.

"And that goes for you, Sol Pincus and you, Herman Schweinler. You were directors of the bank and you not only let him get away with it but you had your fingers in the gravy, too.

"But you're not going to get away with it. You're going to pay! You're going to . . ."

But payment came more swiftly and surely than even Big Nose had expected. The door was burst asunder and a mob of Venizelos' henchmen charged into the room. The banquet hall immediately became a scene of chaos and turmoil as the doughty quartette, led by Serrano's trumpeting roar of defiance, mixed with the opposition gangsters.

High above the din of battle came Venizelos' shrill command to his men. "No guns, boys! Just throw these bums out on their cans!"

With a joyous grin on his lips and the light of battle in his eye, Serrano made answer, "And that goes for us, too! Zowie!"

His hamlike fist ripped through space and crashed into yielding flesh and bone. What had once been a high-bridged Semitic nose, found itself suddenly transformed into a nose of Celtic origin. The Hebe who had been the victim of the blow crashed backwards and down taking with him half a dozen chairs in his meteoric descent. His crumpled body came to rest at last against the banquet table, sending a shower of chinaware and silver to the floor in a jarring crescendo of noise.

Serrano ploughed through the debris, leaped over the unconscious form, reached across the table and grabbed the trembling figure of Morton around the neck. He yanked the banker towards him. His right arm described a short arc through the air and a warm stream of claret gushed suddenly from Morton's nose.

"You're paying now through the nose," chortled Serrano. "Later you're going to pay through the pocket."

His sledge hammer fist drew back for a second damaging blow when a whiskey bottle, wielded by an expert hand collided dully with his skull.

Big Nose grunted, blinked his eyes, shook his head and let the body of the banker slump to the festive board. He whirled with a bull-like roar and closed with his attacker, just as the whiskey bottle was describing a second flashing arc through the air.

Serrano's powerful arms coiled around the body of the gorilla. His muscles tensed convulsively and the yegg lay paralyzed in his arms. Big Nose took advantage of this moment of respite to survey the scene of battle.

The room was rapidly becoming a shambles. Chairs and tables were overturned; dishes, glasses and silverware lay shattered and broken on the floor.

In one corner, his back to the wall, doughty McGinnis wrought havoc with a leg of oak, wrenched from a shattered chair. In the other, Goldstein, his two heavy automatics reversed in his hand, cracked every skull within a radius of six feet.

Directly opposite him stood LeBrett valiantly trying to stave off the attack of half a dozen lunging wolves. But LeBrett's dark face was strangely pale, his blows unbecomingly weak and ineffective. Then Serrano saw the flash of steel!

A bellowing roar of fury sprang from his lips. His muscles contracted, then expanded with the force of an explosion. The man in his arms was lifted clean off the floor and hurtled across the room.

"Hold 'em, Charlie! Here I come!"

Head lowered, arms swinging savagely at his side, Serrano charged across the room with the force of a battering-ram. He tore into the pack of wolves closing in around LeBrett, smashed the ever-tightening circle wide open.

His arms worked like pistons and the fists at the ends of them were like lumps of cement. Blows bounced off his cauliflower ears, others collided solidly with his nose. But nothing could wipe the joy of battle from his lips, the light of conflict from his eyes.

He dodged knives, beer bottles, a stray cuspidor. Skillfully, from long practice in many a barroom brawl, he avoided lunging feet directed at his middle.

And with each blow he delivered, with each bellowing cry of triumph that issued from his battered lips, an evil face before him was suddenly blotched with blood for a moment, then disappeared in the welter of twisted, still bodies on the floor.

A half-dozen police whistles blared stridently, simultaneously. A score of heavy feet pounded down the long hallway outside the banquet hall. With the presence of mind of a Napoleon, Big Nose snapped the lock in the door and turned to LeBrett.

"The bulls! We got to beat it. Windows. Back way. Can you make it?"

"Sure," grinned LeBrett. "A knife in the shoulder, that's all."

"Good lad!"

Serrano's voice rose in a stentorian order. McGinnis and Goldstein obeyed and battled their way wearily to the windows. The door trembled under the assault of the embattled police. And a second later as it caved in under their concerted rush, Serrano lowered his nose over the last windowsill and disappeared.

LeBrett's wound proved to be a superficial one and after a visit to the saw-bones where they were all treated for a varied assortment of bruises, abrasions and contusions, the quartette retired to Serrano's private sanctum at the Frivolity, there to seek what solace they might from a bottle of McGinnis' best.

McGinnis smacked his lips over his liquor, no other thought in his mind than the excellent bouquet of his spirits. To him a battle was a battle—a thing complete in itself, with no further ramifications.

After the second drink, Goldstein went over his guns with methodical care. He liked a brawl as well as the rest, but in a showdown he would far sooner have relied on the cold steel of his automatics than on his fists.

LeBrett, in turn, gazed sourly at Serrano. And on seeing the happy, carefree, smiling expression on that individual's face, his dreary, dour features became more saturnine than usual.

"Well," he croaked, "like damn fools we let you rope us into this. A free invite to a swell banquet. Nuts! Now what the hell did it get us?"

Big Nose turned a fond eye of his on his inseparable ally in crime. "It got you a couple of inches of steel in the shoulder, but I got the joy of socking Morton on the nose."

"You always did get the breaks," grunted LeBrett. "But a hell of a lot of good that does Ruby and the rest of the depositors in the Packers Trust. What are you doing—going in this thing for the hell you can raise or to help those poor suckers?"

His pointed words sobered Big Nose. With a gnarled hand he scratched speculatively at the stubble on his chin. "Now that you put it up to me that way, Charlie," he answered, "I'm going to do something for those depositors. I told Morton he was going to pay and I meant it!"

"How you going to make him?" questioned Goldstein. "The courts gave him a clean bill of health."

"I'm damned if I know. But I haven't let the Tenth Ward down yet. And I'm not going to let it down now."

He applied himself again to the bottle, but oil his brain as he might and did, no inspiration came. He appealed to LeBrett, to McGinnis, to Goldstein for some idea, but that unholy trio was as barren of inspiration as their leader.

The hours dragged by. The bottle was emptied and another opened, but at four a.m. when the session broke up, Big Nose was no nearer the solution of the problem he had been wrestling with the past few hours, than when he had begun.

Only this he knew. Venizelos the Greek, Boss of the Tenth Ward, was mixed up in it somewhere and consequently the solution, when he did arrive at it, was bound to be opposed by bullets and blood.

III

THE PRESIDENT'S ENVOY

LEBRETT'S UNMUSICAL SNORE WAS ABRUPTLY TERMINATED in a strangling snort as a heavy boot in the rear punctuated his slumbers. He rolled over, sat up and scowled heavily as a cheerful voice boomed through the room.

"Come out of the fog," Big Nose bellowed. "Wake up and get a load of this. I got a wow of an idea and you got to help me put it across."

"What? Again?" groaned LeBrett. He flopped back on the bed again, pulled one corner of the sheet over his head and waved a hand in dismissal. "Can't you save it?" his muffled voice pleaded from the depths of the pillow. "Won't it keep for a couple of hours?"

Serrano wrenched the bed clothes from the pajama'd figure. "I said it's a wow," he repeated indignantly. "And when Big Nose Serrano says . . ."

"All right, all right," mumbled the other wearily. "Spill it."

He heaved himself to a sitting position once more, reached for the half-empty bottle that stood within easy reach of the bed and tilted it to his lips. The Adam's apple in his lean throat bobbed convulsively a couple of times, then he set the bottle back on its stand, wiped the back of one hand across his lips and came to attention.

Serrano retrieved the bottle and began to stalk back and forth across the room. Between gargantuan swallows of Two-gun Goldstein's choicest stock, he explained.

"What we need is publicity, see? We got to put people wise to the raw deal these banker gents are putting over on them. When a mob takes a double-crossing rat for the ride that was coming to him, the papers squawk like hell and everybody yells 'murder.' But when one of these slick guys pulls a fast one, the whole deal gets a nice coat of whitewash and everything's jake. Even the poor saps they've robbed sit back on their cans and just wonder, dumblike, what happened."

"Sure," agreed LeBrett patiently. "Don't you see? If you stick up a bank with a Tommy-gun, that's robbery. But if a bank president sells his customers down the river, that's business."

"Yeah, *I* see," answered Big Nose sarcastically. "The idea is, we're going to make the rest of the chumps see it, too."

"How?"

Enthusiastically, Serrano got to the point. As he listened to the bold plan which his friend proceeded to unfold for him, LeBrett reached once more for the bottle. When Big Nose had finished, he shook his head.

"It's a big order, swinging a deal like that. Only a loco'd gent like you could have framed such a crazy deal. But if you land in Leavenworth, or in the bug house, I suppose I might as well be with you. You're on."

The bunting-draped special train slowed down as it entered the suburbs of the city and panted to a halt for a brief stop at a small station, before proceeding to the Dearborn Street terminal. John Varney thrust a massive head out of the window of his private compartment and complacently surveyed his surroundings.

Though a personage of importance in Washington, and a well-known figure in New York, to the teeming populace of the mid-West metropolis he was only a name that frequently decorated the headlines of the daily papers. Now, as the President's special representative to the World's Fair, he would introduce his imposing bulk to the millions of visitors and native Chicagoans who had gathered for the great event.

At the moment, he was too busy congratulating himself on the pompous speech he had so carefully committed to memory, to notice the man who swung up on the flag-draped platform at the rear of the train.

As the special, with a piercing blast from the engine, pulled out of the station on the last lap of its journey, Varney withdrew into his stateroom and put the finishing touches to his immaculately correct formal attire. With a critical eye on the mirror, he had just pinned an important-looking scarlet badge to his lapel when a discreet tap on the door interrupted him. Graciously he opened the portal and beamed upon the intruder.

The smile died abruptly from his face as a broad-shouldered man edged into the compartment and closed the door behind him. Though there was a twinkle in Big Nose Serrano's eye, John Varney found himself staring into the gaping muzzle of a blue-steel automatic.

"What—what is the meaning of this outrage?" he spluttered.

"Sorry to bust in on you like this," apologized Serrano. He cast a critical eye over Varney's clothes and then looked ruefully at himself in the mirror.

"Class will tell, eh?" he shook his head sorrowfully. "Here I had Jake the Tailor working on me all morning and thought I looked like a million bucks. But I got to admit you show me up."

Varney's jaw sagged in speechless amazement as he took in the incongruous figure before him. Despite Jake's best efforts, the idol of the Tenth Ward looked strangely out of place in the role of a sartorial gentleman. But the threatening gun in a hamlike hand made the absurd vision real—too real.

"Turn around, mister. And stick out your hands behind you."

It was incredible—unheard of. The unbelievable audacity of the proceeding made Varney's head reel. But despite the flood of indignant refusals that poured from his lips, he obeyed.

Skillful hands got to work on him and a few moments later, the President's special envoy lay like a trussed fowl on his berth. The strange noises that rumbled in his throat were effectively muffled by the makeshift gag that Serrano had fastened across his mouth.

Three hoarse blasts echoed from the engine of the train. Serrano compared his own topper with Varney's, decided the latter was a quarter of an inch taller and consequently more imposing, and donned it at a jaunty angle. Then he appropriated the scarlet badge, pinned it prominently on his own broad chest and with a polite bow toward the bound figure on the bank, stepped from the stateroom.

A throng of excited, expectant people jammed the Dearborn Street station. They jostled each other rudely, trod heavily upon each other's tired toes and perspired freely, yet despite it all they were enjoying themselves immensely. As three strident hoots of an approaching train sounded in the distance, they milled nervously about and jammed even closer against the ropes that separated them from a group of frock-coated dignitaries.

The central figure of that imposing group, Mayor Kenyon, grunted his annoyance as the police lines gave way before the strain and instead of his isolated dignity, he found himself the center of a pushing, sweating, noisy crowd. He shouted vainly for the Police Commissioner who had been at his side a moment before, but a sea of strange faces had poured like a flood between them. The train rumbled under the shed and a hoarse cheer rose from the throats of the mob, drowning out the frantic orders of the policemen who sought to restore the gathering to a semblance of order.

Mayor Kenyon cursed the throng beneath his breath, and was adjusting the gardenia in his buttonhole when he was interrupted by what he at first thought was the hand of a pickpocket. Closer inspection, however, proved the error of his surmise. It was not the probing finger of a light-fingered gent that had disturbed him, but the more aggressive nozzle of an automatic held firmly in the competent hand of Charlie LeBrett.

"No squawks out of you," a low voice warned His Honor. "Stick to business, do your stuff or else. . . ."

The roar of escaping steam as the locomotive of the Special panted to a tired halt, drowned out the rest of the words. But Kenyon had heard enough. An icy finger of fear played a chill tattoo up and down his spine, and despite the busy blue-coated figures that ploughed through the crowd about him, no appeal for their aid crossed his trembling lips.

The cheers that echoed from the very rafters of the building drowned out any further warning that LeBrett might have uttered, but the ominous steel that prodded the Mayor's ribs was a far more potent silencer than any threatening speech. Obedient to the gun muzzle that urged him forward, Mayor Kenyon advanced toward the train.

Special policemen shouldered their way toward the steps of the first coach; a grinning porter, swelled up with his sudden importance, placed a set of steps upon the platform. Propelled through the crowd by her own escort, a little girl clutching a huge bouquet of roses was pushed forward by scores of eager hands. Then, while the mob screamed themselves hoarse, a tall, broad-shouldered figure appeared upon the platform of the train.

A profane oath, unbecoming to a man of his official position, escaped the lips of Mayor Kenyon as he recognized the hero of the occasion. Others in the crowd, also, gaped in amazement as the favorite of the Bloody Tenth waved his silk topper in greeting to the mob. But to the peasants from West Overshoes, and to ninety-nine per cent of the assemblage, he was the privileged delegate from the President himself.

Serrano accepted the bouquet that was thrust at him by a sadly frightened little girl, tossed a kiss in the direction of a pretty blonde who was gazing raptly up at him and continued to bow.

A particularly savage jab in the rear snapped Mayor Kenyon out of his hop.

"Do your stuff, big boy," LeBrett's voice grated in his ear. "Go welcome the President's understudy and do it up fancy, too."

How it all happened, Mayor Kenyon could not afterward have explained. He was conscious only of a gun barrel, that seemed to grow in size until it assumed the proportions of a cannon, drilling into his consciousness. His voice seemed to come from a great distance as he mumbled a stereotyped speech of welcome and it could not possibly have been his own hand that was enclosed by a huge paw and violently pumped up and down.

As in a dream he marched toward the entrance of the depot, with the rumbling bass of Big Nose's voice bellowing a friendly speech in his ear. He winced unconsciously when Serrano's huge hand clapped him enthusiastically on the shoulder. Then they were outside the building and headed for the line of official cars drawn up at the curb.

Once in the rear seat of the limousine that headed the procession, with Serrano's bulk jammed against the cushions beside him, Mayor Kenyon became suddenly aware that the terrifying cannon no longer menaced him. He drew a deep breath, straightened up and whirled on his unwelcome companion.

But Big Nose Serrano was not to be cheated of one single iota of his fleeting glory. His left hand was buried deep in a side pocket of Jake the Tailor's masterpiece and the harassed mayor learned, as Serrano's body lurched against his own, that the sinister threat of sudden death was still upon him. He collapsed limply back upon the cushions and his lips moved in a silent but fervent prayer.

The streets through which the cavalcade passed were lined with people who burst into noisy tribute at their approach. Serrano beamed his appreciation and flourished Varney's hat with all the intricate gestures of a big league pitcher winding up. Festoons of ticker tape swirled down from nearby buildings and coiled about him. He pawed strands of it from across his eyes, screwed around on the cushions and grinned widely in the direction of the fourth car in the triumphant procession. The grin grew even wider as he saw the expression of that particular car's occupants, Banker Morton, seated between two of the directors of the defunct institution, was visibly upset by the strange turn of events. He glowered fiercely at Big Nose, but apparently he was at a loss how to cope with the situation.

By the time they reached the vast auditorium which had been erected on the fair grounds, Serrano was in high good spirits. Only a faint twinge of conscience reminded him of the man he had left bound and helpless in the stateroom berth, denied all this glory and applause that was rightfully his. But the sad fact was not going to spoil Big Nose's great moment. He was still beaming when he piled out of the limousine and solicitously linked one arm through that of Mayor Kenyon.

The mayor suffered the indignity in stony silence, for at each step they took on their way to the gaily bedizened platform inside, something ominous and hard in Serrano's coat pocket bumped warningly against His Honor's hip. They found their appointed places on the dais and faced the vast sea of faces that filled the auditorium from one end to the other.

Mayor Kenyon rose from his chair, cast a helpless look about him and then took his place before the microphone that would send his voice across the nation to millions of listeners at the same moment that it boomed out from the cluster of loud speakers suspended from the arched roof of the building itself. He squared his shoulders with an effort, cleared his throat portentously and began.

"My fellow citizens, my welcome visitors, and my unseen radio audience. We are gathered here today . . ." Unfortunately for the impressive speech he had prepared, the harassed man glanced over his shoulder and his eyes fell once more on the hero of the day. Kenyon choked, spluttered. Then his body seemed to wilt and he shrugged his shoulders in a dispirited gesture of resignation to his fate.

"Allow me to introduce to you," he managed weakly, "the . . ."

He was saved from further indignity when Serrano rose from his chair and a thunder of cheering drowned out his words. Kenyon gladly relinquished his place on the rostrum and slunk back to his chair, where he proceeded to mop his brow with a large handkerchief.

Serrano stayed the uproar with a raised hand, scraped his feet awkwardly for a moment and then found his voice. His rumbling bass, transmitted by the delicate mechanism of the microphone, trembled the cluster of amplifiers till they threatened to shake free of their fastenings.

Had Mayor Kenyon not become suddenly engrossed in the tips of his own shoes, he might have noticed the presence in the audience of the man who had introduced him to this outrageous farce. For the dour-faced LeBrett had secured a position of advantage directly below the speaker's platform. As the familiar voice of Big Nose echoed through the hall, his hand moved in a pre-arranged signal. From all directions, grim-faced men, with hands plunged deep in coat pockets, elbowed their way through the push and drew closer to the dais.

"Ladies and gents! Due to an unfortunate little accident to the President's special envoy, he was unavoidably delayed. I was delegated to take his place. To those strangers from outside the city who don't know me, let me introduce myself. My name is Serrano—Big Nose Serrano from the Bloody Tenth."

Serrano rose from his chair and a thunder of cheering
drowned out his words.

He paused dramatically and LeBrett was quick to pick up his cue. He started the applause by stamping his feet and every tax payer from the Tenth, every man, woman and child from the stockyards district who was there, burst into rapturous hand-clapping.

Big Nose beamed down fondly on the vast assemblage. Then, like a Roman senator in the Forum, raised his mighty arm and commanded silence.

"Thanks for the tribute, friends. I think I heard only one razzberry. But let's get down to business. I got plenty to say and not much time to say it in.

"First, we're all gathered here to celebrate Chicago. Chi's a swell town. Take it from one who knows. You can get everything you want here and sometimes you get more than you ask for.

"The booze is not too steep and it isn't too bad. Even in the cheapest hotel you can always find a poker or a crap game going on if you look hard enough for it. There're plenty of girls and they're not too up-stage. Business is good, the rackets are good and everybody's happy including the cops and the street-cleaners."

He paused a moment to marshal his thoughts. The audience sat in stunned silence, unable to believe its collective ears. Two hundred special policemen looked questioningly at one another, but the President's special envoy was inviolate no matter what he said.

Up on the platform Mayor Kenyon writhed in agony. But no more acute was it than the suffering of Banker Morton and his two directors.

Serrano launched to the attack again.

"Yes, folks, it's a mighty swell town. And I'm proud of everything in it but one thing. It's a couple of bankers!"

The Chief of the Special Police realized too late that something was radically wrong. He shouted an order to his men and they made a concerted rush towards the speaker's platform. But before they had advanced a scant ten feet, the great audience in the hall arose as one man and swamped their charge.

Hoots, catcalls, whistles, razzberries, echoed and reechoed in the building.

"Let him speak! Let's hear what he's got to say! Attaboy, Big Nose! Tell 'em where to get off, Serrano!"

A thousand pleas, a thousand words of encouragement, a thousand commands to continue assaulted Serrano's cauliflower ears, as he stood like a prophet, before the populace.

Order was restored at last. The police had been put in their place. One more show of opposition and they would have precipitated a riot.

Serrano cleared his throat portentously. He beat on his chest with a hamlike fist, in excellent imitation of an enraged gorilla.

"A couple of chiseling bankers, I say. They took the nickels and dimes and dollars of the poor devils who work in the stockyard. They promised to pay 'em a shyster interest of three per cent. Then they gamble with some of the money and lose it. Then they put a lot more in a bunch of phony investments which comes right back to their private accounts. And with the balance they square accounts with crooked politicians, crooked attorneys and crooked courts."

He hammered on the desk before him by way of emphasis.

"Yeah, they're the slickest bunch of swindlers outside the pen. And what do we do to them? I ask you? What do we do to them? There's some who give 'em banquets. There's some who eat at their tables, slap 'em on the back and ask them how they get away with it.

"But that isn't what we do to 'em down in the Tenth Ward—down in the Bloody Tenth.

"We got telephone poles down there and we got rope. And we still got hacks that know how to make a one-way trip to the graveyard.

"But that's ahead of the story. Folks, ladies and gents, let me introduce to you the banking racketeers in question." He turned his back to the audience and with an imperative gesture bellowed at the speaker's table.

"Step up, Morton—and you Pincus—and you Schweinler. Meet the folks out front."

The three called upon declined the honor. They studiously avoided Serrano's dominating eyes and busied themselves in examining the tips of their polished boots. Big Nose snarled, lunged across the rostrum, yanked Morton out of his chair and flung him towards the front of the platform. Pincus and Schweinler followed in rapid order. Serrano stepped to the fore again, expanded his leather lungs and bellowed at the top of his voice.

"Ladies and gents. Let me introduce to you P. Jay Morton, Sol Pincus and Herman Schweinler—the three bankers who looted the Packers Trust. Give these babies a great big razzberry."

The audience responded wholeheartedly and with a will. An avalanche of hoots and jeers; a whole lexicon of vile epitaphs swept up like an irresistible tidal wave from the vast audience and engulfed the three bankers in their own shame and ignominy.

Newspaper men tore wildly for telephone booths; telegraph keys hammered out the story in staccato dots and dashes. Special messengers ran wildly from the building to report the happenings to higher-ups.

When at last the three pathetic figures had slunk back to their chairs, when at last some semblance of order had been restored, Serrano again raised his hand for quiet.

"Now that you've seen what yellow rats those three gents are, I want to tell every depositor in the Packers. Trust that they're going to pay out—every penny of every dollar. I don't give a whoop in hell if they have beat the rap in the court. I'll find a way of making 'em pay. They'll pay twice. Once through the nose and once through the pocketbook."

He extracted a pint of whisky from his hip and took a long swig. Carefully he recorked the bottle and replaced it. Then, wiping his mouth with the back of his hand, he faced his audience once more.

"And folks, just to show you there ain't no hard feelings, I want you to join me in the chorus of the latest little song I composed. It's hot! Get this!"

And despite the loud groans of LeBrett that threatened to drown him out, he ripped open his collar, threw out his chest, unhinged his jaw and bellowed like a Tetrazzini.

> *"Oh Big Nose went out on a banking crusade;*
> *To clean up the banks and the Tenth Ward to aid.*
> *Oh, when he began he had nothing to do,*
> *But before he got finished*
> *The bankers were through."*

IV
THE RIDE THAT DIDN'T COME OFF

DESPITE A STORM OF INDIGNATION that the formal opening of the great fair had been turned into something resembling a three-ring circus, Serrano's homely speech had a far greater and more serious effect. Ridiculous as his performance had been, the basic truths of his accusations against the bankers opened the eyes of the public.

Laboriously, Big Nose waded word for word through the screaming headlines that sprawled across the front pages of the daily papers. With the more literate members of his mob he even delved into the editorial pages, which he had heretofore thumbed hastily through in his hurry to peruse the sporting sections. Like a steadily growing avalanche, letters poured in to the various editors. Serrano's grammatical errors were forgotten, his audacity in turning a pompous occasion into a riot was forgiven, and in his name the American people demanded a sweeping investigation.

The avalanche turned to a flood; carried by its own momentum it swept over official Washington, thrust international affairs into the background in an insistent demand for action. And on the day that Serrano spelled out the words "Official Inquiry Under Way," his broad thumb tracing each letter across the front page of the *Tribune*, Big Nose and LeBrett threw an inordinately wet and noisy blowout for the gang.

Serrano wasn't the only one who ignored the baseball scores and fight results during those hectic days. The swarthy ward boss of the Bloody Tenth sat in his office over the Athens Pastime and Athletic Club, and meditatively smoked a long black cigar as he read of the results of Serrano's campaign. He finished the account of the investigation that was under way in Washington, sat back in his chair and expectantly eyed the telephone on his desk. He had not long to wait. The cigar had dissipated itself into an acrid cloud of blue smoke that hovered in the vicinity of the ceiling, when the instrument buzzed a strident summons.

Venizelos reached for the receiver.

"Hello? Yeah. I was expecting you to call . . . Sure. I just read the papers. . . . Okay, I'll be here . . . . Good-bye."

He hung the receiver back on its hook, crossed the room and opened the door. There he bellowed down the stairs that led to the speakeasy and poolroom that flourished under the name of the Athens Pastime Club.

"Nick!"

Voices downstairs took up the cry and a moment later a voice answered up the stairwell.

"Morton's on his way over here," Venizelos told him. "Shoot him up the side stairs and then see that nobody barges in on us."

A muffled "okay" drifted up the stairway and Venizelos withdrew once more into his office. He crossed to the window and peered out from behind the opaque green shade that was always drawn across the dusty pane.

Banker Morton was too discreet to park his familiar limousine before the shabby entrance of the Athens Club. It was an inconspicuous cab that pulled up to the curb some ten minutes later and disgorged its distinguished occupant. Morton ducked swiftly across the sidewalk, followed Nick up the side stairs and was immediately ushered into the office of the Greek.

He sank wearily into a proffered chair, refused one of the odorous black cheroots and extracted a cigar from a heavy gold case. When it was drawing well, he leaned back and drummed his fingers on the arm of the chair.

"You read the papers?"

Venizelos nodded.

"What do you think about it?" asked Morton.

"Looks to me like Serrano has started something."

The drumming fingers clenched suddenly into a hard fist that smashed down significantly upon the chair arm. The banker's face twisted in a heavy scowl.

"He started plenty. That scum of the stockyards is going to get me into plenty of trouble if he doesn't stop his clowning."

"Listen, Mr. Morton," answered the Greek. "You can call it clowning if you want to. Maybe Big Nose has got a funny way of doing things. He's pulled crazier stunts than that in the past and got away with it. I know him better than you do. And if he's out to block your play, you can take it from me you got a tough customer to buck."

"What does he know about big business?" demanded Morton indignantly. "An ignorant gangster—that's all he is. What does he know of finance, of banking, of . . ."

"There are times when a gat talks louder than dollars," Venizelos reminded him. "That guy's mob is no bunch of choir boys, either. Every time he sings one of those crazy songs he makes up, there's a chorus of Tommy-guns ready to play the accompaniment."

Morton ran a finger around the inside of his collar.

"You've got a—you've got a handy crew of men yourself, haven't you?"

Venizelos squinted thoughtfully at the ceiling. "My boys know their stuff, all right," he admitted.

Morton gazed unseeingly at the far wall. "It would be worth a lot to me if this Serrano could be persuaded that the banking business is a little out of his line."

"He's a stubborn gent," said Venizelos slowly. "But I think perhaps I can make him see the light."

Morton shifted uneasily in his chair for a moment and then climbed wearily to his feet. "I hope he'll listen to reason. If he does, I'll remember that it was you who showed him the wisdom of attending strictly to his own affairs. I am not forgetting the countless favors you have done for me in the past."

Venizelos grinned. "That's all right, Mr. Morton. Neither am I forgetting what a little friendly advice on investments has done for a certain Mr. Venizelos." He ushered his visitor to the door. "Nick'll have a hack waiting for you. You just go home and watch the papers, see?"

A glance of mutual understanding passed between the two, then Morton was gone. Venizelos waited until he heard the taxi in the street below as it shifted into gear, then picked up speed and pursued its honking way toward the North Shore.

A second summons shouted down the stairs brought Nick to the foot of the steps.

"Round up the boys," ordered the Greek. "Bring them up here. We got a job on our hands."

Serrano's blowout for the mob that night was officially opened by the delivery of case after case of clinking bottles. A grinning headwaiter brought the first half-dozen bottles to Big Nose's table in the far corner of the Frivolity Club and repeated the message that had accompanied the liquor.

"Compliments of Mr. McGinnis, boss. He says a couple of shots of this stuff'll provide the fireworks for the celebration."

With a flourish he opened the first bottle, poured out drinks for Serrano and LeBrett and then hurried off to distribute the glad tidings to the rest of the gang. The two men clinked glasses, then tilted back their heads to test the accuracy of McGinnis' proud boast.

LeBrett was the first to get the benefit of the experiment. He choked, spilled half the amber-colored fluid down the front of his vest and clawed at his throat. His face grew mottled purple as he fought frantically for breath and for a moment it seemed as though his eyes would burst from their sockets.

"Jeez!" he croaked. "What the hell's the matter with Mac? He trying to poison us?"

Serrano put down his empty glass, blinked rapidly and then drew a great gasp of cool air into his lungs. He scratched his ear, ran one finger down the side of his bulbous nose and with an heroic effort achieved a grimace that he believed was an easy smile.

"Why—why, Charlie! Don't you know—uh—good liquor when you taste it?" A sonorous belch that could not be stifled interrupted him. Before LeBrett could call attention to this sign of weakness, Big Nose hurriedly continued. "This is the real thing, I tell you. Bet it just came over the border."

"Over the border from Kentucky," growled LeBrett. "I've tasted potent 'mule' from the mountains, but this stuff would knock a team of mules off their feet."

Big Nose was feeling too well pleased with himself that day to back down now. Deliberately he reached out, got a firm grip on the bottle and poured himself another liberal shot. LeBrett raised an eyebrow.

"I take it all back, Big Nose," he said affably—too affably. "It's good stuff—honest. Have another."

Serrano glared defiantly across the top of the upraised glass. "Ain't I telling you so?"

To hesitate was to be lost, he knew. His head went back and the burning fluid coursed down his shrinking gullet. Only the sudden blare of the orchestra as it broke into a fast foxtrot, prevented the spasm that followed from being heard across the room. LeBrett callously ignored his friend's ill-concealed agony.

"Pour you another?" he offered.

Big Nose hastily shook his head. "Want to dance," he mumbled thickly. "Saw a hot-looking mama at Lefty's table. G'bye."

He lurched to his feet, but before he could make his escape, a short, furtive-looking man sidled up to the table. Serrano looked down at him from a swaying height.

"Hello, Shifty. What's on your mind?"

Opaque blue eyes darted a swift glance to right and left, then a squeaky voice answered.

"I seen your pal Morton fade into the Athens Club today. Thought you might be interested to know the Greek had a big shot like P. Jay calling on him."

Serrano's face twisted in a scowl. "Yeah, I am. Thanks, Shifty."

"Okay. You're welcome."

The little man faded off into the crowd as Big Nose sank once more into his chair.

"So what?" asked LeBrett. "What's it to you, Big Nose?"

"I don't like it—that's what," growled Serrano. This time he reached for the bottle without hesitation, tossed off a shot in grand style and wiped the back of his hand across his lips. As the burning alcohol coursed through his body like liquid fire, the scowl on his face grew even blacker. "I'm beginning to see the light, Charlie. I'm beginning to understand some of the deals that have been pulled off down at the city hall. I always had a hunch the Greek was mixed up in them, and now I think I see the reason."

"I give up, Big Nose. What the hell are you driving at?"

Above a large and flaming nose, Serrano's eyes flashed danger signals. "Listen. That Greek came off the sidewalks of this district. He's one of us, even if I don't like his oily pan. And if he's selling his own ward down the river . . ."

LeBrett nodded his understanding. "You mean he's double-crossing the poor saps that shoved him up the ladder, eh? Suppose he is?"

"That's what you and me are going to find out, right now. If he is, the Bloody Tenth is going to be minus one Greek."

He polished off the last of the bottle, patted his hip pocket and then rose. With an impassive face, in silence, LeBrett trailed off in his wake.

Big Nose's legs were rather unsteady, but his eyes were clear enough as they crossed the sidewalk under the glittering marquee of the Frivolity Club. However, the cautious LeBrett was not going to take any chances of being wrapped about an El pillar. He yanked open the door of Serrano's sedan and hastily slipped behind the wheel. Big Nose climbed in beside him and they were off.

The Venizelos mob were still in session in the office over the Athens Club, when Nick came back to report the celebration at the Frivolity. The Greek received the information with a scowl.

"I guess that queers us for tonight, anyway," he told them. "No use barging down there. His whole outfit'll be in the joint."

He was just about to dismiss the gathering, when there was a commotion down at the door. Half a dozen men looked a question at each other, then

Nick went to the head of the stairs and peered down. He popped back into the room and waved his arms excitedly.

"Big Nose! And Charlie LeBrett!"

A thin smile curled the lips of the Greek. "Nice of them to call, eh, boys? Tell them to come on up, Nick. They're sure welcome."

Heavy footsteps pounded up the stairs and Nick obligingly held open the door. Big Nose swaggered across the threshold and LeBrett edged into the office behind him. Serrano looked over the group and then jerked a thumb at Venizelos.

"Tell the boys to take a run-out. I want to talk to you."

"The boys stay," answered Venizelos shortly.

"Okay, if you want it that way."

"What's on your mind, Big Nose?"

"I got the tip-off that Morton was here today. I'm interested, see? I want to know the connection."

Venizelos suppressed a grin with difficulty. "Just a matter of business," he answered. "What did you think he came for?"

Big Nose planted his feet securely on a floor that threatened to sway a trifle beneath him and glared down at the ward boss.

"Listen, Greek. Your old man used to run a fruit stand down at the next corner. When we was kids, we flew pigeons together off the roofs. Our gang, the kids of the Tenth, shot craps together and then gave the bulls the bird when they tried to chase us.

"Those same kids put you where you are. They've backed you up every time and boosted you to the top of the heap. What I want to know is, are you letting them down now? Are you lined up with guys like Morton and crossing the boys who saved you from selling bananas for a living?"

Venizelos shifted uneasily under the direct question. Beads of perspiration glistened on his oily face. He glared defiantly at his accuser.

"Who's running this ward—me or you? Where do you come off walking in here and shooting off your mouth like this?"

LeBrett backed against the door and his hand crept suspiciously close to his hip pocket. A low growl sounded from the Greek's henchmen and Nick stepped forward. His body was tense and his gun arm crooked in a rigid right angle to his body.

"The boss is right, big boy. Better scram back to your own dump and do your preaching there."

"Yeah?" asked Big Nose softly. "Okay. Only when I go—I'm taking this rat with me."

The last sentence came out with a rush, and simultaneously, an oversized automatic sprouted in Serrano's hand. Its gaping nozzle pointed squarely at Venizelos' vest.

"Not a move out of you gents," warned Serrano, "or your boss gets his—right now."

But they were too many for him. Venizelos fell sideways from his chair as half a dozen gats leaped to avid life. LeBrett's first shot crashed the light overhead as Big Nose charged toward the Greek. Before Venizelos could scramble to his feet and get his own gun into action, a powerful arm wrapped about his body and a huge hand wrenched the weapon from his fingers.

Guns flashed through the blackness and acrid gun-smoke choked the battling men. Serrano raised his voice above the confusion.

"Clear the door, Charlie! Here I come!"

Dragging his helpless prisoner, his automatic clearing the way before him, he ploughed in the direction of the doorway. A hand touched his shoulder and a familiar voice sounded in his ear as Charlie LeBrett, still firing back into the room, thrust him through the portal.

"Down the side stairs, Big Nose, I'll be right on your heels."

A barrage of lead poured down the stairwell as they plunged downward. Big Nose tripped over the trailing legs of the man he was dragging, found his balance and then burst through the outer door into the street.

The window of Venizelos' office banged up and a face peered down at him. But the man held his fire lest his bullet find the body of his chief instead of halting the flight of Big Nose Serrano.

As Serrano shoved his prisoner into the front seat of the sedan, LeBrett raced around the car and climbed in back of the wheel. A spatter of shots poured from the window as Big Nose wedged himself in beside the hapless Greek, then the big car roared away from the curb.

"You're not going to get away with this," Venizelos told the panting Serrano. "My mob'll blow hell out of your joint and you along with it!"

Serrano found his breath at last. "Says you," he retorted. "Maybe they will, Greek, but it won't do you any good."

"Yeah?"

"Sure. Don't play dumb. You know what's happening to you right now."

Venizelos' swarthy face assumed a greenish tinge. "You mean—I'm going for a ride?" he asked, incredulously.

"Looks that way," answered Serrano grimly. "I came over to your place to ask you a question. You didn't answer it, but your guilty conscience gave you away. You're a double-crossing rat—and you know what a double-crosser gets."

Venizelos sank back limply on the cushions. Though the speeding car was traversing busy, well-thronged streets, he knew the futility of attempting escape. He knew, too, the futility of attempting to bargain for his life. Big Nose Serrano, when he was embarked upon one of the virtuous crusades which occasionally transformed his usual lawless life, was not to be bribed with ill-gotten dollars.

A sudden gleam of inspiration struck the Greek. Not with dollars—no. But . . . His eyes narrowed shrewdly.

"Listen, Big Nose," he pleaded. "I'll make you a deal. You want to get Morton with his pants down, don't you? You want to put the skids under him proper—and I can give you a swell steer how to do it. Lay off me now and I'll spill it."

Venizelos' hopes rose as he watched the expression on Serrano's face. He had scored a shot that went home, for Serrano's eyes lit up with interest.

"Yeah? That straight?"

Venizelos started to nod his head, but the movement was never completed. Hands like hams shot out and encircled his throat. Powerful fingers sank deep into his windpipe.

"Bargain with me, eh? Why, you crummy . . ." Serrano vented his just indignation by exerting an even greater pressure on the other's gullet.

"Out with it, mug! Say your little piece!"

Venizelos' eyes popped from their sockets and his face turned a ghastly purple. His lungs threatened to burst and a thousand devils of agony racked him as he struggled frantically for air. Doomed though he was, he had no desire to have his precious life ended in such torturous fashion. Better a swift, merciful slug of lead.

He tried to speak, to signify his willingness to talk. But he could not move. Big Nose recognized the dumb appeal of his eyes and relaxed his fingers a trifle. "Go on."

The Greek pawed feebly at the clutching hands sunk in his throat. "The ledger," he gasped. "Oh, Jeez. . . . Lay off . . . the ledger of the bank . . . Morton's hiding it. . . . If Washington gets it . . . Ease up, for God's sake. . . ."

With a last shake that threatened to roll Venizelos' head from his shoulders, Serrano let him drop.

"So that's it, eh? Thanks for the info, Greek."

Venizelos leaned back and drew great gasps of air into his tortured lungs. His trump card having failed him, he huddled on the seat in a woebegone heap of misery.

LeBrett jammed on the brakes and brought the sedan to a screeching halt as a light winked red before them. A group of pedestrians scurried past the hood of the purring car. Suddenly the back door of the sedan was wrenched open and a cheerful voice broke in upon them.

"Hello, Big Nose. Hello, Charlie? Mind taking me home?"

With a groan of dismay, Serrano turned to his unwelcome passenger.

"Uh—of course not, Grady. Get in."

"Much obliged," answered Detective Sergeant Grady, as he clambered inside. "Who's that with you? Oh, hello, Venizelos."

The Greek jerked erect on his seat.

Big Nose did not miss the curious glint in Grady's eyes as he recognized the Greek. He gritted his teeth in futile rage as Venizelos seized his golden opportunity.

"The boys were taking me home," he told Grady, "but I'll drop off at your place with you, if you don't mind. I've been wanting to see you. I think I got a lead on that Gruber case."

The detective beamed. "Swell. The inspector's been on my neck for a week and if I can't get some action in that direction, my life is going to be plain hell. Come up and have a drink and we'll talk things over."

The red light vanished and a solitary green eye took its place. Serrano and LeBrett exchanged a glance of hopeless resignation, then Charlie stepped on the gas. His aching throat forgotten, Venizelos began an amiable monologue. And despite their rage, his erstwhile captors escorted him politely to Sergeant Grady's home.

V

HIGH FINANCE AND LOW

AFTER HIS ARDUOUS LABORS OF THE NIGHT BEFORE, Serrano slept late the following morning. The sun poured in a golden cascade through the windows of his suite on the twelfth floor of the Royale Hotel.

Big Nose tossed fitfully in slumber. He was dreaming—dreaming of bulls and gunfights. Suddenly, a beatific smile wreathed his mobile lips. In his slumber he had Morton by the nape of the neck and Venizelos by the Adam's apple of his throat. It was a very, very, pleasant dream.

But then an obnoxious insect came to disturb the splendor of the vision. It bored irritatingly into Serrano's ribs. With an impatient hand Big Nose brushed it aside. But the insect was persistent. It bored in again and again with lusty vigor.

Serrano groaned, trumpeted loudly through his nose and opened his eyes just in time to catch the insect red-handed, in the act of gouging a grimy fist into his ribs. He sat up, made a clumsy lurch for the red-haired, freckled-face urchin, who nimbly eluded his grasp.

"Hey, you imp of hell!" he bellowed. "What do you think you're doing?"

"Waking you up, Big Nose," replied Mickey Deegan. "Jeez, Big Nose, how'd you get all dem warts on your nose? Squintin' at frogs?"

Serrano sat bolt upright in bed. His cheeks puffed out, his eyes widened and his voice exploded like the roar of a Bashan bull.

"What's that about warts, you young hoodlum? You're just like your old man, poking that pug nose of yours into trouble."

Mickey grinned at the compliment and altogether unabashed by Serrano's bellowing voice and mock anger, straddled his legs, cocked his head to one side and surveyed Serrano appraisingly as he climbed out of bed.

"Jeez, Big Nose," he piped admiringly. "You got more hair on yer chest than me old man."

Serrano was fog-eyed. He hadn't seen the grinning figure of LeBrett at the far side of the room. He grabbed Mickey by the seat of his ragged pants, hefted the diminutive body up until he glared into the starry blue eyes of the urchin.

"How in the hell did you get in here, anyway?" he demanded.

"Charlie brought me!"

"Who? LeBrett? Just because that guy's got insomnia he brings pests like you around to trouble other people's sleep." He lowered Mickey to the floor and glared around the room, and discovered LeBrett at last. "What's the big idea, Charlie?" he wailed. "What's the big idea?"

LeBrett strode across the room and extracted a flask from his hip. "Here, take a pull of this and snap out of it. The kid's got something to tell you."

Serrano snatched the flask, tilted it to his lips and under the admiring eyes of Master Deegan, emptied it at a draught.

"Now," he demanded, banging the bottle down on his bedside table. "What's it all about?"

"We're being dispersessed," piped up Mickey proudly.

"You're being what?"

"The old lady and all the kids are being put out on the street along with the furniture," elaborated Mickey.

"Rent, eh?" said Serrano, reaching for his wallet. It wasn't the first time he had been appealed to in a like emergency.

"No," answered LeBrett. "Worse than that. Tim Deegan owns that house except for a mortgage. Well, the mortgage is due and he can't meet it. And why? Because he had his dough in Morton's bank."

"And they're throwing him out of his home . . . Why, the dirty rats!"

"Worse than that," agreed LeBrett. "It's some side company of Morton's that holds the mortgage. Slick, eh? The bank closes, they can't get the money to lift the mortgage and so the side company forecloses."

"Like hell they will!"

Serrano's slumber was swept away. He became radiant with dynamic energy. He jammed his derby hard over his ears, jumped out of his pajamas and threw himself into his clothes. He ran a probing hand across the stubble of his chin.

"To hell with a shave," he muttered. "Come on, Mickey—come on, LeBrett."

It was a grim and bitter irony that had given the name to the street on which the Deegans lived with their numerous offspring. True, Mulberry Lane had at least one thing in common with its name. It was redolent with odors. Not with the wide-swept freshness of trees and the open country but with the more pungent smells of reeking garbage cans, dripping lines of diapers and sweaty shirts, stale beer, spoiled fruit. And over it all, like some all-pervading seasoning was the dank and fetid odor of the stockyards, themselves. Get it just right, with the wind from the south and it had it all over a convention of Italians in a crowded subway car.

Serrano's bulbous nose crinkled with distaste as the old, familiar stench assailed him, as he guided his car deftly into Mulberry Lane. Expertly he weaved in and out of the regiment of urchins playing *One o' Cat* in the gutters. He dodged pushcarts, baby carriages, flea-ridden cats and mangy dogs.

On all sides of him, the long row of drab, monotonous, two-story frame houses emptied an overflowing stream of life into the already crowded street.

By the time he brought his car to a grinding halt before number 72, most of the dilapidated furniture of that establishment had been removed to the sidewalk. A crowd of sympathetic neighbors had gathered about the tottery pile of furniture to commiserate with the full-bosomed, titian-haired Mrs. Deegan.

But that elegant lady was not looking for sympathy. With the blood of her illustrious forebears seething in her veins and the light of battle in her eyes, she was aggressively wielding a rolling-pin beneath the florid nose of the marshal who was superintending the dispossess order.

A flock of brats, ranging from the innocent age of two to the Satanic age of ten, clung to her ample skirts. The more precocious ones augmented her irate words by kicking lustily at the shins of the persecuted marshal.

Mickey wiggled his way into the circle, dragging Serrano after him. LeBrett lifted down a commode from the top of the furniture pile and sat down gingerly on one edge of it.

"Here's Big Nose, mom," piped up Mickey.

"Good morning, Mrs. Deegan," boomed Serrano, with an eloquent bow.

"Ah, so it's you, Mr. Serrano," said Mrs. Deegan. "Sure it is I'm sorry to be calling on you so early in the morning, but I'm at my wit's end. This old reprobate, here"—brandishing her rolling pin threateningly under the marshal's nose—"is putting me out of me house and home."

Serrano turned to the marshal. "What's it all about, Hennessey?"

Hennessey shrugged weary shoulders. "You know how it is, Big Nose.

Orders is orders. I get the official papers to dispossess 'em, so what can I do?"

Serrano grunted, turned away from the marshal and surveyed the crew of heavyweights who were engaged in removing the last of the furniture. Backed up only by LeBrett and the redoubtable Mickey, he felt sure that if he started to move the furniture back in again, he would achieve nothing but a few broken bones.

But yet manifestly something had to be done. Mrs. Deegan also, was of the same mind.

"What are we going to do, Mr. Serrano?" she appealed. "That home is all we got. We got no place to go. I can't camp on the street with the children like gypsies. It's that bank—the dirty crooks. Sure, we got enough money to pay off the mortgage, but they won't give it to us. They say there isn't any. Well, who's got it, that's what I want to know."

She glared menacingly around the circle of neighbors as if by some happy miracle Banker Morton had been delivered into her hands.

A few of the brats began crying; others broke away from their mother's restraining apron strings and darted beneath the wheels of charging taxis. Mrs. Deegan screamed at her progeny; heaped curses and abuse on the head of the marshal, then cried out the bitterness and defeat of her soul on Serrano's manly chest.

Big Nose was bedeviled, beflustered and bewildered. He looked appealingly at LeBrett, but the only consolation he received in that quarter was a mocking grin. He had to do something and he had to do it fast.

But first he removed the entwining arms of Mrs. Deegan from around his neck. Then he turned to LeBrett. "Come here, Charlie," he called.

LeBrett arose from the commode and wormed his way to Serrano's side. "So what?"

"Didn't we read in the papers that there was a mortgage on Morton's home?"

"Yeah; so what again?"

"It was overdue, wasn't it, but hadn't been called?"

"Check. What's the idea?"

Serrano ignored the counter-question and came back with another. "Who held that mortgage?"

LeBrett's brows wrinkled in deep thought. He scratched his chin, he pulled his ear. Then his face lit up. "So help me! Venizelos the Greek holds that mortgage!"

Serrano's eyes popped. "Venizelos!" He threw himself suddenly on LeBrett and pounded the other affectionately on the back. "What a break! What a break!"

LeBrett coughed up his wad of cut plug, disentangled himself from

Serrano's embrace and looked acidly at his pal. "Another brain storm, eh? What is it this time?" he asked with heavy irony.

But Serrano's sudden good spirits were not to be dimmed by the other's pessimistic words. He threw back his head, expanded his bellows-like lungs and burst into raucous song:

> *"Oh, Morton was a banker,*
> *A great big business man.*
> *He lived in a marble palace,*
> *But Serrano threw him out on his can."*

"How's that, Charlie? Get the idea? A wow, eh? The idea and the ditty!" But before giving LeBrett time to answer, he boomed out the last line again, laying particular stress on the last word thereof.

His artistic soul satisfied, he got down to business again. He turned to Mrs. Deegan. "Listen, Mrs. Deegan, you park here with the kids, see? Me and Charlie will be right back." He patted her rough and reddened hands. "And don't worry. I'll fix everything for you. You'll be drinking your beer after this out of glasses instead of a can."

He turned swiftly to LeBrett, hooked his arm under the other's and dragged him towards the waiting car.

Despite his undue haste on leaving the scene of the eviction, he pulled up the car to the curb at the head of Mulberry Alley for a moment to inspect the literary efforts of Mulberry Alley's juvenilia, illustrated by appropriate sketches, indited on a convenient blank wall. He was rewarded for his trouble and learned two edifying bits of information. One: That Nigger Joe had a big *umph*, and two: That Banker Morton was a dirty so-and-so.

From firsthand information, Serrano agreed with the latter observation and satisfied with what he had read, he shifted into gear again and continued on his way. And while he careened his way through the crowded streets of Chicago's South Side, he unfolded and elaborated his plan to LeBrett. And for once, LeBrett appreciated the humor, wit and wisdom of the proceedings and approved them heartily.

Some twenty minutes later Big Nose brought the sedan to a halt on the corner of Clark and Fifth. A block away, on the near corner, hung a shabby sign proclaiming to the world that that was the site of the Athens Pastime Club.

The main entrance to the establishment was out of sight, around the corner, but the discreet side entrance, used by such business associates of the wily Greek who found it beneath their social position to enter a public speakeasy, was but a hundred yards away.

This was their objective and towards it, Serrano and LeBrett made their way. No word was passed between them. None was necessary. They had laid their plan and was banking on its utter simplicity for success.

Casually, as if they were mere idlers of the day, they sallied down the sidewalk. But there was a wary intentness to their eyes, their jaws were hard and firm and their hands were ever within easy reach of the guns that bulged in their pockets.

Ten feet from the side entrance, Serrano forged ahead a bit. His hand dropped easily to the side pocket of his coat. His eyes were concentrated on nothing but the doorway. He had complete confidence in LeBrett that he wouldn't be bushwhacked from ahead, behind or the side. He stepped across the threshold of the side entrance into the gloom of the entryway beyond. But despite the darkness there was no mistaking the evil glint of the automatic that had now sprouted in his hand.

If there had been any doubt before, it was immediately dissipated as he rammed home the hard nozzle deep into the navel of Nick the guard.

"One crack out of you and you get it," croaked Serrano laconically.

Nick had a swift vision of the events of the night before and felt that his number was up. He turned a sickly green. His heart bobbed to his throat and he found great difficulty in swallowing it again.

"Honest to God, Big Nose," he whined. "Honest to God, I had nothing . . ."

"Shut up!" The order was emphasized by a more vigorous jab from the automatic.

LeBrett stepped into the hallway and expertly removed the gun from Nick's hip. "What do we do with him?" he asked.

"Take him along," replied Serrano. "It's the only way." He pressed his lips close to the ear of the trembling Nick. "Take us upstairs and tell the Greek you've got Morton with you, see? We'll take care of the rest."

"And one bum crack out of you—one false move—and you get it," warned LeBrett. "Get going!"

With Serrano's gun prodding him on from the rear, Nick got going.

The silent procession came to a halt before the oaken door of Venizelos' private office. Prompted by a savage prod from Serrano's gun, Nick lifted a trembling hand and rapped on the stout panel. From behind the barrier came the sound of a door slammed shut, then the Greek's oily voice.

"Who is it?"

Nick licked dry lips. "It's me, boss—Nick. I got Mr. Morton with me."

A chair scraped behind the door, footsteps sounded across the floor, chains rattled, a key was snapped back in the lock and the portal was swung open.

But instead of receiving his friend and business associate, Banker Morton, Venizelos was greeted by twin automatics held in the hands of his two visitors. His black eyes narrowed suddenly, his right hand twitched and then was still. But those were the only signs of the panic that ate at the Greek's heart.

There was a moment's strained pause; then Venizelos bowed to the inevitable. A sickly smile came to his lips and with a valiant effort he made his voice casual.

"What is this gents, a stick-up?"

Serrano's lips curled in scorn. "You know better than that, Venizelos. Step back in that room. No funny business. This gat here is aching to empty its guts into yours. I owe you that for last night."

At the mention of the events of the preceding night, the Greek paled slightly, despite his iron self-control. The smile died on his lips and the rat-like courage of desperation glinted in his eyes.

He stepped back from the threshold and Serrano immediately pushed Nick across it and followed with LeBrett. Charlie again did the honors and relieved the Greek of his iron. Then the door was closed and locked with an ominous click.

The tension eased. "Back up, Greek," ordered Serrano. "Sit down. I want to talk to you."

At the mention of the word talk, a faint ray of hope animated the Greek's soul. The greasy smile came to his lips again as he sidled around his desk and plopped into his swivel chair.

"Sure, boys; let's talk it over," he agreed. "This rough stuff won't get us anywhere."

"No place but hell," corrected LeBrett heavily.

"Have a drink?" Venizelos waved a greasy hand at the bottles that decorated his desk, but Serrano, for one of the few occasions in his long career, waved the amenities aside.

"What's your life worth to you?"

"My life!—what's it worth?"

"You got it the first time, Greek."

Venizelos stared at Serrano with wide eyes; stared at the two menacing guns leveled at his heart. He ran the point of a dry tongue over dryer lips. "Why, I never put a figure on it before—that way."

"No; then think fast."

The Greek suddenly flared up. "You can't get away with this, Serrano!"

"No? Why not? I got the car parked downstairs. Nobody saw us come in. Nobody will see us go out when we take you and Nick with us. It's as simple as all that. You ought to know. I asked you a simple question, but if you can't answer it, maybe I can help you out. Is that yellow life of yours worth forty grand?"

"I ain't got forty grand," whined Venizelos.

"The hell you ain't. But we'll let that go by, too. Just to show you that I'm a real gent and a sport, I'll make it still easier for you. You got a mortgage on Morton's joint up on the North Side. It's for forty grand. Give me that mortgage and I give you back your life. And I'll throw Nick's in for good measure."

"But I . . ."

Serrano's jocular manner slipped from him like a cloak. His gargantuan nose throbbed violently; his eyes gleamed menacingly. He took a swift step towards Venizelos' desk, leaned across it, gripped the cowering Greek by the slack of his vest and lifted him clear of the chair. He laid the barrel of his gun across Venizelos' face.

"I'll punch out your teeth with this gat," he grated, "if you lie to me again. You got that mortgage and I want it. It's in the safe back there in the corner. Are you going to come clean or do you want me to ram this gun down your throat?"

Serrano's grip tightened on the greasy vest and he shook his victim as if he were a rat. It was a full minute before the Greek could answer.

"Okay—you don't have to get sore."

With a violent heave, Big Nose sent him hurtling across the room towards the corner safe.

"Sore?" he laughed. "Hell, Greek, I was just playing with you. When I get sore, things happen."

Venizelos' answer, if any, was lost as he stooped over the safe and twirled the dials. Serrano stood over him, his arms akimbo, a large grin wreathing his homely pan.

The door of the safe swung open. Then two things happened simultaneously. The Greek darted a snaky hand into the dark interior of the strong box and with an inarticulate bellow, Serrano lunged forward with his foot.

His number 12D planted itself squarely and firmly in the middle of Venizelos' back. The Greek described a graceful arc through the air, then collided with the floor, face first. The gun he had snatched from the interior of the safe slithered across the floor to come to rest at the feet of LeBrett.

Serrano planted the other Number 12D squarely and firmly on Venizelos' bowed neck. "Wise guy, eh?" he taunted. "For trying to pull a trick like that on me, I got a good idea to renig on my bargain and take you along for a ride anyway. But other things first. More important things."

He prodded the Greek in the ribs with the point of his shoe. "Get up, punk, while you got the use of your limbs. It won't be for long, now."

While Venizelos stumbled to his feet, Big Nose disdainfully turned his back on him and stalked over to the safe. He went through it like a cyclone. Files, private letters, bonds, a case of whisky, all went hurtling into the room.

At last Serrano straightened up in triumph. In his hand he held a legal-looking document. He waved it joyously at LeBrett.

"Here it is, Charlie," he chortled. "Now watch."

A swift boot to the rear and Venizelos obediently slouched to his desk. At Serrano's command he reluctantly made over the mortgage to the name of Mrs. Dennis Deegan. Big Nose snatched up the document, then dictated a receipt for forty grand which the Greek laboriously wrote out and then signed.

The transaction completed to the satisfaction of Serrano and LeBrett, they backed their way to the door. And just before making their exit, Big Nose raised his voice in happy song and crooned the words of his latest masterpiece into the burning ears of Venizelos, the Greek.

VI

TEA AT THE MORTONS

IT WAS HIGH NOON WHEN SERRANO AND LEBRETT RETURNED to Number 72 Mulberry Lane. Following them came a second car, bulging with Two-gun Goldstein, Roaring McGinnis and a half-dozen other doughty gunmen. And trailing along a block behind, came a dilapidated, ramshackle junk wagon, drawn by an even more dilapidated, jog-gaited mare.

With a flourish the cavalcade pulled up before the door of the Deegan mansion. The men piled out of the two cars and the poor mare, on seeing the tower of furniture stacked on the sidewalk, drooped her weary head still farther and crossed one hock over the other in a gesture of utter resignation.

Big Nose boomed a cheery greeting at Mrs. Deegan, waved the mortgage on Morton's home under one eye and a legal dispossess notice under the other.

"What's that you got there?" queried Mrs. Deegan sharply. "Can we move the furniture back in?"

"Hell no!" snorted Serrano in grand contempt. "You're through with Mulberry Alley, Mrs. Deegan. Not enough room for you and the kids. Not enough fresh air and sunshine. I'm taking you to a place where there's flowers and birds and trees and grass."

"And sure, you're crazy as a bed bug, Mr. Serrano," answered Mrs. Deegan. "What would the likes o' me be doing in a place like that?"

"Crazy, eh?" grinned Big Nose. "Sure I'm crazy, but I'm getting a hell of a lot of fun out of it. Watch!"

He waved his hand majestically at his men, issued a sharp order and they immediately attacked the pile of furniture and began loading it on the junk wagon. Mrs. Deegan protested shrilly, but at Serrano's assurance that he would not let her down, she watched the proceedings with a skeptical eye.

When the last broken rocker had been tied on the sagging tailboard, Serrano waved Mickey and his squad of younger brothers to the towering mass of furniture. With gleeful whoops they agilely climbed aboard the wagon, fought viciously for a few minutes over points of vantage, then settled down to comparative quiet.

Serrano then ushered Mrs. Deegan into his sedan, whispered a word in LeBrett's ear and climbed himself to the driver's seat of the junk wagon.

From his majestic height he looked down on the old, familiar scene of Mulberry Alley. His barrel chest expanded with pride; his bulbous nose radiated with glory; his wide mouth was even still wider in a cherubic grin.

He flourished his whip majestically, perked the reins, chirped to the mare. With a heavy sigh that wracked her emaciated ribs, the old gray mare lifted her tail, uncrossed her hocks and lurched forward in the traces.

With an ominous rumble and groan the junk wagon moved forward, its destiny and destination guided by the broad and capable hands of Serrano.

Big Nose pulled out into the center of Mulberry Alley and the two cars rolled along in his wake. The mare was capable of no more than a slow, shambling walk and Big Nose permitted her to pick her own way and make her own gait.

Straight for the Loop he headed with the kids behind him showering the pedestrians who stopped to stare with loud and fulsome razzberries. From his place on the sagging driver's seat, his derby cocked rakishly over his right eye, the reins in his left hand and a fuming Corona in his right, Serrano surveyed the passing stream of traffic as from a throne.

He shouted bawdy greetings to passing acquaintances. He whooped at the passing girls and with a flourish of his derby invited them to a fast pick-up.

"And you don't have to bring no roller skates either," he flung back, when they all gave him the go-bye.

The news of their coming preceded them. The curbs of the sidewalks were lined with curious, grinning spectators as they crossed Dearborn Street and rolled slowly up State towards the heart of the Loop.

Traffic was tied up in a snarl. Big Nose was bawled out fluently by irate cops. In turn he cheerfully bawled out impudent cab drivers who tried to cut him off. But all unperturbed by the sensation he was making, he smiled genially on the throngs that lined the street, kept the gray mare going at her even pace and wended his way majestically across the Loop to the North Side.

At Monroe he turned east to Michigan Boulevard, thence north across the bridge at the Wrigley Tower. He induced Nellie to essay a slow trot and with the load of furniture and the kids behind swaying perilously he traversed the length of the boulevard to Chicago Avenue. Here he turned east again to

Lake Shore Drive. The mare reverted to her shuffling walk and Serrano was content.

He was in the Gold Coast—the section of the plutocrats—the snobs—the community of vice-presidents and shyster bankers like P. Jay Morton.

The drive was lined with imposing mansions of marble and stone and landscaped gardens. French governesses wheeled the heirs and heiresses to fortunes along the sidewalk. Ancient dames in silks and satins inspected the strange cavalcade as it swept slowly up the drive through long and disapproving lorgnettes. Mickey and his pals responded, their shrill voices as loud as their remarks were vulgar.

Big Nose had his eye on the numbers of the houses. And after a while a whoop escaped him. He flourished his whip over the mare's buttocks and pulled up a moment later before the canopied entrance to a large and imposing graystone mansion.

A string of expensive, chauffeured limousines extended along the curb before and behind him. Evidently Mrs. P. Jay Morton was entertaining the social elite of the Gold Coast with an afternoon tea. So much the better. This was going to be rich!

Serrano climbed down from the junk wagon and waved to LeBrett and his followers. They piled out of the cars and with Big Nose leading the way, they tramped across the velvet lawn to the ornate entrance of the Morton mansion.

Big Nose jabbed the push-bell with a stiff forefinger. The door was opened almost immediately by a liveried footman. With a supercilious stare he surveyed the group of men encumbering the threshold; his nose crinkled disdainfully as he took in the wagon at the curb, piled high with a varied assortment of junk.

"No," he shook his head in a dour negative. "No junk here."

Serrano followed the direction of his gaze. "Junk!" he exploded. "Why, you poor sap, we're moving that furniture in here."

The flunky's eyebrows elevated and his Adam's apple jerked convulsively. "In here?" he asked in a weak voice.

"Sure. This is Morton's dump, ain't it?"

"If you are referring to Mr. Morton's town house, you are correct."

"Okay! Step aside. We want to see Morton."

The doorman colored a scarlet red. True to his calling he blocked the door. "Mr. Morton is not at home."

"Well, Mrs. Morton will do just as well. Out of the way, guy."

His nibs, the flunky, suddenly found himself face to face with a situation for which there was no precedent. He hesitated just a fraction of a second too long. McGinnis poked out a heavy hand, planted it in the footman's face and sent him sprawling down the long length of the hall beyond.

The mob surged in after him.

Heavy-footed, tobacco-chewing, cigar-smoking, they swept through the house in a vain search for Mrs. Morton. But they uncovered nothing more important than a half-dozen squeamish parlor maids.

But out on the broad, landscaped terrace back of the house, things began to happen.

Mrs. P. Jay Morton was just in the act of serving tea to a distinguished gathering of grand-dames from the Gold Coast, when Serrano and his men swaggered out onto the lawn. Instantaneously, a score of lorgnettes were raised to as many eyes.

With mingled emotions the old biddies appraised the iron hats sitting so rakishly on the heads of the newcomers. Long and forgotten emotions fluttered in their ample bosoms as they noted the swelling chests, the bulging biceps, the sturdy thighs of this band of romantic figures who were descending upon them.

But Mrs. Morton entertained no such sentimental emotions. Flustered, embarrassed, angered, she rose in her wrath as Serrano approached her table.

"What is the meaning of this intrusion, sir?" she demanded haughtily.

"You old lady Morton?" boomed Big Nose.

"I'm Mrs. P. Jay Morton, if that's what you mean."

"It's the same thing, lady," grinned Serrano. "Sorry to bust in on you like this but—" He broke off suddenly, reached down to a platter of sandwiches on the table and took a handful. "Hmm! Liverwurst."

"Liverwurst nothing!" rasped Mrs. Morton. "That's pâté de fois gras."

"It might be herring to you, but its liverwurst to me," answered Serrano. "It goes swell with beer. You ought to try it some time," he advised confidentially.

The color drained from Mrs. Morton's face. She was perilously close to hysteria, but with a valiant effort she controlled herself.

"What is the meaning of this outrage?" she demanded, again.

"Don't get sore," protested Serrano. "I'm not used to being talked to like that by dames." He winked broadly at a fat dowager, who immediately began choking over her false teeth. He whipped out his two official documents. He shoved one into Mrs. Morton's trembling hand and shook the other under her nose. "That's a dispossess order and this here is the mortgage on the old homestead. You're being dispossessed!"

"Being what?"

"Being put out!" boomed Serrano. "Bag and baggage. We're tying the can to you. You and your man servant and your maid servant; and your ass and your sheep; and the strangers within your gates. That's scripture, so you can't take offense. Savvy, lady?"

Mrs. Morton savvied nothing but that she had never been so insulted and humiliated before. She was dumb with horror, paralyzed with chagrin.

"Out," explained Serrano patiently. "O-U-T, out." The word didn't register. Big Nose shook his head sadly and turned to his grinning men. "One o' them damned illiterates you read about. Okay boys, get to work. Might as well begin here. Pile the stuff out on the sidewalk. And tell Mrs. Deegan and the kids to come in. And go easy on that liverwurst, you guys."

Chairs were yanked from beneath clucking females, tables were cleared and the great exodus of the Morton family from Lake Shore Drive was on—the star of the Deegan fortunes was in the ascendency.

With the first batch of outgoing furniture, Mrs. Deegan moved in, still clutching her rolling-pin, the symbol of a rampant democracy. Red-headed Mickey led the charge of her numerous offspring. They swept through the house like an avalanche, skidded across the waxed and polished hardwood floors on the seats of their ragged pants and erupted out into the garden at the rear of the house.

They plundered the flower gardens; they posed obscenely by the side of the nude nymph spouting water in the center of a large pool. They scurried recklessly beneath the agitated skirts of Mrs. Morton's guests as they beat an harassed retreat. In five minutes they undid a year's work of half a dozen gardeners.

Arm tucked protectingly under Mrs. Deegan's, Serrano proudly escorted her through her domain. He showed her the six baths, the three kitchens, the conservatory, the music room. But to all the splendors Mrs. Deegan had only one thing to say: "Holy Mary and St. Patrick! To think of all the scrubbing to keep this place clean!"

The Morton unholstered furniture reposing on the sidewalk, and the Deegan heirlooms decorating the paneled rooms of the mansion, Serrano repaired to the garden again to enjoy a much deserved last liverwurst sandwich.

By his side sat Mickey, laboriously drawing caricatures in a large, black-bound book. Serrano washed down the last of his sandwich with a swill from a pot of tea and looked over the shoulder of the precocious artist.

He saw a long ruled page, compactly filled with small neat figures of large denominations. On the blank sheet opposite it, Mickey was drawing his impressions of Mrs. Plushbottom.

"What's that you got there?" asked Big Nose.

"A book. I found it in a little hole in the wall in one of the rooms upstairs."

"In a hole in the wall, eh? Let's have a look."

Serrano picked up the large ledger, focused his eyes on the complicated array of figures. And just then, with a sly smile LeBrett announced the precipitate arrival of P. Jay Morton.

"And the Greek's with him," he added as an afterthought. "And half his mob!"

VII
THE BLACK LEDGER

WITH VENIZELOS AND HIS CREW OF GUNMEN keeping pace beside him, Banker Morton stormed across the lawn toward Serrano. He shook an apoplectic fist beneath a gargantuan nose and bellowed his indignation.

"This is an outrage! What is the meaning of this performance?"

Serrano grinned. "It's all legal and proper, mister. Ask the Greek here. He signed the papers."

"Because you threatened him. It won't hold water in court," cried Morton.

"No? I threatened him, did I? You can take it from me, Morton, if that oily gent opens his mug in court, he's signing his own death warrant. And he knows it."

Venizelos opened his mouth to say something, then, for the first time, he caught sight of the book that dangled from Big Nose's hand. Speechless, he grasped Morton's sleeve and tugged it violently, pointing at the book. The banker followed the direction of his finger and his eyes bulged. He made a sudden dive for the ledger.

Serrano wasn't quite sure what it was all about, but instinct made him grasp Morton's arm and thrust him violently backward.

"Lay off," growled Big Nose. "Ain't you got no manners?"

"That book is my personal property," cried Morton. "Give it to me immediately." He thrust out an imperious hand. "Hand it over."

A shrill cry sounded from behind Serrano. Mickey Deegan, forgotten in the excitement, broke from the group and raced across the lawn toward the house.

"Ma!" he screamed. "Oh, Ma—they want to take my drawing book off of me! Ma!"

Serrano watched him disappear into the house, then turned back to Morton. "I'll take care of this thing. The book stays here."

Banker Morton looked for a moment as though he meant to fling himself bodily on the burly scion of the stockyards. Then he whirled on Venizelos.

"What are you standing there for?" he almost screeched the words at the Greek and his crew. "*Get that book!*"

Hands streaked for hip pockets, but before a shot was fired, an angry woman, still brandishing a rolling pin, erupted from the house. Mrs. Deegan, completely oblivious to the electric current of danger that charged the atmosphere, bustled up to Serrano.

"What's the idea, Mr. Serrano?" she demanded indignantly. "Can't a body have a moment's peace without someone plaguing the children?"

"Nobody's bothering Mickey, Mrs. Deegan," answered Big Nose, "unless it's Mr. Morton here."

Mrs. Deegan's jaw sagged as Serrano pointed out the man who had become a veritable ogre in her imagination. With a war whoop that must have been a gift from some fighting ancestor, she brandished her shillelagh over her head and sailed into her enemy.

She spared no hair of the distinguished gray head, and those of the Greek's mob who tried to rescue him from the onslaught received resounding whacks for their pains.

"Come in me own house, will you?" she raved at the hapless banker as he ducked her murderous bludgeon. "Take things away from the children, you robber, will you? Out with you! All of you!"

While Venizelos and his crew were not exactly noted for their chivalry, they made no attempt to use their weapons. There was no chapter in the gangland code to guide their actions in such a situation. Though his soul cried out for vengeance, P. Jay Morton was too busy to rally his bewildered bodyguard. Seeing that they stood helplessly by while the whirling rolling pin threatened to dash his brains out, he turned tail and fled.

For once in his life, the dour-faced LeBrett actually roared with laughter. He and Serrano held their aching ribs and, with hoarse cheers of encouragement for Mrs. Deegan, watched the rout. They were completely exhausted and deliriously happy when the last of the Venizelos outfit sprinted frantically out of view.

Despite his mother's militant defense, Mickey Deegan did not get his drawing book. Serrano took it with him to his room at the Royale, ordered a Babe Ruth bat and a catcher's glove to be sent to Master Deegan as a consolation offering, and then went into a huddle with Charlie LeBrett.

As a result, that afternoon found the pair closeted with a bespectacled young man, who possessed two outstanding virtues—he understood figures and he knew how to mind his own business.

With the two men peering over his shoulder, he delved into the mysteries of the ledger. While his attentive audience watched him in awed silence, he covered page after page of blank paper with neat columns of figures, checked and re-checked his calculations and occasionally gave vent to a portentous "Humph."

At last he pushed back his chair, blinked at Serrano through his thick-lensed glasses. "I won't attempt to explain all the details of the transactions that are shown in this ledger. This is the missing book of which you have spoken—there's no doubt about that. It shows clearly how deposits have been diverted, how, after very involved manipulations, most of the money eventually found its way into the private accounts of P. Jay Morton himself. Mr. Venizelos also came in for a large share of the illegal profits."

"You mean," asked Serrano, "that all the dope is right there for anybody to read it? That it says, in plain English, that Morton is a crook?"

The accountant reached for his hat. "Exactly. Now, if you are finished with me, I'll say good day."

A crisp note of goodly denomination found its way from Big Nose's wallet into a neat but threadbare pocket. "That's all. You can go now."

After the door had closed behind the man, Big Nose and LeBrett exchanged significant glances. "No wonder the old boy made a pass at me," said Serrano. "No wonder he hid out that book in his house. There's enough dope there to send him to the pen for years."

"So what?" growled LeBrett. "Are *you* turning copper?"

"Not yet," mused Big Nose. "But with that rat, Morton, I'm almost tempted to."

"What are you going to do with the book?"

Serrano turned on LeBrett with exasperation. "How in the hell do I know?" he complained. "You always ask so many damn fool questions, Charlie. I'm going to put it in the safe now. Something will break over that book yet, if it's all what that bookkeeping guy says it is."

"Morton wants it—wants it bad enough to come gunning for it," cautioned LeBrett.

Serrano opened the safe in the corner of his room, deposited the black ledger therein, slammed the door and twirled the dial. He straightened up with a broad grin.

"So much the better, Charlie," he boomed. "If he comes gunning for it, that'll give me a legitimate excuse to pump him full of lead. What do you say to a beer at Mac's?"

LeBrett admitted that he could stand a round or two and, with Big Nose humming one of his infamous ditties, they sallied forth from the hotel in search of liquid nourishment.

Banker P. Jay Morton didn't come gunning for the book that night or the following day, for the simple reason that he was testifying before the Senate Banking Committee down in Washington.

With laborious care, Serrano and LeBrett spelled out the account of the testimony, word for word. With bitter oaths they realized at last that Banker Morton was getting away with it. With the aid of a high-powered lawyer, ably abetted by certain members of the investigating committee, who continually threw a monkey wrench into the works, he was pulling out of the fire without getting too burned.

The failure of the committee's counsel to pin the rap on Morton was caused chiefly by the lack of all records of certain deft transactions in high finance.

Morton's contention was that the transactions never took place and, consequently, there couldn't be any records of them. And the prosecution was up a certain creek unless they could prove otherwise.

"Do you know," said LeBrett solemnly, "I think that black book you got gives all the missing dope."

"Sure," whooped Serrano. "I just tumbled to that myself."

"What's the play?"

Serrano scratched his off ear. "If nothing breaks in that investigation tomorrow, I think I might take a run down to Washington myself. I've served time in the State Legislature, but I always did have a yen to tell those dumb congressmen what I thought of 'em. And the black book goes with me."

VIII
DEATH BY NIGHT

ALL CHICAGO SLEPT—that is, all the law-abiding citizens thereof. Of the others, a shrug of the shoulders is the only answer. But whether Big Nose Serrano was classified on the books of the Police Department as law abiding or not, he was having a tough time of it.

In his suite on the twelfth floor of the Royale Hotel, he fought futilely to strangle his pillow. He was in the throes of a vague, oppressive nightmare. Some lingering, conscious nerve or sense tried vainly to signal a warning to his sleep-fogged brain.

His sturdy heart had picked up a faster, unaccustomed beat; the palms of his gorilla-like hands sweated and his massive brow was clammy. A needle pricked at his spine. The psychic signal of danger and death that had been beating insistently at his brain for the past five minutes finally struck a responsive chord.

Big Nose came to with a start. Immediately he was wide awake. Long years of danger in bucking cops, killers, machine-guns and gats had taught him that. Every nerve was alive; every sense keen, alert. Immediately he located the alien sound in the room. It came from the direction of the far corner, where his safe was located.

LeBrett's prediction had been right. Morton was coming for his little black book. And if he wasn't exactly coming a-gunning, he was coming at least with cold steel—which was worse.

Slow, insidious footsteps crept up stealthily on the bed. Big Nose lay limp and inert on the sheets. His eyes were closed and his unhurried breath was as sweet and calm as a babe's. But beneath the spread, the steel muscles of his legs were tensed for swift and instant action; the large, ponderous hands were knotted into fists of iron.

The hair in Serrano's nose quivered. He hadn't the slightest idea who the intruders were, but it was as good a guess as any that they were Venizelos' men. They were after the ledger and himself. Though his eyes were closed, he knew that one of the killers was still by the safe—the other was a few paces from his bed. He was coming in slowly, stealthily, and Big Nose sensed the glint of light off cold steel.

There was a song in his heart and a crazy ditty ran through his mind as he timed his movements to the last dangerous split second. Then, just as the killer lunged forward, knife upheld, he whipped around in the bed and lashed out with his feet.

He caught the gunman in the pit of the stomach and, with a convulsive grunt, the night-hawk grappled wildly with Serrano's suddenly convulsive figure.

The swift arc of the knife sang past Serrano's ear and burned a long streak of crimson in his left shoulder. Big Nose lurched over, grabbed the lean knife wrist in the steel fingers of his right hand. The two men struggled there on the bed, silently, bitterly, for possession of the blade.

Entangled in the sheets, Big Nose was at a decided disadvantage. His attacker knew his stuff. There was a fury of murderous desperation in his blows as he battered at Serrano's face.

Breath came in short, panting gasps. Vicious blows were given and taken with a silent intentness. But never once did Serrano's grip relax around the wrist that held the knife.

He heard the second intruder pad across the floor and make for the window. He couldn't bother with him now! If he could only get that damn sheet from around his neck!

He arched his mighty back, threw himself bodily off the bed, the other on top of him. A chair crashed down with an explosive roar. They fought to their feet again. A swift shuffle of straining footsteps across the room to the far wall. The killer had his back to it. Bracing himself with one foot, he lunged forward with the other.

The blow caught Big Nose in the groin and for a second his grip on the knife wrist relaxed.

The blade flashed up again. Serrano twisted and lunged forward, caught the descending wrist in midair, twisted it around and back.

Cool steel caressed yielding flesh, was bathed in warm blood. With a choking gurgle the killer slumped forward and slid slowly down the wall, the heavy hilt of the knife still protruding from his throat.

Panting, sweating, his barrel chest heaving laboriously, Big Nose stared down for a long moment at the man at his feet. He stirred the still form with the point of his big toe, so that the bloody head fell towards the light.

"So it's you, Nick," he whispered softly. "So help me, I never thought you had it in you!"

And that was Nick the Guard's obituary, his eulogy.

With a shrug of his shoulders Serrano turned from the body, stalked across the room to the safe. As he had expected all along it was open—and the black ledger of P. Jay Morton was gone.

Big Nose glanced at his watch, found that it was three in the morning. He immediately got down to business and put through a hurry call for LeBrett and his lieutenants.

By the time they arrived, he had dressed, disposed of Nick's body in a convenient trunk, cleaned up the bloody signs of battle and had consumed a half pint of liquor.

Swiftly he told his allies of the night attack and the resulting disappearance of the black book.

"Venizelos has it now," he concluded grimly. "And we're going right down there and get it back. It means blood and battle, but it's worth it. Are you with me?"

As one man, they proclaimed their allegiance. Then, with a determined, businesslike precision, they unlimbered their automatics, inspected them swiftly, stuffed their pockets with extra clips of ammunition and sallied forth from the hotel.

The four of them piled into Serrano's sedan and with cutout wide open, headed south through the Loop for the Bloody Tenth.

They knew, as a matter of course, that their arrival would be expected. They also knew for a certainty that great preparations were being made at the Athens Pastime Club in view of their coming. Guards were being stationed at all the doors. Automatics were being unlimbered and a grinning machine gun was uncovered from its hiding place beneath a few loose boards in the Greek's private sanctum.

And so, knowing all this, as if it were part of a prescribed ritual, Big Nose did not lead his men into the mouths of roaring cannon. Instead, he brought the sedan to a halt on the street that ran parallel to the one on which the Athens Club faced.

It was but the work of a moment to force the lock of the outside door of a shabby tenement house and with lunging strides, Serrano took the three flights of steep steps that led to the top floor.

He pushed open a trap, climbed up a vertical, iron fire ladder and emerged onto a gravelled roof. The other three followed in rapid order. There was no moon, but by the lights of the myriad stars they made out a sea of chimney pots, broken, irregular parapets, radio aerials and a tangle of sagging clotheslines.

No lights showed in any of the windows in their immediate vicinity, but stretching a long hand to the west, Big Nose indicated a rectangular crack of light that escaped from behind a drawn blind, in the top floor of a building removed from them by three intervening others.

"That's from the Athens Club," he commented softly. "From the Greek's office on the top floor. Venizelos will have his men posted at all the doors on the ground floor. He might have one or two on the roof, but we'll be able to take care of them."

"Sure," grated LeBrett dourly. "It'll be easy enough getting in. The question is, how are we going to get out?"

"On our feet or on a shutter," growled Serrano. "Let's get going."

Despite their bulk, despite the treacherous footing beneath them, they cat-footed it across the roof, negotiated the yawning chasms that marked the air-shafts. They climbed up fire-escapes, recklessly leaped the intervening space between adjoining buildings, skulked around chimneys and so, at last, climbed over the low parapet that surrounded the roof of the Athens Pastime Club.

A shed-like structure in the center of the open space before them marked the hatchway that led below to the top floor. In the heavy shadows around it, a cigarette pulsed and glowed in the night like an evil eye.

LeBrett nudged Serrano. He made certain graphic signs with his hands to indicate that he intended to circle around the roof and come up on the unsuspecting guard from the rear. Big Nose nodded assent.

LeBrett promptly slipped over the parapet again and disappeared from view.

Minutes crawled by—three—four—five.

Then, suddenly, the ruby eye of the cigarette described a wild and erratic arc through the air, as LeBrett came up behind the lounging guard and caught him by the neck in the crook of his arm.

There was a split second of struggle, a hurried scuffle of frenzied feet, then LeBrett's automatic, butt first, cut through the air in a short, vicious curve. It collided with sickening force against the guard's skull. The man crumpled, his knees buckled and without a sound he collapsed into the arms of his attacker.

By the time LeBrett had stretched him out on the roof, Serrano, Goldstein and McGinnis had come up. Without so much as a glance at the unconscious figure, they tried the door in the hatch. It gave beneath the gentle pressure of their fingers.

Guns advanced before them, they crept forward to the landing stage beyond. A flight of iron stairs descended steeply at their feet, terminating at the door to Venizelos' private sanctum. No one was in evidence, but the thin crack of light that slithered beneath the threshold of the closed portal, and the subdued hum of conversation from behind it, told them that the Greek was at home—and not alone.

Serrano led the way down the stairs. Sparks of fire glinted in his eyes; his nose was a flaming torch of wrath and his index finger was wrapped tightly around the trigger of his gun. He paused a moment by the side of his objective, pressed a large, cauliflower ear to the jamb of the door.

Then his hand went out to the knob; silently he turned it. But the door was locked.

Undaunted, he pressed the nozzle of his automatic to the keyhole, waved a warning to his men and squeezed the trigger. A staccato explosion rent the confined air of the hallway but before its reverberating echoes had died away, Big Nose had heaved his massive shoulders to the door and had crashed his way into the room.

A swift, terse order ripped off his lips.

"You Mac and you Goldstein—hold the door. The first rat that shows himself—blow 'im to hell!"

Then, with LeBrett at his side, he confronted the startled tableau gathered around the Greek's desk. Venizelos was there and two others—Pincus and Schweinler, the two swindling directors of the Packers Trust. And before them, in full view, was the fatal black ledger that had already cost the life of one man that night.

A varied score of emotions chased themselves in swift succession across the faces of the Greek and his two associates. Stark fear leaped to their eyes as they took in the menace of the leveled automatics in the hands of the two men that towered over them. But that fear was as nothing compared to the panic that consumed their souls as they read the flaming wrath that smouldered in Serrano's eyes.

But before a man could say a word—either in accusation or defense, a barrage of heavy feet stormed up the stairs from the floor below.

Goldstein's voice rang out, sharp, clear, loaded with death. "Stay where you are, you mugs! The first rat that shows himself gets it between the eyes!"

The rush of men was halted as suddenly as it was born. From below, where Venizelos' men had congregated on the second floor landing, in irresolute indecision, came a swelling chorus of muttered oaths.

Big Nose grinned, but there was no humor in the thing. He hefted the gun experimentally in his hand as slowly his glance traveled from the Greek to the two bank directors. His eyes squinted dangerously. Abruptly he got down to the business in hand.

LeBrett's automatic, butt first, cut through the air in a short, vicious curve.

"Two cut-throats raided the safe in my room tonight. One got killed and the other got that black book on that desk. I've come back to collect it. Any objections?"

Venizelos' lips curled back in a wolfish snarl. His eyes gleamed like twin agate balls of hate. Little flecks of yellow foam collected at the corners of his mouth.

"I'm objecting, Serrano," he choked.

"Oh, yeah? On what grounds?"

"That book don't belong to you."

"No? Well, I'm going to take it just the same."

He took a long stride towards the desk. Venizelos' hands shot out and clutched the ledger.

"You can't get away with this, Big Nose," he screamed in a frenzy. "You'll burn for this!"

The mere suggestion that he might spend an uncomfortable few minutes in the shot squat infuriated Serrano.

"Burn, will I?" he bellowed. "Why you dirty, chiseling, crummy punk! You low-life—"

The back of his hand knocked the Greek's head violently to one side; the palm jerked it convulsively back in the other direction.

"One more crack out of you and you burn right now!"

To emphasize his meaning, he jammed the nozzle of his automatic a full two inches into Venizelos' navel, yanked the ledger from the Greek's reluctant fingers.

"This is just the beginning, Venizelos," he warned. "You sold the ward down the river and in the end you're going to get the dose that every rat gets, sooner or later."

He backed up slowly to LeBrett, whispered a few words in his ear and together they retreated towards the door. From the corner of his mouth he spoke swiftly to Goldstein and McGinnis.

"Most of the mob downstairs are up on the roof now waiting for us to come out. They think they got us bottled up, but we'll cross 'em. They're expecting us to try for a getaway the way we came. But that's where they're wrong.

"I'll blast away at the skyline above to make it look good. You three guys charge down the stairs. Got it?"

The three nodded.

"Okay," grunted Big Nose.

A moment's pause while they edged to the doorway. LeBrett kept the occupants of the room under the leveled menace of his gun, while Serrano made the few necessary preparations before going into action. They were exceedingly simple. He expanded his leather lungs to their fullest, gripped the black ledger tightly in one hand and his automatic lightly in the other—then exploded with a bull-like roar that shook the rafters of the building.

His feet pounded loudly on the hollow floor of the hallway. His automatic leaped to convulsive life. A hot stream of lead splattered up the rungs of the iron stairs that led to the roof.

And on the instant that the embattled foe above returned Serrano's fire en masse, LeBrett, Goldstein and McGinnis plunged down the stairs to the floor below.

Their flaming automatics hammered out a skeleton's dance of death. Nothing could have stood before that withering fire; nothing could have withheld their irresistible charge. Before the half-dozen gunmen at the foot of the stairs knew what it was all about, they were staring wide-eyed into the grinning face of Death as it leaped relentlessly from three spitting automatics.

The first assault successful, Serrano pumped the last of his lead up the iron stairs to discourage reckless pursuit and plunged down after his cohorts.

His voice bellowed triumphantly through the building. He caught up with his men and his ringing voice and vitriolic profanity as he ploughed forward was as effective as a machine gun.

Their blazing guns swept a clear path before them. After that first murderous charge, the opposition was feeble, ineffective.

They hit the sidewalk just as the crescendo wail of a siren announced the approach of the riot squad. But ere the coppers arrived on the scene, Serrano and his three henchmen had disappeared into the secret haunts of the underworld.

The Senate Finance Committee, appointed to investigate the affairs of P. Jay Morton and his bank, was monotonously droning on to a futile conclusion of their affairs. The investigation had been hogtied from the very beginning by its lack of ability to trace some few million dollars of the bank's funds. Though the committee, the press, and the public were morally certain that Morton and his directors were guilty of embezzlement, they couldn't unearth the evidence to prove it against them.

Despite his worry over the damaging evidence in his little black ledger—damaging, if it should ever be produced—a smug smile of satisfaction wreathed the face of Morton. So far, he had faced the ordeal successfully. A few more minutes now of routine questioning and the whole sorry mess would be over.

The special prosecutor was hammering home his last few questions—questions he had asked on an average of every two hours.

"And you're positive, are you, Mr. Morton, that you've produced, for this committee, all the bank's books?"

"Yes, sir; I'm positive."

"Well, let me put the question in another way. Have you produced for this committee all your own personal books, documents and papers that would throw any light on some of the very shady transactions of the Packers Trust Company?"

"I have answered that question before," replied Morton, testily. "The answer is yes."

"There isn't some other little book, kept by yourself, say, or by your secretary, showing what happened to some four million dollars?"

Morton was sweating freely but there was triumph in his eye as he gave his answer in a loud clear voice.

"No, sir; there isn't any other book!"

And then, as if echoing his words, a clarion trumpet of a voice bellowed out a dramatic denial of the banker's last statement.

"You're a liar, Morton, and you know it!"

Never before had the august Senate chambers been so violated by such unparliamentary language. An ominous stillness and quiet fell over the room and the gathered assemblage. Morton looked up, deathly pale, a wild look in his eye. His attorney, to cover his confusion, busied himself with a sheaf of papers on the desk before him. Venerable senators stared; energetic newspaper men sat tense on the edge of their seats, poised for instant flight. For they sensed—for they all sensed that some dramatic revelation was about to be presented to them.

"You're a liar, Morton, and I can prove it," came the bellowing voice again.

A towering giant of a man unhinged himself from a seat in the back row and with long, lunging strides started for the mahogany desk of the Committee. His ears were misshapen and twisted; his eyes were of a fighting blue beneath bushy brows, his mouth was like the excavation for a subway. And his nose! It was a glory to behold! Never before had such an august nose, such a Roman nose—such a nose like the side of a mountain dominated the council chamber.

Big Nose Serrano, clutching the now famous black ledger in one ham of a fist, pounded his way up to the Committee. Squarely he confronted Morton, waved the black book before the banker's startled eyes.

"You're not only a liar, Morton," he boomed. "But you're a chiseling crook. And here's the proof!"

His dramatic entry, his dramatic accusation and the dramatic proof he brought to back it up, created a sensation. With the long-sought evidence now in his hand, the Counsel for the Committee revamped his case, recalled his witnesses and slowly but surely forged a chain of facts that would eventually land Banker Morton behind prison bars.

IX
ON THE DOTTED LINE

SERRANO'S MAD ENTERPRISES HAD SUCCEEDED in making a lot of hell for Morton and the directors of the Packers Trust. But when he was all through he came to the bitter realization that, as yet, he hadn't done a damn thing in fulfilling his promise to the Tenth Ward, that the defunct bank would pay off, dollar for dollar.

Morton was due for a couple of years in the pen, but that put no bread on the table, no beer in the cans of the families who lived along Mulberry Alley.

Big Nose discussed the situation at length with LeBrett and his allies. Something had to be done. Not alone for Serrano's reputation but for the poor devils who were counting on him to get their deposits back for them. And the only thing he could do that would mean anything, was to show them some do-re-mi.

"What's the bank short?" asked Two-gun Goldstein, with shrewd Jewish instinct.

"Four million and a couple of hundred grand," answered Serrano.

"That's a pile of dough in Mexican money," mused Goldstein. "And didn't the story break in the papers that Morton's private bank-roll was over two million?"

"Yeah," growled Serrano. "But he was slick enough to put it in another bank."

A cunning light came into Goldstein's eyes. He rubbed his hands together after the manner of his forefathers since time immemorial. Two-gun Goldstein hadn't worked in his old man's hock shop for nothing.

"Morton's got two million and between Pincus and Schweinler and Venizelos we ought to be able to raise the other two million," he said.

"Yeah," protested Big Nose. "But I already told you they got their dough in other banks."

Goldstein snorted contemptuously, patted the twin guns on either hip confidently.

"What the hell's that?" he wanted to know. "Didn't you get that mortgage from the Greek when he didn't want to fork it over; didn't you get the milk trust to lower the price of milk when they wanted to raise it; didn't you block that playground grab when the City Council had already received their cut for condemning it?"

A light began to dawn in Serrano's brain. "You mean put the screws to 'em?"

"Sure! Those guys are so yellow that the first time you crack 'em over the head with a gun barrel they'll come clean. And if they don't . . ." He shrugged his shoulders. "If they don't, they deserve all that they'll get. What do you say, Big Nose?"

"It's an idea!" boomed Serrano. "In fact, it's the only way out. Goldstein, whenever I'm mixed up in high finance, you sit at me right hand, see? Your old man would be proud of you!"

"Sure," grinned Goldstein. "Where he is, he's got half the haloes and harps in hock."

A definite course of action decided upon, Serrano threw off his lethargy and got down to the planning of the details of the campaign. He kicked out his chair, called his men around the council board and under the stimulating influence of a bottle of McGinnis' best, they evolved their plans.

They were ridiculously simple. As Goldstein had suggested, they counted more on the persuasive power of a grinning automatic than on any moral or ethical argument they could bring to bear on the bankers.

But one joker, Big Nose held up his sleeve. On one point he didn't enlighten his men as he sent them out to bring in the quarry.

He looked at his watch and gave his final instructions. "It's now nine. You, Charlie, it's up to you to get Morton. Pincus is your man, Goldstein. Mac, you get Schweinler. I'll take care of the Greek, myself."

Growls of approval and understanding answered his words. Automatics were brought to light and given a hasty but thorough examination.

"And at eleven o'clock," continued Big Nose, "we'll all gather down at the old Lion Brewery in the ward. Got it?"

"Got it!" they answered in chorus and the mob dispersed, each to carry out his allotted part in the drama directed by Serrano.

Long before the allotted hour, dark figures emerged upon the streets of the Tenth Ward and converged in the direction of the old Lion Brewery. They gathered in little groups about the dilapidated building, clustered in the dim glow of the street lamp before its sheer brick walls and discussed in low murmurs the latest project of Big Nose Serrano.

Each passing moment added to their numbers and it was an ever-growing crowd that milled about the building. The sound of their voices swelled to a low but ominous rumble. Officer Casey, making the lonely rounds of his beat in the warehouse district, turned a corner and then came to an abrupt halt. He tilted back his cap, scratched his off ear and then approached the outskirts of the throng that had invaded his territory. A few questions put to the stragglers on the outer fringe of the crowd made him decide that his duties called him elsewhere. Without seeming to hurry his measured gait, he managed to fade inconspicuously toward a quieter neighborhood.

Inside the sound-proof walls of the brewery, an uneasy but sullenly defiant quartette waited to hear the reason for the unceremonious way in which they had been summoned to the meeting. No telltale sounds from the street outside penetrated the solid walls of the building. And within the strange council chamber, silence was assured by the eloquent presence of glinting, sinister automatics, held in the firm and capable hands of Serrano's henchmen.

Big Nose himself sat in judgment, enthroned upon an empty barrel. The seriousness of the occasion was not marred by the fact that the desk before him had been improvised by the simple expedient of piling up several cases of clinking beer bottles. On the topmost case reposed a bottle of ink and a handsomely engraved gold fountain pen that Two-gun Goldstein had brazenly appropriated from Banker Morton's vest pocket. Big Nose flipped the pages of one of the narrow, leather-bound books in his hands.

At last he faced his prisoners.

"You guys are wondering what it's all about," he announced. "You're going to find out right now.

"I've raised a big stink and showed up all your shady deals. I've put you out of the banking business for good. I've made every decent man and woman in the country hate your guts.

"But in spite of it all, the poor suckers of the Tenth are still holding the bag. They're still out their four million bucks. And even if every dirty-nosed kid spits at you when you ride by, you think you can laugh up your sleeve. Because in the end you got away with it—you still got the dough you stole socked safely away.

"Now, listen, you guys. I got the dope on all of you. Between you, there's just about four million smackers salted away somewhere ready to be handed over on your say-so. And that four million is going to go right back where it came from—into the pockets of the poor slobs that actually earned it. Here's your check books. I've filled in the amounts. All you got to do is sign them and the money goes back into the Packers Trust. Come up here and do your stuff."

A howl of protest greeted the conclusion of his speech.

"Go to hell!" screamed the Greek. The others also voiced their refusal in no uncertain terms.

Serrano glowered and his men ringed closer about the defiant quartette. But even the threat of sudden death failed to impress the prisoners. For four million dollars, they'd willingly charge into a barrage of machine-gun fire. No demand that Serrano had ever made upon them before was so outrageous to their money-loving, dollar-grasping souls. Like cornered rats they glared defiantly at the circle of guns that hemmed in and continued to screech in horror at the proposal.

It was evident that their money lust had overbalanced their senses. The idea of signing over their ill-gotten millions had turned them into howling madmen. They preferred to be shot down, slaughtered like so many trapped animals.

Two-gun Goldstein shouldered his way into the circle. "Let me get to work on them, Big Nose," he pleaded. He brandished his gun and swung its shining barrel in a vicious, raking blow through the air. "I'll make 'em loosen up. I'll make 'em wish they were never born."

He grasped Morton's coat collar and yanked him free of the group. "One at a time, eh, Big Nose? Just let me do my stuff."

But Serrano shook his head. "No, Goldstein. There's been enough rough stuff pulled by our gang. Let him go. Let them all go."

Goldstein's jaw sagged and McGinnis crossed himself. "You nuts?" he wailed. "For God's sake, Big Nose, you gone screwy, too?"

"I said 'let them go,' " repeated Big Nose grimly. "Open the door, one of you guys."

McGinnis wailed aloud and Goldstein wrung his hands in utter misery. Reluctantly one of Serrano's gunmen approached the door and shot back its massive bolt.

The four prisoners stood for a moment in stunned silence, too taken aback by their release to move. They seemed to find the use of their limbs at the same moment and, with Banker Morton in the lead, dashed frantically for the portal.

Big Nose stood back and watched the rush, saw Morton charge across the threshold and then lurch to an abrupt halt. His arms flew wide and he staggered backward, bumping awkwardly into the trio who were hard on his heels.

At his appearance in the doorway, the mob in the street surged threateningly forward. A terrible cry of vengeance poured from their throats. Under the gleaming street light, they brandished a formidable array of homely weapons. Baseball bats, over-sized bricks, iron bars, stout broom handles wielded by irate housewives, were whirled over the heads of the throng. Banker Morton's face went pasty white as he saw the glow from the lamp post reflected on the gleaming steel of stilettos.

"We're waiting for you!"

"Come out and take it, you . . ."

"Let me at him!"

"Kill the thieving . . ."

A pop bottle, flung by a scrawny childish arm, struck the brick wall to Morton's left and shattered into a thousand tinkling fragments. With a cry of horror, he drew back from the threatening mob. At the movement, they rushed forward, bellowing.

Serrano swung the big door shut and slammed back the bolt as the four men retreated into the brewery. The cry of the maddened throng was abruptly stifled, but it still rang, in terrifying echoes, in Morton's ears.

"They only want what's coming to them," said Big Nose. "It's up to you. Either you sign those checks, or . . ."

Morton covered his face with his hands. Schweinler and Pincus cringed piteously into a corner. The livid face of Venizelos worked spasmodically.

Serrano walked back to his desk. "Step up, gents. Who's first? Or do I have to throw you out of that door?"

"No, no! For God's sake—no!" The words tore from Morton's throat in a shriek of mortal agony. "I'll sign!"

His shoulders sagging, his spirit broken, he staggered over to the desk. His eyes were blank wells of despair and horror. Big Nose thrust the fountain pen into his limp hand and shoved over the opened check book. As in a daze, Morton scrawled his signature, let the pen slip from his nerveless fingers and tottered feebly toward the back of the room.

"Next! You, Pincus!"

Each man in turn helplessly signed away his fortune.

Four wealthy men had entered the Lion Brewery that night. Now four frightened paupers huddled together in their mutual misery.

Serrano tore the checks from their folders, handed them to LeBrett. "Cash these the first thing in the morning, Charlie, and see that they're credited to the Packers Trust. And tell the mob outside to scram home. You come back here in the morning after the bank opens." He looked about at his henchmen. "Better make yourselves comfortable, boys. I think we better stay here for the night."

A couple of the men fashioned bunks with the aid of crates and old burlap bags. They were soon snoring lustily away. Another sat down before the door, leaned back, placed his automatic within handy reach and proceeded to make his vigil endurable with a pack of cigarettes.

McGinnis explored his pockets, then triumphantly produced a greasy, ear-marked deck of cards.

"How about a little stud, Big Nose?" he suggested. "We can use matches for chips and it'll help to pass away the time."

Goldstein dragged over some empty casks and the trio gathered about the crates that served as a desk. Serrano rifled the pasteboards with expert fingers. He grinned at the disconsolate quartette that sat silently in the corner.

"Want to take a hand, boys?" he invited. "On the cuff, see?"

His invitation brought no response.

"Aw, forget 'em," mumbled Goldstein, "and get down to business. You sent me to the cleaners last game we played and I'm out for blood." He raised one corner of his hole card a trifle, peeped cautiously at it and then rubbed his hands. Solemnly he produced a match and deposited it on the center of the crate. "Get a blue," he announced, and the game was on.

Gold rays of sunlight pierced the grimy windows of the Lion Brewery. The man at the door stretched his cramped legs and flipped another butt onto the already littered floor about him. Big Nose yawned prodigiously, rubbed his bloodshot eyes and yawned again.

Goldstein thumbed over a heap of matches. "Fifty-five, fifty-six, fifty-seven," he counted. With the aid of his fingers and a grimace that betokened intense concentration, he did some fancy figuring. "That makes three grand you owe me, Big Nose. Three thousand, two hundred and eighty-six dollars and four bits. I'll knock off the four bits," he added generously.

"Maybe you better leave it on the score," answered Big Nose seriously. "Your old man would turn over in his grave if he knew you handed money away like that."

"That's all right," said Goldstein affably. "I ain't squawking, am I? I—"

A heavy fist hammered on the door and the guard climbed to his feet to admit Charlie LeBrett.

"It's in the bag, Big Nose," he announced. "The tellers are hopping around like monkeys in their cages and the bank examiners are doing their stuff. The doors of the Packers Trust are due to open Wednesday and every flatfoot the Commissioner can spare will be on the spot ready to handle the push."

"Swell," boomed Serrano. "Well, we can let these mugs go, then."

He flung open the door and looked out into the street. Except for an occasional truck that rumbled past, the cobbled thoroughfare was deserted. He hailed his prisoners. "Okay, you can scram."

Disheveled and bleary-eyed, they shuffled to the portal. P. Jay Morton and his two allies peered warily across the threshold before they ventured forth. Venizelos stopped long enough to glare at Serrano.

A long arm shot out and a huge hand clamped down on the Greek's shoulder. Big Nose spun him halfway around and then slammed the door shut once more.

"I've changed my mind," he said grimly. "You're not leaving here—like this."

The opening of the Packers Trust was a never-to-be-forgotten occasion. Inside the building, sweating tellers thumbed over sheaf after sheaf of crisp new bank notes and slipped them through the wickets. A barrier of blue-coated figures at the doors stemmed the tide of humanity that clamored for entrance, allowing the depositors to pass inside only in orderly files.

Outside in the street, traffic was hopelessly snarled as the crowd overflowed the sidewalks and ignored the mad hooting of taxicabs and clanging trolleys that demanded passage. Cameramen and reporters wormed through the throng.

Sweating, cursing policemen earned a year's pay in one morning, as they sought to bring order out of chaos. It was not until the fever of excitement had abated somewhat, that they finally herded the crowd into block-long lines on the sidewalk. Then, with a renewed outburst of horns and sirens, the tangle of cars and trucks got under way.

A few minutes after traffic had resumed again, came another delay. A slow-moving procession of cars turned the near corner and rolled silently down the street to a death's-time march. An open touring car, piled high with dewy floral tributes, led the cavalcade. It was followed by a hearse, shrouded in black.

Majestically, impressively, the creeping cars filed past the Packers Trust Building. Immediately behind the ebon hearse, its top down, came a resplendent touring car. Seated alone on its back seat, in dignified and appropriately solemn state, was Big Nose Serrano.

Above his bulbous nose, his eyes were moist with unshed tears. His hands were crossed in pious attitude and his head was bowed as if in silent prayer. And from the crook of his right arm, there dangled a huge, lily-studded wreath. In gilt letters across its band of gauze, were inscribed the touching words:

To Venizelos the Greek
—Our Pal

But nobody there but LeBrett, who viewed the passing of the funeral cortege to the Greek's last resting place, knew that Serrano's eyes were dim—not with tears of grief but of laughter; knew that Big Nose's head was bowed—not in reverent awe but in order to study the *Racing Form*, which he held cupped in the palms of his hands.

N.R.A.—No Rats Allowed

Big Nose goes to bat for the good old Tenth Ward again and comes through hell and high water with loaves of real bread and a cheer for the N.R.A.

BIG NOSE SERRANO HOISTED HIS STEIN, buried his proboscis in the frothy foam and sipped the bitter beer with a meditative air. With large, cauliflowered ears he listened attentively to the dynamic voice emanating from the loud speaker of the radio. He grunted in appreciation.

And the grunt was answered by an anguished groan from the man opposite him. On the other side of the battle-scarred table lounged Charlie LeBrett, more surly, more dour-faced than usual. And with good reason, too. Charlie had a fifty-buck bet riding on the Giants to win the third game of the series—and the big boy insisted on listening to a talk on economics.

Hell! What did he care about politics—about the depression! He had protested, loudly, emphatically and profanely. But Serrano would have none of it. For the past hour he had guarded the radio with a sledge-hammer fist, a convenient bottle of rye and a heavy right boot—size 12D.

When Fitzsimmons was batted out of the box, LeBrett never knew; but on the other hand, Serrano got an earful of wise talk.

The President was speaking—making the concluding appeal of his address. . . .

> It is not for me that I ask you to do this. It is for yourselves, your friends, your neighbors. For your support of the N.R.A. will bring this country out of the valley of depression into an era of social justice, industrial harmony and economic security.

Serrano kicked his shoes off the table, snapped off the radio and reached for the bottle of rye.

"That's what I call a man, Charlie," he boomed. "A real President with guts!"

LeBrett was not impressed; he wailed.

"Yeah; but what about the game? Say, you mug, I got fifty smackers riding on that game and . . ."

Big Nose poured himself a shot of booze, then shook the bottle belligerently before LeBrett's startled nose. "To hell with the game! That's the trouble with you, Charlie. Always thinking of boozing"—he neatly downed the drink at a gulp—"of gambling—of running around with fast women."

"Rats!" exploded LeBrett wrathfully.

Big Nose ignored the interruption. He poured himself another drink, kicked back his chair and rose, glass on high. "You should be like me, Charlie—social-minded, see? Interested in the big things; interested in—uh—well, never mind." He waved his glass through the air in an eloquent gesture. "I'll admit I was elected to the Assembly on the Republican ticket, but I'm for Roosevelt, see—and the N.R.A. Here's to him!"

This sincere tribute duly solemnized by the shot of rye, he sat down again. He cleared his throat portentously, was on the point of launching forth into a dissertation on social economics when, fortunately for LeBrett, he was interrupted by the advent of Pete Swoba.

Swoba was a labor organizer, one of the few honest ones, and with the announcement of the President's New Deal, had had his hands full.

Now he entered the back room of McGinnis' speakeasy in the manner of a man who fears far more that which is behind him than that which lies ahead. His head was screwed far around on his neck so that he could survey the bar in the main room and his right hand dangled suggestively in the neighborhood of his hip.

Serrano and LeBrett recognized all the signs. Unconsciously their muscles tensed and instinctively they eased their gun hips away from the table. Swoba carefully closed the door behind him, then approached the table.

"So what, Pete?" greeted Serrano. "Why the dramatic entrance?"

Swoba grinned at the two men as he kicked out a chair. He poured himself a shot of booze, downed it before answering.

"I thought I spotted three torpedoes trailing me."

"And why would three torpedoes trail you?" asked LeBrett.

Swoba grinned again. "That's the story, Charlie. That's why I came to see you and Big Nose."

Serrano sighed ponderously, resignedly, but there was an eager light in his eye as he hitched up his chair closer to the table. "Sounds like trouble, Pete. Let's have it," he urged.

"It is trouble," answered Swoba. "And . . ." The door was pushed violently open before the assault of three burly shoulders. "And here it is!"

Three ugly-faced gorillas marched across the threshold. Narrow of eye, low of forehead, bat-eared, they were distinctly of the killer type. Serrano took them in with one comprehensive glance, didn't recognize them. Imported gunmen, was his mental comment. And by the same token, the three lollygows failed to recognize Big Nose and his inseparable ally, LeBrett.

The odds were all in favor of the home-town boys.

Serrano's bulbous nose began to itch and quiver, and on seeing this sign, LeBrett prepared himself for action. But the three newcomers failed to appreciate the significance of this phenomenon. With a contemptuous disdain they ignored Serrano and LeBrett completely and concentrated their attention on the labor leader.

Hands thrust into the pockets of their coats they hemmed him in.

"We want you, Swoba," said the leader, a pale-eyed gorilla with an underslung jaw.

And it was then that Serrano entered the argument. With a prodigious sigh he heaved his massive bulk out of the chair. "Just a minute, gents," he purred. "What's this all about?"

One of the gunmen whirled on him. "Keep out of this, fat-face, or I'll plaster that nose of yours around your ears!"

And thereby he signed his own death warrant. For he had committed the sin of sins, had cracked wise about Serrano's nose.

LeBrett grinned like a demon, knowing full well what was to follow. With an effort Serrano mastered his murderous impulse. Only the sudden, radiant glow that emanated from his nose, told of the terrific emotion under which he was laboring.

"You're tough, eh, mister?" he grated, rocking back and forth on his heels.

"Tough enough to handle you," shot back the other.

"Uh-huh—what's the name, mister—I didn't get it when . . ."

"What the hell do you want to know the name for? You're not going to do anything about it."

"No? I was going to give you a break, you punk. I was going to put it on your tombstone. But you wouldn't have it. This is what I'm going to do!"

Two hundred and ten pounds of bone and muscle leaped through space as if shot from a cannon. Two hundred and ten pounds of bone and muscle backed up Serrano's sledgehammer fist as it crashed into the gunman's face.

Then many things happened simultaneously. The would-be tough guy collapsed in a gory heap against the far wall; the table crashed back under the savage impulse of LeBrett's sudden kick; and glistening automatics flashed to light.

But the venomous rods of Serrano and LeBrett were already grinding at ribs, while the guns of the killers were only half out of their pockets.

Serrano snorted through his nose like a bull elephant. His outraged organ glowed and dilated to the scent of blood.

"Fat-face, he called me!" he grated. "Cracked wise about my nose, he did, the rat!" The nozzle of his gun ground deeper into yielding flesh. "And what do you say, punks?" His left forefinger, like a hickory limb, went up to his schnozzola. "It's a big nose, it's a warty nose; it's a nose that spreads all over my face. But to you, punks, it's the nose of a cherub, see?" He emphasized the statement by digging the snout of his gun an inch deeper into yielding flesh. "It's a delicate nose, a refined nose—a dainty little nose no bigger than a flea's!"

Then he relaxed, rocked back on his heels. "You punks came in here asking for murder. You're going to get it. But first, just to keep the records clean, the name is Serrano—Big Nose Serrano. Maybe you heard of me?"

The two gunmen shifted uncomfortably from foot to foot, made sickly attempts at grins.

Said one: "Yeah, we heard of you but we didn't know we was busting into anything you were interested in."

"I'm interested in everything that's crooked in this town," growled Serrano. "On the other side of the fence. What's the racket?"

His question was answered by a heavy silence from the two gunmen. It was broken a second later by Swoba's voice.

"It's a rotten racket, Big Nose. These three rats are Taggart's men. Imported gunmen from Detroit. The punk you smashed out of the picture is Lou Mancuso; this one here"—indicating the yegg on his right—"is Mannie Heiner and the other is Monk Gordon."

Serrano frowned, pulled at a cauliflowered ear with a huge paw. "Toughs from Detroit, eh!" He spat disdainfully in the direction of the nearest cuspidor. "Well, Pete, I don't like any of 'em, the place they come from or the mug they work for. What lousy racket is Taggart pulling that he has to import trash like this?"

Swoba became fluent and virulent. "He's scabbing and strike breaking. These lice do his dirty work. That's what I came to see you about."

"Yeah?" queried Serrano. "Where do I fit in?"

"It's the Tenth Ward," answered Swoba. "The Consolidated Baking Company wouldn't sign the N.R.A. code. I pulled the men out on strike. Schultz imported a bunch of scab bakers, got Taggart to strong arm for him and Taggart imports these mugs to break a lot of innocent skulls."

Serrano wasn't half so interested in the last statement as he was in a former one. His eyes glowed with a fanatical fire.

"So Schultz wouldn't sign the N.R.A. code, eh?"

"No!"

"And Taggart and these cheap killers are backing him up?"

"That's the idea!"

Big Nose suddenly became savage. His lips snarled back from bared teeth. "Like hell they are!" His mighty left arm shot out, grabbed Heiner by the lapels of his coat and yanked the gunman to him. Swiftly he relieved him of his automatic, then planting that same left hand full in Heiner's face, he sent him reeling drunkenly backward towards the door.

LeBrett had his cue. He performed the same operation on Gordon. And then between the two of them—LeBrett dragging the groggy Mancuso to his feet and Serrano planting his 12D in the seat of the latter's pants—they sent the last of the trio hurtling out of the door.

"You guys are getting a break," bellowed Serrano after them. "And tell Taggart that if he's bucking the N.R.A., he's bucking me."

He pocketed his rod, took a long pull out of the bottle, then turned to Swoba.

"Now, Pete, give me the dirt. What's it all about? What do you want me to do?"

They pulled up their chairs again and the three of them went into executive session.

Tom Taggart, chief of as ruthless a mob of gorillas as ever intimidated a city administration, started to listen to Heiner's report with a perfectly good Corona-Corona between his lips. By the time his hired gunman had finished, the cigar was in shreds and Taggart's usually anæmic complexion was a choleric red.

"So you made a bum out of the job, eh?" he grated.

"But, Jeez, chief . . ."

"Shut up."

Taggart's snake eyes took on a smoky film. Twin pulses beat violently in his throat above his tightly fitting collar. On more than one occasion he had tangled with Big Nose Serrano, to his own disadvantage. But this last affront—this last interference with his legitimate business could not be tolerated.

He turned back to the three gunmen cowering before him and his eyes were venomous.

"So you let him take your rods away and throw you out on your cans, eh?"

"But he had the . . ."

"Shut up!" roared Taggart again. He chewed viciously at the mangled end of his cigar; his manicured nails beat a savage tattoo on the polished surface of the table before him.

Once more he spoke and his voice cut like acid.

"Listen, Heiner—I'm giving you another chance. You know what it is."

"Sure, chief! Get Swoba, like you said!"

"To hell with Swoba!" snarled Taggart. "You mugs said you were killers and by God I'll give you work to do. Get Serrano—or else! And get him now. He'll still be up at McGinnis' speak. Get going."

In the back room of the speakeasy Swoba gave Big Nose all the details of Taggart's dirty work.

"So you see the kind of stuff they're pulling," he finished. "My own number's up. That mob won't stop short of murder. And the men I called out on strike are getting leery. Not that I blame them much."

Serrano grunted, then spat on his hands and rubbed his palms together.

"Looks to me like you need a couple of good guys to back you up. Charlie, here, is just spoiling for action. And me—well, I never liked Taggart's mug anyway. What do you say, Pete?"

"You mean it, Big Nose? On the level—you going to back us up?"

"With both hands," Serrano assured him. His eyes twinkled. "And a gat."

"That's what we need, I guess. What'll we do for a starter? You're the boss from now on, Big Nose. What you say, goes."

Serrano rubbed his bulbous nose with a stiff forefinger and squinted reflectively at the far wall. "Hmm. You say your crew's getting cold feet, eh? That's bad. . . ." Suddenly he turned to face Swoba again. "Listen, Pete! You go out and spread the word around that I'm on your side of the fence. Get your strikers down to Floral Hall tonight—say at ten o'clock. Let me talk to them."

"That don't give me much time," answered the labor leader. "But I'll do my best. I better get going right away, eh?"

"Yeah," agreed Serrano, scraping back his chair. "Me and Charlie better scram, too. I'll have to make up a speech. Come on."

They left their table and stalked into the main room of the speakeasy. As they headed for the door LeBrett laid a hand on Serrano's arm. "Wait a minute."

He walked over to the bar where the proprietor himself was busily dispensing drinks over the shining mahogany.

"A bottle of Scotch, Mac. And none of that mouth wash you're handing out, either. Dig into that private stock of yours."

McGinnis looked injured. "Why, Charlie. You don't think I sell . . ."

"Dig," broke in LeBrett gruffly.

Obediently McGinnis ducked out of sight behind the counter and then emerged with a dusty fly-specked bottle. He shoved it across the bar and spat in the general direction of the nearest gabboon. "Take it," he grumbled. "And I hope you choke."

LeBrett picked up the bottle and presented it to Serrano. "Here. It might help you with that speech. You'll need it—I've heard you try to sling fancy words before."

"Bah!" Serrano snorted contemptuously at the insult. But the bottle looked good. He held it up to the light, squinted through the amber glass and licked his lips. "I can use this, anyway. Come on, mugs—let's get going."

Clutching the bottle firmly by the neck he led the way through the outer door. The others followed him out into the dim areaway beyond. Big Nose began to mount the steps that led to the sidewalk and the light from the nearest street lamp gleamed on the bottle in his hand.

Suddenly a sharp explosion ripped through the night. It was followed instantly by the tinkle of falling glass as the bottle shattered in his fist. For a split second Big Nose stared stupidly at the jagged neck of the bottle still clutched firmly in his fingers. Then he understood.

"Taggart's crew!" he bellowed. "Drop!"

As one man the trio flung themselves face down to the ground. They were not an instant too soon. From the window of a parked car on the opposite side of the street something black and shiny poked out at them. Then with a staccato clatter the sub-machine gun went into action.

Lurid stabs of flame streaked across the gutter. Steel-jacketed bullets sprayed the areaway and splattered off the front of the speakeasy. They ricocheted off the iron railing, bounced off the bodies of the three. A shower of tinkling glass sprayed down upon them as the trio streaked for their own guns.

In a moment the street was alive with whistling steel and singing lead. Gun-smoke drifted up in swaying, tinted clouds. Their automatics barked in swift retaliation and the machine-gun answered with burst after burst of avid steel.

The areaway became a hot spot as the gunner in the car began to get the range. To hesitate meant suicide. Serrano scrambled to his feet, gun blazing.

"At 'em!" he roared. "Come on, guys!"

With Swoba and LeBrett hard on his heels, he barged up the steps and raced across the gutter. With their guns growing hot in their hands the trio swept down upon the car and sprayed it with a fusillade of leaden bullets.

A howl of pain and rage told of at least one casualty as with seemingly charmed lives they charged across the street. The driver of the ambush car shifted hurriedly into gear and gave her the gas.

As it pulled away from the curb Serrano emptied his gun at the rear tires. But the careening car made a poor target and its red tail-lights faded rapidly into the distance. It roared down to the corner of the block, slewed wildly around and disappeared.

Big Nose lowered his smoking gun and cursed.

"Got away, the rats!"

"Winged one, at least," answered LeBrett. "Those guys don't waste much time, anyway. Looks like we're in for plenty hell from now on."

Windows banged up and cautious heads poked out to learn the cause of the excitement. A curious crowd gathered on the far corner. Then a blue-coated figure broke through their ranks and pounded down the street toward them.

"Better get going, Pete," advised Serrano. "Me and Charlie'll get another bottle of booze. We'll knock it off back in Mac's place—it's safer. See you at Floral Hall."

The oncoming copper shouted an unintelligible order. Swoba faded in the opposite direction and Serrano and LeBrett ducked back into the speakeasy.

Big Nose paused a moment at the bar.

"If a bull pokes his nose in here, you didn't see a thing, McGinnis. You don't know what all the shooting was about, see?"

"I get it," answered the man behind the bar. "You mugs pay for that window, though, or I'll hand you over."

The threat brought a broad grin to Serrano's face. McGinnis was a friend of long standing and his truculence was only a pose.

"Window—hell, you old skinflint," he retorted. "Never mind the window. Trot out another bottle of that Scotch and bring it into the back room. The last one got in the way of a bullet."

In the safety of the back room, he and LeBrett shared the bottle while an irate policeman badgered McGinnis with questions.

Serrano was in high spirits, but LeBrett was solemn.

"I tell you Taggart's no fool, Big Nose. Look how fast he sent those mugs back here. And it wasn't Swoba they were after this time. They got a good look at that homely mug of yours before they cut loose."

"What of it?" demanded Serrano. "Hell, Charlie, we been shot at before. You getting the jitters now?"

"Not on my own account. But you're all the time poking that snozzle of yours into trouble. Why can't you—"

A sharp rap on the door interrupted him. The portal opened and McGinnis poked his head into the room.

"Did you get rid of the bull?" asked Big Nose.

"Yeah. He just faded—and plenty hot under the collar, too. Such language. For a uniformed officer—disgraceful, I'd call it.

"But that ain't what I came for. You're wanted on the phone, Big Nose."

Serrano tossed off another shot of whiskey, scraped back his chair and rose. "Wait here, Charlie. I'll be right back." Then he trailed out into the other room. He jammed his huge bulk into the narrow booth and picked up the receiver.

"Serrano talking—shoot."

"No more shooting—I hope," the voice over the wire answered him.

It was a familiar voice and as he recognized the harsh, grating tone Serrano's eyes narrowed. The tip of his nose got red and twitched.

"Taggart, eh? What do you mean by that crack?"

"Just what I said. Listen, Serrano, there's no sense in us bucking each other. We're both saps if we do. Suppose we talk things over? Maybe we can get together?"

Taggart could not see Serrano's hands clench, could not see them knot into hard fists. The voice that answered him showed no change of expression.

"Go on—I'm listening."

Encouraged, Taggart continued. "I got a good racket, see? As long as you and LeBrett got to cut in on the deal, you might as well get in the gravy. There's plenty for all of us. Now, suppose you come down to Schultz's office. I'll give you my proposition and you can think it over. What do you say?"

Serrano thought fast. It sounded fishy, all right, but he wasn't the kind to sit back and play them close up to his vest.

"Sure," he said at last. "Yeah. I'll be down. Wait for me."

He hung up the receiver, then marched back to LeBrett. He took the glass from his friend's hand and set it on the table.

"Forget the bottle, Charlie. We're going places."

"Yeah? Where?"

Serrano told him of the phone call from Taggart. And as he talked, LeBrett's face twisted in a scowl.

"And you're chipping in with that rat?" he asked incredulously.

"Of course not, you chump. But I want to see just what that gent has up his sleeve."

"Sounds like a trap. Don't go, Big Nose."

Serrano hauled him out of his chair. "Trap or no trap, I'm going down there with my eyes and ears wide open. Of course, if you'd rather sit here on your can and swizzle . . ."

That settled the matter. With a groan LeBrett patted his hip pocket and then nodded.

"Of all the thick-skulled, dim-witted, stubborn . . . Aw, hell! Come on."

A short half-hour after having received the call from Taggart, Big Nose Serrano, followed by his doughty lieutenant, LeBrett, was ushered into the private sanctum of Mr. Carl Schultz, owner of the Consolidated Baking Company.

Big Nose and his ally tarried on the threshold of the room a moment and surveyed the three men gathered round the polished mahogany table in the center of the floor. Taggart they recognized immediately; likewise Alderman McLaughlin. The blond, blue-eyed Dutchman they took for Schultz.

Big Nose shrugged massive shoulders, hitched his belt, patted the automatic in his coat pocket and lumbered forward.

"Well, Taggart," he grated. "Here we are. What's it all about?"

The eyes of the two men clashed audibly for a moment, then Taggart forced a sickly grin to his face. He indicated the gentleman on his right. "Meet Mr. Schultz. You know the alderman."

"Yeah," grunted Serrano, "I know him. But never mind the song and dance. First you send a couple of torpedoes gunning for me, then you say you want to talk it over. Talk what over?"

McLaughlin removed the cigar from his mouth and jerked it toward two vacant chairs. "Sit down, boys. We got plenty to talk over. No use getting sore!"

Big Nose laughed. "Who—me sore! Forget it, Mac. When I'm sore, you'll know it and it won't be in a letter, either."

He and LeBrett kicked out the indicated chairs and sat down. "Well, we're waiting, gents. Speak fast! We got important business on for tonight."

Mr. Schultz wiped his gold-rimmed glasses with a nervous hand.

"By any chance has it anything to do with the strike at my bakeries?" he asked in a high falsetto.

Big Nose turned on him, surveyed him contemptuously from head to foot.

"So what?" he demanded belligerently.

Schultz coughed apologetically and turned with a helpless gesture to Taggart.

"That's what we wanted to see you about, Big Nose," said the latter in a conciliatory voice. "Sort of a truce, see?"

Serrano trumpeted through his nose and LeBrett spat disdainfully over his shoulder.

"There'll never be any truce between you and me, Taggart," growled Serrano.

"But there's big dough in this," put in McLaughlin.

"To hell with your dough," rapped Serrano.

The conference was rapidly coming to a bitter termination even before it got under way.

LeBrett stepped into the picture. "Let's hear his proposition, big boy," he urged. "Then we can tell him to go to hell properly."

Serrano shrugged. "Okay by me." He tilted his hat far back on his head, leaned back in his chair. "Well, gents, what is it?"

Mr. Schultz gave the nod to McLaughlin and the alderman took up the burden of conversation.

"It's this way, Serrano. Mr. Schultz's bakers have gone out on strike. Mr. Schultz brought in other bakers but Pete Swoba is making a lot of trouble for him. We want to know whether you will back up Taggart—you know—preserving the peace and law and order."

Serrano grinned at first; then slowly the grin changed to a scowl. The wide nostrils of his nose began to pulsate, his hamlike hands clenched into hard fists on the table.

"So that's the proposition, eh?"

"Yeah. There's big dough in it for you."

Serrano nodded, turned to Schultz. "What did the men go out on strike for?" he shot out.

"Why—why . . ."

"I'll tell you why," boomed Serrano. "Because you wouldn't sign the N.R.A. code—that's why! Because you give 'em starvation wages, work 'em long hours. Because you've tied up every bakery in the Tenth Ward and—backed by a greasy politician like McLaughlin and a cheap gunman like Taggart—you've boosted the price of bread two cents!"

Mr. Schultz turned pale, then red. The cord that held his glasses broke in the convulsive grip of his fingers. His watery blue eyes bulged from their sockets.

"How—how dare you insult me like that?" he stormed.

"Dare?" mocked Big Nose. "Why you two-bit chiseler, you haven't heard anything!" He rose suddenly from his chair and, with a weary sigh, LeBrett prepared for action.

Serrano towered over the table. With a righteous eye he glared around at the trio. Then he threw back his head and the room trembled to his bellowing laughter. For a full minute he was unable to restrain himself; then he was sober again, deadly, venomous. His voice grated like jagged ice.

"So you want to make a strikebreaker out of Serrano, eh? Want to make a lousy scab out of me for pay, eh? Want me to sell the President down the river, eh?"

He lunged forward suddenly, planted his massive right hand, fingers extended, full in Mr. Schultz's apoplectic face and sent that outraged dignitary sprawling out of his chair.

Taggart dove for his gun, but LeBrett's rod had him covered before he could complete the draw. Big Nose threw an appreciative grin at his lieutenant, then turned to the council board again.

"Now you rats will listen to me," he boomed. "Listen to my proposition! I wouldn't take on your dirty work for all the dough in the State Street Bank. And what's more, I'm backing up Swoba to the limit!"

He turned to Taggart, jabbed a stiff forefinger into the gang chief's navel. "When you import a crummy bunch of killers from Detroit to run the Tenth Ward, you're bumping up against me, see—and it means war!"

He turned to McLaughlin, snapped the tip of the alderman's nose with a crooked forefinger. "And when you, with your crooked politics and graft cover up Taggart, you're digging your own grave, see!

"The Tenth Ward is my ward—the bloody Tenth. I'm seeing that everybody in there gets a break. There'll be no gorillas running loose there, committing murder for pay; there'll be no rise in the price of bread. There'll be no slackers on the N.R.A."

He waxed eloquent, swung around on Schultz, who was painfully climbing to his feet.

"By God, Schultz," continued Serrano. "I'll run those bakeries for you and I'll run them under the N.R.A. My own N.R.A.—*No Rats Apply!*"

He paused a moment. The wrath that had consumed him a minute before slowly disappeared. His savage scowl gave place to a cherubic grin. He rocked back on his heels, arms akimbo.

"And to celebrate the event, I'll sing you a little ditty, gents." LeBrett groaned, but Serrano ignored the protest. "Yes, sir, a little ditty I just made up for the occasion. Get this, Charlie, it's a wow!"

LeBrett knew the utter futility of prayer or protest. He shrugged his shoulders wearily and prepared himself for the worst. No wit abashed by his unappreciative audience, Big Nose threw back his massive head, expanded his bellow-like lungs and broke out into full-throated song.

His husky basso shook the rafters of the room and these were the words of his lay:

Oh, the striking bakers will win their fights
In the coming battles for their rights.
For Big Nose turned down Schultz's pay
To fight under the banner of the N.R.A.

"That's a riot, eh, Charlie? That'll panic 'em, eh?" But without giving LeBrett an opportunity to comment on his operatic efforts, he waved his arm in the signal of retreat. "Amscray, son! It's time for us to shove off."

His retreat to the door covered by the gun that still glistened in LeBrett's hand, he again assaulted the ears of his unwilling listeners with his song. And on the final booming, defiant note, the door slammed to behind their backs.

As a one-man grapevine, Pete Swoba did a swell job. And the name of Big Nose Serrano was something to conjure with in the Tenth Ward. Despite the fact that Taggart's gorillas had made life hell for the striking bakers, the news that Serrano had cut in on the deal brought them hot-footing down to Floral Hall.

Long before the appointed time they began to arrive, singly, in twos and threes, and then in droves. The long rows of benches were rapidly filled and by the time Serrano and LeBrett arrived the small auditorium was jammed.

They were spotted the moment they entered the door and met by a hearty cheer. Serrano beamed at the reception and even the taciturn LeBrett was awed by the size of the crowd.

"Jeez, what a turn-out. You better look out, Big Nose, or some promoter'll sign you up. You'd draw a million dollar gate at the stadium."

Serrano's wide smile changed to a frown as he addressed his companion. "This is serious business, you mug—not a circus."

"Yeah?" retorted LeBrett. "It'll wind up like a three-ring circus if you're mixed up in it. You mark my words. . . ."

"Better mark mine. This is going to be some speech, Charlie. Knock 'em right out of their seats. Just watch me."

Pete Swoba bustled down the aisle to meet them.

"Come on right up on the platform. This way, gents."

He led the way through the cheering crowd. It was a triumphal progress. Hoarse shouts and shrill whistles echoed from the rafters. Serrano bowed right and left and his smile widened until it threatened to reach his ears. Eager hands reached down and hauled him up onto the rostrum.

The crowd continued to cheer. Swoba had to hold up both hands in an eloquent plea for silence as he advanced to the front of the platform. When at last his voice could be heard he made his brief speech of introduction.

"Hold it!" he begged. "Gentlemen, I'm not going to take up your time.

You came here tonight to listen to somebody else. I've already talked to all of you at different times—telling you to stick to your guns. I know what you've been through. But now you're in for a new deal. Mr. Serrano has thrown his hat into the ring and I'm ready to take a back seat.

"It's going to be a different story from now on. I won't waste any more time. He can tell you all about it himself. Gentlemen—I present to you . . ."

He got no further. As Serrano rose the crowd burst into an uproar again. Big Nose advanced to the edge of the platform and beamed at his audience. His mighty chest swelled out and the tip of his bulbous nose wiggled in delight. He enjoyed the ovation to the full, but at last his smile faded and he cleared his throat with a portentous "Hmm."

The cheering died into silence. His audience leaned forward, breathless and still, eager for the words of wisdom that were to pour from his lips.

"Gents," he began solemnly. "I ain't much on making fancy speeches. I wish I could hand out words like the President did over the radio. That was talking, boys, and no mistake. And it wasn't empty words, either—he said a face full.

"Gents—this N.R.A. business is the real McCoy. Know what it means?"

He paused dramatically, but a swift chorus answered him.

"Sure!"

"Of course!"

"Sure we know, Big Nose! Ain't that what we're fighting for?"

Serrano waved his hands. "That ain't what I mean, boys. I got it figured out this way. The N.R.A. calls for men—regular guys. N.R.A. means—No Rats Apply!"

A mighty cheer greeted his interpretation. It was picked up, repeated, shouted back and forth across the hall. It became a slogan on the instant—a war cry.

Serrano beamed again.

"That's right, ain't it? That's what I told Tom Taggart."

At the mention of their hated enemy, the assemblage growled. A low murmur swept through the hall and then left an ominous silence in its wake.

Serrano pounded a hamlike fist in a huge palm and his eyebrows drew together in a scowl.

"That ain't all I told him, gents. I told him plenty. I told him I was pitching in with you guys and from now on—it was war. As I told you before, I ain't much on fancy speeches. I can argue better with this. . . ." He patted a significant-looking bulge in his coat pocket. "I'm a law-abiding citizen, gents. . . ." He paused to scowl at LeBrett, who had chosen to guffaw at the statement. "Yeah—a law-abiding citizen. But that don't mean taking any shellacking from Taggart and his mob of two-bit gunmen.

"It's war, boys. War! We're fighting for the good old N.R.A.!" He waxed eloquent. "Fighting for the N.R.A.! For the good old U.S.A.! For the good old Stars and Stripes!"

He began to pace the platform. His face grew red with excitement and carried away by his own voice, he waved his arms wildly about him.

"Remember Valley Forge! Remember Gettysburg! Remember the Argonne! Remember your President!"

His classic speech was never finished. It was a riot. As he had predicted to LeBrett, it knocked them out of their seats. They cheered. They yelled. They stamped their feet. They pounded each other on the back. They wept.

Serrano ran a forefinger around the inside of a wilted collar. With the back of his hand he wiped great beads of perspiration from his brow. Then he waved his arms again, windmill fashion.

"War!" he bellowed. "We'll run Taggart and his push out of the city! Out of the country! You with me, boys?"

A thunderous ovation echoed from the rafters of Floral Hall. The striking bakers acclaimed their new general with straining lungs and hoarse, dry throats. When at last they stopped for sheer lack of breath, Serrano continued.

"Just one more thing. As a wind-up to my speech, I made up a little ditty. Want to hear it?"

They did.

"Okay. Get this:

> *Oh, the striking bakers will win their fights*
> *In the coming battles for their rights.*
> *For Big Nose turned down Schultz's pay*
> *To fight under the banner of the N.R.A."*

There was a roar of appreciation. Then a voice took up the refrain. Another joined in. Then another—and another. In two minutes the entire assemblage was shouting the chorus. Serrano's booming voice led them through his masterpiece. He kept time with a hamlike hand. Others marked it with the stamp of heavy boots.

They sang it over and over again. They were halfway through their fifth repetition when the front door of Floral Hall suddenly burst open.

The refrain died abruptly into an ominous silence. Serrano stood frozen on the platform, mouth agape. Then a single voice broke the stillness—the voice of Charlie LeBrett.

"I told you," he wailed. "I warned you it'd end in a circus. See—here come the clowns!"

He pointed at the doorway, pointed at the ugly-looking crew who had jammed their way across the threshold.

At the head of Taggart's mob of gunmen stood Mannie Heiner. Flanking him on either side were Gordon and Mancuso, the others in a pack at their heels. Heiner squinted at the platform. One corner of his lips curled up from bared teeth.

"Clowns, eh? Climb off that platform, you mugs! The meeting's over!"

For a moment no one moved. Then slowly Big Nose Serrano stepped down from the rostrum. A concerted gasp of astonishment and chagrin broke from the assembled bakers and Heiner's crooked grin widened.

But LeBrett understood. He charged down from the dais and followed Big Nose up the aisle. Serrano paid no heed to the growing murmurs of the disappointed crowd. He marched straight up the aisle and halted only when he was directly before the grinning Heiner.

"You're not giving orders here—I am," he announced. "And my first one is—wipe that grin off your pan."

The grin vanished, all right. But it was replaced by a snarl.

LeBrett hitched his coat around a trifle and let his right hand droop at his side.

"Why didn't you leave him be?" he asked Serrano. "He looks worse now. My God, but he's an ugly gent."

"I sure am, beautiful," snapped Heiner. "And a tough one, too."

The crowd of striking bakers began to get the idea. They ceased to murmur and closed in behind their new leader. Anxiously they awaited developments.

Serrano stepped forward a pace. His chin jutted forward aggressively into the snarling face of Heiner.

"So Taggart sent you here, eh, tough guy?"

"Yeah. The meeting's finished, see? You're going to bust it up, right here and now."

Serrano didn't need a second invitation. He proceeded to do just that. His huge right hand, open, shot out and covered Heiner's scowling face. With a vicious push he sent the gunman flying backward into the arms of his henchmen.

That was the signal for all hell to break loose. Heiner's scream of rage was drowned out by a full-throated roar from the entire crowd. The Taggart mob streaked for their guns. Others fell upon them to wrest the deadly weapons from their hands.

LeBrett saw the lights gleam on Gordon's automatic and his own belched lurid flame. Gordon's gun dropped from a bleeding, shattered hand. Screaming curses, Heiner rushed at Big Nose, tugging at the weapon in his pocket. It was never drawn. Serrano's huge fist caught the gunman flush on the jaw with a resounding crack.

Heiner's eyes rolled, went glassy. His arms flew wide and his knees buckled. Big Nose whooped and with a mighty bellow he began to sing his little ditty. The battling bakers caught up the song once more and with the chant welling from their lips they plunged into the mêlée.

It was a mad, gory free-for-all. Automatics were useless at such close quarters. Big Nose Serrano was in his natural element. A sea of arms and bobbing heads seethed about his tall form. A Taggart man charged him and he stiff-armed him with a jolt that rocked the man's head on his body.

A hard fist smacked into his oversized nose and warm blood spurted in its wake. He stemmed the fountain of blood with a ragged sleeve and delivered retribution in the form of a wicked left hook. Two of the man's henchmen charged Big Nose simultaneously. He knocked them into a heap with one sweep of a mighty arm.

LeBrett went down under a tangle of flailing arms and legs, bucked a man off his back and scrambled once more to his feet. The tide of battle had swept him from Serrano's side and he vaulted over seats and jumped once more into the thickest of the fray.

With Big Nose battling like a dozen furies and cheering them on, the bakers lost their fear of Tom Taggart's sinister crew. They seized chairs and splintered them joyously over the heads of cursing gunmen. They swept down, a yelling, screeching tornado, upon the mob by the door.

The walls of Floral Hall trembled. Some one broke out into the street, blasting frantically on a police whistle. That decided the Taggart crew. One, nearest the door, broke for the street and safety. At his example the others charged frantically for the exit.

Serrano and his cohorts were exultant with their victory. In order to escape, Taggart's men had to run the gauntlet of smashing fists and chair legs wielded by muscular arms. Bruised and battered, knocked about until they were heartily sick of the mission upon which Taggart had sent them, they struggled for freedom.

Monk Gordon, tattered and bleeding, was the last to retreat. Serrano aided him on his way with a heavy boot that sent him flying over the threshold, then turned to his equally tattered but triumphant cohorts.

"Great stuff, gents! It was a swell meeting—but now you better scram. The cops'll be here any minute."

Even as he spoke, from somewhere outside came the far-away screech of a police siren. Whooping and cheering, the bakers began a triumphant exodus from Floral Hall. They jammed through the doorway and poured out into the street, the refrain of Serrano's ditty still welling from their lips.

Big Nose sucked a bleeding knuckle. He grinned at LeBrett. "You know, Charlie, ever since I was a kid I always liked a circus. This was a swell one, don't you think?"

LeBrett flung away the remnants of a chair which he had shattered across the shoulders of Taggart gunmen, spat on his hands and tucked in the tail of his shirt. The police siren shrilled nearer.

"That scram business means you and me, too. Come on, Big Nose—let's fade."

Serrano had laid down the gauntlet to Taggart; he had promised Swoba and the striking bakers that he would back them up. Both gestures demanded action. And with this in mind, he master-minded all through the following day in the back room of McGinnis' speak, trying to evolve some course of action that would lead his men to victory.

It was not until late at night and after he had consumed two bottles of McGinnis' best that inspiration struck. With a joyous whoop he kicked back his chair, staggered to his feet and pounded LeBrett affectionately in the ribs.

"Lay off!" protested Charlie. "What's eating you?"

"An idea," boomed Serrano.

"Yeah," retorted LeBrett sourly. "Another one like addressing the bakers."

"Ixnay," grinned Big Nose. "We're going into action, this time. Listen! How would you like to take a crack at Taggart?"

"How would I like a million bucks?" answered LeBrett with heavy irony.

"Swell! That's all I wanted to know!"

Without another word, Big Nose lumbered across the room to the telephone set against the far wall. He dropped a coin into the slot, dialed a number with a grimy finger. His conversation, when the call was answered, was short, sweet and to the point.

"Hello, Goldstein? Serrano. Want to take a crack at Taggart? Swell. McGinnis' back room, right away. And bring the mob."

Three more times he repeated the operation and on each occasion he was assured that his listener was only too eager to take a crack at the unpopular Mr. Taggart.

These preliminary details attended to, Serrano returned to the table. But to all LeBrett's questioning he had but one answer. "Wait!"

And they didn't have long to wait. An hour later, in response to Serrano's call, the back room of McGinnis' joint was thronged with a motley crew of gunmen. Three mobs were present—Goldstein's outfit; the boys that slung a rod for The Flash; and the gorillas that took orders from Art Gotz.

On more than one occasion before they had temporarily forgotten the bloody feuds that were waged between each other and had united under the banner of Serrano. And they were prepared to do so again.

The meeting was called to order with a shot of booze all around. This formality attended to, Big Nose took the floor.

"Boys," he began, "first I want to thank you for responding to the call. Now that that's over I'm going to give you the low-down."

Chairs scraped and then were silent. The muttering rumble of conversation subsided. All eyes focused on him, all ears concentrated on his words, Serrano continued.

"It's the bakers' strike at Schultz's bakeries. I don't know whether you know what it's all about, but here's the story. Schultz has gobbled up all the independent bakeries in the Bloody Tenth. Those who wouldn't sell, those who wouldn't line up with him were bombed out of business with the aid of Taggart and a crew of imported gunmen.

"It was the same thing with the little neighborhood bakeshops. Either they bought their bread from Schultz or they found real pineapples in their pineapple cake.

"Taggart knew his stuff. He got the bread business tied up in the bag in the Tenth for Schultz—and then the Dutchman raised the ante two cents a loaf. Get it?"

The men were not so interested in the economics of the situation as they were in the fact that Tom Taggart had his hand in it. That was bad. After their muttering clamor had subsided Serrano continued.

"And another thing I got against Schultz. He wouldn't sign the N.R.A. code. He's paying starvation wages to his men and selling lousy bread at two cents above the scale.

"Pete Swoba, here, called the men out on strike. And then the fun began. You know all about that. Well, I promised Swoba I'd back him up and I got to make good. And that's why I called you in. I need your help."

The three gang chiefs assured him that it would be forthcoming and Serrano continued.

"Schultz thinks he's in the bag because he's got Taggart and his cutthroat mob guarding his bakeries and beating the hell out of the strikers. But we're going to show him he's screwy. We're going to put the fear of the devil himself into that Dutchman."

Swiftly he outlined his plans. And as he talked, the assembled mobs waxed enthusiastic. Here was a leader after their own heart. Nobody but Big Nose Serrano would have even considered the audacious plan he unfolded to their willing ears. Serrano was no piker. When he did things—he did them in a big way.

"You get the idea?" he finished. "Are you with me?"

They were. Figuratively, they spat on their hands and hitched up their belts. Literally, they gave their weapons a quick going-over, announced the fact that they were ready and sallied forth on their mission.

Marcy Street was dark and deserted at that hour. It was a neighborhood of dingy, dilapidated warehouses and ramshackle buildings long since fallen into disuse. But the low, rambling structure that was the largest of the Consolidated Bakeries was an oasis of light in the blackness.

Inside, amid the noisy hum of machinery, overworked bakers labored far into the night. Outside, squatting on the front steps, lounging about the walls of the building, were Taggart's crew of gunmen.

Theirs was a dreary, monotonous vigil. They prayed for something—anything—to happen. And this night, their prayers were answered.

The roar of powerful engines suddenly shattered the stillness of Marcy Street. With exhausts wide open, a cavalcade of speeding black cars swept down upon the bakery. They came to a skidding halt before the building and spewed a crew of armed men out onto the sidewalk.

The Taggart mob shouted the alarm and streaked for their rods. In return, the mighty voice of Big Nose Serrano boomed out the signal for action.

Then all hell broke loose!

Guns barked ominously, stabbing the darkness with streaks of livid flame. Fire answered fire as the Taggart men blazed back in swift retaliation. In a moment Marcy Street was a mad vortex of struggling men, growling guns and whistling bullets.

The guards at the bakery grouped themselves into a knot about the door and pumped lead as fast as their fingers could jerk the triggers of their guns. But there was no stopping Serrano and his cohorts that night. They poured a merciless fusillade into the tangle on the steps of the bakery, wreaking heavy toll.

Men cursed and fought; screamed and died. With the irresistible force of a juggernaut, with Serrano whooping a battle cry at their head, the combined mobs under his command swept up to the doorway. The Taggart phalanx broke and scattered wildly in all directions. It was a panic—a mad, complete rout.

The massive doors of the Consolidated Bakery gave way before the victorious invaders. They burst inward and a horde of men, brandishing guns, erupted into the building. Bricks shattered windows and others climbed in through the jagged apertures.

Panic swept through the bakery. The whirring machinery, neglected, came to a dead stop. White-aproned bakers milled madly about, stumbling, bumping into each other, crying aloud in mortal fear as they sought the exits.

But every possible way of escape was blocked by hard-faced, steely-eyed gunmen. The terrified bakers ran in crazy circles until the booming voice of Big Nose Serrano bellowed out above the din. Then they backed into a miserable huddle against the wall, their flour-whitened hands raised high in eager capitulation.

"Silence!" roared Big Nose. "Nobody's going to get hurt. Stop making such a racket!"

The uproar died down at last. At least, it died down enough to make his voice audible through the vast room where the Consolidated bread was manufactured.

Serrano turned to his three allies. "Okay, boys. You know what to do. Get all this bread out of here and on the trucks. And while your boys are dumping that cheap stuff into the river, I'm going to show these bakers how to bake some real bread."

Orders were rapped out and with speedy proficiency the mob attacked the towering stacks of bread. When the work was well under way, Big Nose turned to the row of frightened bakers.

"Who's the master-mixer?" he snapped.

A thin, anæmic individual, with drooping mustachios stepped a foot forward from the line.

"Okay, long-horns," barked Serrano. "March. Lead the way to that mixing machine."

The master-mixer led the way down a flour-coated aisle, came to a trembling halt a moment later before a massive thing of shiny steel, belts, cogs, conveyors and receptacles. He indicated it with a mute hand.

Big Nose grunted, looked around, saw the rows of barrels containing flour, the crates of eggs, the cans of milk, the pounds of butter.

A wide grin spread over his face.

"Okay, brother. Now we go to work. How many eggs do you put in a batch of bread?"

"Two dozen," came the trembling reply.

"Make it twenty!" boomed Serrano.

"How much butter?"

"No—no butter."

"What—no butter?" bellowed Big Nose. "The hell you say. We're making bread, you punk—not hard-tack. Come on, get busy. Dump in some flour— get going—you got a lot of work to do. By God if you can't make bread, I'll show you how to make cake."

Under the bull-like voice of Serrano the master-mixer went to work. Never was such bread baked before in Mr. Schultz's bakery. Eggs went into the mixer, butter, sugar, cream. And as a final touch to his creation, Big Nose dumped a bushel of cracked nuts and a crate of raisins into the hopper.

The machinery turned, the ovens roared, the mixer worked at top speed.

"We're making bread, you punk—not hard-tack," Serrano
told him.

Batch after batch of Serrano's manna was turned out in huge, over-sized loaves. They were a trifle heavy, a bit indigestible, but each glorious loaf contained enough calories to run a dynamo for a year.

Big Nose was proud of his creation—and rightly so. There was no dumping of this divine food in the river. No. As fast as the hot loaves came out of the oven, they were loaded onto the delivery trucks of the bakery—and delivered—not to the retail stores—but to the hungry poor of the Tenth Ward, with Serrano's compliments.

And for once the Bloody Tenth breakfasted on cake!

On the second night after Serrano's raid on the bakery, there was a heated council in Schultz's office. Mancuso and Heiner had trailed along with their boss, but it was Taggart himself who was under fire. He sat sullenly in his chair and listened to Schultz's tirade in sulky silence.

The owner of the Consolidated Baking Company paced nervously back and forth and his squeaky voice was raised in indignation.

"Tell me, what am I paying you for? What do I pay your hired hoodlums for? Just to let this Big Nose Serrano make monkeys of us?

"He raids my bakery and you sit back and do nothing. Why? You've got to stop him. I don't care how, and I'm willing to pay—God knows I'm paying you plenty now—but you've got to stop him."

"Yeah," broke in McLaughlin. "You got me in a spot, too. The papers are squawking. They know I'm backing you and it looks bad."

Taggart cursed—a foul, obscene oath. "What the hell you want me to do?"

"Do?" squeaked Schultz. "Anything. Something. I don't care how far you go. I've told you that already."

Taggart waved both hands in an exasperated gesture. "I know—I know. But this guy Serrano's a different proposition. It ain't like giving the works to a bunch of striking bakers. These guys carry rods and they know how to use them."

The conference was getting no place. Schultz looked ready to burst into hysteria. McLaughlin gnawed his finger nails. The two cannons shifted uneasily in their seats and Taggart just glowered.

The silence was broken by the shrill buzzing of the telephone on Schultz's desk. He snatched the instrument and piped a shrill "Hello." Then he passed the phone over to Taggart. "For you."

The others remained silent as Taggart answered.

"Yeah. Silver talking? Go on—spill it . . . yeah . . . where? . . . how many of them? . . . Right . . . Good work, Silver . . . Yeah, I'll handle it . . . So long."

When he hung up the receiver, his scowl was gone. There was a gleam in his snaky eyes that boded no good for some one. The others waited for his explanation.

"That was one of my men. He just got the dope that Swoba and Serrano are meeting tonight. LeBrett'll be there, and a couple of the strike leaders. They're meeting to figure out what they'll do next."

"What'll they do next?" shrieked Schultz. "My God—"

"Aw, keep your shirt on," retorted Taggart. "They ain't going to do any 'next.' I'm going to get those three. Alive, see? Kidnap 'em."

"You just said they were tough customers," growled McLaughlin. "What do you want to take chances for?"

"I'm hired to bust up this strike, ain't I? That's the way to do it, dumb guy. Hold those three. And then unless the strike is called off—well, figure it out for yourself."

They did. Schultz patted him on the back and beamed.

"That's more like it. Get all the men you need, eh? After all—three men are only three men. Get a dozen gunmen—get twenty—get a hundred if you want them. There's a bonus in this for you if you succeed."

"Count it out, then," answered Taggart. "Come on, you two," he beckoned to Heiner and Mancuso. "Let's round up the boys. I'm heading this expedition myself."

With loving fingers McGinnis polished the glasses lined up behind his bar. A cheery whistle piped from his lips. It was late and the last customer had long since weaved his way out through the door. But the labor meeting was still in session in the back room.

McGinnis glanced up at the clock and shook his head. Why the hell didn't Serrano finish his business and scram? McGinnis wanted to get home. He'd just go in there and remind . . .

The whistle died abruptly on his lips. His eyes flashed to the door as it swung sharply inward and unconsciously his hand moved out and wrapped itself about the neck of a heavy bottle.

Tom Taggart stopped just inside the threshold, a gun in his hand and the rest of his pack crowding hard on his heels. The gaping muzzle of his automatic swung around to line up on McGinnis' third vest button. The latter froze, the bottle paralyzed in his hand.

"Not a squawk out of you, guy," ordered Taggart. His eyes narrowed. "Where's Serrano?"

McGinnis gulped hard at the Adam's apple that rose in his throat and threatened to choke him. Suddenly he found his voice.

"Big Nose!" he bellowed. "Look out . . ."

He ducked behind the bar a split second before Taggart's bullet gouged splinters from the mahogany. Taggart mouthed a horrible oath, then spotted the door leading to the back room. Gun ready for a vicious burst, he led the charge. His men barged after him and crashed headlong against the portal. It fairly burst from its hinges and the gunmen piled into the back room.

Serrano and his companions never had a chance. Big Nose's chair scraped back and he leaped to his feet—to face the ready muzzles of a half-dozen automatics. A ring of glistening steel hemmed in the rest. They never moved from their chairs.

Serrano's face flamed a livid, blotchy crimson. He looked around the circle of snarling, vicious faces that surrounded the conference table. Then he stared into the sneering face of Tom Taggart.

"Fast work, eh? Looks like you rounded every cheap, two-bit gunman in the whole damn state. Now—what?"

"Plenty," Taggart assured him. "You been screwing up the works long enough, see? Now you're through."

"Meaning?" Serrano glanced once more at the gunmen who pressed closer about them, fingers itching on the triggers of their guns. "What's it going to be, Taggart, a slaughter?"

Taggart looked aggrieved. "Of course not. Nobody's going to get hurt. At least, not if you mugs obey orders. We're just going to take you some place where you'll be safe, see? Just to keep you out of mischief.

"Now, not a sound out of you punks. You're going to walk out of the door and get into the cars out on the street. And you're not going to make a single phony move. If you do . . ." There was no need to finish the threat. "Now get up and reach for the ceiling. All of you."

Swoba was nearest the door. Setting the example, Taggart jammed his gun into the labor leader's ribs and nudged him toward the door. "March, bozo."

Swoba marched. The yegg nearest Serrano jammed the nozzle of his own gun against Big Nose's spine. LeBrett, with his own escort, was the next to go. The two strike lieutenants were herded enthusiastically on their way. Left alone, except for the rod whose gun dug deep into his broad back, Serrano hesitated.

To march meekly out, with his hands up in the air, was a bitter pill for Big Nose to swallow. Yet he knew, even as he hesitated, that resistance would be fatal.

"That means you, too, big guy," growled a voice behind him. "Step on it."

"I'll see you in hell for this," grated Serrano between clenched teeth.

"Nuts," was the answer. "Get going."

Each step was torture. The humiliation of his position ate like acid into Serrano's soul. With lagging feet he shuffled through the doorway and entered the speakeasy. Outside in the street, the sound of an auto horn urged them to speed up. Taggart, elated at the success of his raid, was anxious to get off.

Cocky because the notorious Big Nose Serrano was his prisoner, the yegg failed to notice anything amiss in the speakeasy. But Big Nose caught a glimpse of the mirror behind the bar. And what he saw reflected there brought a swift gleam of hope into his eyes.

He swerved slightly and drew near to the counter. Slowly he marched down alongside the bar. He had progressed half its length when a head raised cautiously over the mahogany and then, like a jack-in-the-box, McGinnis bobbed up from cover.

The gunman never knew what hit him. The menacing automatic suddenly was gone from Serrano's back and he whirled about just as his erstwhile captor crumpled in a limp heap to the floor.

McGinnis ruefully surveyed the jagged remnants of the bottle that remained in his fist. "That's the second bottle of that Scotch busted all to hell," he moaned. "My best stock, too."

Serrano didn't wait to hear his complaint. Snatching the gun from his hip pocket he raced for the door and plunged out into the areaway beyond.

Three cars were drawn up at the curb, their engines running. They were loaded with the gunmen and their prisoners. Only Taggart still stood on the sidewalk, holding open the door of the first car and waiting impatiently for his prize captive.

From the shadows Serrano charged out, blazing away at Taggart as he came.

But the gang boss' impatience saved his life. Just as Serrano cut loose he leaned forward to beep the horn once more. The whistling lead fanned his ear and he dove headlong into the car. Serrano's yell of frustrated rage was drowned out by the roar of three motors. Taggart didn't wait to find out what had screwed up the works. The foremost car swerved sharply away from the curb and careened down the street, the others in its wake.

Waving his arms and bellowing curses, Serrano raced out into the gutter. He dared not fire into the cars for fear of wounding his friends. Vainly he looked about for a cab, but there was none in sight.

The winking red tail-lights of the last car rounded the corner and left him capering, impotent and helpless, there in the gutter.

Serrano had completely forgotten the N.R.A.—the bakers' strike—everything save that Charlie LeBrett had fallen into the hands of Tom Taggart. For the past hour he had been in heavy session with The Flash, Goldstein and Gotz in McGinnis' back room. There had been only one subject before the house—how to rescue LeBrett and the others, if they hadn't already been taken for a ride.

Serrano made the final decision. It was his plan to make a bold attack on Taggart's stronghold up on Rush Street. If it was too late to help LeBrett, at least they might have the satisfaction of sending Taggart to hell along with him.

The men were just on the point of rising from the table, when a soft tap sounded on the door. Four hands flashed to as many hips as Big Nose crossed to the portal in two long strides. Standing far to one side of the jamb, his automatic covering the opening, he swiftly flung the door open.

Instead of a barrage of hungry steel, the quartette stared down into the excited face of the red-headed Mickey Deegan. It was easy to see that the kid had news—important news. Big Nose swept him into the room and closed the door behind him.

"Well, kid—what's up?" he asked.

"Plenty, LeBrett . . ."

Serrano snatched him up by the slack of his coat.

"What about LeBrett?"

"I know where Taggart's got him and the rest."

Serrano restrained himself with an effort. Gently he lowered the kid to his feet.

"Let's have it, son, fast."

"He's got 'em down at that old warehouse of his on the river. You know the place. The dump he used to run his booze into."

Serrano's lips were grim, his eyes flashed fire.

"Yes, I know the place," he grated. His eyes narrowed in sudden thought for a moment, then he reached for his hat. "Come on, boys—let's scram. You, too, Mickey, I can use you."

As one man the three gang leaders followed him to the door.

"What's the racket?" asked Goldstein.

"We're going down to that warehouse and yank LeBrett and the others."

"Alone?" queried Gotz.

"Yes, alone—with the help of the kid and our guns! I got an idea. I'll spill it on the way down."

Swiftly they barged out of the speakeasy and a minute later had crowded into The Flash's car. They careened away from the curb with a roar. With Flash's foot all the way down on the gas pedal and hitting a steady sixty-five, Serrano unfolded his plan of campaign.

"I know that dump of Taggart's. The rear end juts right out into the river. There's a big sliding door and a smaller one. He used to use the back end of the building as a warehouse for his booze, the front as a hang-out for his mob. If he's got LeBrett there and the rest, the place will be lousy with guards. We got to draw those guards off some way. And I got an idea.

"Across the street from the dump is a bunch of old, wooden shacks that have fallen all to hell. Now listen, boys, and you too, Mickey. You got a big part to play. This is the low-down. We'll pull up a block away from the warehouse. The kid beats it over to the wooden shanties and gets everything set for a big blaze. We four cut down to the river and swim for the back door of Taggart's joint. Mickey times us. When he figures we're there, he gives the shacks the works with a match and sees that there's plenty blaze."

"That's easy," chortled Mickey with excitement. "Those shanties will make a swell bonfire."

"Then," continued Serrano, "when all of Taggart's men are watching the blaze from the front of the joint, we'll charge in the rear and rescue LeBrett and the others. Get it? Simple, eh?"

"Simple as a shot of booze," gloated Gotz.

"Like taking beer away from a brat," said The Flash.

"So easy," commented Goldstein, "that we won't even get a chance to pump some lead into Taggart."

"Don't be too sure of that," warned Serrano. "Those guys ain't free, yet."

Some twenty minutes later, the careening car skidded to an abrupt halt by the waterfront. Before the spinning wheels had stopped turning, Big Nose and his cohorts had piled out.

It was a dark night, with no moon. The few intermittent stars that showed between the scud of racing clouds were pale and watery. A solitary street lamp far down the dockside, glowed dismally as it creaked on rusty hinges in the gusty breeze.

"Amscray, now, kid," ordered Serrano, throwing a fond arm around the ragged shoulders of the guttersnipe. "You know your stuff. Pull it off for me tonight—and Big Nose is a pal of yours for life."

The red-headed Mickey looked up into the massive face of Serrano. One grimy hand patted Big Nose reassuringly on his belt—as far up as he could reach.

"Don't worry, Big Nose," he piped in an eager voice. "I won't let you down."

A lump arose in Serrano's throat—a lump he found hard to swallow. "I know you won't, kid. Give us plenty of time to swim down to the back of Taggart's, then give those dumps the torch."

The hands of the two met in sober earnestness, then with the light of great deeds in his blue eyes, Mickey broke away, sped across the street on diminutive feet and disappeared in the dark shadows that marked his base of operations.

Big Nose watched him for a moment, then with a tremendous heave of the shoulders, turned to his men. "What a gangster that kid is going to make—what a gangster! Well, let's get going, boys. Straight for the river!"

They started off on a dog trot, furtive shadows in the night. Swiftly they ducked down a Stygian alley that led between two warehouses, dodging from shadow to shadow. They raced like the wind, but they made no sound. The stillness of the night was broken only by the gusts of wind around sharp corners, and the persistent groan and creak of ships chaffing against their moorings.

It was a mad and impossible enterprise they had embarked upon, but such was the power of Serrano's personality that not one of the men entertained a suspicion of failure.

They had to succeed—even if their mad scheme hinged on the work of a ragged, half-starved kid.

Two minutes later they broke out of the alley into a small, open square. From the far side of it projected a short, dumpy pier. The oily wash of the river lapped against the scummy pilings with a million muted tongues. Straight to the water's edge Serrano led his men. He squatted down and hurriedly kicked off his shoes and coat. His men followed suit. Then he pointed across the dark water, squinted down the rows of piers and warehouses that jutted out into the stream.

"See that building with the slanting roof? The sixth one from here?"

The men nodded.

"That's the joint! After me, boys—and if it comes to throwing lead, remember the good old N.R.A.—a new variation—No Rats Alive!"

He ran lightly across the loose planking of the dock to the water and threw himself forward. His muscled body described a perfect arc through the air, then cut the water cleanly without a splash. In rapid succession, Flash, Gotz and Goldstein dove in. They were all powerful swimmers and though the current was against them, they made rapid progress upstream. Despite Serrano's head start, Flash was the first to pull himself up onto the rear landing stage of Taggart's headquarters. Two minutes later, like grim spectres, the other men followed him.

Their first concern was with their guns. They went over them carefully and dried each part, then examined the cartridges to see that all was in perfect working order. When this important detail had been attended to, Big Nose gave the order to lay low.

"It's up to the kid, now," he said. "We got to wait for him."

They crouched there, side by side in the dark, guns drawn, waiting. Would Mickey fail them? The success of their venture depended upon the kid. Minutes dragged by slowly. A wharf rat dove into the water with a sudden plunk and cut a slimy trail to the shore. Eagerly the men pierced the darkness ahead toward the row of wooden shanties.

Suddenly a sharp, indrawn breath from Goldstein! A spark, a splutter, then a tiny tongue of flame showed itself before them. The ball of fire glowed sinisterly for a moment, then with a sudden vicious burst shot upward. Involuntarily the men crept forward. A sharp gust of wind swept off the river, caught the hungry flame and fanned it like a bellows.

With an ominous growl the avid flames broke loose with a shower of sparks and engulfed one of the shanties. Tongues of licking fire shot high into the air and a heavy pall of smoke streaked with orange and crimson, billowed in a thick, sulphurous cloud.

The wind, as if enjoying the spectacle, zoomed in from all quarters and in two minutes the entire row of shanties was a blazing, seething inferno. Mickey had been right! They went up like a box of matches, painting the dull, overcast sky a vivid crimson.

"The kid came through, boys," growled Serrano exultantly, creeping forward. "Now it's up to us."

His men were right with him. They never hesitated. Swiftly they advanced to the rear door of the warehouse. Big Nose tried it. It was locked. Mutely he signaled his men and four shoulders applied silent but mighty pressure to the oaken panel. Once, twice, in concerted surges of power. The third time, with a sharp rending of wood, the lock gave way.

They paused for a moment, tense, waiting, their guns ready. Nothing happened! Either the ruse of the fire had effectively drawn off the rear guard or whatever noise they had made had been drowned in the roar of the flames that filled the air with a vibrating roar.

Slowly Serrano pushed open the wrecked door and the four slipped into the warehouse. The billowing flames of the fire filled the place with a lurid, pulsating glow. It was deserted. Directly ahead of them, facing the front of the building was a heavy oaken door.

"You, Gotz," ordered Big Nose, "guard that door. It leads to the front. Any one that comes in there—get him. But get him quiet. You know your stuff."

Gotz nodded grimly and took up his position at the forward door.

Along the left-hand side of the warehouse were two other portals. Big Nose nodded towards them and his remaining two men stepped forward with him. They forced the lock of the first. The room beyond was empty. They attacked the second. Softly it opened inward on well-oiled hinges. A heavy, opaque gloom greeted them. Serrano entered, closely followed by his two men. Silence for a moment, then some one stirred, followed immediately after by a weak voice—the voice of Swoba.

"Okay, Taggart—we're ready for it. Get your dirty work over with."

"There's going to be no dirty work," said Serrano in a low voice.

A startled silence; a gasp. Then: "What—by God, it's Serrano!"

Big Nose struck a match and the tiny flame exploded in the darkened room like a bomb. The light revealed a small, ten-foot, iron-sheeted cell with no outlet save the door by which the rescuers had come. Stretched out on the floor at the far end, bound hand and foot, were Swoba and his three lieutenants. There was no sign of LeBrett.

Serrano put into words the question that was uppermost in his mind while he sliced at the bonds that held the prisoners with a long knife.

"Where's Charlie?" he demanded of Swoba.

Swoba struggled to his feet. "Up front! He's having a special little session with Taggart. . . ."

"You mean they're giving him the business?"

"Just a sample," whispered Swoba bitterly. "We all took a beating, but I guess Charlie's in for plenty!"

The blood in Serrano's veins turned to flaming acid. His nose flared dangerously and his eyes narrowed. If Taggart had gone to work on LeBrett—if LeBrett was . . . Big Nose cursed savagely under his breath. His massive fist tightened around the butt of his automatic as he turned to Flash.

"You three guys get Swoba and his men out of here," he said tersely. "I'm going after Charlie."

"Ixnay," protested Goldstein. "You can't pull that off alone."

"No?" snorted Big Nose. "Watch me. One guy will have a better chance of crashing the front end of this dump than half a dozen. Get this mob out of here—get 'em away. Then you three wait for me outside. If I don't come out within ten minutes with Charlie, come in and get me!"

Reluctantly the men obeyed and preceded by the liberated prisoners, filed out of the warehouse and disappeared into the night beyond.

Big Nose watched them go, then paused a moment in the darkness before advancing. Outside he heard the crescendo wail of sirens as the fire-fighting apparatus pulled up with a roar and a clang before the blazing shanties opposite the warehouse. Now was the psychological moment.

For the first time Serrano opened the doorway in the center partition that led to the front part of the building.

Unlike the other doors it was not locked and opened easily to his pull on the knob. He passed silently through it and found himself in a short corridor. A thin beam of light along the floor at the far end attracted his attention. On silent feet he approached it and stopped before still another door. Voices came to him thickly from within. He pressed his ear to the jamb and listened.

What he heard caused his heart to pound and his nerves to tense—Taggart's gloating voice answered by the defiant one of LeBrett; then Schultz's high falsetto drowned out by the booming bass of McLaughlin.

Big Nose grinned wickedly to himself. This was turning out better than he had dared hope for. The three of them together! All to the good! He would settle that business now.

He waited no more. His finger constricted around the trigger of his automatic. Slowly, carefully, his left hand went out to the knob. It turned silently in his fingers. Then, with a mighty heave of his foot, he kicked the portal wide and his massive frame filled the doorway.

A quartette of startled faces looked up at his explosive entrance. Taggart's hand flashed to his hip but was arrested midway, as Serrano calmly covered him with the leveled nozzle of his gun. Schultz's glasses dropped away from his popping eyes and McLaughlin's heavy jaw sagged open.

Only LeBrett enjoyed the situation. A slow grin of pure enjoyment spread over his face.

Serrano answered it with one of his own. His eyes twinkled and with an easy, nonchalant movement he closed the door behind him.

"Hi, Charlie," he called. "Okay?"

"Sure," answered LeBrett. "I been expecting you to call all evening."

"Got here as soon as I could," answered Serrano.

They spoke in casual, matter-of-fact voices, but there was death in Big Nose's eyes. In one swift glance he took in the room, saw that the only door was behind him; saw that LeBrett's hands were tied behind his back.

He moved forward slowly.

Taggart's evil face was distorted with baffled rage and fury. His white hands knotted convulsively on the table as he glared from red eyes at Serrano. His thick tongue wetted thin lips as he tried to give utterance to the profanity that welled in his soul.

LeBrett's grin grew.

"How the hell did you get here?" The words came, strangled and incoherent from Taggart's working lips.

"Easy," answered Serrano. "Through the back door. Thought it about time I paid you a little social call."

"Yeah?" sneered Taggart. "Glad you're here. You'll never get out the way you came in."

Big Nose grinned. He scratched the tip of his nose with the nozzle of his gun.

"Now you're talking big, Taggart—too big for a little rat— If I were you, I wouldn't bet that way. If Charlie and I don't get out that back door, they'll bury us all in the same hole!"

"Yeah?"

"Yeah?" beamed Serrano affably. "Oh, I almost forgot to tell you. I set those dumps on fire across the way. And before I broke in on your little party here, I took the liberty of releasing Swoba and his mob."

The full import of these words was slow to sink in, but when it did, it yanked Taggart half out of his chair. A terrible mask of hate fell over his face

Then, with a mighty heave of his foot, he kicked the portal open.

and with murderous eyes he glared at Serrano.

"Sit down!" grated Big Nose and all the mocking humor had gone out of his voice. "I'm running things here, now."

Fuming, choking with rage, Taggart subsided into his chair.

"That's better," laughed Serrano easily. "Don't get hot, or a hunk of lead will cool you off. I never miss when I'm shooting at rats like you."

"So what?" snarled Taggart.

"That comes later as far as you're concerned," answered Big Nose grimly. "First I want to speak to Schultzy, here—and McLaughlin."

"You can't get away with this, Serrano," began the alderman sullenly.

"Shut up, you," snarled Big Nose. "Your turn comes later. Squawk too much and they'll take you out of here on a shutter!"

McLaughlin subsided and Serrano turned to Schultz. He played with his gun suggestively, for a long moment studied the pale face of the bakery owner from somber eyes.

"Do you want to die, Schultz?" he suddenly shot out.

"Die?" echoed the other.

"You heard me," growled Serrano. "Die with a slug of lead in your guts. At that it's a damned sight better than the way you starve your help. Well, speak up. Do you want to croak or no?"

"Of—of course not," sputtered Schultz.

Big Nose snorted. "I didn't think you did. Well, there's just one thing that will save you."

Schultz looked helplessly from Taggart to McLaughlin, then back to the menacing barrel of the automatic in Serrano's hand. "Die—I—I don't want to die."

"Then pick up that phone!" snarled Serrano. "Call the *Tribune*, savvy— and get the editor on the phone. Then tell him that you made a mistake—that you're going to sign the N.R.A. code. Tell him that you're going to raise wages and shorten hours. And tell him that you're going to reduce the price of bread two cents a loaf."

"But . . ."

Schultz got no further. Serrano leaped forward, his left arm described a swift arc through the air and his open palm lashed across the baker's face.

"Grab that phone, damn you, or by God you get it now!"

Schultz grabbed the phone.

Three minutes later he hung up and there were large beads of sweat on his forehead.

"Just one more thing, Schultz," grinned Serrano. "You're going to keep that bargain. If you ever think of changing your mind—think of me—and it will change it back again. I'm being nice to you, Schultz—very nice."

Big Nose shifted the gun in his hand and searched in his pocket for a slice of cut plug. He chawed off a massive quid, rolled it contemplatively in his mouth for a moment and then spat obliquely towards a distant cuspidor. He turned to McLaughlin.

"Your number is up, Mr. Alderman. I'm giving you the tip for what it's worth. If you take my advice you'll scram to hell out of town. I'm giving you one chance for your lousy life. If you're not . . ."

He broke off abruptly. He had noted the sudden dilation of LeBrett's eyes, had seen the swift, convulsive movement of Taggart's clenched fist on the table.

Serrano's nerves tensed; an icy finger played a skeleton's dance down his spine. Some instinct warned him that the door behind him had moved, that it was slowly opening inward. With LeBrett's hands tied, he was caught between two potential fires!

To turn and face the new menace meant instant death from Taggart's rod, which would leap to frantic life the instant he shifted position. He smiled, grimly, bitterly. Tiny beads of sweat popped out on his forehead. The icy hand of death again raced down his spine.

It seemed to his straining nerves that hours passed while he confronted Taggart like a graven image. His agile mind raced with lightning speed. He realized that no matter what he did, it was a gamble for life.

And then it was that LeBrett made the decisive blow. Doubling his feet under the table, he suddenly sent it crashing forward into the pit of Taggart's stomach. The gang chief sprawled wildly.

And on the instant Serrano whirled, sidestepped, convulsed his finger on the trigger.

The sharp crack of two automatics blended into one deafening roar as a sizzling hunk of lead burned its way through Serrano's sleeve. A guttural scream came from the doorway, followed by a dull crash of a falling body. His lead had found its mark. Peering through the blue haze of smoke that drifted through the room he recognized the fallen figure, Lou Mancuso!

Suddenly a loud commotion sounded from the front of the warehouse. Aroused by the shooting, Taggart's mob was pounding down on them. Emboldened by the coming of his men, Taggart snarled a vicious curse, leaped to his feet and charged straight at the huge figure of Serrano.

Big Nose's arm described a swift arc through the air. The barrel of his automatic landed with a sickening thud on Taggart's skull. Without a sound the gang chief slumped heavily to the floor.

Serrano hurtled his fallen body, whipped out his knife and hacked away at the bonds that held LeBrett. A moment later his ally was free and armed with Taggart's gun.

The yells of Taggart's men were echoing in the corridor as Big Nose took his stand beside LeBrett. His eyes gleamed with the joy of battle, his nose radiated a furious energy and he whirled on Schultz and McLaughlin.

"Under the table, you mugs. Lively, now, if you want to save your lousy hides. There'll be hell popping in a minute."

With a squeal of fear the bakery owner scrambled under the overturned table and cowered there. McLaughlin flung a bitter curse at Serrano, then followed suit and wedged his bulk in beside the shivering Schultz.

Big Nose whooped joyously.

"Great stuff, Charlie," he roared. "Give 'em the works! Hurrah for hell! N.R.A. *No Rats Alive!*"

Heavy feet pounded toward the door. LeBrett flicked a cigarette to his lips, lit up and inhaled greedily.

"The slogan's changed, eh? Big boy, it suits me a damn sight better. Here they come! Now for some action!"

Howling and cursing the mob charged into the room but their very numbers hampered them. Big Nose and LeBrett went into action as one. Stabbing flames of vivid orange fire split the haze, lighting up the scene with a weird, unholy glow. The staccato explosions of the flaming rods reverberated through the room and the screams of the wounded added to the din.

The foremost gunman straightened out with a jerk as a heavy slug from Serrano's gun ploughed its searing path through his belly. A bitter oath rose to his lips, then faded into a strangled, blood-choked gurgle. He fell heavily and the battle cry of Serrano boomed out above the confusion.

LeBrett's gun barked twice and each time, a Taggart henchman howled shrilly above the din of battle. A smashing slug tore a deep furrow over Serrano's eye and a crimson stream trickled crazily down his face. Even as he wiped the blood away with his left hand his gat barked again and another of his attackers gasped out his last tortured breath.

The room became a shambles. Bitter, acid curses mingled with the groans of the dying and Serrano's war-whoop roared out clarion above it all. But the tide of battle was slowly turning. Even two such deadly fighters could not expect to hold out long against the superior numbers of the mob.

Big Nose grinned encouragingly at LeBrett.

"We'll take a couple more of the rats along with us, anyway, son," he roared. "Come on, you punks! Take it or give it! We're waiting!"

The pair backed up to the corner where the still groggy Taggart was climbing to his feet with the support of the wall. He stood there a moment, swaying drunkenly in the pall of gun-smoke before Serrano spotted him.

With a joyous whoop, Big Nose pounced upon him, clutched him in his powerful arms and swung him around in front as a shield.

"Out of the way, mugs!" he roared. "Try to stop us and it's curtains for Taggart, here!"

The dazed eyes of the gang chief cleared rapidly as he realized his predicament. The savage nozzle of Serrano's gat dug deep into his ribs.

"Call off your dogs," Big Nose grated into his ear, "or I'll blow you to hell!"

Taggart complied with alacrity. His mob backed off sullenly, guns ready for the first break on the part of the hated duo. Slowly, carefully, Serrano edged for the door with LeBrett bringing up the rear. Only the bitter oaths of Taggart broke the silence of those tense moments. Back, back to the door and down the corridor went the raiding party and their prisoner, the mob following at a respectful distance like a pack of hungry wolves at bay.

Taggart tensed, but Serrano's arms were like bands of steel and the snarling gang chief knew it was death to make a break.

They backed out onto the jetty at the rear of the warehouse, fell into the arms of The Flash and Gotz and Goldstein.

"Lord!" exclaimed Gotz. "Look who they got! Taggart!"

"Yeah," grinned Serrano, "Taggart and the end of the bakers' strike! If you want the rest of his mob, go in and get 'em. They're trailing us ten feet behind."

His men leaped eagerly forward, but Big Nose hastily countermanded the order.

"No—better save it, boys. Schultz and McLaughlin are in there somewhere and they might get knocked off by mistake. Taggart's the rat I wanted anyway. Let's scram to hell out of here. There's a speed boat tied up at the end of the dock. Get her going."

The mob jumped to obey. As the powerful engine leaped to life, Serrano, still dragging his unwilling victim, backed up, swept Taggart clear off his feet and dropped with him into the stern of the launch. He swayed perilously a moment, then regained his balance and the boat shot away from its mooring.

A howl of rage rose from the pack at the end of the dock. Cheated of their prey, their chief kidnapped from their very stronghold, they made the night hideous with their howls and curses.

In answer to their profanity Serrano's voice boomed out across the rapidly widening stretch of water between them.

"N.R.A.—you punks! *No Rats Alive!* Get me?"

And to make sure they did, he grabbed Taggart's collar, jerked him to his knees and let the screeching mob on the dock have a last good look at their leader.

Hell's Gangster

Big Nose Serrano gets wind of a labor kick-back racket—then a murder seals the bargain and Big Nose goes on the warpath as never before.

SERRANO WAS DRUNK—VERY DRUNK! But that in itself was not unusual. The tragic element about the situation was the fact that he was plastered—not on bootleg stock—but on the real McCoy.

His prodigious nose was aglow; his wild eyes were suspiciously dim as he leaned his massive bulk against the polished mahogany of McGinnis' speak. Pardon, gents! McGinnis' Tavern—officially licensed by the city, county, and state to dispense hard liquor to the thirsty, under the law.

For a second, Serrano's bleary eyes focused on the neatly framed license, suspended behind the bar. He stared, his nose got redder, he choked, and then to drown the fit of coughing he helped himself liberally from the bottle of Scotch that decorated the bar.

Like a man who has witnessed the last miracle he turned wearily to

LeBrett who slouched somberly at his side along the brass rail.

With drunken ardor, Big Nose punched LeBrett affectionately in the ribs. LeBrett growled and applied himself to the bottle. Serrano ignored the protest and wheezed an alcoholic breath in his companion's face.

"Well, Charlie," he boomed, "it's all over."

"What's all over?" LeBrett wanted to know in a sour voice.

"This life of ease and sin, of ours," elaborated Serrano with an expansive gesture of his hamlike fist. "This life of booze, bullets, and blood we've been leading. This life of machine guns and murder! This life of—"

"Okay! Okay! Don't rub it in," interrupted LeBrett impatiently. "So what?"

Serrano looked at LeBrett from sorrowful eyes and slowly shook his head. "The same old Charlie, eh? Always crabbing my act—always rushing me—never giving me poetic feelings a chance to express themselves."

LeBrett winked broadly at McGinnis, spat disdainfully at the nearest cuspidor, turned to Serrano.

"Nuts to all that," he said succinctly. "The booze is out—Mac, here, has got his license. I ask you again—so what?"

Serrano shook his head again. "Cripes, you take it hard, Charlie," he said. Then he grinned and once more his hamlike fist beat an affectionate tattoo on LeBrett's ribs. "So what, Charlie, you ask? Well, I'll tell you. We're retiring from the rackets, see? We've got our pile—so what the hell? We'll devote our dough to charity—to—to philanthropy."

"You mean *your* dough," edged in LeBrett sardonically. "Go on. Then what?"

Serrano had no ready answer to the last question. He ran a stubby fist over the stubble on his chin, pulled reflectively at the lobe of his left ear, trumpeted hoarsely through his hairy nose.

"Then what?" he boomed in a voice that set the bottle and glasses to dancing. "Why, when the dough is gone we turn honest, see? Make an honest living."

With a world-weary shrug, LeBrett turned to McGinnis. "There must be something to this bottled-in-bond stuff. I've never seen him that bad before." Then to Serrano. "Don't make me laugh, big boy. How long do you think you would last swinging a pick? Not in a barroom brawl—but in a ditch?"

Big Nose ignored the heavy sarcasm in the other's voice. "Maybe I'll become a dick—a private—"

LeBrett's glass shattered against the bar. His eyes popped open in pained surprise. Then he saw the humor of the situation. He laughed.

"Sure. I get it. You become a dick and send up every crooked shamus on the force. By God and I think I'd give you a hand. Not bad, Big Nose!"

Serrano expanded under this subtle flattery. His gorilla chest expanded; his bulbous nose glowed with pride. "Didn't I tell you I had ideas?" he demanded.

LeBrett's lips curled with scorn. "Confine them to dames, Big Nose—not dicks." He hooked his arm under Serrano's. "Come on, you pick-and-shovel artist—the whistle's blowing. Let's scram."

Serrano waved a vague farewell at McGinnis and under the steadying pressure of LeBrett's arm staggered towards the door.

Then he slipped out into the night and onto the point of a gun!

Shabby cap pulled well down over his eyes, his thin, emaciated body stooped slightly forward, the gat-goose confronted the two drunks as they staggered out of McGinnis' Tavern. A short, stubby, bulldog automatic glinted ominously in his right fist—a fist that trembled slightly.

Serrano stiffened, was immediately sober; LeBrett's eyes narrowed, his muscles tensed for swift and instant action.

The snout of the gun edged forward a few inches. A cracked muffled voice emerged from beneath the brim of the cap.

"Dough!"

"Oh! A stick-up, eh?" purred Serrano.

"Dough!" croaked the voice again, a terrible urgency in the word.

Big Nose was very sober. He noticed that convulsive trembling of the hand that held the gun. No gat-goose, this.

"There are enough cheap gunmen in this town without you trying to crash the racket, bud," he said softly. "The town's lousy with torpedoes—and for an amateur, it don't pay. If you want a—"

His hand went to his breast pocket as if to extract his wallet, then like a flash of light it descended in a swift arc. His hard knuckles, crashed against the wrist that held the gun. The automatic clattered to the sidewalk, where the point of LeBrett's shoe expertly dispatched it to the gutter.

With an inarticulate cry, the stick-up artist pivoted, started to bolt. Big Nose yanked him up short by the ample slack of his coat. The gunman's cap fell off and with a flash of defense he threw back his head and glared at Serrano. Then his expression changed.

"Jeez! It's Serrano!" he breathed.

Serrano's eyes narrowed then opened wide with recognition. And with recognition a swift look of pain came over his face.

"By God if it isn't Turner! Flash Turner!"

LeBrett whistled expressively.

"It's this way, Big Nose," began Turner. "I didn't mean to . . ."

"Of course you didn't!" boomed Serrano. "Anyway, what the hell!" In one illuminating flash he knew only too well what had motivated Turner, without having the other explain. He tucked his arm protectingly under the other's. "You're hungry as hell, Flash—and I'm starved. Between us we could eat an ox. There's a hashhouse down here that makes a specialty of steaks. Let's go."

Turner hesitated.

"I got the kid around the corner," he explained.

"You mean Ruby?" questioned Serrano.

Turner nodded. "Yeah—and she's hungrier than I am."

"Lead the way," intoned Big Nose. "We'll all eat!"

Despite the ravages the past year had wrought, Ruby Turner still showed the class that had at one time made her the toast of gangdom. Though there were dark circles under her velvet eyes they still showed the spirit and fire of the old days; though there were hollows of hunger in her cheeks, they couldn't mar the lovely contour of her face.

And though for Serrano's tastes there could have been more meat on her bones, she still had a figure that was like a hop-eater's dream.

She started to edge away when Turner approached with his two escorts. Serrano's booming bass halted her. She stood poised for a second like a frightened deer, then turned, hurriedly up to meet the three men.

It was the most natural thing in the world for her to flee to the comforting embrace of Serrano's encircling arms.

"Big Nose!" she breathed and despite the catch in her voice, there was a world of relief in her words.

Serrano held her close to his huge chest for a long moment and a sudden lump appeared in his throat as he felt her body tremble against his. She and The Flash *had* been up against it!

"It's okay, babe," he said at last. "We eat now. You can tell me all about it later."

They started for the hashhouse, but so intent were they on each other that they failed entirely to note the dark, slouching figure that kept step behind them.

They ate. They all did justice to the steak and the French fries. And over the coffee, The Flash and Ruby told their story. It was pathetically simple in general outline; in detail, exceedingly interesting to Serrano and LeBrett.

A little over a year ago, The Flash and Ruby had been attached to Serrano's mob. Then they had seen the light—at least they had thought so—had had their union duly solemnized by the genial Father Ryan of the Tenth Ward and had decided to go straight.

With the net result that when their supply of ready cash ran out—they starved.

"At first the dicks wouldn't give us a break," elaborated Turner. "Either they didn't believe we were on the up and up or they wanted to make it tough for us. I'd no sooner talk myself into a job than they'd talk me out of it."

"Some cops are like that," admitted LeBrett bitterly.

"Well," continued Turner, "we finally convinced MacBride—he's the only right dick on the force—that we were on the level. Things eased up a bit then. We thought we'd be able to make a go of it.

"And then this last turned up."

Serrano hitched his chair closer to the table and mouthed his cigar aggressively. "Okay, let's have it."

"The dirtiest racket of them all," grated Turner bitterly.

Big Nose grunted impatiently. "Is what?"

"The kick-back racket—the labor racket!"

Serrano's eyes nodded and he shook his massive head soberly.

"I've heard of it—dirty, eh?"

"Lousy!"

"What's the set-up?"

"Simple as A-B-C. Either you kick back a buck out of a three-dollar day's pay—or you don't work. It's tough on a guy with a family. Four days a week at twelve bucks. Eight bucks left when you pay a four-dollar bonus for the privilege of sweating and starving."

"That does sounds pretty nasty," growled Serrano. "I always did hate chiseling."

Turner smiled bitterly and raised his hand in protest.

"Don't get it wrong. There's nothing chiseling about this racket. There's millions in it. Figure it out for yourself. Every poor slob who is lucky enough to have a job has got to kick back one third or he's out. If he don't like it, there's a hundred other hungry bums willing to kick back fifty per cent for a chance at a job.

"You don't know what it is to be hungry; you don't know what it is for the missus or the kids to be hungry."

There was a far-away look in Serrano's eyes. "No, maybe I don't," he admitted. "Maybe it would do me a lot of good if I did."

"I've talked to a lot of boys in the Tenth Ward," continued Turner. "Good lads, who've backed you up before, Big Nose. They're all wailing the blues; they're all up against the same proposition—but what the hell can they do?"

LeBrett looked at Turner shrewdly.

"What the hell did you do?"

"Who me? I refused to kick back, slapped a collector down—and in return got the sweetest shellacking from a mob of gorillas a guy ever took."

"And on top of that," put in Ruby, "he got fired off the job. Not only that job but off every other. He never got another chance to slap down a collector.

And to make it sweeter, they sent a couple of gorillas around to tell me that if The Flash did any more kicking, they'd settle the argument with a machine gun."

"So that's the way it works," mused Serrano. "Tough guys, eh?"

"Yeah—and they mean it."

"And then what?"

"And then we starved," said Turner savagely. "After starving for a couple of months I went around to see Castagni—he's the field man for the racket. We had a nice little scene. We called each other a lot of nasty names and I was eased out with a gun in my navel. He delivered his little song and dance to me in person. 'If I thought I could buck the racket—they'd bury me!' "

"When did this happen?" asked Serrano.

"A week ago."

There was a savage glint in LeBrett's eyes. With an admirable insight into Serrano's psychology, he said: "And you thought it easier to go into the stick-up business than to buck the racket. Is that it?"

Turner nodded, lowered his eyes. Then he snapped his head erect and the fire in his eyes matched the one in LeBrett's.

"I was hungry," he said simply. "So was Ruby. But if you two boys want to buck the racket, I'm with you all the way." Ruby put a protesting hand on his arm but he brushed it aside. "Listen, babe," he implored. "This isn't going off the straight and narrow. It's a lousy racket; it ought to go!"

"Right!" intoned Serrano solemnly. "It's a lousy racket. It preys on the poor. It takes the milk out of the mouths of babes; it takes the bread out of the mouths of hungry kids. It's a starvation racket and it's got to go."

He waxed eloquent. His chest expanded, his fists clenched, his eyes glinted to the old savage fire and his gargantuan nose was a wondrous thing to behold.

"We'll buck it, Flash!" he boomed. "No, by God, we'll do more. We'll break it! Now give me the set-up back of it."

A new animation appeared in Turner's face. Even Ruby had reacted to Serrano's stirring words. Her eyes shone brightly and the hot blood coursed swiftly through her veins as she realized that once more she and her man were enlisted under the banner of Big Nose Serrano.

Turner hitched up his chair and lighted a cigarette.

It was the last conscious thing he ever did!

The door to the hashhouse opened suddenly, noiselessly. A short squat figure stood silhouetted in the opening on straddled legs. A slouch hat was pulled low over his killer eyes; his cheeks had the waxen pallor of the hop-head—a hop-head coked to the ears.

But the glinting, blue-steel Luger in his hand was steady—steady and as sure as death.

Turner sat facing the door. He was the first of the four at the table to realize what was happening. He looked up, saw the man in the doorway and involuntarily half rose in his chair.

That act signed his death warrant!

The Luger snapped up. The torpedo's finger constricted on the trigger. A savage spit of orange flame jetted from the long barrel. Lead crashed into Turner's body, ate avidly through bone and gristle.

The impact of the wasps of death sent Turner crashing back but, even before the echo of the shots had died away, Serrano and LeBrett had sent their chairs crashing. As if by a miracle two guns sprouted simultaneously in their hands.

Simultaneously the twin automatics leaped to an avid, death-dealing life. The hashhouse resounded to the growl of their guns, and the chaos of noise as the customers scrambled for cover beneath the tables was drowned as they continued to hurl lead.

But no more than the first two shots were necessary. The joint fire had converged unerringly to a spot exactly in the center of the torpedo's forehead. As if by a miracle a third eye appeared there. A ruby eye, this, that glowed with an ever-increasing sinister brightness as the light faded and was extinguished from the other two.

The killer crumpled forward, went down slowly, joint by joint, as if pulled to the floor by invisible hands. A sudden gush of blood welled from his mouth and his descent was accelerated. He crashed, arms outflung, smashing his face on the floor.

Chaos, pandemonium, reigned in the restaurant. Outside an automobile engine came to life with a throaty roar. The door was suddenly assaulted once more. It crashed inward. A second torpedo, the submachine gun in his hands already pumping death, charged through the opening.

Big Nose and LeBrett met his advance with a blast from their automatics. The charging gunman failed to see the body of his companion on the floor. He tripped over it, staggered, the typewriter still roaring its song of death.

The elaborate crystal chandelier overhead went out with a crash of broken glass.

Serrano's automatic spewed its last ounce of death. The machine gun was suddenly stilled. And the sudden, appalling silence that followed was punctuated by the crash of a second body.

Once more the machine out on the street roared to life. A police whistle shrilled; shouting voices filled the air.

In the darkness, Serrano heard the suppressed sobs of Ruby. He felt for Turner, found him.

"Got you bad, Flash?" he asked in a hoarse voice.

Chaos, pandemonium reigned in the restaurant.

"All the way," answered Turner. He essayed a laugh that was racked with pain. "What—what do you think—of the racket, now, eh?"

"Plenty!" grated Serrano. "We got to get you out of here."

Turner shook his head in the darkness. "You'll—never get me out—I'm done. Only one thing—before I go. You'll go through with it—eh, Big Nose—what you said before—about busting the racket?"

Serrano gripped the hand of the dying man in two tremendous paws.

"I wouldn't back out now for a million, kid," he promised.

Turner heaved a sigh of relief. "That makes it easier." He paused, gathered his strength for one last supreme effort. "Just one more thing—take care of the kid—she always did have a—soft spot for you, Big Nose— So long, Ruby—kiss me, Ruby—I'm going!"

It was a full two minutes later before Serrano had the heart to break that embrace of death. The cops were already pounding down the sidewalk outside.

"We got to scram out of here," he whispered hoarsely to LeBrett. "The back way. Through the kitchen. If anyone gets in your way, slap 'em down!"

Serrano forced a roll of bills on Ruby and established her in a secluded hotel on the South Side. An hour later he was back once more at McGinnis' Tavern in sober session with LeBrett. A bottle of Scotch stood before them and, though Big Nose helped himself liberally to its contents, this time he did not get drunk.

The bitter acid of the hate that seethed within him, the grim resolve to finish the job to which he had dedicated himself within the past hour, were effective antidotes to the alcohol.

They had discussed the painful passing of Turner, they had discussed Ruby, they had discussed all they knew and had heard about the kick-back racket.

After a momentary silence Serrano looked up, turned to his ally in crime with a wry smile.

"Well, you win, Charlie," he said. "There goes all my good resolutions to hell. I guess I never was slated for a pick-and-shovel job anyway. There's still plenty in the rackets to hold our interest."

LeBrett nodded somberly. "Right," he grunted. "And if you ask me, if you're still thinking about charity, cleaning up this mess is pure—is pure filan—filan . . . aw, hell—you know—it's the right thing to do."

Serrano didn't smile; he nodded his head in sober agreement.

"Right! Now let's get down to ways and means."

However, before they had an opportunity to discuss their course of procedure, the door to McGinnis' opened to the broad shoulders of Detective MacBride.

Big Nose waved him an affable greeting. LeBrett shoved the bottle in the detective's direction as he ambled over to their place at the bar.

" 'Lo, Big Nose—hi, Charlie," he drawled, a quizzical light in his eye.

"Have one on me," suggested Serrano.

"Don't mind if I do." MacBride poured himself a liberal four fingers, held his glass up to the light and squinted speculatively through the amber fluid. "No, I don't mind if I do," he reiterated. "Here's to two dead gorillas. May they stay dead long."

Big Nose promptly filled his own glass and held it on high. "And here's an answer to that, Mac," he said. "Here's to the lad that tried to go straight— the lad that got the two gorillas."

MacBride nodded. "Sure, I'll drink to that." The three men raised their glasses and the toast was downed. This formality attended to, the detective placed his glass carefully on the bar and wiped his broad mouth with the back of his hand. "That toast of yours is all right, Big Nose," he said quietly, "only it's screwy as hell. How Turner could have filled that rat with the machine gun, when the first rat had already filled him with lead, is a hot one. Maybe you can answer it?"

Serrano shook his head, grinned. "I'm no dick, Mac. That's your job."

"Sure. Know anything about the shooting down at the Eat Shop?"

"Not a thing, Mac; honest, not a thing."

MacBride's lips twitched into a half smile. He poured himself another drink. "I didn't think you would. But I'm not asking too many questions. I'm satisfied that Turner rubbed out Fink and Denton before they got him. That's my story and I'd advise *you two* to stick to it."

"Okay, Mac," grinned Big Nose. "That makes us all Elks. If ever I get to be police commissioner, I'll make you chief inspector."

MacBride didn't smile. He spoke soberly, sincerely. "And I'd be damned glad to work under you."

Serrano slapped him affectionately on the back. "Thanks, Mac. Coming from one of the few honest coppers on the force, that means a lot. Listen. There's a racket in this town that I'm interested in—damn' interested. Interested so much that I'm going to clean it up. You know what I mean—the racket that got Turner—the kick-back gyp. Monk Lannigan is the muscle man and front for it, I know—but where's his protection—his connections?"

Detective MacBride poured himself another drink, looked furtively around the barroom.

"What do you mean you're going to clean the racket up?" he asked slowly.

"Just what I say," answered Big Nose. "You know me. If it takes a little moral persuasion, I got that; if it takes a few machine guns—" He paused and his eyes took on a steely glint. "Well, I got that, too, Mac. I'm going to kill the racket if I got to kill everybody back of it. Who's giving it protection?"

"It's dynamite," cautioned MacBride.

"You're telling me? Who's back of it?"

MacBride shook his head. "I don't know. I wish I did. If I did I'd tell you. Only this. It's somebody high up. So watch your step." He turned, started towards the door, paused and turned back again. "And here's wishing you luck, Big Nose. If I get anything, I'll pass it on."

Serrano and LeBrett didn't wait for a tip-off from MacBride before going into action. They had enough leads of their own to start on. It was Serrano's philosophy of warfare to always take the offensive and it was with this policy in mind that eleven o'clock the following morning saw them entering the shabby portals of the Crescent Building on Clark Street.

They paused in the lobby just long enough to learn that the Labor Protective Organization occupied a suite of offices on the fourth floor, then wedged into the dilapidated elevator and were whisked upward.

The third door down the corridor was adorned by a bold brass plate. Serrano jerked a derisive thumb.

"Get that, Charlie? Labor Protective Organization. Bet Lannigan thinks that's funny as hell. But by God, he won't think it's so damn' funny when I get through with him."

LeBrett didn't second the motion with idle words. He spat on his hands and hitched up his pants. Then Big Nose grasped the door knob and flung the portal inward.

Directly across the outer office was a glass-paneled door which bore the inscription:

MARTIN LANNIGAN, *PRES.*
PRIVATE

Serrano uttered a low growl and started for it. But between him and his objective was a low wooden railing, its center opening blocked by a lantern-jawed, narrow-eyed individual. A battered felt hat perched at a rakish angle on his head and his shirt-sleeved arms were crossed pugnaciously across his chest.

Big Nose waved an impatient hand. "Out of the road—you."

The other stood his ground.

"Oh, yeah? Who the hell are you—and what do you wa—?"

Big Nose Serrano's answer was effectively simple. One great paw of a hand yanked the man's hat down over his eyes; the paw's mate shot out toward his belt buckle and sent him careening wildly backward.

"Big Nose Serrano's got a date with Mr. Monk Lannigan," Serrano's booming voice flung back over his shoulder. "And anybody tries to stop me'll get his face smeared."

With that, he yanked open the door marked "PRIVATE."

Half a dozen men were in the office when he swaggered across the threshold. Six pairs of eyes stared at the doorway. Six men stiffened to rigid immobility as they recognized Serrano and LeBrett. Yet no one made a sound.

Big Nose stood for a moment, arms akimbo, thoroughly enjoying the sensation caused by his precipitate arrival. Then, while LeBrett posted himself against the door jamb, wary-eyed, with his hand near his gun pocket, Serrano toured the room.

"Harry the Heel, eh?" he stopped before a shabby, shifty-eyed little man. "So you quit peddling hop for a bigger racket, eh?"

He reached out, grabbed the little man's nose and tweaked it with an agile twist of his wrist. Harry the Heel fell back, rubbed the aching member with tender fingers, and mouthed curses.

Serrano moved on to the next man.

"Handsome Joe Piani—decked out in yellow shoes and stinking with cologne. Now, that's what I call gilding the lily, beautiful."

He chucked Piani under the chin and leered. The manicured hands of Piani clenched into hard fists and his eyes spat hate. But a glance at the silent figure of LeBrett, tense and watchful in the doorway, kept his arms rigid at his sides.

Serrano turned to the man who sat behind the desk in the center of the room.

"Nice crowd of protectors you got here, Monk."

Lannigan pursed his lips and ran a hand over his sleek black hair. "I saw that you didn't need an introduction," he said. "But I don't suppose you came around here just to look up some old friends."

"No, I just heard about the sweet racket you got."

Lannigan's eyes narrowed slightly. He buffed his nails against the lapel of his coat. "I get it. But it's no go, see? You had your innings in the old days and I didn't try to chisel in. And if you think you can muscle in on this set-up, you're nuts. You can go to hell."

"Muscle in!" bellowed Serrano. "You think I want to cut in on the dirtiest, rottenest . . ." He strode wrathfully toward the desk and brought his huge fist down with a bang that sent papers flying in all directions. "I'll tell you why I came here. I don't like your dirty racket. I'm out to smash you. And I'll do it. I'm giving you fair warning, so you can fold up before the fireworks start."

Some one laughed—a jeering, mocking laugh. Lannigan permitted himself a wry grin at the boastful words before his face grew cold and calculating once more. Then he shook his head.

"That's a lot of ——!"

Serrano's face grew purple and the nostrils of his huge nose flared twin danger signals.

"Oh, it is—is it? You're cocky because you got a political set-up behind you on the deal. But you can take it from me, Mr. President, that when the lid blows off, those guys go sky-high along with the rest. I've bucked the big boys before and made 'em eat dirt. I've taken crooked bankers off the Drive and dumped them in the gutter. I've eased crooked judges off the bench right into the hot seat. And I'll see you and the rest of the protectors in hell."

The silence that followed his bombastic speech was rudely shattered by a derisive razzberry. With a hoarse cry of rage Serrano whirled to see the sneering face of Castagni at his elbow. Serrano trumpeted loudly through his nose, aimed a terrific swing, and had the satisfaction of feeling his knuckles crunch deep into bone and flesh.

Castagni crashed over backward, arms wide, liquid scarlet spurting from smashed nose and torn lips. And on the instant, hands streaked for hip pockets.

"Hold it!"

Hands froze in coat pockets as eyes sought the doorway. LeBrett had not moved, but now the light glinted from murderous blue steel in his right hand.

"Not a move out of you mugs," he warned. He stepped aside and jerked his head at the portal. "Come on, Big Nose, let's scram."

But Serrano was seemingly oblivious to the fact that the room was charged with dynamite. He strolled easily to the door, then turned once more to look at the ring of scowling faces.

"Just a minute, Charlie, and I'll be with you. But I just had an inspiration."

LeBrett knew what was coming. He groaned aloud. "Forget it, Big Nose," he begged. "Let's fade—quick."

But Serrano was not to be cheated of his glory. Striking an attitude in the doorway, he drew a deep breath.

"A new ditty, gents. It just came to me. Here—how do you like this?"

He tilted back his head and burst into full-throated song:

> *"Lannigan, Lannigan, don't pull no shenanigan*
> *Or I'll throw you out on your fat can again.*
> *For I've busted D.A.'s and crooked judges,*
> *A gat's the answer to all my grudges.*
> *Your racket is through, and if you think I'm wrong,*
> *Let me hear you laugh at this little song!"*

He glared at Lannigan as if challenging him to crack so much as a smile but that individual was taking no chances, either with Serrano or with the gun in LeBrett's hand.

Big Nose relaxed again, gave Lannigan the razzberry, and turned to LeBrett.

"Pretty swell, eh, Charlie? We can scram, now. So long, punks. I'll be seeing you—at the other end of a gat."

Then, with LeBrett keeping a wary eye on Lannigan and his cohorts, he swaggered arrogantly through the door.

Despite Charlie LeBrett's nervous finger on the trigger of his automatic, Big Nose was in high good humor when they emerged into the sunshine of Clark Street once more. He had amply satisfied—for the moment—the two dominant cravings within his expansive soul—his lust for action as personified by a healthy sock to the jaw; and his creative-poetical instinct as embodied in his bawdy but memorable lyrics.

"What a sock! What a ditty!" he gloated as they pounded up the sidewalk.

"Yeah?" sneered LeBrett. "But what did it get you? You can't bust that racket with a sock or a song. If I hadn't been there to back you up with my gat, they'd have thrown you out on your fat can!"

"Yeah?" growled Big Nose. "And I would have wrecked the joint. The trouble with you, Charlie, is that you have no soul—no *esprit*"—he looked doubtfully at LeBrett from the corner of his eye, as if fearful that his ally would challenge him as to the meaning of the word. Serrano wasn't exactly sure of it himself.

But LeBrett was used to such outbursts. He weathered the storm with an air of weary patience.

"Yes!" boomed Serrano, confident of himself once more. "You lack *esprit*, Charlie. As some punk poet once said, a sock to the nose is sufficient unto itself and a song is a joy forever."

"Sure," agreed LeBrett the practical. "Last night, Flash Turner was bumped off; today Ruby's a widow. What do we do outside of calling Lannigan names?"

These barbed shafts from the vitriolic tongue of LeBrett sank deep into Serrano's hide. He sobered up, pawed at one cauliflowered ear with his fist, erupted a stream of brown tobacco juice into the gutter, and squinted speculatively after it.

Evidently he found the answer in the horse droppings that decorated the street and had little difficulty in reading it. After a moment's consideration he grabbed LeBrett and hustled him into the cigar store on the corner.

Serrano spent a laborious two minutes thumbing over the telephone directory, raised his shaggy head triumphantly, at last. He dragged LeBrett out into the street again, hurled him into a cab.

"Drexel Building, bud," he called out to the driver. "Step on it."

Deposited at the Drexel Building, Big Nose and LeBrett once more ascended in an elevator. This time they alighted on the twentieth floor and after a long walk down intricate corridors stopped before a frosted, double glass door.

A neat legend printed on one pane in gold leaf proclaimed to the world that this was the office of the Cook County Builders Association. On the other pane was a long list of names, with various cryptic symbols after them.

Serrano ran his thumb down the list, then up again, stopping at the topmost name.

"Jay Hugo Cleveland," he rumbled. "*Pres.* I guess that means president and the bozo we want to see."

His hand went out to the knob but LeBrett held him back. "I know you're the master mind," he said caustically. "But what's the play? Do you sock this Jay Hugo Cleveland, *Pres.*, in the jaw and sing a song about it; or do I play it blind?"

Serrano looked at his ally with scornful tolerance. "The trouble with you, Charlie, is that you have no imagination. How the hell do I know what the play is? We might both take a sock at Jay Hugo, or he might fall on our necks, or he might . . ."

"I get you," groaned LeBrett. "We play it blind."

"Right!" rumbled Big Nose. "Take your cue from me."

He twisted the knob of the door, pushed the portal inward, and with an arrogant swagger barged into the resplendent reception room of the Cook County Builders Association. LeBrett's hand sank innocently to the pocket of his coat as he followed in after him.

Big Nose sized up the place with an all-inclusive glance.

"Swell dump," he grunted, then confronted the rather flustered but still hoity-toity reception clerk.

Big Nose winked at her. " 'Lo," he said familiarly, hitching one mammoth hip on the edge of her glass-topped desk. "We want to see this here Jay Hugo Cleveland."

The already supercilious nose of the receptionist elevated still higher. She made a vain attempt to wither Serrano with a disdainful glance.

"Mr. Cleveland is in conference," she replied in a tone of voice she had acquired from the English butlers in the movies.

Serrano's brow puckered into a puzzled frown. "Well, what of it, sis? Tell him Serrano wants to see him—Big Nose Serrano."

"I'm sorry, but . . ."

LeBrett had long since wearied of the argument. He had spied a door on the right decorated with the name of the gentleman in question. He yanked Serrano by the arm.

"To hell with the dame," he growled. "Here's the door. What are you waiting for? We've barged into better places than this."

Mr. Jay Hugo Cleveland looked up with an annoyed frown as Serrano and LeBrett unceremoniously violated the sanctity of his private office. The two men on either side of him ceased talking at the abrupt entrance. The one removed the cigar from his mouth and smoothed back the three stray hairs that decorated his otherwise bald dome. The other individual, bull-necked, low-browed, and with a sneering mouth, clenched his cigarette in an ash tray and hitched himself forward on his chair.

Recognition between the latter and the two invaders was instantaneous and mutually distasteful.

"I'm sorry but I'm in conference," began Cleveland with strained patience. "If you'll give the girl . . ."

"To hell with the girl," grinned Serrano. "She's more interested in putting on the ritz. Now that we're here, we'll stay. And if you're in conference, so much the better."

Mr. Jay Hugo Cleveland wasn't used to such brutal methods. He colored a choleric red, half rose from his chair. The bull-necked individual intervened.

"Let me handle this, Mr. Cleveland," he said.

He hoisted himself out of his chair. LeBrett waited patiently until he was squarely planted on two feet. Then, with a sudden, vicious, straight-armed movement, he planted his broad hand—five fingers extended—full in the face of the bull-necked one. He heaved and his victim went sprawling backward into his chair once more.

"Sit down, Slavin!" croaked LeBrett. "You'll handle nothing. I don't like your guts, so don't get tough." Delivered of this little speech, he turned to Serrano. "Okay, Big Nose—the floor is yours."

Serrano grinned appreciatively, kicked up two chairs. He draped his huge form into one while LeBrett commandeered the other. Big Nose took up the burden of conversation. He confronted the gentleman opposite him.

"You're Cleveland, eh? And Jed Slavin we both know." He turned inquiringly to the third of the trio. "Where do you fit in?"

The eyes of the two men met and clashed for a moment.

"I'm Harry Yaeger, Commissioner of Labor—and you're Serrano, eh?"

"Yeah—Big Nose Serrano and Charlie LeBrett. So the party's complete."

Mr. Cleveland toyed nervously with the watch chain across his vest. "I—

I'm afraid I don't understand," he said.

"You will," answered Serrano. "I understand there's a racket in this town—the kick-back racket—that's worked a lot on construction jobs. Well, it's a dirty racket. It's got to stop. We came up here to see what you were going to do to stop it."

Cleveland coughed apologetically. "We were just discussing that situation, when you—ah—intruded."

LeBrett looked at Slavin, then at Cleveland. He jerked his head in Slavin's direction. "What the hell is he doing here?"

"Mr. Slavin is trying to break up this racket you speak about," answered Yaeger.

Serrano's lips curled in scorn, then he threw back his head and erupted into laughter. "What! That lousy scab and strike breaker! It's my guess, if anything, that Slavin's mixed up in the racket."

Slavin's lips pulled back in a snarl and he leaped from his chair. The corner of Serrano's coat jerked up suggestively.

"Easy, punk—easy," he warned. "Mr. Cleveland wouldn't want your guts spilled all over his nice, new carpet."

Slavin subsided in his chair with inarticulate rumblings.

Commissioner Yeager protested. "You've got Slavin wrong. He's been hired by Mr. Cleveland to do what he can to stamp out this kick-back racket. He's cooperated wholeheartedly with my office. Between the three of us we expect to get results."

Serrano sneered. "Yeah? When? You'll never get results with Slavin, even if he is on the level, because whoever is behind this racket is consolidating it with machine guns. And Slavin ain't the kind of a guy to face that kind of music."

It was Cleveland's turn to sneer. "And I'm to intimate that you are—is that it?"

Serrano pounded his chest, gorilla fashion. "Right, mister, the first time!"

"You want Slavin's job?" continued Cleveland, sarcastically. "It pays two hundred per month."

Big Nose looked at him from round, startled eyes. "Two hundred . . ." Then he laughed, short and bitterly. "I'm taking the job whether you give it to me or not. And as for the two hundred, you can stick it. I told you the racket has got to stop and I came up here to see what you're going to do about it. You've told me about Slavin. That's a joke. It's out. What else?"

Serrano's bass voice dominated the table. Despite himself, Cleveland was impressed.

"Why—why there's nothing else. We're up against a difficult situation—

we've done the best . . ."

"Why don't you throw these kick-back collectors off the jobs?" demanded Serrano.

"We've tried that—with disastrous results," answered Cleveland.

"Such as?"

"Sabotage. Machinery wrecked, engineers beaten up and intimidated, construction delayed and destroyed."

Serrano turned to Commissioner Yaeger. "Who's the protection back of it?"

Yaeger stroked the three stray hairs on his head and shrugged. "I don't know. But I'm afraid we'll have to beat this racket, despite its protection. Why are you so interested in it?"

"For lots of reasons," answered Serrano. "Because I don't like Lannigan; because I don't like Slavin; because a pal of mine got bumped off last night. But mostly because the racket preys on a lot of poor slobs who've got to work for a living, because it takes the food and clothing and coal away from a lot of poor, hungry kids and women."

Cleveland's lips curled in scorn. "Very commendable. And what do you propose to do to break up the racket?"

Serrano rose slowly from his chair. He looked down on his questioner from hard eyes.

"Do, mister?" he echoed. "Well, I'll tell you. I'm going to buck brass knuckles with gats; I'm going to buck gats with machine guns. And when I'm through it won't only be the muscle men they'll be burying. The higher-ups back of the racket—the protection and the brains are going to get theirs, too." He started for the door followed by the stolid LeBrett. On the threshold he paused, turned, and addressed himself to Slavin. "And as for you, scab, whenever you want to resign, your resignation is accepted."

Serrano knew that he was definitely committed to a war on the kick-back racket. He had flung the gauntlet of battle into Lannigan's teeth; he had laid down the law to Cleveland. And he realized that even if he had wanted to drop the matter, it was too late.

Lannigan wasn't the one to ignore the challenge. He commanded a sweet bunch of rods and there was bound to be trouble. And since it was inevitable, Big Nose wanted to get in the first blow. But how? The obvious course was to go gunning for Lannigan but, after a moment's consideration, he vetoed it.

He would get Lannigan in due time; but first he had to uncover the set-up back of the racket. He reviewed his two interviews of the day and had to admit dourly, to himself, that all he had accomplished was a lot of talk. And no one knew better than Big Nose that talk was cheap.

Of course he had slapped down Castagni; and LeBrett had put Slavin in his place, but those two items were small-time stuff. Serrano realized that before going into action he had to get the low-down on the racket from the inside.

He attacked the bottle again for inspiration and after a long session an idea dawned in his brain. He promptly began to put it into execution. He got in touch with Detective MacBride with the net result that later on that evening he had secured himself a job as a steel worker on a skyscraper that was being erected in the heart of the Loop.

"Didn't I tell you I was going to make an honest living?" he chortled gleefully to LeBrett.

But Charlie wasn't impressed. "Sure—an honest job with a pair of .45's slung under your armpits!"

Serrano was on the job the following morning as the whistle blew. What he didn't know about erecting steel girders on a skyscraper would fill a book. But he had the nerve and the bull strength to get by without breaking his neck from a thirty-story fall or without getting run off the job by the union foreman.

By the second day Big Nose had learned his job pretty well, and by the end of the week he had learned a lot of other interesting and more important facts. He got it from the men on the job, in whispered asides from the corners of their mouths. Who collected the kick-back and how; what happened to those who made a stink about it; the shabby funerals of the few hardy souls who threatened to squawk to the police.

It was all very bitter and disillusioning. Serrano had had rackets of his own. But this graft, which stole pennies from the poor, turned the blood in his veins to acid.

He gritted his teeth, swung steel girders into place, hammered home hot rivets and bided his time. Bided his time to pay day.

It came on the following Friday. Big Nose had learned that the men were paid off during the lunch hour and that, immediately after receiving their slender envelopes, they lined up at another shanty window to pay tribute to Lannigan and the moguls of the kick-back racket.

Ten minutes before the noon whistle blew, Serrano climbed down from the steel skeleton of the skyscraper. A devil glinted from his steel-gray eyes; his rugged jaw was jutted forward aggressively. But in his heart was a song—a wild, bloodcurdling song of battle.

There would be no kick-back that pay day and to make sure that he kept his word, Big Nose retired for a moment out of sight behind the dynamite shack.

Here he swiftly whipped out his automatic from his shoulder holster and gave it a quick once over. Satisfied that it was in perfect working order, he thumbed back the safety, then dropped the gat into the pocket of his overalls.

His grimy fist stayed with it and his index finger was wrapped lovingly around the trigger.

The whistle blew. Big Nose stepped from behind the dynamite shack. Already the men were piling off the job and heading for the pay-off window. But Serrano gave this procedure but a casual glance. He was far more interested in a little tin shanty some hundred feet away from him.

As he watched, two burly individuals erupted from the dilapidated door and took up positions on either side of the portal. The head of a third gent appeared at a small window cut in the side of the building.

Serrano grinned to himself and the song he was mentally singing increased to a rousing tempo. The thing was a set-up—a push-over. Just three of the mugs—and after a week of slinging steel beams, he felt that he was equal to at least a dozen of them.

A scowl on his lips, his battered felt hat pulled well down over his eyes, he headed for the kick-back window. In his greasy overalls, four matches decorating the band of his hat, a pair of worn gloves protruding from his hip pocket, he looked like a typical workman to the collectors.

A big bruiser, yeah; but one that would come through like all the rest!

Big Nose maintained the pretense until he was within a few feet of the window. He grunted something to the effect that "this is a hell of a shakedown" to make his act look good, then buried his right hand in the grimy pocket of his overalls as if in search of his pay envelope.

His hand came out but instead of a couple of crumpled bills the menacing snout of a blue-steel automatic bulged in his hand.

"There's goin' to be no . . ."

He never finished—then.

One of the gorilla guards made a flash for his hip. Serrano never asked any questions. His long right leg shot out like a piston and with remarkable precision he sank the point of his number 12D into the pit of the gunman's stomach.

The man doubled up like a jack-knife, bounced off the ground, sailed five feet through the air, and collapsed with a crash against the flimsy sides of the kick-back shack.

There was fire in Serrano's eyes. The hairy nostrils of his nose flared and quivered. His teeth showed in a hard grin as he weaved swiftly forward, half crouched, keeping one eye on the man behind the window—the other on the remaining guard.

He came up to the latter, jutted his jaw forward aggressively.

"There's goin' to be no . . ."

This time it was the collector who made the phony move. And again Serrano never asked any questions. The heavy automatic in his hand came up in an arc as swift as light. The long cold barrel crashed into the guard's chin. And on the downward stroke Serrano jabbed it through the window and into the collector's teeth.

"As I was saying pal, when your buddies made the mistake of interrupting me—there's goin' to be no kick-back today." He removed the point of his gun a few inches from the purple face of the collector. "So help me!" exclaimed Serrano. "What a break! Why, if it ain't my old friend Castagni!" A menacing snarl came into his voice. "Rat, I'm giving you one break for your life. Come out of that cage with your hands up! Come out a-shooting and you'll get what Fink and Denton got last week. And if you're too paralyzed with the load that's in your pants, I'm crawling through this window for you."

Castagni's snake eyes were two venomous slits of hate. His swarthy skin turned a pukish yellow and while his thin lips worked a thin stream of yellowish saliva drooled down from the corners of his mouth.

It was a full twenty seconds before he could speak, and when he achieved that accomplishment his voice was strained, brittle as ice.

"Goddam you, Serrano, you'll get yours . . ."

Big Nose lunged forward. In their stark cruelty, his eyes matched Castagni's. Deliberately, without a word, he elevated the nozzle of his automatic some three inches to a point in the center of Castagni's low forehead. Then, with even more deliberation he dragged the point of the gun downward, bearing down hard.

Castagni went white—a white in startling contrast to the stream of crimson blood that spouted in the trail of Serrano's gun.

"Come out of there, damn you!" grated Serrano. "Or I'll stop that yellow heart of yours from pumping that blood!"

Castagni came out of there, his hands elevated, his lips mouthing obscene curses. Big Nose backhanded him in the teeth, sent him crashing back against the shack.

Castagni was down and he stayed down.

The first advance of the men had come up by now. They stared at the fallen gunmen with wide, unbelieving eyes; stared even more incredulously at the towering giant that straddled over them, the nozzle of his automatic dripping blood. The word spread like wild fire and in a few minutes the kick-back shack was swamped.

Big Nose grinned, waved a grimy hand at the men.

"No kick-back today, boys!" he boomed. "I've persuaded these three chiselers that they've made a mistake. Bring the pay roll home to your old ladies." He prodded the fallen Castagni in the ribs with the point of his shoe. "And if you ever see or hear of this rat demanding a cut of your pay again— just let me know. Just let Big Nose Serrano know—and it'll be lilies for Mr. Castagni."

• • •

Monk Lannigan leaned back in his swivel chair, took a deep drag from his cigarette, and then, tilting his sleek head, blew twin spirals of smoke toward the ceiling.

The quiet of his office was abruptly shattered when the door burst violently inward and a disheveled, bloody figure staggered into the room. The cigarette dangling from Lannigan's thin lips jerked and ashes sprayed down over his vest. Castagni flung himself into a chair, placed his aching head in his hands, and mumbled scorching oaths.

Lannigan carefully brushed the gray flecks from his clothing before he spoke.

"Trouble?"

His lieutenant's battered features writhed in a hideous scowl. "Trouble?" he repeated hoarsely. "Murder! He damn' near killed me!"

"So I see. Snap out of it. Who did it? Where's the pay-off?"

Castagni leaped to his feet and paced the floor, his arms waving jerkily. "There ain't no pay-off. He slammed us around, beat the hell out of us, and told the men the kick-back was out."

Lannigan drummed his fingers on the polished surface of the desk. "Oh, he did, did he? Just to get the record straight, would you mind telling me who the hell you're talking about?"

"Big Nose Serrano—the bastard—"

A strange light flared in Lannigan's eyes. He digested the information in silence a moment, then reached for the telephone on his desk. Twice he called a number and each time issued a curt order over the wire. Then, while his sullen henchman subsided to a mumbling tirade of curses, he leaned back in his chair and waited.

The two men he had summoned arrived together. They looked curiously at the disheveled Castagni and then turned to their chief for orders.

Lannigan inspected his finger nails with a critical eye. "You know, Piani," he remarked, "this guy Serrano is getting in my hair."

"Yeah?" Piani exchanged glances with the man beside him.

"Sure." Lannigan looked out of the window. "Big Nose Serrano's working now. An honest laborer, so Castagni tells me. On the new Shotwell Building."

"You don't say!"

Lannigan was silent. After a brief hesitation, the pair realized the interview was over and shuffled from the room. When the door had closed behind them Castagni, too, received a curt dismissal.

"Better go home and soak your head in cold water. You'll be on the job again next pay day."

• • •

Despite his elephantine bulk, Big Nose Serrano picked his way across a narrow girder with all the grace of a ballet dancer. The brilliant afternoon sunshine flooded the skeleton structure and a blithe whistle piped from the lips of this new recruit to the ranks of honest labor.

From the narrow ribbon of street some twenty stories below came the subdued rumble of traffic. Around him busy trip hammers beat a rhythmic tattoo of steel against steel. The steady clatter was music to Serrano's ears and he felt blissfully at peace with the world.

Then abruptly his calm serenity was shattered.

Something whined past his ear and splattered against the upright behind him. Big Nose had heard that eerie wail before. He flung himself forward, clutched the girder and peered downward.

One glimpse was enough.

Three alien, menacing figures climbed rapidly upward. The brilliant sunshine glinted on murderous weapons. Death-dealing trigger fingers sprayed lead at Serrano as he scrambled wildly for safety.

The song of the riveters died abruptly as his comrades saw his peril. They clung wide-eyed from their perches and shouted hoarse cries of warning.

Big Nose reached a cross beam, leaped to his feet. His gun came out and with a roar of defiance, he blazed back at his attackers. A huge steel hook, swinging at the end of its cable, struck his elbow as the automatic leaped to avid life. Trailing wisps of gray gun-smoke, the weapon flew from his fingers and described a mad parabola in space.

Like a pendulum the hook swung outward once more, but the damage had been done. Cries of triumph echoed from the killers as they saw their victim left weaponless on his precarious perch. A barrage of lead flattened against the girder as Serrano raced across the narrow beam.

He reached a wooden stage. A young lad faced him there, mouth agape, paralyzed by fright. One rigid hand grasped a bellows. The other clutched a pair of tongs and the glowing rivet he had just removed from the fire. Big Nose pounced upon him.

He yanked the tongs from the lad's nerveless fingers, whirled about and glared across the skeleton framework of the building. A snarling face looked back at him. And with the crash of gunfire ringing once more in his ears, Big Nose swung back his arm.

The red-hot rivet screeched through space. A bleat of terror—a scream of mortal agony—then shocked silence. Horrified eyes saw a limp, lifeless thing, that had once been a man, go hurtling off into space.

Serrano's full-throated war cry rang out. And in swift retaliation, his remaining attackers went into action. Lead sprayed at the bold figure silhouetted against the sky. And each bullet whined ominously closer as the pair raced toward him.

Serrano glanced down at the canyoned street, far below. Then with the flaming courage that had marked his swashbuckling career, he braced himself for the coming impact and bellowed a last challenge.

In that moment every detail of the drama in the sky became vividly clear. He saw the dark figures of his enemies converging upon him. He heard the shouts of his fellow workmen. He saw them scramble toward the killers, but knew that they would be too late. Then it came, the shock for which he had braced himself.

An unerring bullet seared a furrow across his forehead. Warm blood spurted in its wake, cascaded over his eyes. Even as his hand flew up to brush it away, the world was suddenly dissolved in a blinding red mist. He staggered, swayed, struggled frantically to retain his balance. But the crimson universe only spun the faster and with a sickening nausea at the pit of his stomach, he whirled around and pitched headlong into—nothing.

His clawing arms and legs threshed the empty air. Then, with a crash that knocked the very breath from his body, he struck something solid.

For a split second he clung desperately, his arms wrapped around a reassuring bulk. Then his head cleared and he knew that he dangled from the cable hook. From his precarious grip he swung in wide arcs through space.

A shrill scream of rage burst from his enemies. As he swung with breathtaking speed toward a girder, he saw the contorted features of one of the pair. Puffs of smoke marked the man's gunfire but the dangling figure of Big Nose made a poor target.

Serrano's legs jerked up, his knees stiffened. With the force of a battering ram his heavy boots shot out, caught the gorilla in the pit of the stomach.

The man's arms shot up in a wild, imploring gesture to heaven. His still-smoking gun described a wide arc as it sailed from his hands. Then, his arms clawing wildly at the empty air, he toppled backward, turned slowly over, and went plunging down, headfirst, for the dizzy earth twenty stories below.

An exultant rumble burst from Serrano's throat! What a fight! What a man he was! Even though he figured that he didn't have a chance in hell, he gloried in the combat. He hadn't done so badly. No gun and yet two of his enemies were already down. Two down and one to go!

And now for the last. The return swing of the cable swung him far out over the yawning abyss that was outlined by the skeleton-work of the skyscraper.

Big Nose wrapped his long legs around the hook and set himself for the return swing of the pendulum. He was at the apex of the arc—now he was stopped for a fleeting second—now with ever-increasing acceleration he swooped down on the return journey.

Serrano's boots caught the gorilla in the pit of the stomach.

Lead droned ominously over his head; steel-jacketed bullets whined sinisterly past his ears. Clutching fingers of death plucked at his shirt.

Serrano was conscious of something warm and sticky that ran down his arm. His left hand was numb, his fingers were slipping. The spurting blood from the wound on his head blinded his eyes again with a red mist.

And then abruptly the bottom dropped out of the world for him. The cable played out on the run and at express speed Big Nose was plummeted earthward. How he held on was a miracle. Story after story flashed by in blinding succession. The granite earth below rushed up to meet him with sickening speed.

Then abruptly his speed was slackened. His head cleared. He was at the fourth floor level—third—second—then with a gentle bump he kissed the earth.

But only for the fraction of a second. The devilish threnody of a sub-machine gun shattered the unnatural stillness of the air. A molten stream of hot lead battered and ricocheted off the steel girder behind which Serrano had landed.

He threw himself backward into a slight excavation. From off to his right the savage snarl of an automatic answered the song of the Thompson. Big Nose risked a swift glance over the rim of his hole and saw enough to arouse all the fighting instinct within him.

A half-dozen of Lannigan's men had been waiting for him on the ground. And now, with murderous wariness they were closing in on him.

Big Nose grinned to himself. Dogs, yellow dogs, he grated to himself. What the hell were they waiting for? He didn't have any gun. Why didn't they charge? Then an idea struck him!

Yellow, were they? Well, by God, their yellowness would be their finish.

Big Nose snaked across his excavation to the far side. Abruptly he leaped out of the hole, flung himself behind a pile of cement sacks just as the gunners got range.

He dodged for a stack of lumber—from the lumber to the lee of a truck—and from the lee of the truck he disappeared. But only for a matter of seconds.

Before the gunmen had discovered his hideout, he, himself, barged wildly out of the explosives shack. Three long sticks of yellow dynamite were in his left hand and he weaved and crisscrossed as he charged down on his enemies. A challenging bellow erupted from his bloody lips.

Nothing could have stopped him! But he had the business to stop the others. Abruptly his right arm swung back over his head, shot forward. A yellow stick of dynamite hurtled through the air, straight for the head of the machine gunner.

That individual ducked. The dynamite crashed into the steel girder behind him. A blinding concussion—a cataclysmic roar and, with the first explosion still shattering his eardrums, Big Nose hurtled his other two sticks full into the center of the fleeing mob of gorillas.

Chaos! The earth shook; the steel skeleton of the skyscraper trembled. But none remained of Lannigan's mob to report back the catastrophe to their chief.

Hot drinks—hot dames! Hot music and, a crowded house. The Golden Slipper Night Club, down on State Street, was busting things wide open, was blowing off the lid.

And why?

Because Big Nose Serrano was blowing in the first honest dollars he had ever made. Many a time he had sweated over the barrel of a hot rod in the collection of a bank roll but never before had he punched a time clock and at the end of the week collected twenty-seven fifty.

He went nuts. The dough burned a hole in his pocket. He ordered champagne at eighty per case and had the house drink on him. He showered the jazz band with tens and twenties just to keep 'em steamed up. Check girls, cigarette girls, the bouncing blondes of the floor show—anything, in fact with skirts and a pair of legs came in for his largess.

For Serrano was not only celebrating his first week of honest toil—he was commemorating his first decisive victory over Lannigan and his racket.

LeBrett was there, Ruby, McGinnis, Two-gun Goldstein, and all the rest. Serrano's row of reserved tables, set against the far wall, looked like a board of directors' meeting of the elect of gangdom.

The party was just well under way when Oscar, the soft-footed head waiter insinuated himself up to Serrano's table.

"Phone call for you, Mr. Serrano," he said obsequiously.

Big Nose removed his hand from the silk-clad knee of the bit of fluff beside him and looked up.

"Yeah—who is it, Oscar?"

Oscar coughed apologetically into a napkin. "I told him you were occupied but he was insistent. It's Mr. Monk Lannigan."

Big Nose pushed back his chair with a loud, scraping noise. A happy grin spread over his homely pan. "Yeah? So it's Lannigan, eh? Sure, I'll speak to that baboon. And when I get finished will his face be red!" He stooped down, wheezed an alcoholic leer into the blonde's face. "Save the next struggle for me, babe. Be right back."

He shoved off in the wake of Oscar and, as he weaved across the dance floor in his ill-fitting tuxedo, the tail of his shirt escaped the confining clasp of his belt and waved coyly in the breeze.

"What a man!" murmured the blonde ecstatically. "What a man!"

Big Nose was back three minutes later and, though by now his tie was perched somewhere behind his left ear and beads of sweat bedewed his brow, a cherubic grin wreathed his lips.

He nodded to LeBrett and the two of them went into a private conference by the band stand.

"It was Lannigan, all right," began Big Nose.

"Yeah?" answered LeBrett suspiciously. "What did he want?"

"Wanted to see me."

"In a lead kimono, eh? So you told him that you would be on deck at the Silver Slipper from now till closing time."

"Exactly," boomed Serrano.

"The hell you did!"

"Sure. Lannigan's coming up to join the party."

"To join it or wreck it?"

"Ixnay," answered Big Nose shaking his head. "He's got too much savvy for that. He knows the boys are all here. Listen, Charlie, I got a hunch that baby's leery. He wants to talk business. We'll let him talk. But this is the point. Tip off the Barber and Lang to spot him coming in and to spot him going out. They're to pick him up when he leaves, trail him to wherever he's going and report back to us by phone.

"I got a hunch that when I get through making a monkey out of Monk Lannigan, he'll report back to his protection. And I want to know who that is. Got it?"

LeBrett nodded. "Got it. All of which means I better oil the gat."

At the height of the festivities, Monk Lannigan entered the Golden Slipper, flanked on either side by two doughty torpedoes. His entrance was announced by an ominous roll from the trap drum. At a cue from Serrano the lights were dimmed and in the dazzling beam of a baby spotlight, Lannigan made his way to Serrano's table.

A sudden hush fell over the crowded club. Some psychic instinct warned the revelers that they were sitting on a keg of dynamite. And knowing Serrano of old, they more than half suspected that the fuse was already lit.

Lannigan withstood the battery of all eyes with a supercilious smile but he and his men made quite sure as they approached that their hands were in full view.

The invading trio came to a halt by Big Nose's chair. Lannigan flung his eyes disdainfully up and down the table. His glance was met by sullen, bitter stares from the assembled mob.

"Celebrating, eh?" he sneered.

"Just a little party—at your expense," mocked Big Nose.

Lannigan frowned, flicked the ash from his cigarette with his little finger.

"My expense?" he echoed. "I don't get it."

"No, but you will later," answered Serrano. "Nice of you to drop in on us. What's it all about?"

Lannigan again permitted his eyes to meet the row of challenging ones ranged around the table. He jerked his head significantly towards the rear of the dance floor.

"We can't do business here. A little privacy . . ."

"Yeah?" taunted Serrano. "Nuts to that! When I do business I'm just like a goldfish in a bowl. There's nothing you can tell me, you can't tell the boys. Either you make your little speech now or you scram the hell out of here."

His bulbous nose crinkled and he sniffed the air suspiciously. "Did some one . . ." He broke off abruptly and turned to Piani, one of Lannigan's guards.

"Jeez, Piani, are you still using that cheap cologne? You smell like a six-bit floozy!"

A hot wave of color crawled slowly up Piani's swarthy cheeks. He dug his nails into the palms of his hands and held them there. Serrano turned back to Lannigan.

"Well, what is it to be, big shot? Do we deal or don't we?"

Lannigan shrugged. "Have it that way if you want."

"I want!" growled Big Nose. He turned to Two-gun Goldstein who was seated opposite him. "Vacate, Ike! Where's your manners? Give the big shot a seat!"

Lannigan's eyes were venomous as he circled the table and appropriated the chair vacated by Goldstein. He leaned back in it casually, trying to affect an ease and nonchalance he far from felt. Even under the best of circumstances an interview with Serrano was a tough proposition; but now, with the grinning mob hemming him in, it was still tougher. Still, he had his orders from the higher-ups and he had to go through with it.

Big Nose shoved a bottle of Scotch across the table to him with a magnanimous gesture. "Oil your tongue, Lannigan—and then speak fast."

Lannigan poured himself a drink, downed it with an avid gulp.

"It's this way, Serrano," he began. "We're neither of us getting any place bucking each other. I thought maybe we could get together on this."

"Get together on what?" demanded Serrano.

"Don't be dumb—you know."

"So what?"

"Well," began Lannigan slowly, "I got a couple of propositions to make. The first—throw in with me and my mob—I'll give you complete charge of the collection end and a ten per cent cut."

Big Nose was beginning to get hot under the collar. His bulbous nose glowed an angry red but with admirable restraint he controlled himself. LeBrett, however, saw all the signs of an imminent explosion and eased himself round in his chair so as to be able to cover Piani and the other guard in case of fireworks.

To cover his mounting wrath Big Nose took a hurried swig at the bottle.

"That's proposition number one, Lannigan. What's the other?"

Lannigan toyed with his glass a moment, buffed the nails of his hand against the lapels of his coat. "The second deal is simpler and easier," he began. "A slice of jack now for you to keep your nose out of the racket!"

That last reference to Serrano's nose was unfortunate but Big Nose ignored it for the moment. His eyes glinted narrowly.

"So that's the story, eh?"

Lannigan nodded.

"Only half of it," replied Serrano. "Who's your protection, Lannigan?"

Lannigan smiled acidly. "We're not talking connections. You got two propositions. Do we deal?"

Big Nose shrugged. "How much dough is in it for me on the second set-up?"

"Fifty G in these times isn't a bad bit of change to pick up," replied Lannigan.

Serrano agreed emphatically. "Hell, no! I know where fifty grand could do a lot of good. Got it on you?"

Lannigan nodded and with the nod, a swift, sudden, and savage transformation came over Serrano. His chair went back with a crash. He was on his feet and a blue-steel automatic had sprouted in his fist.

Piani and the second guard were a fraction of a second too late. LeBrett, with a businesslike proficiency had them covered before their gats were half out of their holsters.

"Okay, Big Nose," he sang out quietly. "The floor's all yours."

Serrano had completely ignored the two torpedoes. He was concentrating with a furious intentness on Lannigan. The angry red of his face matched the pallor of the other's; the scorn and contempt in his eyes challenged the flaming hate in Lannigan's.

Then Serrano laughed, a short, bitter laugh. His left hand reached across the table. Pincer-like, his mammoth thumb and forefinger contracted on Lannigan's nose. With a savage relish he twisted the protruding organ.

"So I'm to keep my nose out of it, eh—for fifty grand!" he trumpeted. "That was a bum crack, Lannigan. You ought to know that my schnozzola is too big to keep out of any crooked deal!"

He gave Lannigan's proboscis a filial tweak, then rocked back on his heels. A deathly silence had settled over the table. Lannigan never moved.

He sat there, unbudging, like some implacable image of incarnate hate. Only his eyes told of the raging hate that burned in his breast.

Big Nose broke the appalling silence at last.

"Frisk him, Two-gun! His gat and his roll!"

Two-gun Goldstein rubbed his hands together gleefully. "To hell with his gun, Big Nose. The dough is what we want."

Standing behind Lannigan's chair he deftly slipped his hand beneath the gangster's coat. And it was a tribute to Goldstein's skill that when his hand appeared a moment later it held the two items in question.

He dropped Lannigan's automatic into his own pocket, questioned Serrano with his eyes.

"Count it," ordered Big Nose.

Goldstein flipped open the wallet and exposed a roll as big as Carnera's neck. With agile fingers he thumbed over the crisp, golden-backed bills.

"Fifty grand," he announced. "And a couple of hundred in small stuff."

"Small stuff, eh?" grinned Serrano. "Okay, Goldstein—give that back to Lannigan for carfare. That's his style."

Goldstein obeyed. He divided the sheaf of bills, tossed the fifty grand on the table before Serrano, and stuffed the wallet and the remainder into Lannigan's pocket.

Serrano rocked back on his heels and leered down on his victim. "That's the way I handle rats like you, Lannigan," he taunted. "And you're getting a break. It's a damn' sight easier to part with fifty grand than with your life."

His left arm shot suddenly forward, grasped Lannigan by the lapels of his coat, and yanked him to his feet.

"Hey, Steve!" he bellowed to the back of the room. "Spotlight! Spotlight for Mr. Lannigan."

Steve obligingly came through and a moment later the two principal actors in the little drama were bathed in a silver noose of light. Serrano grinned appreciatively into the sea of faces that were turned towards him. These little scenes were right down his alley.

"Ladies and gents!" he boomed. "I want you all to meet Monk Lannigan—the cheapest chiseler that ever walked down State Street. Give this punk a great big razzberry."

The house responded with a will. Lannigan was buried under an avalanche of Bronx cheers and catcalls.

When the little tribute had somewhat subsided, Serrano took the floor again. "But, ladies and gents, I've made him see the light." He chucked Lannigan under the chin with the nozzle of his automatic. "Or maybe it was the gat that made him see the light. No matter.

"Lannigan's conscience-stricken, ladies and gents. Conscience-stricken to the extent of fifty grand. Out of the bigness of his heart he's just donated that amount to the five hundred neediest cases.

"Big-hearted Lannigan—at the point of a gun! More razzberries, gents!"

Again his audience responded vociferously. Big Nose had to raise his hand to command silence. A cherubic grin spread across his face from ear to ear.

"To commemorate the occasion," he boomed, "I've composed a little ditty." He turned to the orchestra leader. "Professor—strike C."

A discordant wail in high C trilled from the flute.

Big Nose grinned. "Swell!" Then he expanded his bellow-like lungs, trumpeted through his nose, cleared his throat with a resounding gargle, and then shook the rafters of the Golden Slipper with his foghorn bass.

And this is the song he sang:

> *"Oh, Lannigan came to Big Nose*
> *Loaded with fifty grand.*
> *He said 'It's yours, Mr. Serrano,*
> *If you'll give me a hand.'*
> *But Big Nose knew Monk Lannigan*
> *For a dirty rat,*
> *So he lifted the chiseler's bank roll*
> *At the point of his gat."*

He broke off suddenly and turned to the audience. "Follow me, everybody! Everybody join in the chorus.

> *And to the Monk, Serrano said:*
> *'Your number's up and your racket is dead!'"*

The house applauded him to the echo. Feet were stamped, hands clapped, bottles rattled. The Golden Slipper shook in noisy appreciation of Serrano's poetical effort.

But as an ominous obligate to the boisterous acclaim, came Lannigan's words from between white lips.

"You asked for it, Serrano—and so help me—you're going to get it!"

Three minutes after Lannigan's exit from the night club, Oscar again called Serrano to the phone. He was back at his table a minute later and once more he went into executive session with LeBrett.

"That was the Barber on the phone. Lannigan's got a dozen gorillas parked outside waiting for me. Lang has picked up Lannigan and is trailing him."

"Swell," gloated LeBrett. "What's the play?"

"Wait till Lang reports," answered Serrano. "Then you and I are going to blast our way out of here. Can do, eh, Charlie?"

"And how!" grated LeBrett. "I'm aching for a little gun play. My finger's getting rusty on the trigger."

The party proceeded at the same hilarious tempo for the next half-hour as if nothing had happened in the past and as if nothing was expected to take place in the future.

Then for the third time, Oscar called Serrano to the phone. He was gone but a few moments, but when he came back there was the eager light of battle in his eye. He nodded significantly to LeBrett, then addressed the party at his table.

"Sorry, folks, but Charlie and I got to leave you for a while. We'll be back by and by. Keep the glasses full."

He turned abruptly and LeBrett followed him across the dance floor. "Where'd he go?" asked Charlie.

"He put in a couple of phone calls then beat it back to his office in the Crescent Building."

LeBrett grunted. "And where are we going?"

"To the same place," answered Serrano grimly. "But first we got to get out of here. Through the kitchen and out through the cellar is our best bet. There's a sidewalk trap. We'll spring that on 'em and then it's going to be gun to gun. Let's go!"

He led the way through the swinging doors that led to the kitchen. At their entrance a fiercely mustachioed chef bustled up to meet them, brandishing a skillet.

"Hey, you—you stay outside where you belong, eh?" Then he recognized Serrano and the skillet was hastily lowered. "Ah, Big Nose! You want a special steak, maybe?"

"Not tonight, chef. We're just scramming out the back way." Serrano winked broadly. "There's a dame hanging around out front—thinks I gave her a stand-up. You understand."

The fierce handlebars went up on either side of a flashing smile. "Sure, I got you. Go 'long."

They strode through his steaming domain, opened a small door at the back, and entered a small vegetable cellar. Instead of clicking on the switch beside the door, Serrano lit a match. They picked their way past crates, burlap bags, and cases that bore intriguing liquor labels. Then, stooping at the far end, Serrano felt above him for the iron trapdoor that opened onto the sidewalk.

"We pop out, make a break for the other corner. If they don't spot us—swell. If they do—you know your stuff."

LeBrett nodded grimly. The last feeble flicker of the burning match reflected from businesslike automatics. Then it died out and left them in total darkness.

"Here goes, Charlie. One . . . two . . ."

A mighty heave of Serrano's broad shoulders and the trapdoor swung upward. Swiftly they ascended a short flight of steps and peered over the side of the iron cover.

Despite the many passers-by they instantly picked out their men. There were three of Lannigan's torpedoes in sight and the nearest, lounging before the corner drug store, was a scant thirty feet away.

Serrano and LeBrett broke from cover and on the instant, the look-out spotted them. Steel sprouted in his fist and he raced toward them, firing as he ran. The other two heard the crash of gunfire and came barging into the fray.

LeBrett stumbled into a nearby doorway and snapped back a scorching blast of lead. Serrano hurdled the gutter and wedged his huge bulk between two parked cars. His own gun joined the chorus with a deafening crescendo.

They never knew afterward just which one's bullets stopped the charging look-out. The torpedo rocked back as the slugs slammed into his body. Then he plunged forward and hit the pavement in a crashing dive.

The whole street went to pieces like a bomb exploding. People fled in all directions, screaming. The rest of the Lannigan murder squad sprinted around the corner in hot pursuit.

A bullet shattered the window of the car behind which Serrano had taken refuge. Tinkling glass sprayed over him and the adjacent curbing. LeBrett's gun filled the doorway with blasts of vivid flame.

The nearest Lannigan rod pumped a frantic burst at the portal. Then suddenly he dropped his smoking gun and wrapped both arms around his belly. Doubled up in agony, he lurched forward and then collapsed against a hydrant.

A taxicab turned in from State Street, started to slow down. Then the driver saw what he had blundered into and gave his bus the gun.

But before he could pick up speed again, Serrano charged from cover and leaped onto the running board. The nozzle of his automatic ground into the shrinking body of the driver.

"Hold it! Brakes!"

Then he bellowed over his shoulder.

"Come on, Charlie! Run like hell!"

Clinging to the cab with his free hand, he raked the street with singing lead to cover LeBrett's escape. The hail of bullets sent the remaining torpedoes scurrying for safety.

LeBrett raced up, panting. He swung open the rear door of the cab, piled inside, and Serrano stumbled in after him. The driver needed no further orders. The instant that menacing gun muzzle was removed, he jammed the gas pedal down to the floor boards.

With hoarse cries of rage Lannigan's gunmen erupted once more into the street. They fired frantically after their fleeing quarry. But the result served only to heighten the din. Crouched on the back seat of the cab Serrano heard the shrill blast of a police whistle above the roar of the guns. Then the sputtering exhaust of the taxi drowned out all other sounds as they sped down the street, careened around a corner, and made their get-away.

Big Nose and LeBrett alighted from their cab a block away from their objective. Serrano flung a bill at the driver and waved him on his way with the point of his gun. Then, in the lee of a tall building, he and LeBrett held a hurried, whimpered consultation. Decided on their course of action, they continued down the block toward the Crescent Building.

They stopped short one building of their destination, pushed through the narrow all-night door and were immediately confronted by the burly and suspicious figure of the night watchman.

"We're looking for the offices of the . . ." began Serrano.

And LeBrett finished the statement for him by neatly clipping the watchman over the head with the butt of his automatic. The man's eyes rolled far up into their sockets, his jaw sagged open, he clawed wildly at the air for a moment, then collapsed into the waiting arms of Serrano.

Big Nose and LeBrett carried him up to the second floor and deposited him gently on the floor of the Gent's Room. It was but the work of a minute to tape his wrists to his ankles and to tape his mouth.

Then, their first preliminary move carried out successfully, they climbed swiftly to the roof of the building. It abutted directly onto the roof of the Crescent Building and, after dodging several chimney pots, a tangle of radio aërials, they located the trapdoor that led below.

They pried it open noiselessly, descended into a well of blackness, their guns probing the darkness ahead of them. Swiftly, warily, like jungle beasts tracking down a kill, they made their way from floor to floor, counting the stories as they went.

A few minutes later they were peering intently down the dark corridors of the fourth floor. From around the corner, off to their right, the Stygian gloom was lessened by a faint effulgence of light.

Serrano's elbow prodded LeBrett in the ribs. They took a firmer grip on their guns and advanced cautiously down the corridor. They paused again at the turn, looked warily around the corner. Hot breath whistled against Serrano's teeth. For lounging before the lighted door of the Labor Protective Organization stood Piani.

LeBrett was for moving forward immediately to the attack, but Serrano held him back. He frowned a moment in deep thought, then fished a penny box of matches from his pocket. Removing one of the sticks he broke it between his fingers.

The resultant snap was plainly and distinctly heard down the corridor. Piani stiffened, his hand went to his hip, he listened intently. Nothing! Only somber silence. After a moment he shrugged and relaxed.

Again Serrano snapped a match. Again Piani stiffened but this time a heavy Luger slid off his hip. Head low, swaying from side to side, his gun arm pulled in close to his ribs, he tiptoed swiftly down the hall.

Serrano's massive bulk was high-powered dynamite; LeBrett's tense muscles were high-tension steel. Their assault was sudden, swift and silent. Serrano's right hand throttled Piani's throat; LeBrett's froze onto the Italian's gun wrist. Simultaneously their lefts descended, gripping their guns, to bounce joyfully off Piani's perfumed hair.

He never had a chance; he never knew what hit him. He collapsed without a protest.

"Never mind the master mind. Take a look at these two items of interest." It was Serrano's challenging voice, and at the words, Monk Lannigan's head snapped erect from the papers on his desk. And the items in question were both interesting and apparent. The first was the gun in Serrano's hand that pointed unwaveringly at Lannigan's head; the other was the limp body of Piani, who was sleeping like a baby in LeBrett's arms.

Lannigan's eyes narrowed and his thin nostrils dilated wide. Twin pulses began to beat in his throat.

Serrano grinned crookedly at him. "Don't get nervous, Monk. Just a little social call. Thought we'd repay the little compliment of that reception committee you left for us at the Golden Slipper."

Lannigan ran the point of a dry tongue over drier lips.

"Sure," he croaked. "Sit down. Too bad the boys slipped up."

"Too bad for you," corrected Big Nose.

"Well—let me have it," clipped Lannigan. "I can take it."

Serrano shook his massive head. "Maybe you can—and maybe you can't. We'll see later. But your time isn't up yet."

He dropped his automatic negligently into the pocket of his coat, kicked out a chair facing Lannigan. LeBrett dumped the still sleeping Piani unceremoniously into a corner and pulled up another chair facing their enemy.

Lannigan examined the tips of his glistening finger nails. The color slowly returned to his face. He straightened up in his chair, looked squarely at Serrano. Twin devils of hate glinted out of his eyes. When he spoke his voice was slowed and unhurried, deadly with venom.

"You're dumber than I think you are, Serrano, if you don't give it to me now. My gat's just aching to splatter your guts."

"Thanks for the tip-off," grinned Serrano. "But it ain't news. I'll gamble on your missing."

Lannigan extracted a monogrammed cigarette from a silver box on the table. He flicked a lighter and lit up with a steady hand. With twin streams of smoke trailing from his nostrils he beat a monotonous tattoo on the polished surface of his desk.

"So what?" he said at last. "If I don't get it now—why the call?"

"Not anxious to get rid of us, are you?"

Lannigan's brows contracted. "Not too anxious. But I happen to be busy. If you came here just to slap Piani down—well, the door's behind you. Don't slam it on your way out."

Serrano leaned back in his chair, squirted a brown stream of tobacco juice over Lannigan's Oriental rug, wiped his mouth with the back of his hand.

"Sorry, Monk, to take up your time but we're sticking. When we laughed you out of the Golden Slipper, you put in a couple of phone calls. I'm curious as hell to see who's coming to keep the appointment you made."

"Oh, so that's it," said Lannigan in a soft voice, shaking his head from side to side.

And in answer to the shake a new voice insinuated itself into the conversation. It was harsh, commanding, dynamic.

"Stick 'em up—and keep 'em up!"

A grim, electric tension filled the office for a moment. Then slowly Serrano and LeBrett reached for the ceiling.

Lannigan laughed softly, shook his head again.

"Not yet, Fagin. Save it. Where are the boys?"

"Be here in a minute," came the gloating answer. "What a break."

Footsteps sounded behind Serrano and LeBrett and a moment later Fagin came into view. His pin-point eyes were hot and he licked his lips in hungry anticipation. The heavy gun in his hand was steady and unwavering as he took up a position by Lannigan's side.

"It's all over, Fagin," said Lannigan quietly. "All over with these two rats. When the boys come, you'll take these two gents, weight 'em down with lead, and drop 'em on the city dump."

Serrano sneered, the sneer changed into a grin, the grin into a happy laugh.

"Yeah?" he taunted. "A hell of a lot of swell gunmen you got, Lannigan. Fagin's so dumb he forgot to thumb back the safety on his gat."

Fagin's beady eyes shifted for a fraction of a second, but that second was sufficient. Both Serrano and LeBrett fired through the pockets of their coats, without drawing their guns. Three streaks of orange flame crisscrossed. Three explosions crashed through the room, so close together that it sounded like one report.

Plaster erupted from the wall behind Serrano's head. Fagin jerked forward, a surprised look in his eyes. He coughed once, then crumpled gracefully like a ballet-dancer and draped his inert body on the floor.

Big Nose was on his feet. His smoking rod was in his hand.

Through white lips, Lannigan spoke. "You rat!" he said.

"Say it again and I'll chisel it on your tombstone," shot back Serrano. "Too bad we can't wait for the boys. But I don't think our lead would last out to get 'em all."

He grunted to LeBrett and they backed slowly to the door. On the threshold he paused. "You asked for trouble, Lannigan, and you're going to get it. This is just the beginning."

"You rat!" breathed Lannigan again, and on this tender tribute, Big Nose slammed the door.

Down on the street again, LeBrett headed for the corner and the nearest cab. Big Nose, however had different ideas. He checked LeBrett's stride and swung him into the heavy shadows of the doorway of the building by which they had entered.

"What's the idea?" croaked Charlie. "Lannigan's mob will be here any minute."

"So what?" growled Serrano. "Nervous?"

"Nuts," answered LeBrett. "But if you're going to commit suicide, I know a lot of better ways. What the hell are you stalling here for?"

"Because, dumb guy," answered Serrano patiently, "the mug or mugs who are going to keep that appointment with Lannigan got to go in through that door. I want to get a peep at 'em—and maybe more."

A cab abruptly swerved into the curb and pulled up before the Crescent Building. Serrano's elbow ground into LeBrett's ribs. Their hands sank to their pockets and wrapped around the butts of their guns.

As they watched from narrowed eyes a familiar, bulky figure climbed out of the interior of the hack, stood for a moment by the driver's seat while he paid off the clock.

Big Nose wheezed hoarsely into LeBrett's ear.

"So help me! It's Slavin the Scab! What a break! We're playing this monkey for all he's worth!"

With a clash of gears the cab pulled away. Slavin headed for the door of the Crescent Building and Serrano and LeBrett shifted forward out of the shadows. Swiftly they moved down on their quarry.

"What's your hurry, Slavin?" croaked Serrano.

Slavin whirled and his hand dropped to his hip.

"Too slow!" mocked Serrano. "Look at this one."

He sank the nozzle of his automatic an inch into Slavin's navel.

"What's your hurry?" he asked again. "And where you going?"

Slavin didn't answer. With surly defiance he glared back at Serrano. LeBrett wiped the snarl off his lips with a back-hand swipe across his mouth.

"We're in a hurry, too, punk. The big boy asked a question. Answer it!"

Slavin fought back the string of invective that foamed to his lips. "What the hell's the big idea?" he demanded in a strained voice. "Can't a guy go out for a cup of coffee?"

"That's lousy," answered Serrano. "A punk like you don't go for coffee in a cab. You got to think faster than that, Slavin. Lots faster and lots better."

Two black sedans turned the far corner. LeBrett nudged Serrano. "Let's roll, Big Nose. Lannigan's mob. We'll take this rat with us."

Serrano grunted, shifted his gun from Slavin's navel, up under Slavin's coat to a point under his heart.

"March, Slavin!" he ordered in a menacing voice. "Straight down to the corner. We're just three pals, instead of one, out for that cup of coffee. Make one phony move, one phony pass, and I'll blow the shirt clean off you."

Slavin marched. With Serrano and LeBrett on either side of him and two guns nudging his ribs, there was no other alternative. And under the same escort he was ushered into a cab that stood waiting at the corner.

"Meredith Hotel, bud," called Big Nose to the driver. "And never mind the traffic lights."

Their captive became visibly alarmed. "Hey! What the hell is this—a ride?"

"Of course not," chided Serrano. "At least, it won't end in one if you loosen up."

"I don't know what you're talking about. So help me—it was just like I said. I only wanted a cup of . . ."

"That's your story and you're smeared with it," answered Serrano cheerfully. "But when we get you in the hotel, I got a hunch your memory's going to come back—fast."

Content to bide his time, he settled back comfortably on the cushions. He whistled blithely for the rest of the trip. But Slavin was not deceived by his high good humor. He squirmed uneasily on the seat and in his eyes showed the stark light of a nameless fear.

The cab drew up under the marquee of the Meredith Hotel. Big Nose swung open the door, climbed out onto the sidewalk, and shoved his hand deep in his pocket in search of the fare. Then, suddenly his hat sailed from his head and kited across the sidewalk.

Diagonally across from the cab, parked on the opposite side of the street, a car belched lurid flame. LeBrett flung himself to the floor of the cab and even as he fell he clutched Slavin's ankle and jerked him off the seat.

With a hoarse cry the driver scrambled from his perch. Big Nose's hand snapped from his pocket, came out clutching his automatic. He shoved it around the back of the hack and sprayed lead at the death car opposite.

A fusillade of bullets peppered the taxi. Its window shattered with a rain of tinkling glass. LeBrett poked the nozzle of his gun through the jagged aperture and fired back. In a moment the street was raked by a crisscross of deadly missiles.

Serrano's finger jerked convulsively on the trigger of his gun. The man sitting beside the driver of the parked sedan suddenly slid limply from sight.

"One gone, Charlie!" whooped Big Nose. "Give 'em hell!"

As his war cry resounded above the din, another slug plucked the sleeve of his coat. A burning pain stabbed his arm and he swore roundly.

LeBrett fired again before he glanced at his companion.

"Wing you, Big Nose?"

"Bah! A scratch! Hey—you—get back in there!"

Slavin crawled out of the cab on his hands and knees, dropped to the sidewalk. The toe of Serrano's Number 12 boot caught him in the ribs and sent him sprawling.

"Get back—I said!"

A muffled cry rang out across the way. LeBrett's deadly fire had found another victim.

"Come on, Charlie!" bellowed Serrano. "Let's rush the mugs!"

But as LeBrett scrambled out onto the pavement the motor of the sedan leaped to sudden life. Their ambush a failure, they were getting more than they had bargained for.

The sedan shot away from the curb and headed up the street. Shouting in triumph, Big Nose hurdled the gutter and peppered the fleeing car as it picked up speed.

He had the satisfaction of seeing heads bob from sight, smashing a taillight and knocking the license plate askew. Then at last, with a sigh, he lowered his smoking gun.

"Looks like we're in top form today," he grinned at LeBrett. "Bet those mugs . . . hey—where's Slavin?"

They both spotted him at the same instant, saw him sprinting up the street as fast as his flying legs could carry him. LeBrett's gun jerked up and he tried to stop the fugitive with a warning splatter of bullets.

But fear lent Slavin wings and as the leaden pellets caromed off the sidewalk at his heels he sped on in mad flight. With a last burst of speed he rounded the corner and disappeared.

Reviewing his activities the next day, since he had given Flash Turner his word that he would bust up the kick-back racket, Big Nose admitted to himself that there had been plenty of gun action.

This was all to the good as far as it went. A number of unlovely and unwanted individuals had cashed in and checked out. But it didn't go far enough. Of course there was still Lannigan and the pack of gorillas he still commanded. But Serrano was loath to have the final show-down with him until he knew the powers back of him.

He reviewed many possibilities to attain this information but finally decided on the oldest and perhaps most efficient method.

He paid a visit to Ruby Turner and laid his proposition before her.

"It's this way, Ruby," he concluded. "You've got the class, you've got the savvy—you've got everything that Charlie and I haven't. You can get by where we'd get nothing but a dose of lead."

Ruby smiled at him fondly, let her hand rest on his.

"You don't have to sell me the job, Big Nose. I'm way ahead of you. It's mine." Her eyes suddenly hardened and her lips set into bitter lines. "I'm not forgetting what happened to Flash. I'm tickled to death to take a stab at it. I only wish I was using a gun instead of—"

"Instead of your sex, eh, baby?" grinned Serrano. He patted her hand clumsily. "Don't you worry about that. What you're going to do is worth a lot more than a lot of cheap gun play. And if you come through—well, I'll see that you're in at the pay-off."

"Okay," said Ruby. "Let's have it."

Big Nose shifted the wad of cut plug in his mouth, looked around the room for a cuspidor, and, not finding any, shifted the wad back again.

"It's this way, kid," he began. "There's a certain punk by the name of Jed Slavin. A bad egg. I got a strong hunch he's mixed up in this racket on the pay-off end." He recalled his abortive efforts of the night before and growled deeply under his breath. "Well," he continued, "I want you to verify my suspicions."

"Sure, but how?" asked Ruby.

"By getting next to Slavin. That should be a cinch for a girl like you. Slavin don't know you and, if I know anything about that dirty egg, he'll tumble like a load of brick for your class. You know Goldie Ryan, eh?"

Ruby laughed. "Who don't?"

"Swell," answered Big Nose. "Get in touch with Goldie. Tell her it's worth a yard to me for you to get a knockdown to Slavin. She can fix it up for you and from then on it should be a cinch."

Ruby nodded her head thoughtfully. "And if this mug Slavin is mixed up in the racket—then what?"

Serrano patted her hand and winked at her knowingly. "Just let me know the dirt," he cooed. "I'll do the rest."

"Okay," said Ruby quietly. "I'll give you action!"

And Ruby did—sooner than Serrano had any right to expect. It was two days later. Big Nose and LeBrett were doing a heavy master-mind over a bottle of rye in his hotel room, when the kid barged into the apartment. There was a glint in her eye and excitement had flushed her cheeks a glowing rose color.

"Say, babe, you look the nuts," complimented Serrano.

Ruby flashed him a smile.

"That's what Slavin thinks, too," she cracked.

Serrano and LeBrett straightened in their seats.

"You've contacted him already?" asked Serrano.

"Contacted him?" derided Ruby. "Say, that big bum's propositioned me already."

"What a gal!" grinned LeBrett. "Can't say that I blame him, though. That's the first sign of sense I've ever seen from Slavin."

Serrano busied himself with the bottle and ice and hurriedly mixed the girl a drink. He pressed the drink into her hand, then demanded eagerly.

"Well, babe, what's the dirt?"

"Plenty, Big Nose," she answered. "Your hunch was right!"

Serrano's nose quivered and his eyes glinted with expectation. "Go on, kid," he urged.

Ruby sipped her drink. Then: "Not only is Slavin part of the racket—but here's the important angle. I got it right from the big slob himself that he's getting one of his cuts tonight. Five grand. That was part of his sales talk in the proposition."

She shuddered as she recalled Slavin's greasy hands reaching out for her.

"Five grand," she murmured under her breath, in a strained voice. "And The Flash was bumped!"

Big Nose threw one arm clumsily around her slender shoulders. "Forget, it, kid," he urged. "When we get finished with this deal, Flash will have plenty of company in hell."

Ruby brushed a furtive tear from her eye.

"I was nuts about that lad," she said simply. Then forcing back the sentiment, she continued in a cold, hard voice. "Five grand. Dominick is taking it up to Slavin in his room at the Empire tonight."

"What time?" barked LeBrett.

"Ten."

Serrano turned to LeBrett. "Got that?"

LeBrett looked at him dourly. "I've already picked out a casket for him."

Big Nose grunted, turned back to the girl.

"You've done swell, kid," he complimented her. "And when this little deal is finally settled that five grand pay-off is going to be yours."

Ruby stared at him. "Do you think I'd touch that dough? If you do, you're screwy. I went in on this game on one promise from you."

Serrano's brows wrinkled. "And what was that, kid?"

"That when the pay-off came—it would be with lead. And what's more, I'm holding you to it!"

Serrano looked at her fondly, with a deep appreciation in his twinkling eyes.

"Jeez, babe, I could go for you myself in a big way," he sighed heavily.

Ruby flashed him a provocative smile. "Yeah—why don't you try it some time?"

But before Serrano could recover, she had slammed the door behind her.

Big Nose stared for a long moment unseeing at the blank door. So long, in fact, that LeBrett had to snap him out of his mental hop.

"Well, big shot?" he taunted. "Are you promoting a dame—or death?"

Serrano turned slowly, reached for the bottle, took a long pull. He rubbed his horny hands together with satisfaction. "Both, Charlie, my boy—both. What a ditty I could make about that gal."

LeBrett groaned. "Save it," he pleaded. "Save it till we get Slavin mastermined."

LeBrett got a break for once for Big Nose momentarily put aside his song and concentrated on the problem that confronted them. For a long hour the two men imbibed freely from the bottle in silence, their brows knitted in twin scowls of concentration. And then their favorite source of inspiration brought results.

Serrano's huge fist banged down on the table. "I got it, Charlie," he whooped. "And a neat set-up, too. Listen, who've we got in the push that Slavin don't know? I mean a couple of guys he won't recognize. Guys with a little finesse. I'll need three of 'em."

LeBrett rubbed his nose with a lean forefinger and squinted speculatively at the ceiling.

"Well, there's Puccini—he's smart. And Sullivan and Murdock. They do?"

Serrano rubbed his hands together in satisfaction. "Swell. There's the phone—use it. Get them up here on the run. And tell them to dress like gents for once in their lives—not like a bunch of bums."

He reached for his hat.

"And where in the hell do you think you're going?" demanded LeBrett.

"Who me?" answered Serrano with a broad wink. "I'm going to see a man about—five grand. I'll be back by the time the boys get here."

Though the lobby of the Empire Hotel was well crowded at that hour, Serrano took no chances. His three recruits, apparently strangers to one another, mingled with the groups that occupied the palm-spotted lounge. He himself leaned against the cigar counter, busy with a cigarette. Across from him, on the other side of the revolving doors, LeBrett perused the sporting columns of the *Evening Gazette*—or at least, appeared to.

Big Nose kept one eye on the door, the other on the clock. And when the hands of the latter pointed to ten to ten, he spotted a familiar figure as it got out of a cab and headed for the hotel entrance. Serrano flicked away his cigarette and nodded to LeBrett.

LeBrett moved forward slowly, the open paper still before his eyes, as if still trying to dope the last race. And just as Dominick had cleared the doorway, he bumped into him—oh, so innocently.

"Watch where you're going, you . . ."

Dominick never finished the reprimand. His jaw sagged open and he sucked in his stomach away from the nozzle of LeBrett's automatic that was jammed into his navel.

The open newspaper was an effective shield.

Serrano strolled over, casually; the other three men bore down from the rear.

Big Nose spoke tersely, savagely, and to the point.

"Take it easy, kid! Just a stick-up! There's enough lead aimed at you to sink a ship. We're all going out the way you came in."

Dominick turned a sickly yellow, stuttered something inarticulate, felt the point of LeBrett's gun eat deeper into his gut. For a moment he swallowed plaintively at his Adam's apple.

"Well, rat, do you want it now!" snarled Serrano. "Or—"

Dominick gambled on the "or."

He turned slowly and with feet that dragged wearily across the tiled floor of the lobby headed for the door again, surrounded by his unwelcome bodyguard. They hit the sidewalk in mass formation and on their approach a dark blue sedan parked at the curb purred to life. Two-gun Goldstein was behind the wheel and, seeing that Dominick was due to pull a flop at any minute, he hastily jerked open the rear door.

Big Nose and LeBrett booted their prisoner into the rear compartment, crowded in close after him. The others followed, and Ike slipped into gear and rolled away.

The blinds were already drawn and once in traffic Serrano got to work on the ashen pay-off man. First, he lifted the five grand from him. Then he extracted a heavy roll of adhesive from his pocket and, with the touch of an artist, effectively bound and gagged the prisoner. It was all over in two minutes, without a word having been said.

Then Serrano called to Goldstein. "Okay, Ike, you can head back to the Empire."

Goldstein obediently turned the first corner and started to circle the block. Big Nose called to him. "You can handle this punk alone, Ike. You'll have to give him smelling salts to revive him. When you've put him away, drift back to the Vendome. Don't come up but stick around the lobby. We'll pick you up."

Goldstein grinned, nodded, and a moment later, once more pulled up before the Empire. Big Nose, LeBrett, and the other three alighted, and with a wave of his hand, Goldstein slipped again into the traffic.

Back in the lobby of the Empire, Serrano turned to Sullivan. "Okay, son. Do your stuff! And make it look right."

Sullivan patted his breast pocket, his hip, waved a jaunty farewell at the remaining quartet, and headed for the elevators. When the gilded cage had disappeared up the shaft, Big Nose turned to Puccini and Murdock.

"Everything's gone swell so far. You two know your stuff. Make no mistakes. Get him out of here in a hurry and over to the Vendome. We'll be there before you. But you won't see us. Go through the act and make it look legit."

"Don't worry, Big Nose," grinned Puccini. "I once took a correspondence course in detecting. Thought it might help me in my business."

"Yeah?" said Serrano. "Come through on this deal and I'll see that you get a diploma."

The little session was over. Serrano and LeBrett took up positions of advantage behind the line of potted palms. Puccini and Murdock lounged around the cigar stand. And thus for a matter of five minutes they waited.

Then the elevator door opened and Sullivan emerged. A broad grin was on his face. He headed straight across the lobby for the door and as he passed the two waiting men, he said from the corner of his mouth: "Bag! Be down in two minutes."

Sullivan's estimate was exactly correct. Two minutes later to the dot the hulking figure of Slavin disgorged from the elevator. A black Corona was fuming between his thick lips and he seemed not to have a care in the world.

With the air of a man who has just completed some very profitable bit of business, he strolled for the door. Puccini and Murdock moved forward at his approach, blocked his way.

"Just a minute, buddy," said Puccini, pushing a hand against Slavin's chest.

Slavin scowled. His right hand lowered to his hip.

"Hold it!" clipped Puccini. "Take a look at this."

He opened the palm of his left hand, exposing a flat, silver shield.

"Federal cops!" he said tersely.

"Yeah? So what?" demanded Slavin.

"Don't get tough, bud," said Puccini. "We just want to give you the once over."

"Well, get it over with," growled Slavin. "Maybe you'll know me the next time you see me."

"Sure," said Puccini. "But not here. Drift over to the Gents' Room."

Storm clouds gathered on Slavin's brow. "What the hell is this—a shakedown?" he demanded.

Puccini got tough—just the correct amount. "It'll be a knockdown if you ask for it. If there's nothing on your conscience, what the hell are you worrying about? Over to the Gents' Room, you—and walk as if you liked it."

Slavin shrugged sullenly. "You guys are nuts. You got me wrong. Somebody's given you a bum steer. I'm in a hurry."

"Nuts!" said Puccini expressively. "Are you coming or do you want a scene?"

"Okay, weisenheimer," growled Slavin. "Let's get the act over."

They drifted across the lobby to the Gents' Room. Murdock locked the door; Puccini ran expert fingers down Slavin's hips and up under his armpit.

"Pack a rod, eh? Tough guy?"

Slavin sneered. "You can't get me on that. That's no Federal rap."

"Too bad," grunted Murdock.

Puccini's fingers were at Slavin's inside pocket. They came out a moment later clutching a heavy wallet. He balanced it in his hand a moment, looked speculatively at the sullen face of his victim.

"Carry plenty of dough on you, don't you?"

"What the hell's that to you?"

"It might be nothing—and it might be everything," answered Puccini softly. "You're sure this is honest money, eh?"

"Sure it's honest," growled Slavin.

"We'll see. If it is, your okay, we owe you an apology and my informant is going to catch hell. If it isn't . . ."

He flicked open the wallet, extracted a thick roll of bills. Then his lips curled in a disdainful sneer.

"Wise guy, eh?" he taunted. "In a hurry—had an appointment."

Slavin stared at the money in his hand.

"Why—why, what's the matter?"

"Matter? This dough is as phony as hell. Why you dumb chump, even a blind beggar could spot this green goods by the feel."

"You're nuts!" snarled Slavin. "It's a damn', lousy . . ."

"Yeah?" cracked Puccini. "Look for yourself. Take a feel of it." He stuffed the roll into Slavin's trembling fingers.

Slavin took a look—took a feel. The color drained from his face.

"Why the dirty two-timing . . ."

"Sure," agreed Murdock. "They all say that. Come on. You can tell it all to the inspector."

Puccini deftly removed the gun from his hip and dropped it into his own pocket. He hooked his arm under Slavin's; Murdock fell in on his other side. In a daze, Slavin staggered towards the door. Halfway there he stopped, held back.

"Say—can't we get together on this? I've been crossed."

"I'll say you have."

"Can't we fix this?"

Puccini looked at Murdock; Murdock looked at Puccini.

"I got some real dough maybe you boys would like to look at," put in Slavin eagerly.

"Maybe," replied Puccini warily. "Anyway it won't hurt to talk it over, eh, McKee?"

"Naw," answered the bogus McKee. "Let's take him up to the hotel."

The scene shifts to a suite on the twentieth floor of the Hotel Vendome. Puccini set the stage with a bottle of Scotch and three glasses. The three men drank in silence. Then, when this preliminary formality had been attended to, Mr. Puccini did his damnedest to earn that diploma Serrano had promised him.

"You're in a spot, Slavin," he began judiciously. "If you ask me—a damn' tough spot."

"Don't rub it in," growled Slavin.

"I'm not. I'm just telling you that Uncle Sam is getting hard-boiled about the green goods game. And these Federal 'pens' aren't all they're cracked up to be."

Slavin squirmed uncomfortably on his chair.

"Did you bring me up here to tell me that—or to talk business?"

"We'll come to that," answered Puccini. "I just want to give you the lay, so you won't think we're unreasonable."

Slavin wet his dry lips. He had heard that approach before. He had sour visions of seeing all his illegal profits from the kick-back racket of the past year go by the boards. And thoughts of the kick-back racket snapped something in his mind.

"Don't get me wrong, you guys," he pleaded. "I'm no millionaire. I tell you I was framed."

"Maybe you were," admitted Murdock. "The bird who gave us the office about that phony roll of yours sure knew his onions."

Slavin leaned forward eagerly; his lips worked convulsively. "That dough was planted on me!" he growled. "Who spilled the dirt to you?"

Puccini smiled cynically. "The chances are the same guy who planted it on you. But that's no alibi."

Slavin ignored the latter statement and gave vent to his righteous and wrathful indignation. A lurid string of profanity rolled off his lips. He calmed down sufficiently at last to make himself coherent.

"The dirty, double-crossing rat! Sold me down the river, eh? Why? Just because I was getting a lousy ten per cent cut for all the dirty work I did. I'll get that snake if it's the last thing I do."

"Yeah?" said Puccini. "Do you mean that?"

"Mean it?" roared Slavin. "Do you think I'm going to take the rap for that bunch of cutthroats?" He sobered abruptly, and a cunning look came into his eyes. "What if I do mean it?" he demanded.

"If you do, we can deal," answered Puccini.

Slavin's heavy jaw set into a hard line, his eyes narrowed, and his lips twisted bitterly.

"I mean it, alright—what's the proposition?"

Puccini gave it to him straight from the shoulder.

"Rat!"

Slavin stared at him blankly.

"You mean rat on 'em?"

Puccini jumped up from his chair. "Sure I mean rat on 'em, you punk. What the hell do you think I mean? Don't be dumb. We've got you with your pants down. Well, we're willing to give you a break—we're willing to deal.

"Washington's interested in other things besides counterfeit money. Right now it's damn' interested in this labor racket. That's something Lannigan didn't know when he framed you. Washington is going to clean it up whether you play ball or not.

"You got a chance to get off with a couple of years if—"

"If I what?" asked Slavin sullenly.

"Give me the dope on who's backing Lannigan."

Slavin nodded. "So that's it, eh? It's about time some of the big shots took a rap."

"Sure, it is," encouraged Murdock. "They're making you the goat. Give us what we want and maybe we can fix it that you get clean in this."

A cunning avarice fought with the gleam of hope in Slavin's eyes.

"And what about the dough?"

"To hell with the dough!" snapped Puccini. "Come clean on this labor racket and we'll forget that."

That settled the argument as far as Slavin was concerned.

"I don't guess you'll put that in writing," he said with a leer, "but here's what you want. Harry Yaeger is the big shot. He's Labor Commissioner for Cook County. He and Cleveland, president of the Builders Association are back of the racket. Lannigan is their front." His lips snarled with hate and malice. "Framed me with a load of green goods, did they? Okay, coppers! Get this. There's a meeting of the three of them at Lannigan's house tonight! And when you get 'em I hope you give it to 'em all the way."

He rose hurriedly.

"I'm in the clear now, eh?" he asked eagerly.

With a straight-armed right, Puccini threw him back into his chair.

"Don't be dumb, guy," he taunted.

And on this admonition, Serrano and LeBrett made their entrance from the adjoining room of the suite. Big Nose held a complicated mechanical apparatus in his hand, that consisted mostly of a cylindrical recording disc, coils of wire and a battery.

He pranced up to Puccini, threw his arms around him.

"Baby, do you win your diploma—and how!"

And it was then, for the first time, that Slavin realized that he had been framed. Framed—not by Lannigan—but his old enemy—Big Nose Serrano.

It took a matter of seconds for this startling information to sink in. Then, with an animal-like roar he lunged from his chair.

LeBrett's and Murdock's fists collided on either side of his jaw at precisely the same moment. Slavin's bulk described a short arc through the air and crashed to the floor. And such was the weight of the double shock, that it required half the bottle of Scotch to revive him.

Ten minutes later, the party, now augmented by Ruby and Two-gun Goldstein, and with Slavin crowded in their midst, left the Vendome. They crowded into two cars parked at the curb.

"Jeez, where we going?" moaned Slavin, as Goldstein got under way.

"Going?" echoed Serrano. "Didn't you say there was a meeting on up at Lannigan's dump? Well, use your own imagination!"

Slavin went white.

"For God's sake, Big Nose—give me a break. He'll—he'll kill me!"

Serrano shrugged. "Somebody will sooner or later and it might as well be Lannigan."

Slavin turned on Ruby with venomous eyes.

"You—you did this to me—you bitch!"

Ruby's open palm whipped across his lips.

"Did you just tumble to that, punk?" she spat. "And the name isn't bitch. It's Mrs. Flash Turner—widow!"

On the blood-sucking profits of his vicious racket, Monk Lannigan had acquired for himself a swell dump on the South Side in a hoity-toity neighborhood. It was close to one o'clock when Serrano's cavalcade roared through the deserted streets and slid to an abrupt halt before the joint.

The boys alighted, and after a whispered consultation, Big Nose ordered Ike to stand guard at the front of the house, Puccini and Murdock at the sides and Sullivan to the rear.

His men placed to his satisfaction, he and LeBrett on either side of the quaking Slavin, with Ruby bringing up the rear, he marched brazenly across the sidewalk and up the short flight of steps that led to the entrance to Lannigan's bungalow.

Two guns gaped avidly at Slavin's ribs as Big Nose, Ruby, and LeBrett flattened themselves against the house on either side of the door.

"Now do your stuff, punk," ordered Serrano in a hoarse whisper. "Give the play away and you get it now! Behave and maybe I'll see that Lannigan doesn't get you. It's your only chance."

The fear of death had sealed Slavin's slobbering lips. Big Nose's broad thumb shot out and with energetic pressure he squashed the bell-push by the side of the door. A faint and distant jangle sounded deep in the house.

They froze there, tense, expectant, the pale light of the stars glinting frostily off the blue barrels of the automatics. Slavin's knees were buckling, but even greater than the fear of Lannigan's wrath was the fear of immediate death from the twin guns aching for his middle.

Footsteps sounded behind the barrier. A vagrant beam of light shone out onto the porch as the corner of a curtain was pushed back. Serrano, LeBrett, and the girl were lost in the shadows. Only Slavin's heavy face was evident to the scrutiny from within.

Then a key clicked in the lock, a chain rattled. Big Nose and LeBrett set themselves for action. The door opened and the nasal whine of Castagni drilled into their ears.

"What the hell do you want, Slavin?"

Slavin hesitated a fraction of a second. And in that brief interval he almost felt hot lead eating at his vitals.

"Listen, Castagni," he whispered hoarsely, playing the part Serrano had allotted him. "Who's that hanging across the street?"

Castagni's reaction was prompt and natural. He slipped out his gun, stepped forward a foot and stuck his head forward a few inches beyond the jam of the door.

And those few inches were fatal.

Big Nose kept his gun on Slavin while LeBrett kissed the innocent Castagni over the head with the barrel of his rod. The blow was neat and expertly delivered to the place where it would do the most good. Castagni never knew what hit him.

His knees turned to water, he crumpled, the gun slipped from his nerveless fingers, and he sagged to the floor.

"He's out for a long time," whispered LeBrett. "What shall I do with him?"

"Take his gat and heave him out on the porch. We'll lock the door behind us when we go in."

LeBrett executed the order promptly and with precision, then followed the others across the threshold. He locked the door, dropped the key into his pocket.

Serrano was laying down the law to Slavin.

"You know the room this meeting is in. Take us there." Slavin moved forward but Serrano's massive fist yanked him back. "Not so fast. When you get there, I'll try the door. If it's locked—you know. Get it? And when Lannigan asks 'Who is it?'—you tell him, 'Slavin.'

"Then your act ends!"

"Got it!" growled Slavin.

"And what I said before about getting the heat turned on, goes double now. No mistakes."

Slavin whined that there wouldn't be any and again moved forward. The menacing trio were right behind him. Evidently he was familiar with the house, for he moved swiftly across the darkened rooms with surety.

They crossed the large entrance hall, passed through a door at the far end and entered the library. It, too, was dark, but a thin crack of light along the floor at the far side, marked still another door.

And as they tiptoed towards it, the vague rumble of masculine voices assailed their ears.

LeBrett's gun found Slavin's spine as Serrano's hand found the knob of the door. He tried it slowly, silently, but the portal was locked. He stepped back, prodded Slavin in the ribs with the point of his automatic.

Slavin understood. Like the trapped rat that he was, he looked furtively around him but there was no escape. Certain death hemmed him in on either side; and an almost as certain one lay before him.

He took a deep breath and his trembling fist beat a halting tattoo on the door. On the instant all talking ceased beyond the barrier. Then Lannigan's voice called out.

"Yeah? Who is it?"

Slavin answered as the pressure of the two guns against his ribs increased.

"Slavin."

A chair scraped; footsteps sounded across the floor, a bolt rattled.

The portal swung inward and Lannigan found himself confronting Slavin and a whole lot more. Ruby had commandeered Castagni's gun and now held it against Slavin's spine. The twin automatics of Serrano and LeBrett concentrated on Lannigan and the three men seated at the table beyond him— Jay Hugo Cleveland, Harry Yaeger, and Serrano's old friend, Polecat Piani.

Lannigan went white but he said not a word. For a long second he gazed into the gaping nozzles of the guns. Then he shifted his glance to Slavin's yellow face. The air was charged with dynamite—super-charged. For he must have read the answer there to the unspoken questions that raced through his mind.

With a supreme effort he controlled his voice.

"Where's Castagni?" he asked casually.

"Don't fret about him," growled Serrano. "He's out. Back up, Lannigan."

Lannigan backed up, and with Ruby prodding the reluctant Slavin before her, the invading trio entered Lannigan's den. Again LeBrett shut and locked the door, dropping the key in his pocket to join the other.

"The game's up, Lannigan," boomed Big Nose. "And that goes for you, Yaeger—and you, Cleveland. The racket's through!"

There was a deathly silence in the room as eyes met eyes—clashed and held. The color had come back to Lannigan's face. But heavy beads of sweat had popped out on Cleveland's forehead, and the flesh was visibly crawling along the bald dome of Commissioner Yaeger.

Piani was the only one who seemed to take the situation as a joke.

"Yeah?" he sneered. "Says you!"

"Wrong," corrected Big Nose, with a happy grin. "Says Slavin, here. He's squawked. I got it all down on a dictaphone record. It's a cinch. It's a natural for a twenty-year stretch if you don't get the chair!"

Piani must have figured that the last supposition was the correct one. He achieved a lightning draw. Orange flame spat from two guns. Twin explosions rocked the room.

Slavin clamped his hands to his middle, doubled up, and collapsed like a bag of flabby guts.

Piani went down slowly, the evil red spot on his shirt front ever-widening. The still smoking gun hung limp in his hand as his body sagged. He caught onto the edge of the table with his left hand. Joint by joint he folded up; then, like an exhausted swimmer, his head disappeared behind the table.

Yaeger and Cleveland looked at his dead face with horrified eyes. But Serrano complimented LeBrett with an appreciative grin. Silence.

It was broken a moment later by Lannigan's hard voice.

"Well, that's that. Too bad about Piani. But Slavin got his. And in the gut, too."

Serrano nodded soberly. "Yeah; nice shooting." He spoke to the dead body. "Thanks, Piani—and you too, Charlie. You both saved me a nasty job."

"But—but this is—murder!" panted Cleveland.

"Call it anything you want," growled Serrano. "Flash Turner was murdered, too. And he didn't have the chance Piani had. And I could name a dozen others you buried because they wouldn't kick-back to you in your lousy racket.

"But it's all over gents!" His voice turned to liquid acid, ate deep into the souls of his listeners. "Piani's gone—clean. Slavin's gone—not so clean. There's only you three left—Lannigan, Cleveland, and Yaeger."

"But good God . . ." began Cleveland.

"Shut up!" snarled Serrano.

A heavy, running footstep sounded outside in the library. Serrano and LeBrett stiffened. Twin devils flamed to Lannigan's eyes. A heavy fist battered the door.

"It's me, chief—Becker? Anything wrong?" came an anxious voice.

"Everything's wrong," answered Serrano. His wrist stiffened and his finger constricted on the trigger. "Call your shots, Lannigan."

Lannigan's body was devoured by an all-consuming hate. He leaned heavily against the table for support.

"Why shouldn't I?" he said calmly. "As you say—the racket's through. I might as well—"

He suddenly heaved himself forward. The table went over with a crash, collided into Serrano's knees. Lannigan was on the floor behind the barricade. Piani's gun was in his hand and it was spouting lead.

Bullets crashed through the lock of the door.

Big Nose was down, shooting from his hip. With a flash shot, LeBrett blasted the rod from Yeager's hand, whirled in time to get Becker as he crashed through the door.

The shooting abruptly ceased. The room was suddenly still, deathly still. Slowly, wearily Serrano climbed to his feet. He put his hand under his coat and it came away red.

"Can you imagine that snake pulling that gag—and getting away with it?" he demanded with a grin. "Plugged me, too!"

"Bad?" asked LeBrett, keeping a wary eye on Yaeger and Cleveland.

"Not so bad that I won't survive," replied Big Nose. "So Lannigan went out fighting. More guts than I thought he had. Well, that makes things simpler. This is a real clean-up, isn't it? Too bad I gave up soliciting business for the undertakers."

He turned to Yaeger.

"So Commissioner, you're a gun-toter, too. I ought to turn the heat on you just for luck. Do the job up right." He scratched the point of his bulbous nose with the nozzle of his gun. "And you, Cleveland—what a sweet job your tailor is going to have."

"You mean you're—"

"Yeah. But before I send you two gents to the cleaners, I'm going to do a little cleaning up myself."

He righted Lannigan's desk, stepped unceremoniously on the dead gangster's chest, and ripped open the drop drawer. He rummaged around in the contents a moment, then came up with a check book.

He tore off two blanks, presented one to each of the two men.

"I figure between you you've cleaned up a quarter of a million in the racket. Split it anyway you want. Make out the checks to the Five Hundred Neediest Cases."

The men looked at him, dumbfounded.

Serrano lurched towards them.

"Well—what is it to be?" he rumbled threateningly. "A quarter of a million—or this?"

And to emphasize his words he up-tilted their noses with the end of his gun.

"And considering what Slavin got and Lannigan and Becker, you're getting off easy. This is a nice quiet dump. We can park here till the checks are cleared.

"Of course, if you both figure like Lannigan did, that the racket was through anyway—" He shrugged his heavy shoulders philosophically. "I still got two ounces of lead left."

The checks were signed, sealed, and delivered. And accompanying the contribution was the following soul-touching ditty:

> *The guys that collected all this jack*
> *Have gone to hell and they won't need it back.*
> *There's blood on each buck,*
> *   And maybe you think I'm screwy,*
> *But I'm a phil-an-thro-pist—*
> *   And that ain't no hooey!*

Lead and Lyrics

I
THE SET-UP

THE ROYALE HOTEL DID ITS BEST TO LIVE UP TO ITS NAME. It was a resplendent, gingerbread affair with much polished marble and onyx. There were costly Oriental rugs on the floors, heavy velour drapes hung in the doorways—and the place was lousy with gaudy uniformed, gold-braided flunkies.

It was definitely the policy of the Royale to frown on poverty. From the manager down to the lowliest doorman, the help had been trained to turn up a supercilious nose at any one who didn't smack of the Gold Coast.

And Red McGuire didn't smack of the Gold Coast. As a matter of fact, along with a raft of other young McGuires (Black Irish fighting stock), he originated in the Stockyards Ward—the Bloody Tenth.

All of which, if the head doorman at the Royale had known, he might have acted differently. But he didn't know. So when young McGuire swaggered up to the main door of the hotel, all the doorman saw was a ragged, dirty-faced kid. The seat of the urchin's pants was out, there were no knees to his stockings, and the thatch of red hair that escaped from beneath his grimy hat was a rakish halo to his reckless blue eyes.

"Scram, kid," said the flunky in accents as haughty as the word permitted.

But Mr. McGuire didn't scram. He had to see a guy—a guy in that hotel. He was going places and he was in a hurry. No mug in a uniform and brass buttons was going to stop him. Mr. McGuire entertained a great scorn and disdain for any uniform.

He kept right on going for the door. The doorman should have known better again; but he didn't. He made a heavy-handed lunge for McGuire. McGuire hadn't dodged taxis in the Bloody Tenth for nothing. He side-stepped adroitly and with the speed, finesse, and accuracy that only a guttersnipe can display, kicked the flunky smartly in the shins.

He got through the revolving door without further trouble.

In the lobby he side-stepped a frowning porter, thumbed his pug nose inelegantly at the bell captain, tripped over an indignant matron's train and skidded down a long stretch of polished marble straight for the bar of the hostelry.

But here he met with disaster. His advance was abruptly checked by the heavy hand of Grogan, the house dick.

"Get out," growled Mr. Grogan.

"Lay off. I got to see a guy," protested McGuire.

"Beat it, kid," rumbled Grogan heavily.

"But I tell you this is important, see? You house dicks are too big for your jobs. Take your hand off me. I gotta . . ."

The little session was creating quite a scene. A ring of amused spectators hemmed in the kid and the detective. Some one laughed and Mr. Grogan lost his temper. He made the fatal error of pushing Mr. McGuire. Mr. McGuire recoiled backward, recovered, squared off and started his rush forward.

And it was at this psychological moment that a towering mountain of a man loomed in the doorway leading to the bar. His ears were misshapen—long since cauliflowered by a score of men who were artists at their job. His eyes were wild and reckless, his mobile mouth as sensitive as a woman's. And between these two features an enormous, gargantuan nose pulsed and glowed with a fierce energy.

Big Nose Serrano!

And behind him, blocked by his massive width of shoulder, stood his never-failing ally through hell or high water—the dour-faced, saturnine Charlie LeBrett.

Now, with a frowning disapproval, his massive head cocked judiciously to one side, Big Nose watched young McGuire square away at the burly Grogan.

"The kid's good," he said in an aside to LeBrett. Then he exploded. "Lead with your left, Red—lead with your left!" He lumbered forward across the lobby. "How many times do I got to tell you never to lead with your right?"

Young McGuire looked up at him sheepishly. "I was outweighed here, so I thought I'd change me style," he offered.

Serrano ran the back of a hard fist across his nose. "Yeah?" he said skeptically. "Well, don't. Now watch. See—here's how it's done."

Abruptly, he threw up his hands, sank his head between his shoulders. He confronted Grogan.

"Listen, mug, when a pal of mine comes to the hotel, I want to see him. Get it?"

Grogan nodded sulkily.

"Swell," rumbled Serrano. "Now get this!"

Swiftly he feinted with his right, crossed a neat left to Grogan's chin. Dempsey couldn't have done it more cleanly. It was a mere love tap but Grogan staggered wildly back, pawing futilely at the air for balance.

Big Nose felt better after that. With a pleased, childish smile on his lips and his bulbous nose radiating his unalloyed joy, he turned to Mr. McGuire.

"You wanted to see me, Red?"

"Yeah," answered McGuire worshipfully. "Gee, Big Nose, you got a sock! You just tapped him and he took the count."

"Let's get out of here," growled LeBrett, eying the ring of spectators with a jaundiced eye.

Serrano turned an innocent eye on him. "What's the matter, Charlie? If you think your left—"

Like a man who had the weight of the world on his shoulders, LeBrett heaved a patient sigh. "The left was the nuts," he said dryly. "But cut the clowning. You're always pulling a hippodrome!"

Serrano eyed him from beneath shaggy brows, then punched him affectionately in the ribs. "True to form, eh, Charlie? Always crabbing the act. The trouble with you, Charlie, is that you've got no soul—no—no *esprit*." He pronounced it *es-prit*, looked cagily at LeBrett from one eye to see if the word had gone over.

LeBrett never moved a muscle. "Do we speak to the kid or don't we?" he asked woodenly.

Serrano shook his head sadly, as if there was no more he could do about it, and tucking his arm under the kid's, led the way to the bar.

Young Red insisted that on Mondays—wash day in the McGuire household—he always rushed the growler for Mr. McGuire's better half; and that the can invariably arrived home half-empty. Thus assured, Serrano set before him a half-dozen hard-boiled eggs and a tall glass of beer.

Somewhat fortified by the beverage, the kid began his tale.

"The old lady wants to know if you can spare twenty, Big Nose. It's for the rent. It's a week overdue now and unless—"

"Sure, don't I know?" interrupted Serrano. He slipped a bill of large denomination into the kid's grimy palm. "That's the hell of landlords. How's the old man?"

"Bad," answered McGuire laconically, with an odd tightening of the jaw.

"Hitting the bottle again?" asked LeBrett.

Young McGuire shook his head. "Wrong, Charlie. Hit *with* a bottle."

"A brawl?" questioned Big Nose.

"Murder," said the kid. "A dozen gorillas jumped him. They beat him up bad. The old man gave 'em hell while it lasted, but they put him in the hospital."

Serrano's hard blue eyes narrowed, his hairy nose dilated. He and Terry McGuire had cracked more than one bottle together—more than one thick skull for the greater glory of the Bloody Tenth. And now McGuire, Sr., was in the hospital because a squad of gorillas had gone to work on him. He had to do something about that.

"What's the story, kid?" he asked.

"Trouble down at the yards," answered Red. "Pop says the company's importin' a lot of gorillas to beat the election."

"Election?" puzzled Serrano. "What election?"

Red McGuire looked disdainful. "Sure—you know. This N.R.A. business."

Big Nose was still bewildered and LeBrett elaborated with characteristic brevity. "Section 7A. The Midwest Packing is forming its own union with a mob of imported gunmen."

Serrano nodded his ponderous head sagely up and down, ran a gnarled fist over the stubble on his chin and chastised the cuspidor with a yard or so of tobacco juice.

"Imported gorillas," he mused in a hushed voice. "Gunmen!" The ancient light of battle flamed to his eyes. "You know, Charlie," he continued, his voice edged with eagerness, "it's been a long time since I swung a beer bottle or a gun."

LeBrett poured two stiff four-fingered jolts from the bottle that decorated the table.

"Yeah," he drawled. "It is a neat set-up. Either you join the company union—or else. A lot of good lads in the Tenth took the 'or else.' Mac's in the hospital."

Serrano poured his drink down his cast-iron gullet, then shook his head. "You don't have to sell me on the idea, Charlie," he said. "Who's back of it?"

"Skovac. And back of Skovac is Lasker—"

"And back of Lasker is Raymour," finished Serrano. "Is that it?"

LeBrett nodded. "All three bad eggs. You interested?"

Big Nose beamed fondly on his ally. "Charlie," he said, "I've been praying for something like this. I'm getting rusty"—he punched himself in the stomach—"flabby"—he flexed his brawny arms—"I'm getting soft." He patted his hip for the reassuring bulge of his automatic. "From now on we're in this up to our ears. What do you know?"

LeBrett shrugged his shoulders, dragged deep on his cigarette, then waved the butt vaguely through the air. "They tell me Skovac's called a little meeting for his boys down at Webb Hall for tonight. Going to deliver a lecture on the best way to use the boot and a pair of brass knucks."

Serrano rubbed the side of his nose with a broad forefinger and a faraway light gleamed in his eye. LeBrett saw it, groaned.

"Don't say it, Big Nose," he begged. "I been looking forward to a nice, quiet evening."

His plea fell on deaf ears. "Who said it won't be a nice quiet evening?" Serrano demanded. "We're just going down to Webb Hall and listen to Skovac's speech. We won't say a word—not a word." He laid a bill beside the check, scraped back his chair. "Come on, let's go."

Red McGuire crammed the last egg into his bulging cheeks, mumbled around it. "I'm with you, Big Nose."

"The hell you say," retorted Big Nose. "You're going to beat it right home to your old lady."

They paraded through the lobby, emerged through the revolving door on to the sidewalk. Serrano repeated his command.

"Fade, kid. And don't forget to tell your old man that he needn't worry. Big Nose is on the job. Scram!"

McGuire mumbled something that sounded like "hully chee"; then with an expression of extreme disgust, thrust his hands into his ragged pockets and shuffled off down the street.

Serrano watched his retreating form for a minute with an admiring eye. "The kid's got the makings," he told LeBrett. "A chip off the old block."

II

LEAD PROMISE

THE FOREMOST CAB OF THE RANK AT THE CURB PULLED UP. Its door swung open as Serrano and LeBrett crossed the sidewalk.

"Where to, mister?"

"Webb Hall," answered Big Nose as he climbed inside. Still emitting an occasional groan, LeBrett followed, plumped down on the cushions beside him.

The cab swung out from the curb, pulled out into the stream of traffic. LeBrett started to groan again, then broke off abruptly. "I just thought of something," he announced with sudden satisfaction. "We can't get into that meeting, Big Nose. Skovac handed out passes, and we ain't got any. Let's tell the cabby to head for the Bijou instead—there's a new burley show opening there tonight."

Serrano scowled. He glowered in silence as the cab sped down a block, swung around a corner, turned right again. Then suddenly he leaned forward and shoved back the glass panel that separated them from the driver.

"Don't pull right up to the hall, buddy," he ordered. "Stop half a block this side of the joint."

It was LeBrett's turn to scowl.

"What the—?"

"Never mind. You'll see," Serrano assured him grimly.

Nothing more was said until the taxi pulled up. Serrano rustled his pal out, followed him to the sidewalk. Then his hand went into his pocket, came up with a bill. He waved it under the driver's nose.

"Want to earn this one?" he asked.

The cabby's eyes took in the denomination of the bill, went wide. His head nodded so vigorously it threatened to fly off his shoulders.

"You'll get it," promised Big Nose. "Just stay here for a minute. Leave your engine running."

He took LeBrett's elbow, steered him across the sidewalk and parked him well in the shadows of a darkened doorway. Then he peered out from their vantage point, looked up and down the street.

From all directions, men were converging on the lighted marquee over the entrance of Webb Hall. Singly, in twos and threes, Skovac's gorilla squad was headed for the meeting. A pair of typical specimens ambled down the street toward the watching Serrano. He stepped swiftly back.

"You know what to do, Charlie. Get set!"

He spat on his huge palms, rubbed his hands together.

Footsteps rang hollowly on the pavement, drew nearer. The two unsuspecting gorillas marched abreast of the shadowy doorway.

Long arms reached out from the gloom, iron hands clamped down. The pair were whisked from the sidewalk and jerked unceremoniously into the blackness beyond.

For a hectic moment the silence in the shadowy doorway was broken by hoarse oaths, by the thud of fists, by the sounds of a brief but violent struggle. Then the two gorillas, each with an iron fist at the back of his collar and its mate clutching the seat of his pants, were propelled swiftly across the sidewalk and popped into the waiting cab.

Serrano flung the promised bill at the driver. "There you are, buddy. Get going!"

He slammed the door shut as the taxi jolted away from the curb. As it picked up speed a hand clawed at the rear window and a pale and twisted face glared back at them. Serrano flung a derisive razzberry after it, then he turned to LeBrett and triumphantly waved a crumpled slip of yellow paper.

"I got mine, Charlie. You get yours?"

The whole incident had been accomplished so swiftly, so quietly, that it had drawn no attention. LeBrett produced his loot, regretfully held up two ragged bits of paper. "Mine got torn in the scuffle." Carefully he licked the ragged edges, lovingly pasted the pass together again. "There, that'll hold long enough to hand it over at the door. Did you notice, Big Nose, that these damn things are yellow? I never realized before that Skovac had a sense of humor."

Arm in arm, clutching their precious tickets, they headed for Webb Hall. As they mingled with the others, drew near the entrance, LeBrett turned suspiciously on his companion.

"Remember, you said we were just going to listen."

Serrano looked injured. "I said so, didn't I? You know me, Charlie."

"Yeah," retorted LeBrett. "That's just the trouble."

They turned up their coat collars, pulled the brims of their hats well down over their eyes. They got past the busy ticket-taker at the door without any trouble, filed into the big auditorium. The long rows of wooden seats were pretty well filled, but Big Nose jostled and elbowed his way down the aisle, wedged into a space big enough for a midget and shoved until there was room for LeBrett beside him. Blithely he ignored the comments of his outraged neighbors. He was in high good humor, at least for the moment.

He screwed around on his seat, looked back toward the door, then dug his elbow into LeBrett's ribs.

"We got here just in time, Charlie. Look, here comes Skovac himself."

LeBrett looked. They knew Skovac—knew him well. They had tangled with him, and with the mob of scab strike-breakers that he ruled, in the past. And Skovac's memory of those days was not one that he cared to recall. LeBrett summed him up now in one word. "Ape!"

It was a brief description, but an expressive one. Skovac shambled down the aisle with his satellites at his heels. His abnormally long arms dangled loosely from his shoulders. Beetling brows jutted out over close-set eyes and his small ears stuck out from a bullet-shaped head.

As he mounted the raised wooden dais at the end of the hall his motley crew of gunmen, strong-arm crew and other riff-raff raised a hoarse cheer. Serrano fought a sudden impulse, lost—thrust his tongue out and made a loud and inelegant noise.

The heads in their vicinity swung immediately about to glare. Up on the platform Skovac peered, scowling, in their general direction. LeBrett brought a heavy hand down on the back of Serrano's neck, ducked him out of sight, held him there.

Skovac searched the audience for a long moment with a cold stare. Then at last he took his place behind the speaker's stand, cleared his throat. LeBrett eased his hold and Serrano straightened up, his face flushed.

"What the hell's the big idea?" he demanded.

"You damn fool," answered LeBrett, "there's only two of us. Peace and quiet—nerts! I don't feel like being slaughtered. I think I'll go take in that burley show, after all."

Serrano pulled him back as he started to rise. "Hold on, this show'll be better. Remember Terry McGuire."

LeBrett subsided, as Skovac began his little speech.

"Gentlemen." Serrano grimaced. "Gentlemen," Skovac's hoarse voice filled the auditorium, "I didn't get you here tonight to make any fancy speeches. And I'm not going to tell you what the traveling salesman said to the farmer's daughter, or anything like that. We're here on business.

"You boys were hired for a job and I'm going to tell you how we're going to handle that job. But before I get down to practical details, I'm going to give you the straight dope on the whole set-up. You know the employees of the Midwest Packing have been squawking. They're damn lucky they got jobs, but they're growling just the same."

LeBrett, watching Serrano's face closely, suddenly tramped hard on his companion's toe. At the warning, Big Nose's jaw set at a grim angle.

Skovac went on, his language, as he warmed up to his subject, becoming more natural. "These mugs want a union, see? Well, they're going to get a union. Only they got to be kept in line. That's where you guys come in.

"You're going to be members. You're going to have membership cards and all that stuff and you'll rate just as much say-so as these other mugs. I'm warning you right now, the union meetings ain't going to be no picnic. But you're going to take your orders from me. I'm backing you up. I ain't naming no names, but the higher-ups are backing you. The sky's the limit. If the opposition gets tough, a couple of cracked skulls will talk louder than words."

"Not when I say them!"

Serrano's booming voice rang out through the vast hall. For a moment a tense, ominous silence filled the auditorium.

It was broken by a low groan from Charlie LeBrett. "I knew it!" he wailed.

"Who said that?" shouted Skovac.

Serrano shook off LeBrett's restraining hand, climbed deliberately to his feet. Every eye in the place swung to focus on his face.

"I did, punk. Me—Big Nose Serrano. What are you going to do about it?"

Skovac's face darkened. At the ends of his long arms his hands clenched into fists. "You got something to say?"

"Plenty," Big Nose assured him. "And I'll tell you right now. You're a dirty, lousy scab, Skovac. You'd sell your grandmother down the river for a measly quarter. You're out to break the skulls of overworked, underpaid men just because some blood-sucking millionaire's out to squeeze them harder; just because somebody pays you blood money to do it." He flung his arms wide in a reckless, impassioned gesture. "And these yeggs you've collected, these scum—what I said about you goes for them. Double!"

The hushed silence that had fallen over the assemblage, stunned at his audacity, was broken by a low growl. It grew, swelled to a menacing roar. Someone leaped to his feet and the action jerked them all out of their seats. As one man, the outraged gorillas converged on this brazen intruder in their midst. On the platform, Skovac shouted in a rage: "Get him!"

In an instant, the interior of Webb Hall was pandemonium itself. With an ominous roar the mob of strikebreakers surged forward.

LeBrett fell automatically into place, back to back against Serrano's broad shoulders. Guns sprouted in their fists. The charge was checked.

Big Nose poised himself lightly on the balls of his feet, swept his heavy automatic around in a slow arc. From smouldering eyes he surveyed the rabble hemming him in. Then his lips curled in magnificent scorn. He raised his booming voice.

"Listen—you mugs! This is a gun—and I know how to use it! It's aching to empty its guts into some of yours. Now if any of you think I'm bluffing . . ."

He left his threat unfinished—but Death hovered ominously in the room. The tension in the hall built up, charge upon charge, until an explosion was imminent.

"We got to get out of here," grated LeBrett into Serrano's ear. "All hell is going to pop!"

"We'll get out," answered Big Nose, "but first . . . stick by me, son." He started to edge out into the aisle.

"Where you going?" moaned LeBrett, lock-stepping after him.

"I got a few words to say to Skovac," answered Serrano heavily. Then he grinned. "And a ditty to sing."

Charlie opened his mouth to protest, then snapped it shut again. He knew from bitter past experience that when Serrano had one of his new musical creations to sing, all hell or high water wouldn't stop him.

LeBrett's finger tightened around the trigger of his gun. What a combination! Lead and lyrics!

But Serrano saw nothing funny in the situation. Boldly—the menacing nozzle of his gun clearing a way for him—he marched up to the platform. With sullen, deep-throated rumblings, the push fell away before his advance. Then with surprising agility for one of his bulk, he vaulted up to the dais. In three long strides he crossed over to Skovac.

Their eyes clashed almost audibly. The crowd in the packed auditorium waited with bated breath for the explosion. And Big Nose did not keep them waiting long. His long left arm shot out, caught Skovac by the slack of his vest and yanked him forward.

"Listen—punk!" snarled Serrano. "This is your first warning—and your last! I'm a man of peace, but unless you call off your dogs—it'll be lilies for Skovac! Get it?"

Skovac's thick lips curled back from yellowed teeth. "I get nothing! If you're looking for hell, I can make plenty of my own. Why, you—"

"Okay!" snarled Big Nose. "I'm starting now!"

Abruptly he released his hold on Skovac's vest. His left arm shot back—then forward with the crushing impact of a battering ram. Skovac took the iron-shod fist on the chin, threw his hands wide, staggered back, then collapsed in a grotesque heap at the far side of the platform.

Serrano stared at him a moment, hopeful that he would rise. But Skovac was out—cold. Then, with a shrug, Big Nose turned to his audience. He executed a mock bow—cleared his throat with a portentous rumble, and expanding his leather-like lungs, broke into full-throated song.

> *"Lasker's a bum and his men are just scum.*
> *They'd plug a poor guy for a quarter.*
> *But Big Nose came to call when they met in Webb Hall*
> *And told 'em to lay off or there'd be slaughter."*

The last notes of the unmelodious ditty were drowned out by a new sound. From outside in the street, came the high-pitched wail of a police siren. Then another—and another.

With magnificent disdain, Serrano ignored them. "How was that, Charlie?" he called to LeBrett.

"The berries," growled Charlie. "You'll be singing it from a cell if we don't get out of here."

"We're going—but you wouldn't hurry a gentleman, would you?" grinned Serrano.

Then, with their leveled guns covering their retreat, they backed warily across the stage and slipped out a rear exit.

In the comparative peace and quiet of McGinnis' back room, they discussed their initial move in their latest campaign. Serrano set down his empty glass of Scotch, beamed fondly up at McGinnis.

"You should have been there, Mac," he chortled. "That song of mine wowed 'em!"

"Sure," grunted LeBrett sarcastically. "It brought the police. Well, now that you've expressed your poetic temperament, I guess I can turn in."

"Like hell you can!" boomed Serrano. "You got a date. We're going places tonight."

McGinnis' eye twinkled. He patted his apron-covered paunch. "If you're on the warpath again, Big Nose, let me in on it. I'm getting fat—sitting on my can around here. And I'm aching for action. What's up?"

Over another bottle, Serrano outlined his campaign. McGinnis listened eagerly, waited in silence until he had finished. Then at last he nodded, started to untie his apron. "Looks like a brawl," he commented dryly. "Count me in. And say—Goldstein was around last night. Wanted to know what you were doing. The Hebe's a handy guy in a brawl and you could use him. Shall I give him a buzz? And where do we go tonight?"

Big Nose grinned fondly at him. "You stick here for now, Mac. Me and Charlie are just going to pay some social calls. But get in touch with Goldstein and the Greek. I may need you boys before I put the skids to Skovac. He's a tough baby." He poured himself a last drink, gurgled it noisily down his throat. "Come on, Charlie, let's get the bus and scram."

LeBrett made a face, dabbed at his blinking eye. "I got a date—with a bed," he said sourly. "That's official."

Serrano shook his head sorrowfully at McGinnis. "A little action and he's got to go to bed!" he snorted. "How about some Peppo tablets, sunshine? Or a truss? Jeez, it must be hell to get old!"

LeBrett kicked back his chair, stalked to the door. He yanked it open, glared at his pal for a long, disdainful moment. "Well, what the hell are you waiting for?" he demanded angrily. "Is your fanny glued to the chair?"

Serrano grunted, winked broadly at McGinnis and lumbered meekly after him.

III
THE KID MAKES A BULL'S-EYE

MIKE LASKER, RACKETEERING LABOR BOSS AND MASTER STRIKEBREAKER, occupied a suite of dingy offices in the dingier Court Building up on North Clark Street. The locality was a little bit out of Serrano's territory, but now that he had tasted again the salty blood of battle, that wasn't going to stop him.

Once launched on one of his holy crusades, nothing short of a blast from a machine gun could do that.

And thus it was that a half-hour after leaving McGinnis', he tooled his sedan expertly to the curb before the shabby entrance to the Court Building. He eased his automatic from his shoulder holster, examined it swiftly with an expert eye, then dropped it casually into the side pocket of his coat.

"This is just a social call, Charlie," he said to LeBrett, seated beside him. "But don't let it get out of hand."

"Hell, no!" grunted LeBrett. "This is one time where we're going to mix business and pleasure—and like it. Let's go."

Always a sartorial gent, Serrano cocked his iron hat at a more jaunty angle, then with an unlit cigar jutting aggressively from his mouth, slid from behind the wheel. Shoulder to shoulder with LeBrett, they pounded across the sidewalk, breezed through the door of the building.

And as it slammed shut behind them with an ominous bang, the dirty, freckled face and wide eyes of Red McGuire stared after them from the rear of Serrano's sedan.

At the head of a long flight of wooden stairs, Big Nose and LeBrett pulled up short before a glass-paneled door. Light shone from behind it and through the closed portal came the hum and drone of heavy voices.

"Looks like Lasker is in session," grunted LeBrett, fingering the gun in his pocket.

"Yeah—but did you read this?" answered Serrano disdainfully. With a stubby forefinger he indicated the legend painted on the glass panel of the door.

MICHAEL LASKER
LABOR PROTECTIVE AGENCY

He snorted; his bulbous nose twitched and his gorilla chest threatened to burst the buttons on his vest. "Looks like we got to do a little protecting on our own."

Savagely he wrenched the knob of the door with his left hand, kicked open the portal with a heavy foot. Backed by LeBrett, he marched across the threshold.

His eyes flared wide, then as suddenly narrowed. The grin on his face broadened to a happy smile. And by his side, the saturnine LeBrett began to whistle unmusically through his teeth the opening bars of "Just Before the Battle, Mother."

For their arrival had evidently been expected. They were greeted, not only by Lasker and a dozen of his gorillas but by the menacing guns bulging in their fists.

Serrano rolled his cigar from one corner of his mouth to the other, punched back his derby and rocked back on his heels. He nodded briefly at

Lasker. " 'Lo, punk," he said. Then slowly he swung his shaggy head around on his bull neck and surveyed the row of menacing faces confronting him. "Nice lot, eh, Charlie?" he commented. "Just out of Sunday school." Then his voice hardened. "Why, if it ain't our old friend Peanuts Corbin!"

He took a long stride across the room, pulled up short before a rat-faced individual in a slouch hat. With a magnificent contempt he ignored the heavy automatic in Corbin's fist.

"Still slinging a gun for pay, eh, rat?" he snarled. Abruptly he took the knot of Corbin's tie, yanked it tight and hard up against the gunman's Adam's apple.

Corbin went blue in the face—then white. His upper lip quivered and little beads of sweat popped out on his forehead.

"You'll never die that way, scum!" grated Serrano. "You'll get yours with a slug of lead."

"Try that again and by God—"

"Nuts! You haven't got the guts."

Big Nose turned to the next man, crooked his forefinger and plucked him under the nose. "Cocky Smith—and Blackie Schwartz—and Joe Vogel!" He turned, swaggered back across the room to Lasker, hitched his bulk onto a corner of Lasker's desk. "You're dumber than I thought, mug, if you think you can run this racket with that outfit."

Lasker's tawny eyes were twin opals of hate. With an effort he controlled the twitching of his lips. "It's a nice routine, Serrano," he said heavily. "Go ahead. Make a monkey of yourself. It's your last play!"

Serrano laughed. "Last?" He scraped a match across the top of Lasker's desk, applied it to the tip of his cigar. With a sigh he erupted a heavy cloud of blue smoke. "Hell, Lasker, I'm just beginning. Me and Charlie came up here to give you a break. Your racket is through, see? You're washed up. If you want to take it that way—swell! If you don't . . ." He turned to LeBrett. "What do you say, Charlie?"

"I'm hoping he don't," grated LeBrett.

Lasker's thin lips pulled back in a sneer. "And you're getting your wish. You two mugs have made one wrong play too many." His gun edged up an inch and his finger tightened perceptibly on the trigger. "Take 'em, boys."

Serrano and LeBrett were taken. That is, their guns were expertly frisked from their pockets.

Big Nose flicked ashes across Lasker's immaculate vest. "That takes a load off my mind," he sighed wearily. "I hate to take advantage of rats. That makes the odds about even." Coolly he counted noses. "Yeah, that's about right. Me and Charlie against you and the mob. Well, when does the funny stuff begin?"

Lasker licked his thin lips wolfishly. "Just as soon as Skovac gets here.

He wants to work out on you a little before you get it." Slowly he stood up, kicked back his chair. Then, with a sudden movement, he sank the nozzle of his gun deep into Serrano's navel. "Your number is up, big boy," he said in a hard voice. "You've tangled with me for the last time."

Their eyes met and held, clashed audibly. Serrano's nostrils dilated wide and Lasker's finger was white and tense on the trigger.

Death trembled in the room!

Death from the gaping nozzle of Lasker's automatic—and Death from yet another source! Big Nose and LeBrett were lined up, their backs to the door. Confronting them, facing the portal, was Lasker and his men. In the rear wall, behind the mobsters, was a window.

And there, peering through the dirty glass, was the even dirtier face of Red McGuire. And more important still, clutched in his grimy right hand was a long barreled, blue-steel Smith and Wesson.

There was something familiar about that gun. Big Nose could have laughed out loud. With a mighty effort he controlled the impulse, caught the kid's eye, then turned casually to LeBrett. One glance was enough to tell him that his ally had also seen the rescuing angel at the window.

"It's a pretty set-up," grinned Serrano. "What do you say?"

"I'm not asking for any more," answered LeBrett. "This ought to be good."

"It'll be better when Skovac gets here," snarled Lasker.

Big Nose beamed on him fondly. "Want to lay odds?"

"Sure!" snarled Lasker. "Only it's going to be hell to collect from a stiff!"

"Don't I know!" mocked Serrano. Casually he raised his arm, inserted his little finger in his ear—pointed his thumb at the light overhead—and gave the kid the nod.

Young McGuire got his cue, and three things happened simultaneously— or almost simultaneously. Holding the heavy revolver in his two hands, he elevated the muzzle, drew a swift bead on the large light fixture and squeezed the trigger.

Flame and lead erupted from the nozzle—and with a crescendo tinkle of breaking glass, the room was plunged into darkness. Young Red had scored a bull's-eye.

Fearing a rear attack, Lasker's men whirled at the crack of the revolver. Their guns belched and a withering cross-fire converged on the fire-escape where the kid had been but a moment before.

Big Nose was swift to take advantage of the momentary confusion. His fist was still at his ear. Now, with the crushing force of a pile driver, it shot forward. It was as expertly aimed as McGuire's bullet and Mr. Lasker's jaw crumpled beneath the blow.

LeBrett deftly caught the automatic as it dribbled from the racketeer's nerveless fingers. Then, flat on their stomachs, he and Serrano began a hurried retreat to the door.

The attack of the gunmen shifted from the window to the portal. Lead crisscrossed the room. The swaying smoke of gun fire hung over the scene like a shroud.

But LeBrett held his fire until he and Big Nose were across the portal. Then he squeezed lead very rapidly in a vicious blast to check a premature rush on the door.

They hit the stairs running, skidded down the long flight, and as the outer door slammed shut behind them, Serrano's booming bass floated back in derisive challenge.

> *"Lasker's scabs are after the packers*
> *Because the bosses slip 'em a few lousy smackers.*
> *With brass knucks and cannons they think that they're swell,*
> *But Big Nose Serrano will send 'em to hell!"*

"How's that, Charlie?" he bellowed. "Right out of my head!"

"I'll say you're out of your head," grunted LeBrett the unappreciative. "The car—fast!"

Young McGuire himself swung open the door of their sedan as they swept across the sidewalk and with the crescendo scream of police sirens drowning out the crash of guns that still echoed from Lasker's office, they got away from there.

IV
SERRANO LAYS DOWN THE LAW

MR. MCGUIRE'S STORY WAS SIMPLICITY ITSELF. As Serrano raced the sedan north on Michigan Boulevard, he elaborated on the details. After delivering the bill to his old lady, he had picked up Serrano's trail at McGinnis'. And knowing Big Nose of old, he knew that hell was about to pop. He had decided to be in on the popping.

He had followed Serrano and LeBrett to the garage and while they were inspecting the tires, had slipped into the back of the car. Later, when they had gone up to Lasker's office—and nothing had happened—and they hadn't come down, he had decided that something was wrong.

He had investigated, via the rear fire-escape, armed with the Smith and Wesson he had found in the car.

"I ought to lam you for disobeying orders," growled Big Nose. Then, as

McGuire's eyes went wide in hurt surprise, he brought his ham-like hand down on the kid's shoulders in a whack that sent the breath whistling from his body. "But I'm going to buy you a beer instead!"

McGuire recovered from a fit of coughing, came up beaming. "Then I'm one of the boys now, eh, Big Nose?"

"You sure are." Serrano turned solemnly toward LeBrett. "There's a new partner in the firm now, Charlie. Shake on it."

Ceremoniously, LeBrett enclosed a grimy paw in his own calloused one, pumped the kid's thin arm up and down. McGuire's skinny chest puffed out, strained at the one button that held his ragged coat together.

"I'll take that beer down at McGinnis' joint, Big Nose," he said easily. "Let's go."

"Not tonight—it's too late. I'm taking you right home to your Ma. But get all dolled up bright and early, kid. There's another social call on the list—a real society visit this time—and now that you're a partner you better come along. I'll be around to pick you up." Serrano, amused with the new set-up, chuckled. Then he sobered. "But this time, Red," he added warningly, "no sling-shots, no water pistols, no stink bombs—and no sub-machine guns."

When Serrano's big sedan pulled up before the McGuire tenement at ten the following morning, Red was already ensconced upon the littered stoop. He had, in fact, been waiting impatiently there for the past three hours, not daring to leave his post.

He hurdled down three steps, then remembering his lately-acquired dignity, slowed down to a bold swagger as he crossed the sidewalk. He greeted his partners with the proper formality and accepted a seat beside his idol at the wheel. Big Nose surveyed him critically. The dolling-up that he managed consisted mainly of a vain attempt to plaster down an unruly red thatch with copious applications of water. The result was not exactly successful, but Serrano nodded his approval.

"You look swell, kid. Raymour'll be tickled to make your acquaintance."

The car got under way, headed toward the fashionable precincts of Lake Shore Drive. McGuire's newly-acquired nonchalance left him. His mouth gaped.

"You mean—you mean Old Man Raymour—the Big Boss of the Midwest?"

"Sure. I told you we were crashing into society today."

Red's favorite expression came muffled, strangled. "Hully chee!"

This was something he hadn't bargained for. Being the partner of Serrano and LeBrett was going to be a far different matter from what he had fondly expected. He subsided back against the cushions to ponder this new angle.

The journey was made in silence. Big Nose, well pleased with the hectic start of his latest crusade, was occupied with no more serious a problem than finding a word to rhyme with "union." He wondered whether "onion" wouldn't do, in a pinch. LeBrett, from his solitary grandeur on the back seat, was critically comparing the feminine ankles and calves revealed by a brisk breeze from the Lake. Young McGuire was constructing a mental picture of Old Man Raymour from what that gentleman's employees had said about him. He conjured up a saturnine, grinning face with green eyes and sharp horns projecting from the forehead. He was a little doubtful, though, whether the guy really did have a long tail.

They swung at last into a graveled driveway, pulled up before an imposing gray-stone mansion. Serrano led the way up the steps to the front door, squashed a broad thumb on the buzzer beside the portal.

A few moments later the door swung inward and a liveried butler peered out at them. When his eyes fell upon Red McGuire, they blinked three times in rapid succession.

"Mister Raymour in?" demanded Big Nose.

"Er—I'll see," answered the butler, uncertainly. "You have an appointment, perhaps?"

Big Nose squared his broad shoulders belligerently. "Appointment, hell," he snorted. "Big Nose Serrano and the—uh—committee are calling. He'll see us."

The flunky took another look. "Just a minute, Mr. Serrano. I'll see if he's in."

He started to close the door.

That was a mistake. It didn't quite close, blocked by Big Nose's size twelve boot. Serrano shoved the portal roughly inward. His huge hand shot out, grasped a handful of mauve cloth and brass buttons that was the butler's coat front. He heaved, raised the gasping flunkey to his tiptoes, thrust his glowering face into the other's terrified one.

"Nobody closes doors in my nose, you," he growled. "It's a swell nose, a handsome nose, a nice nose. Maybe you don't like it?" he inquired hopefully.

Knowles, the Raymour butler, did not know what was common knowledge in the Bloody Tenth Ward. He did not know that Serrano was extremely sensitive about the prodigious organ that had given him his nickname; did not know that although Serrano joked about it freely himself, it was sudden death for the stranger who dared a wisecrack. Fortunately for Knowles, he was spared the test of his diplomacy.

"It's a lovely nose, really," a low, musical voice broke the tense silence.

Serrano dropped the flunky back to his heels, whirled abruptly about. A slim, patrician girl was descending the stairs that led from the floor above.

She was clad in a simple dress of blue and her honey-colored hair was drawn back into a loose knot at the nape of her neck. Big Nose watched her admiringly as she approached.

"Well?" she inquired coolly. "Surely you didn't come here to get Knowles' opinion of your good looks?"

Despite her calm demeanor, Serrano sensed the twinkle behind her gray eyes. Unabashed, he executed a flourishing bow. "No, ma'am. I don't give a—I don't care what the gent thinks. We came to see old man Raymour."

She made a slight gesture to Knowles, who gratefully vanished from the scene. Red McGuire could not resist the impulse to thumb his nose after the butler's retreating back.

"Old—ah—Mr. Raymour is my father. I'm Joan Raymour."

Serrano bowed again. "Pleased to meet you, Joan. Let me make you acquainted with Charlie LeBrett and Mr. Red McGuire."

The girl acknowledged the introductions, then turned to a door at the end of the hall. "My father's in the library," she said over her shoulder as she led the way. "He'll be delighted to see you."

"And how," grunted LeBrett under his breath.

They filed inside after her, entered a large, luxuriously-furnished room. A stout, pompous, gray-haired man sat behind the broad mahogany table that served him as a desk. He looked up as they entered, stared at the incongruous trio.

"Mr. Serrano, Mr. LeBrett and Mr. McGuire," Joan Raymour told him. She turned to Big Nose. "Speak up."

As she stepped aside, Big Nose stalked up to the table. He looked curiously at the man who was the big boss, the head of the Midwest Packing Company. He looked at the pouches under Raymour's eyes, at the thin, close-set lips, at the sleek paunch that bulged out to touch the table edge. The girl was promptly forgotten.

"I'm Big Nose Serrano—from the Tenth Ward," he boomed. "Maybe you've heard of me, mister."

Raymour glared. "I have. Lasker called me up this morning. I've heard all about your crazy antics." He scraped back his chair, climbed to his feet. "But you're going too far when you come barging into my home. Get out!" He pointed an imperious finger toward the door.

Serrano's bulbous nose twitched, turned a shade deeper crimson. It was a warning signal, had Raymour known it. With an effort Big Nose controlled himself.

"Not yet—I'll go when I'm damn good and ready," he retorted. "Listen, Raymour, I'm giving you a break. I came up here to talk to you, to appeal to you. You're piling up a mess of trouble. Give your workingmen a break and you'll do yourself a favor at the same time. Give them decent wages, give them shorter hours, give them better working conditions. Give them their union—on the level, not peppered with Skovac's gorillas."

Raymour's flabby face grew mottled. His hands clenched on the table top. "How dare you come here and talk like that to me?" he demanded. "I'll call the police and have you thrown out like the hoodlum you are. I'm running my own business and no bully ward boss is going to poke his nose into it."

The word "nose" was fatal. Serrano quivered in every mighty muscle. He leaned across the table, prodded a rigid forefinger deep into Raymour's navel.

"I gave you a break, but you wouldn't take it. You think that because you got millions you can get away with murder. You use your dirty dollars to hire thugs like Lasker and Skovac to do your dirty work for you." His voice rose to a thunderous bellow. "You're not going to get away with it, Raymour. I'll smash Lasker, just like this." His huge fist smote the table a mighty blow that set papers and inkwell dancing. "I'll wipe out Skovac and every last one of his cutthroat crew. And then—God help you!"

He swung abruptly on his heel, marched toward the door. Raymour, two degrees removed from apoplexy, glared after him in impotent speechless rage.

With LeBrett and the irrepressible Red swaggering in his wake, Serrano strode through the hall. As he reached for the knob of the front door, he pulled up to an abrupt halt as a voice floated after him.

"Mr. Serrano, you forgot to say good-bye. Is that nice?"

He turned, thrust his companions aside and walked back to meet the girl who had followed them. The angry flush died from his face.

"I'm sorry, sister," he mumbled sheepishly. "I forgot he was your old man."

"I've never seen anyone talk back to him before," she told him. "It was a rare treat, really."

Serrano brightened again. "I hadn't ought to have said what I did," he explained. "But I got hot under the collar."

"Father's all right," she assured him. "I don't know what this is all about. But if you knew him as well as I do, you'd know he's got a big heart under his domineering manner."

Serrano brazenly chucked her under the chin. "You know, sister, you and I are going to get along. I'll give you a buzz sometime. So long, baby."

He waved an airy farewell, ushered his partners outside and followed them. A blithe whistle piped from his lips as he clattered down the steps, wedged behind the wheel of the sedan, sprayed gravel from the wheels as he headed out of the driveway.

Young McGuire voiced his thoughts aloud. "Ain't she a lulu?"

The whistle died on Big Nose's lips. He looked suspiciously at the kid's face, saw the freckled countenance set in a dreamy, reminiscent grin. "What the hell you grinning at?" he demanded.

"She winked at me," breathed Red ecstatically. "A real big wink, just as I was going out the door."

Big Nose steered dexterously with his left hand, waved an admonishing forefinger under the kid's snub nose. "Nix, kid, lay off. The partner business don't hold good where the dames are concerned. She's mine, see?"

V

THE SNATCH

"THE POOR WORKINGMAN," SNORTED LEBRETT.

"I always did like blondes especially," sighed Serrano.

"Old Man Raymour's her father," reminded LeBrett.

"I don't care if she's the daughter of the devil himself," answered Big Nose. "If they have a little of the Old Nick in them, the better."

"She's kidding the pants off you," said LeBrett sourly.

"I tell you this baby's regular—the real goods." Serrano was indignant. He rolled off the bed where he had been lying, indulging in romantic day dreams, and began to pace the floor of their room. He stopped in mid-stride and glared challengingly at his partner in crime. "A century against a shot of rye says I can date her up—tonight."

LeBrett hooked a long leg over the arm of his chair, squinted thoughtfully at the half-filled glass in his hand. "Of all the sucker bets—go ahead, big boy, do your stuff."

Serrano stalked to the telephone, thumbed through the book to the R's, found the number. Inserting a pudgy forefinger, he dialed it, jammed the receiver against a cauliflowered ear and waited impatiently for the call to go through.

A buzzing voice came over the wire at last. He scowled at the wall over LeBrett's head.

"You *would* answer. Listen, you, tell Miss Raymour that Mister Serrano's calling. And don't tell me that she's not in or I'll come up and break your damn neck."

He drummed his fingers impatiently on the base of the instrument. A few moments later the wire buzzed again. The drumming ceased abruptly.

"Hello, baby. This is Big Nose Serrano. Feel like stepping tonight? What do you say we go places?" He paused, held his breath, then beamed broadly at LeBrett. "Swell," he boomed heartily into the telephone. "Listen, I'll wait for you in the lobby downstairs. I'm at the Royale. Make it snappy, eh?"

He hung up, swaggered across the room, took the unfinished drink from

LeBrett's hand and tossed it off in one gulp. "Now what have you got to say, you old crepe-hanger? Where's my hat and coat? She's coming right over. You can buy me that drink later."

"It'll keep." LeBrett shrugged. "She ain't here yet."

Down in the ornate, palm-decorated lobby, Serrano tossed away the stub of his fourth cigar. For the tenth time in as many minutes he looked at the clock over the clerk's desk and the scowl on his face deepened. He started for the elevators, gave vent to an explosive "damn!" and turned back. LeBrett was waiting upstairs and Big Nose was in no mood, just then, for any "I-told-you-so's." Once more he fell to pacing the lobby.

His bitter meditations were interrupted by a heavy hand that clamped like a vise on his arm. He turned his head and looked into the face of Detective Marty Flynn.

"Sorry, Big Nose," explained the detective. "But you're wanted down at headquarters."

"What the hell—what's up?" demanded Serrano.

"I'll explain on the way," answered Flynn. "Let's go."

"You'll explain right now. Speak your little piece, Marty."

Flynn waved his hands helplessly. "Be reasonable, Big Nose. I can't help this—orders is orders. Old Morton Raymour's daughter is gone and—"

It was Serrano's turn to grip the other's arm. "Say that again!"

"His daughter is gone and their butler says she went to meet you. The old gent's wild, says to find you both. Where is she, Big Nose?"

Serrano groaned. "I wish to God I knew. But I'll find her, if I have to bust the town wide open."

"You're coming with me. The other boys'll find her, don't worry."

Serrano didn't budge. The glimmer of an idea awoke in his brain. His jaw set at a grim angle. "I got a hunch, Marty. I think I know where to look."

Flynn shook his head. "No, you don't. I'm taking you to headquarters. Raymour's got plenty drag and I don't want my job knocked out from under me. I know you, Big Nose, and I hate like hell to—"

Before Serrano sensed his intention, Flynn made a swift move. There was a sharp click and a slim bracelet of cold steel encircled Big Nose's wrist. Flynn nudged him toward the door.

"Don't blow up, Big Nose. I got to do it."

Serrano's brain seethed. Blindly, mechanically, he stumbled from the hotel, allowed Flynn to herd him across the sidewalk and into a waiting cab. They got under way with a jerk that sat him down hard on the cushions. The jolt was all he needed to crystallize the milling thoughts that ran riot through his consciousness.

He could not let himself be led, like a sheep, into headquarters. He could not be held there, impotent, helpless, while others searched for Joan Raymour. He had to get away from Flynn, immediately.

He rubbed his nose with his free hand, scratched behind his ear, then reached casually for his pocket. "Got a match, Marty?"

His easy manner fooled Flynn, for a moment. But that moment was all Serrano needed. His hand flashed up, the glow from a street lamp shone for a moment on blued steel, then his arm came down in a short, vicious arc. The heavy butt of his gun struck Flynn's temple with a brief thud and the detective collapsed limply on the cushions.

"Sorry, Marty," Big Nose muttered as he fumbled in Flynn's pockets. "But *I* had to do *that*."

The driver had not heard the single dull thud of the blow. The cab sped steadily through the streets. Serrano's probing fingers found the key, inserted it in the lock of the handcuffs and clicked the bracelet open.

The first intimation the cabby had that something had gone amiss was the icy touch of steel at the back of his neck. His hands froze on the wheel as Serrano's gruff voice sounded in his ear.

"Slow down at the next corner."

He did as he was bid. As his foot eased off the gas pedal, Serrano swung open the rear door, stepped onto the running board and landed, staggering, in the gutter. He brandished the weapon, bellowed after the cab. "Keep going!"

As the winking red tail-lights of the taxi disappeared down the street, Big Nose sprinted for the cigar store at the corner. He wedged himself into a telephone booth, dropped a coin into the slot and dialed the number of the Royale Hotel.

In a veritable hail of gravel, the big sedan roared up the driveway and pulled to a sudden halt before the entrance to Raymour's home. Serrano and LeBrett piled out of the machine, barged up the steps and found the door open. Men milled around in the hallway, reporters representing every paper in the city. The door to the library was closed and Knowles, pallid and perspiring, stood guard before it.

The abrupt entrance of Big Nose Serrano produced a sensation. The newshounds leaped at him in a mass.

"Big Nose—what's the dope?"

"What happened?"

"Where is she?"

Serrano brushed them impatiently aside, shouldered his way to where the butler stood petrified at his post. "Get out of the way!"

If the devil himself had suddenly popped up before him, Knowles could not have moved a finger. He stood like a graven image, gaping, helpless. With a low growl Serrano plucked him away from the door, grasped the knob.

"Stay here, Charlie. Keep everybody out."

He swung the portal inward, stepped across the threshold and closed it behind him. Seated at his desk was Raymour. His flabby jowls were ashen, his pouchy eyes lackluster. They focused unseeingly on the broad form of Serrano for a moment, then, as recognition flooded them, Raymour leaped to his feet with a cry.

"You!" he pointed a trembling finger. "Where's my daughter? Where's Joan?"

"I haven't seen her."

Raymour's eyes rolled wildly. "You're lying. She sneaked off to meet you. Where is she?"

"I told you I haven't seen her."

Raymour collapsed like a pricked balloon. He sank back limply into his chair. Serrano strode across the room, confronted him coldly.

"I got a good hunch who's got her, though."

Raymour bounced up again. "Who—for God's sake?"

"Your own hired killers—Skovac and Lasker."

"You're mad." Raymour ran his hands wildly through his hair. "Why would they kidnap Joan?"

Serrano shrugged. "Lots of reasons. Pin it on me and get me out of the way, for one. Bleed you white, for another. Or—you got drag in this town—they could force you to back up their play until they ran every racket in the city. Take your choice." He looked coldly into Raymour's stricken face. "They wouldn't take her to Lasker's office. Where would they go?"

Raymour's bloodless lips alone moved. "The garage," he mumbled. "Skovac has a place down by the river—an old garage at the corner of McMaster and Lowe. His headquarters." Suddenly he found the use of his limbs. He stumbled toward the telephone on his desk. "The police—"

Serrano jerked the instrument from his trembling hands. "The hell with the cops! This is my job. I'll get her back for you."

Swiftly he dialed a number, the number of McGinnis' cafe. The cheery voice of the Irishman answered him. "Get Goldstein—get all the boys you can round up," ordered Serrano. "Load 'em with artillery and shoot 'em down to McMaster and Lowe. We're going to clean up Skovac and his rats."

He banged the receiver back on the hook. McGinnis would ask no questions. Big Nose grasped Raymour by the elbow. "Come on, mister. You can have a ringside seat for the finish. It'll do you good. It'll give you an idea what you were monkeying with when you hired Skovac and Lasker."

He steered the hapless man toward the door, out into the hall where they were instantly surrounded by the frantic reporters.

"Trail along if you want to," Serrano told them, as LeBrett cleared a path to the outer door. "You'll get a yarn that'll fill the front page."

VI

THE KISS-OFF

AS HE TURNED DOWN MCMASTER STREET, Serrano slowed his speed until the roar of the powerful motor died to a low hum. He thrust his arm out of the window, waggled a huge hand. The trailing reporters took the warning, dropped back as the sedan slid onto the rendezvous.

A half-block from their destination three cars were pulled up at the curb. McGinnis had responded faithfully to the S.O.S. Big Nose eased the sedan in ahead of the foremost car, piled out onto the sidewalk. He and LeBrett were promptly surrounded by McGregor, Ike Goldstein, and the mob that Serrano had ruled in the hectic, flaming days of Prohibition.

Big Nose was in his element. He knew these men, knew they would follow him through hell and high water. His eyes gleamed as he saw they were bristling with weapons. He beamed fondly around at the ring of familiar faces.

"Just like old times, eh, boys? We're going to have a swell blowout, together, just like in the old days. Only we got a job to do, first." They gathered closer about him, waiting for orders. "There's a dame in that place," he warned them. "We got to think of her first. If they don't put up a fight, I'll massacre the first one of you that starts something. But if they do get tough—give 'em hell."

A low, subdued cheer answered him. He brandished his automatic. "I'll lead the band. The rest of you take your cue from me."

Old Man Raymour was forgotten, left in the parked sedan. Well in the van of his cohorts, Serrano strode down the gloomy street, headed for the ramshackle old garage on the corner. Stray gleams of light showed from beyond its sagging shutters. Lounging against the door, smoking a cigarette, stood one of Skovac's men.

Some sixth sense warned the lookout of Big Nose's approach. The cigarette dropped in a hissing shower of sparks as he whirled around. The glow of light from the corner street lamp illuminated the features of Big Nose Serrano.

The guard waited for no more. Without warning, without challenge, he blazed away. The staccato report of his gun echoed in the silent street and Serrano's hat was whisked neatly from his head.

Big Nose's decision had been made for him. His gun convulsed, belched flame—and the lookout toppled limply from his post. Serrano's war whoop rang out above the crash of gunfire and at the signal, his eager crew came running to the fray.

The ancient door was riddled with a fusillade of bullets, assaulted by burly shoulders. It burst inward under the impact and Serrano and his men barged into the garage.

Skovac's gorillas met them with flaming lead. In an instant the building was a chaos of spitting guns, of shouts and curses, of milling men. Big Nose heard the voice of Skovac himself, yelling orders in a hoarse voice above the din. With swinging fist and spouting gun, he battled his way in that direction.

"Lay off him!" he bellowed to his comrades. "He's mine!"

Skovac saw him coming. Serrano saw the swift fear flash in the strikebreaker's eyes, saw his gun muzzle come up and gape hungrily in his direction. Their guns roared as one. A bullet ploughed a burning path across Serrano's temple. Warm blood spurted from the wound, trickled into his eyes, dissolved everything into a blinding red mist. He dabbed at the crimson stream with the back of his hand and as his vision cleared, he saw Skovac lying limp and twisted on the floor of the garage.

From somewhere up above came a single, shrill scream—abruptly choked off. Big Nose's head jerked up as he swept a glance about him. Through the blue cloud of gun-smoke that hung like a pall in the air, he saw a rickety flight of stairs leading upward. LeBrett covered his charge for the stairs.

The wooden slats creaked under his weight as he pounded upward. He burst open a door at the head of the stairs and found himself face to face with a wild-eyed, disheveled Lasker. Big Nose's finger constricted on the trigger and a hollow click echoed in his ears. His gun was empty.

Lasker's face contorted in savage hate. Slowly, deliberately, he drew a bead on Serrano's belt buckle.

"You've butted in for the last time, Big Nose," he said hoarsely. "Now—take it!"

A streak of blue and gold flashed across the room. A white hand struck Lasker's elbow. His gun exploded and plaster sprayed down from the ceiling. Then the useless weapon flew from Serrano's fingers, struck square on Lasker's scowling brow. His knees buckled and he slid limply to the floor.

Big Nose shoved his unconscious body out of the way with a callous boot, turned to the girl. Her dress was torn, her hair cascaded in tousled glory over her bare shoulders, but her eyes were shining.

"You're a wow, sister," he said admiringly. Then, as the highest compliment he could offer, he added: "You'd make a swell partner, baby."

And Joan Raymour, heiress to the Midwest Packing millions, asked softly: "Do you really think so, Big Nose?"

The crackle of gun-fire downstairs had ceased and heavy footsteps clattered up the stairs. They were instantly surrounded. The horde of reporters belabored Serrano with a barrage of questions. He stayed them with an upraised hand.

"I got an inspiration," he announced. "I'll give you the whole story—in a little ditty I just made up. It goes like this." He threw back his shoulders, winked at the girl and burst into rollicking song.

> *"A bunch of rats all armed with gats*
> *Shanghaied a swell-looking lady.*
> *They were mugs that I hate,*
>   *so I crashed the gate*
> *And rescued a million dollar baby."*

The reporters whooped in glee, snatched out notebooks and begged for an encore. Modestly Serrano obliged and while he rocked the room with his booming bass, scratching pencils recorded the immortal lines for posterity.

As the last note died away, there was a stir at the head of the stairs. The men there parted and old man Raymour, forgotten in the excitement, stepped into the room. His hands came up, trembling, as he stumbled over to meet his daughter.

Big Nose watched their happy embrace with thoughtful eyes. He rubbed the side of his gargantuan nose with his forefinger a moment, then he brightened.

"Yeah," he announced. "I almost forgot. You can run a statement from Mr. Raymour. The employees of the Midwest Packing Company are going to have their union. They're going to get a higher wage scale, shorter hours, better working conditions. Their spokesmen will arrange the details with Mr. Raymour tomorrow. Ain't that right, Mr. Raymour?"

For an instant the color rose in Raymour's face like the red fluid in a thermometer. Then slowly it subsided again. He looked at his daughter, then faced the reporters. "Yes, that's right. I'll sign that statement."

LeBrett sighed. "It was fun while it lasted," he said regretfully. "One of you mugs take care of Lasker there. I see he's coming to. And you, Big Nose, I owe you a drink. Let's go, I could use one myself."

"Just a minute," said Serrano. "You don't owe it to me, yet." He crossed over to Joan Raymour. "Baby, I promised this push a blowout. It'll be in Clancy's Hall tomorrow night. A swell affair—soup and fish and everything. Will you come?"

She nodded, smiling.

Big Nose beamed. He took LeBrett's elbow. "That's settled. Let's get that drink. And after we have that one, we'll have another. And another. And another . . ."

Gangster Stories, March 1932

The Eavesdropper

WELL, HERE HE IS, TONY FELDMAN HIMSELF—he's a pretty tough guy but a good egg at heart. He chews tobacco, spits, swears an' has an "avid eye for a shapely thigh." Can't say that we blame him much for that. Though he doesn't weigh any more than a hundred an' thirty pounds, he's got hair on his chest and a sock in either fist. He's confessed to us that the favorite character of his creation is Big Nose Serrano—pullin' the Robin Hood stuff. There's a lot of dark an' shady spots in Feldman's past history and we have a sneakin' suspicion that at some time or other, he has tried to pull a Serrano stunt himself.

Feldman has but one ambition—to get a bankroll and then heave his Underwood at the nearest editor's head (I hope I'm not around at the time). He's got a yen to go places an' do things an' if five G will buy him a forty-foot yawl, he expects to pull a Columbus an' head for places unknown. Before he goes, however, we're going to see that he stocks us up with a year's supply of gun-slingin', hell-roarin', high-powered action stuff.

He has asked me to express his thanks and appreciation to all the correspondents of the Eavesdropper for their interesting letters. Good or bad, he can take it on the chin if need be. But if those gobs promise to stop squawking about "Gangsters *vs.* Gobs," he'll turn out another high sea episode and give them all a break.

You'll be seeing Tony's stuff in a lot of issues from now on.

... excerpts from ...

The Eavesdropper

Flowers for Feldman
(and a few weeds)

Gangster Stories, December 1929

Dear Harold:

Glad to see you back in the game! Your Red Band series is a knockout, particularly the GANGSTER STORIES magazine. It has more variety and excitement in it than any other magazine on the market. I liked the quality of romance and glamor that the stories have. It makes them stand out in contrast to the usual underworld stuff one reads.

The novel "Black River" is a corker. Give us some more of Feldman's stuff.

Yours as ever,
HORACE EVANS,
Saranac, N.Y.

Gangster Stories, June-July 1930

Dear Mr. Hersey:

I have been reading GANGSTER STORIES since they first came out. The stories are very interesting, and are written by men who obviously know what they are writing about.

I like Anatole Feldman's stuff best of all. I hope he had a good time in Portugal. If he would write some tales about the Whitechapel District in London, it would sure give the readers some new and pleasant surprises.

The Red Band and the Blue Band Magazines seem to be growing and gaining momentum out here on the West Coast. Well, they deserve their popularity.

CHUCK MARTIN,
Fresno, Cal.

Dear Editor:

I have been reading GANGSTER STORIES ever since it first started, and I thought it was—and is—about the swellest magazine on the stands to-day. And Anatole Feldman is about the greatest writer I know, too.

Good-naturedly yours,
BILL SEYMOUR,
Brooklyn, New York.

Gangster Stories, August 1930

Dear Mr. Hersey:

GANGSTER STORIES is the only mag I ever got a real kick out of. "Tony" Feldman? Is that guy an author? Oh, Boy! Can he write!

Well, so long now, yours for semi-monthly Gangster Mags.

ALBERT BURKE,
110 Eutaw St.,
E. Boston, Mass.

Dear Mr. Hersey:

Since I'm in the writing game myself, I don't ordinarily write editors telling them what I think of stories. But Anatole Feldman's "Serrano of the Stockyards" has made me break my rule.

It's a marvellous story! Wonderful character, action, and plot. Good humor, alternating with tense dramatic action, and at times almost poignant drama. I try to put fast action in my own stories for you, but Feldman's got us all beat!

I'm hoping to see some more novelettes—book-length—about Serrano.

Sincerely,
RICHARD CREDICOTT,
1467 S. Carroll Ave.,
Freeport, Ill.

Dear Mr. Hersey:

I have had the pleasure of reading the Red and Blue Band magazines since first published. The stories are very interesting and are written by authors who know what will keep a reader interested in a story.

I just finished the May issue of GANGSTER STORIES and I wish to praise Anatole Feldman on his good work in writing "The Three Racketeers." It is about the best I have read so far. Let's hear more from Anatole.

WILLIAM LIPSCOMB,

134 Cushing St.,

Providence, R.I.

Gangster Stories, October 1930

Dear Editor:

I am an authorized News Dealer, and have been selling and reading GANGSTER and RACKETEER STORIES magazines, since they first made their appearance. They are now two of the most popular sellers of that class of magazines that I deal in.

Long before they are due on the stands, I have inquiries concerning them. This is what first gave me the idea to read them myself, which I now do, and find them most enjoyable.

I find the months that stories appear by Seymour Rice, Jr. (who incidentally was born and raised in this city), and Anatole Feldman, more copies are sold, than in months when the issues do not contain stories by them. One customer even went so far as to glance at the table of contents, find no tale by Feldman, and Rice, then flatly refused to purchase the magazines.

ISADORE THEODORE COHEN,

12th and McGee,

Kansas City, Missouri.

Gangster Stories, November 1930

Dear Sir:

I like all the stories in GANGSTER STORIES. I read it clear through, without stopping. The best story I read was "Serrano of the Stockyards" by Anatole Feldman, and the Kid Friel stories by Arthur J. Burks.

I wish you would publish all the Blue Band magazines 12 times a year instead of ten times a year.

As ever an ardent reader,

ALEXANDER J. RUSSO,

5050 Argyle St.,

Chicago, Ill.

P.S.—I'm hoping to see some more book-length novelettes about Serrano.

Dear Sir:

I am a reader of GANGSTER STORIES, and I sure do like them. Just my weakness, especially Feldman's stories, as he is my favorite author.

CLEO P. WILLIAMS,
710 E. Church Street,
Tarboro, N.C.

Dear Editor:

Give us some more stories like "Serrano of the Stockyards." I think it was great.

GEORGE L. BAKER,
R.F.D. Box 399,
Fresno, Cal.

Gangster Stories, January 1931

Dear Sir:

Since you invite criticism, you shall have it, because I'm considered quite a critic.

I read a great number of different "mags" because I handle them, and criminal and all detective stories are my favorites; since I started reading GANGSTER, MOBS and GANGLAND, they head the list. Why? Because stories must be exceptionally good, that is, interesting from start to end to satisfy me, with action, mystery and crime.

I'm a member of the International Detective Agency and such stories interest me and also teach me things.

"Serrano of the Stockyards" was good. It wasn't overdone with action or impossible outcomes of such close calls as "The Gang Buster." Anatole Feldman ruined this good story with over action, too much bravado, and entirely too many slang phrases and cuss words. I doubt very much if the gangsters really use such language in real life. Is it necessary to spoil a clean story by using such words as bastard and slut, and also so many lousy crumbs? No doubt many of your readers are girls, youngsters and even ladies. I wonder what they think of Anatole. Cut out the rough language or you'll be ruining your otherwise wonderful stories.

Next to Serrano I like the Kid Friel Stories. They are ok. Then again, there's no "stinking skunks" or "lousy crumbs" to spoil your liking for the story.

I hope this full letter finds space in your "Eavesdropper," and Anatole reads the hints. I'm not a minister's son, nor a little devil, but a critic. Success to your "mag" for cleaner and exciting stories.

TRUEX CUDAHY,
Depew, N.Y.

Gangster Stories, April 1931

Mr. Editor:

Big Nose Serrano used to be a favorite of mine until this last story where I found that he has given the old moll the air, and taken a new one. After how he used to blab about how he loved her. Horse radish, the louse is like all the rest of the punks. Tired of one, chuck her out into the cold and get a new one. Well, Mr. Feldman, Big Nose Serrano is a back number with me. How about writing some good stories with a lot of humor in them. See you on the hot seat.

Sincerely yours,
EDWARD DAVIS,
846 Grand Ave. N.S.
Pittsburgh, Pa.

Gangster Stories, May 1931

Dear Sir:

I read your GANGSTER STORIES and find it very interesting. I sure like the story by Anatole Feldman, "Percy the Gunman." In fact all your stories are good.

I'm a booster from Chicago and proud of it. Here's hoping you have room enough for my letter. I believe all your stories have a kick and a lot of your readers will agree with me.

Yours,
A Steady Booster,
KID POLLACK of Chicago.

Gangster Stories, June 1931

Gentlemen:

Feldman wrote a good story about "Percy the Gunman" in this issue. Please hurry with the next issue so I can read another one of Feldman's stories to my shipmates. I am,

Sincerely yours,
"PICKLES" HEINZ.
(Former all-Navy heavy-weight champ)

Dear Sirs:

Have just finished reading "The Gunless Gunman," by Anatole Feldman and it sure was a wow. Also liked "Final Curtains," by McCandless. Give us more stories like these and we won't fail to buy GANGSTER STORIES.

Yours for success,

JOHN MATHEWS,

920 Texas St.,

Redlands, Cal.

Dear Editor Hersey:

I've been asking for Big Nose Serrano stories right along; this doesn't mean that I fail to enjoy the others as I sure do; I just eat them up; although everyone has some special character that they enjoy better than the others. I have several. Big Nose, Spot Dirk and that fighter whose name I fail to recall at the time being. Shoot more of these in as they are among the best characters you have.

JACK KRONBERG,

150 Mappa Street,

Eau Claire, Wisconsin

Dear Mr. Hersey:

Have been reading GANGSTER and GANGLAND for a long time and would like to say I enjoy your stories so much that I have dropped quite a few other magazines that I used to purchase as regularly.

My favorite author is A. Feldman. I think he is a "wow." "Percy the Gunman" was a swell story.

Wishing you all the success in the world, I remain

A constant reader,

STANLEY JACOWSKI,

110 Sussex St.,

Jersey City, N.J.

Gangster Stories, July 1931

Dear Sir:

I just finished reading February GANGSTER STORIES and I got a thrill out of every story. I liked "The Gunless Gunman" best although they were all good. Give us more of Tony Feldman's stories. They can't be beat.

Yours sincerely,

FRANCES EMBRY,

7401 Huntley St.,

Tampa, Florida.

Gangster Stories, September 1931

Dear Editor:

"Gun Glory," by Anatole Feldman, was a swell story but I always feel as though I can depend upon good old Anatole to give us something good.

Just another Frail looking for a thrill,

PEGGY VANDER,
Baltimore, N.C.

Dear Friends:

"Dames, Dice and the Devil" is a fine story, a good moral.

Sincerely,
IRISH MAC,
Washington, D.C.

Dear Sirs:

I have been a steady reader of your GANGSTER, GANGLAND, and RACKETEER magazines. I especially like stories of Big Nose Serrano—he is Red-Hot. Why don't you write more stories of him? I think everyone will agree with me that he is a swell character.

Yours respectfully,
WILLIAM FRANKS,
Port Huron, Mich.

Dear Editor:

I just finished reading the May issue of GANGSTER STORIES and I think it was a swell number. I never miss an issue for I get more of a thrill out of this mag than I do from any other book.

I'm just a girl, 23 years of age, but believe me, my brothers knew what they were talking about when they told me to read GANGSTER STORIES. I like Feldman's stories the best, because you never know what is going to happen next. Well, more power to your magazines,

I am,
EMMA RAISH,
Onalaska, Winnipeg.

Gangster Stories, November 1931

Dear Mr. Editor:

I am a consistent reader of GANGSTER STORIES and have just finished your September issue.

Anatole Feldman seems to be just a little off stride this month with "Legacy of Crime," while George Allan Moffatt scores first with "The Punk."

I find that Mr. Feldman will be with us again next month and also Big Nose Serrano, more power to both of them.

Respectfully,

CHAS. H. JAQUAYS,

1211 N. Park St.,

Kalamazoo, Michigan.

Dear Sir:

I like Feldman, Margie Harris and Burkholder in the order named: Feldman for his wildness of plot, Harris for her logical, well planned and well written stories, and Burkholder for his naturalness.

Yours truly,

C.M. AKERS.

Dear Sir:

I am a constant reader of GANGSTER STORIES and I am very much interested in them.

The last one I read was perfect. I liked the story "Spawn of the Spider" by Anatole Feldman. That story, I thought, was the best I have ever read yet, and I read every month's issue.

I remain,

WILLIAM COOKE,

104 Sabin St.,

Pawtucket, R.I.

Gangster Stories, December 1931

Dear Hersey:

Your October issue of GANGSTER STORIES sure was a wow. All the stories were great but I liked Feldman's latest Serrano story the best.

Keep up the quality and quantity of your stories and you'll have a steady reader as long as you live (that is, as long as the magazine lives and I hope that'll be forever).

A TRUE FRIEND,

From Houston, Texas.

Dear Editor:

I am an honest to goodness GANGSTER STORIES reader and admit there is none better. It's really the "Canary's Eyebrows" and I don't mean "if." I only wish it were a weekly magazine so I could read good stuff straight through. I don't think there has ever been a story in your mag that needs to be criticized.

Well here's hoping you come back with a lot more of Anatole Feldman stories, they're hot stuff.

Another Booster,
ROBERT HOFFMAN,
27 Harlon Ave.,
Rosslyn, Va.

Editor, Ole Kid:

I've read some issues of GANGSTER STORIES and they *are* great.

I've finished reading the August issue, and am anxious to obtain the next issues. "The Spawn of the Spider" by Anatole Feldman was Okee Tokee and I haven't a single criticism to make about it.

Why don't you put in air stories about gangsters? Hoping you do,

Yours,
ADOLPH KIRBELIS,
13 Seneca St.,
Pittsburgh, Pa.

Dear Ed:

I'll have to give Tony Feldman a big hand for that yarn, "Legacy of Crime."

I'd like to meet Tony Feldman in the street, he's all right, but the more a guy gives me the more I want.

Yours Truly,
BABY CANNONBALL COLLIE,
Newark, N.J.

P.S. Two of Tony Feldman's stories are worth a buck—as "Legacy of Crime" and "Dames, Dice and the Devil."

Gangster Stories, January 1932

Dear Sir:

I am a constant reader of your magazine and like your stories very much; in fact, those written by Anatole Feldman are great. Wishing your GANGSTER STORIES the best of success,

I remain,
Yours truly,
WILLIAM ZIMATH.

Dear Sir:

Have been a reader of GANGSTER STORIES, GANGLAND and RACKETEER for over a year and, after reading one, look forward to the next issue. The stories in these magazines are cleverly written, intensely interesting and in many ways true to our present everyday life.

Have just finished reading GANGSTER STORIES for October, and think "The Undertaker Calls" is unusually clever and different from the usual run of stories. "Horses, Hoboes and Heroes" with the return of Big Nose Serrano is a peach of a story. Let us have more of these. Serrano is a great character.

Why don't you publish your magazines twice a month? I am sure such a plan would go over big.

> A "Smoky City" Booster,
> MORLEY C. ROBINSON,
> 6533 Shetland Ave.,
> Pittsburgh, Pa.

Dear Mr. Hersey:

Feldman's "Horses, Hoboes and Heroes" is a masterpiece.

> FREDERICK A. PLOURD,
> c/o Gen. Del.,
> Malden, Mass.

Gangster Stories, February 1932

Dear Sir:

I just want to let you know how much I appreciated Mr. Feldman's story. From time to time, we in this country get small items of news concerning a shooting in one or two of your big cities. Judging from these items and Mr. Feldman's story, I think they are just about level on points. I'd nearly forgotten. The story I mean is "Heels of Industry," in the May issue. Anyone would have to go a long way to read a story as good as that, and if any of your discontented readers want better—well, words fail me.

Will you do me the favor of printing this letter, and let your regular readers see what an outsider thinks of your magazine.

> Yours sincerely,
> "AN ENGLISH READER,"
> Battersea, S.W. 11,
> London, England.

Editor, Gangland:

Having read practically every gangster magazine on the stands, I have come to the conclusion that the Blue Bands are the best. My favorite author is Tony Feldman. His "Percy the Gunman" was the best story I've ever read.

Well, here's to the success of the Blue Band.

Sincerely,

MR. ARTHUR SALINA,

21 West Smith St.,

Iron Mt., Mich.

Dear Sir:

I have been reading the mag you publish for about four months, but you never heard from me because I don't like to argue. I like to stay on the sidelines and listen to the chin music.

Having tried all three of your mags. I know what I'm talking about when I say your books are swell, but sometimes your writers lay down on the job and write a lot of lousy junk.

Feldman is my pet author and you did not have him in this issue. It burned me up. "Black Ice" was swell and "King Joe Dies" was good but the flatfeet took the spotlight in the end and I don't like it.

EDW. PALOWSKI,

THE "POLOCK."

1414 W. Division St.,

Ed. Note—Don't burn up, Eddie, because here's Tony Feldman back with us again in this issue and he's bigger and better'n ever!

Gangster Stories, March 1932

Dear Editor:

Well, here's to "Big Nose" and GANGSTER STORIES, the magazine with a lesson in every story.

HOWARD NYBERG,

807 N. Perry Ave,

Peoria, Ill.

Dear Ed.:

I've been reading GANGSTER STORIES for the last couple of years, but lately they all write about Anatole Feldman. I'll admit he's good but he can't beat C.B. Yorke when he writes about "Queen Sue." More luck to Mr. Yorke and his "Queen Sue" novels. I am a booster for C.B. Yorke.

A READER FROM

St. Paul, Minn.

Dear Editor:

I don't know of anyone better at writing GANGSTER STORIES than Anatole Feldman. Boy, how he does write!

Yours truly
CLARENCE TUSEN,
Columbus Ave.,
Albert Lea, Minnesota.

Gangster Stories, April 1932

Dear Editor:

I am writing these few lines to ask your advice regarding a matter of "Death or Thanks," and hope that you will help me make a right decision.

You see Ed. it was like this, last night, December 31, 1931, I bought a copy of the February issue of GANGSTER STORIES at the news stand, and came home. I bathed, dressed and had dinner, then because it was only 9:30 p.m. I sat down and started to glance through GANGSTER STORIES. The first story was "Hell-Bent for Election," by Anatole Feldman. Well I was going to a New Year's party, but it did not begin until about 11 p.m., so I said to myself, "Well I'll just start this story and see what Big Nose Serrano is up to this month."

I started to read—and about thirty minutes ago—I heard people shouting and auto horns blowing—I looked up quick and hell it was midnight. Now Ed. I missed out on a swell party, but maybe if I had gone to the party I'd have got drunk, or maybe I'd have drunk some poison booze, but then again if I'd have gone I might have met some swell red-haired moll, so I don't know whether I should put Anatole Feldman on the "spot" or give him a vote of thanks.

Please help me to make a decision, also allow me to wish you a very happy and prosperous New Year! And now you'll pardon me I'm sure—for I must scram into bed and read Margie Harris' "Squeeze Play," also C.B. Yorke's "Business at Midnight," for if anyone knows how to write a story that will hold one spell bound, Anatole Feldman, Margie Harris and C.B. Yorke are the ones. I call them, "The Unbeatable Three!" Happy New Year to them all!

Sincerely,
"A Lover of Good Stories!"
R.W. LEE,
1470 Main Street,
Hartford, Conn.

Gangster Stories, May 1932

Dear Sir:

I have just finished reading the February issue of GANGSTER STORIES. It is the best number I have read since the January issue. The story that is the berries is "Big Nose Serrano." That guy has enough guts for three, and the way he handles a mob is nobody's business.

GANGSTER STORIES is interesting and thrilling. It also shows what a gangster is up against beside the bulls. You can give him credit for one important thing however, and that is he will stick by his pals.

Yours truly,

JOSEPHINE WILLIAMS,

405 Russell St.,

Hammond, Indiana.

Dear Editor:

I get a big kick out of your mag an' get one every time I can spare two bits. Just got through reading the January issue and had a big laugh reading it, especially the ex-racketeer's letter to "Eavesdropper." I have often noticed that generally Big Nose Serrano is well liked. I think he packs a wallop. Please give us more of this guy.

A.E. VADNOIS,

8282 Belmont,

Detroit, Mich.

Hello, Everybody:

This is Helen Costello. Just a word to Tony Feldman. Atta boy, honey, you're right after my own heart. I read your stories every time there is one in the Blue Band mag, or to be plainer, I mean your gangster mag.

"Hell-Bent for Election" is the best story I've ever read and bless yo' heart, honey, I've read plenty of 'em in my twenty-one years. I would sure like to see your "Hell-Bent for Election" on the moving picture screen, that I would.

So give us more about Big Nose Serrano. Hot pants and all. Thanks for listening.

MISS HELEN COSTELLO,

4012 North Ashland Blvd.,

Chicago, Ill.

Gangster Stories, June 1932

Dear Editor:

After reading GANGSTER STORIES for over a year I can sincerely say that GANGSTER STORIES comes out every month with the cream of the crime stories. When I finished reading your present issue, with such excellent stories like "Hell-Bent for Election," and "Business at Midnight," all I could say was oboyoboyoboy.

I believe your magazine is performing a public duty by taking the glitter and romance out of crime and showing it up as it really is. A good many of the gunmen and gangsters of today are under twenty-one. Most of them would have stayed out of the racket if they had known what they were going up against.

My favorite authors are C.B. Yorke, Anatole Feldman, and Margie Harris. I'm positive that these are the ace writers today of crime stories.

I first came across GANGSTER STORIES in a police station where I had gone to get out a pal. It's so good even the cops read it!

Very truly,
SAM EPSTEIN,
1705 South 2nd St.,
Philadelphia, Pa.

Dear Editor:

Geez! What a mag. Where'd yuh git it anyway? It's the grandest mag out. I have just finished my first copy. That novelette "Hell-Bent for Election," by Anatole Feldman was a knockout.

Very truly yours,
HARVEY S. SLAY,
2725 Stockton St.,
Winston-Salem, N.C.

P.S. Why not publish GANGSTER STORIES weekly?

Dear Sir:

Lately I have become interested in a new hobby. Yes, you guessed it! I sure fell for those red-hot stories in your gangster mag.

Believe it or not, the "Head of the House" said that reading those stories would influence my own mind toward the gang idea, but, no kidding, it does just the opposite by giving you the real low down on the "Crime doesn't pay" angle.

Not very often can an author make a hero from such as "Big Nose Serrano," but when he is put in the light of the gang-buster he deserves a salute from anyone, so here's mine, Anatole Feldman.

You sure rate with the other writers of GANGSTER STORIES and I will sure keep buying mags as long as you keep up to snuff with your future stories.

Respectfully yours,
JACK LAURITZEN,
704 Mfg. Bldg.,
c/o A.L. Barnett, Pitts., Penna.

Greater Gangster Stories, April 1933

Dear Editor:

Received my February issue of GANGSTER STORIES, and was more than pleased with the great stories it contained. Anxiously awaiting "The Crime Crusade," the sequel to "Hell-Bent for Election."

Wishing you continued good luck and success, I remain, as ever, a true Gangster Fan.

> Faithfully yours,
> FREDERICK A. PLOURD
> Rear 89 Madison St.,
> Malden, Mass.

Dear Sir:

I just want to let you know what a wow your books are. Especially the stories written by Feldman. Boy, oh boy, they sure give me a thrill. In fact I read almost all the books you publish. If I had to starve to get the dough to buy your books, I'd do it. May your books be printed forever.

> MARY.

Greater Gangster Stories, June 1933

Hello, Everybody:

This is Edward Blair. Just a word to Tony Feldman. Atta boy, baby—you're right after my own heart. I read your stories every time GREATER GANGSTER STORIES has one in it. "Little Big Shot" is by far the best story I've ever read and bless your heart, baby, I've read plenty in the forty years of my life. I would sure like to see "Little Big Shot" on the moving picture screen, that I would. So give us some more stories like "Little Big Shot" and "Suicide Sal."

> Yours truly,
> WILLIAM BLAIR,
> 850 London Road,
> Bridgeton, Glasgow,
> Scotland.

Dear Editor:

I've searched all over for a magazine that tells all of the interesting angles of gangland. But I won't have to worry any longer. GREATER GANGSTER STORIES fills the bill perfectly. You've got two of the best writers I've ever read, I mean John Gerard and Tony Feldman. Keep them working their typewriters overtime and you'll always sell plenty of magazines. Anyway you can depend on me for a sure sale every month. Keep up the good work.

Yours truly,
FRANK RIORDON,
Detroit, Michigan.

Dear Editor:

Wow! What a pack of reading matter GREATER GANGSTER STORIES has for March. The only trouble with you palookas is this—GREATER GANGSTER STORIES should be a twice-a-month publication. It keeps a guy chewin' his nails tryin' to keep hopped up until the next GREATER GANGSTER issue.

You can tell Anatole Feldman for me that he pushes a mean pen and what I mean, he's one great big angel. Margie Harris also is a honey. I'll bet when she starts with that old typewriter it's curtains for someone. Her latest success, "Always a Gent," has a great big wallop, too.

I've been readin' GREATER GANGSTER for nearly three years and haven't missed a single issue. So keep 'em comin' and comin' fast.

Respectfully,
AL R. OSBORNE,
204 6th Avenue So.,
Fargo, North Dakota.

Dear Mr. Editor:

I am taking this opportunity to ask a favor of "Anatole Feldman" and "you."

I have been following Big Nose Serrano's record very closely, and although he is a racketeer of the higher grade, I notice that he is always out to help the kiddies—and the poor.

Now, Mr. Editor, our country has fallen into a very deplorable condition, our politicians are crooked, our poor are starving, a great percentage of our fellow citizens are classed as criminals because they sell liquor, and our youths are turning into dope fiends and vicious killers, and all because of prohibition.

Couldn't Mr. Feldman persuade Big Nose Serrano and his very able assistant, Charlie LeBrett, to start a real honest-to-God campaign for the repeal of the 18th Amendment?

Think of the millions of people that it would put back to work—breweries, glass factories, bottle works, bartenders, waiters, musicians.

I know that you and Mr. Feldman could persuade Big Nose Serrano to help us out.

As ever,
RALPH W. LEE,
79 Mulberry St.,
Hartford, Conn.

Greater Gangster Stories, July 1933

Dear Editor:

Why don't you give us a story by Anatole Feldman every month? Listen, that mug can write and how. After seeing his picture I know WHY he can turn out better gangster stories than anyone else. Why, oh, why can't we have at least one story a month by this master of the art?

ART JORDON,
Birmingham, Alabama.

Dear Ed:

If you'll pardon my English I'd like to tell you mugs that I think you're just plain lousy. Where do you get that stuff—GREATER GANGSTER STORIES? Say, I could write better gangster stories myself. You guys must be a soft lot—why I've got a kid sister who's ten times as tough as most of the mugs in your stories. Anatole Feldman and Margie Harris know a little bit about the real gangsters, but most of the others must have received their training in a wet nursery. Come on, let's have some real blood and thunder stories or I'll have to go back to reading fairy tales for excitement.

"BLACKIE" BRANNON,
Butte, Montana.

Greater Gangster Stories, August 1933

Ye Editor:

I've got two things to be thankful for. GREATER GANGSTER STORIES is back and so is real beer. I'm not sure which one I like best, but I'm telling you that they're both the real goods. Say, when I finished Feldman's "In the Bag" I was going 'round and 'round. What a smashing ending that had—just like an O. Henry story. Shake that guy's hand for me—he sure can write a great yarn. I hope you have at least one story by Feldman every month. And don't forget about Margie Harris either. She's got the stuff, too.

Yours truly,
EUGENE BROWNSON,
Albany, New York.

Dear Editor:

This is the first time I have ever written to an editor to tell him what I think of a magazine, but I'm so enthused about GREATER GANGSTER that I've just got to get this off my chest. First I think Margie Harris and Parke Levy are natural story-tellers. They have something to say and know how to say it. For some reason I didn't like Anatole Feldman's "In the Bag." Maybe

I'm wrong, but that's the way it struck me. I don't mean to tell you how to run your own magazine, but I would like to suggest that you use nothing but straight gangster stories with all gangster characters. Gang war—that's what we like.

Keep your hand on your rod and keep right on ripping out great magazines.

Luck,
BILLY MARKS,
Jersey City, N.J.

Ye Editor of Gangster:

I suppose you receive many letters telling you what a swell story writer that guy Tony Feldman is. Well, this letter isn't going to be any different, other than to pan you for not having him write a whole issue once in a while. If you would let Tony write an issue one month and Margie Harris and Walt Dinghall the next month I would be satisfied.

This gangster stuff is interesting to read about, but don't ever get the idea that I have ambitions of becoming one. I have a good job with a fruit company and make trips to South America about every other month, and let me tell you I see plenty of tough eggs in my racket. It's fun to read your mag and compare the lousy mugs I know to the characters in GANGSTER. Keep up your work . . . it's entertaining.

WALTER I. PERAZZA,
Tampa, Florida.

Greater Gangster Stories, September 1933

Dear Editor:

The type of gangster story I like best is gang wars with a good newshound in it, crooked politicians and real honest to goodness detectives. Something like Tony Feldman's "Big Nose" Serrano stories. They're hot and how!

Well here's wishing lots of luck to GREATER GANGSTER STORIES.

Yours truly,
JOHN OBESTER,
Dunlo, Pa.

Dear Editor:

My search for a real honest-to-goodness thrilling blood-thirsty gangster story magazine has centered around GREATER GANGSTER STORIES. The stories are just the kind I enjoy, and best of all your new feature of real gangster chiefs is a ten strike. My favorite author is Anatole Feldman and my favorite gangster Al Capone. I have only one kick to register and that is please do not inject too much sex into the stories. Gangsters have their love affairs, but do not describe such things too fervently.

I have tried hard to find, unsuccessfully, something important to complain about.

Please give us sane, probable stories with just the average number of killings and please do not make all cops on the beat dumb and flat-footed and all crooks deformed and ugly.

Sincerely,

BENJAMIN CHESTER CWALINA,

744 N. Kenwood Ave.,

Baltimore, Md.

Greater Gangster Stories, November 1933

Editor:

I particularly liked that story—"Gun Gospel," by Anatole Feldman. He's a great writer, he is. Mother says he writes a lot for your magazine, and she is crazy about his stories. Well, I'm goin' to like him too, and that is saying a lot, from me.

Sincerely yours,

HAROLD G. WOODWARD,

903 Gates Street,

Columbia, South Carolina.

Greater Gangster Stories, December 1933

Dear Sirs:

I have heard some of my friends remark that twenty-five cents is too much to pay for any magazine. My answer to that statement is, a person gets just what he pays for and your magazine proves that statement is true. The stories are superb and offer one much knowledge on the life of the gangster, his environment and the hardships he has to contend with in orienting himself to the life of ruthless killing, proving the old adage, that crime doesn't pay. I have just finished reading your November issue and find all the stories within merit my approval. I'm glad to see that Anatole Feldman is offering another Big Nose Serrano story in your next issue, and I can truthfully say I'll be looking forward to reading it when it arrives on the stands.

Just an Ardent Reader,

J.B. MARTIN,

1558 Hunter Ave.,

Columbus, Ohio.

Dear Editor:

This is my first letter to your magazine and you can bet your life it isn't my last, for I am sure that there isn't another magazine on the market that can compare with yours. I have been reading this magazine ever since it began and I certainly hope I will continue to read it forever. I especially want to read "The Return of Big Nose Serrano" by Anatole Feldman. I would gladly pay even more than the usual amount if I only could get a copy of the issue. Please let me know how I can receive one.

Wishing you the best of luck and happiness, and hoping to hear from you, I am,

> KIKI UTIENI,
> 584 Morris Ave.,
> New York City.

Greetings, Editor:

I am a regular reader of your magazine and I thought I would sit down and give you my opinion of GREATER GANGSTER STORIES. Your magazine is my choice from the hundreds on the stands and I want to thank the best staff of editors in the business.

I like Anatole Feldman best of all. He turns them out with a real bang.

> Yours as a reader reads it,
> JACK TENCZAR,
> Jewett City, Conn.

Greater Gangster Stories, February 1934

Dear Editor:

The story I like best in the December issue is "The Door of Death" by James Franklyn. The next best story was "N.R.A.—No Rats Allowed" by Anatole Feldman. There is always some one who is trying to work against it and it is interesting for people to read this story because the man who wrote it is trying to prove to the people that you have to line up with the N.R.A. People trying to work against it defeat their own ends sooner or later.

> Sincerely,
> MR. ELMER GREEN,
> 8½ Park Street,
> Cortland, N.Y.

Dear Editor:

Your "N.R.A.—No Rats Allowed" by Anatole Feldman sure "clicked" with me . . . modern as some of these d—— futuristic furniture and with just about as many odd and interesting quips and twists.

Yours truly,
F.M. LE MAL,
1526 Henrietta Street,
Pekin, Ill.

Dear Editor:

I bought GREATER GANGSTER STORIES more by chance than anything else, but believe you me I'll be a regular reader from now on.

I liked "N.R.A.—No Rats Allowed" better than any other story. I don't think I've ever read a more timely or a better story in any magazine. The other stories all pleased me but Anatole Feldman's was best of all.

GREATER GANGSTER STORIES has made a new friend.

Yours truly,
JAMES CONWAY,
Milwaukee, Wisconsin.

Dear Editor:

Your December issue of GREATER GANGSTER STORIES was a pip. I enjoyed every story and find it hard to tell you which one I liked best. "N.R.A.—No Rats Allowed" by Anatole Feldman is without a doubt one of the finest stories I have ever read in any magazine. Anatole Feldman certainly knows his gangland.

Suggestions? I can't make any except that I hope you keep right on giving us the fine stories you always have—that's my answer. Keep up the good work.

Sincerely,
HAROLD MARTIN,
Detroit, Michigan.

Dear Sirs:

I have been a constant reader of GREATER GANGSTER STORIES for some time now and I am taking this opportunity to tell you how much I appreciate your magazine.

I think Anatole Feldman, Margie Harris and Walt S. Dinghall are the best authors I have ever read. They know what they are writing about and how to write it.

MARION WEST,
Louisville, Ky.

Dear Editor:

So Anatole Feldman has joined the NRA? Swell. "No Rats Allowed" was a splendid story, and Big Nose Serrano got a "great big hand" from me when he turned out all that nice bread and them lusty cheers for the good old NRA. This story had just enough humor in it to make it very savory, and I reveled in it.

MRS. FRED B. GIBSON,
Columbia, S.C.

Greater Gangster Stories, March 1934

Dear Editor:

I have just finished reading your January issue and it is the best ever. Let's have more of the characters Milly McNaught and Spunky Alden. Bring them back on police or Federal work—anything, only give us more stories with them in it. No story I have ever read before had so much action packed into it. Frank Seaton certainly outdid himself on that last story, "When Spunky Hit Redbank."

For once Anatole Feldman has been outdone in packing thrills and action into a story and that doesn't happen very often. "Nuff said!"

P.S. How's chances of another Serrano story by Feldman?

Respectfully yours,
A.G. ADAMS,
48 Danforth Street,
Portland, Maine.

Dear Editor:

I had some trouble getting your December issue of GREATER GANGSTER STORIES but when I finally got it I was fully repaid. It was a wow.

I am decidedly against serials; they become too monotonous. But I am in favor of a series of stories such as the Big Nose Serrano ones. It takes me at least one story to get acquainted with a character and after I do I feel as though I knew him personally.

RICHARD MOLDEN,
2404 Cedar Street,
Sioux City, Iowa.

Greater Gangster Stories, May 1934

Dear Editor:

I've just put your March issue of GREATER GANGSTER STORIES down and I want to tell you that I've never enjoyed any issue of any magazine quite so much as I did that number. Anatole Feldman's "Born To Kill" sets a new high in gangster stories. Boy, how that baby can write. I liked Walt. S. Dinghall's "King Mob" next best. He's another old favorite who never fails to come through with a thriller that is a thriller.

Keep up the good work and although the gangster as such has disappeared from our midst GREATER GANGSTER STORIES will continue to be a best seller.

Sincerely,

HAROLD TREADWELL,

Detroit, Michigan.

Dear Editor:

What's happened to Anatole Feldman? Here he was the star author on our list and he turns out a punk story like "Born To Kill." I can't understand it at all. Maybe I'm wrong but I certainly didn't like that story.

"King Mob" and "Ballots In Blood" were more to my liking. I'd forgive any other author except Feldman but somehow his turning in a bad story is unforgivable. Until Tony Feldman turns out another Big Nose Serrano story I'm disgusted.

Yours truly,

BETTIE GOODHEART,

Denver, Colorado.

Dear Editor:

Well, Big Guy, you've done it again. Yessir, you've hit the nail right on the head. I read every story in your March issue and I haven't a single kick coming. Two bits is a lot of money these days but you can just bet your shirt that you guys give us our money's worth. You make some of those stories in other magazines look like kid stuff.

My favorite author is now and always has been Anatole Feldman. Next comes Margie Harris—and I liked the March issue even though she didn't have a story in it.

Luck to the Big Guy,

FRANKLIN CROMSON,

Duluth, Minn.

Dear Big Guy:

You asked for criticism so I'm going to give it to you. Now don't get me wrong when I say that I didn't like your March issue. I still liked it better than any other magazine on the stands but I don't think it measured up to what GREATER GANGSTER STORIES has always stood for. I didn't like John Gerard's "Ballots In Blood"; and I didn't think Tony Feldman's "Born To Kill" was up to par. The shorter stories were all right, but just all right.

You can do better,

BILL DALEY,

Louisville, Ky.

Dear Editor:

Just a quick line to tell you what a swell book you've got in GREATER GANGSTER STORIES. I buy it religiously and my one hope is that this fiction book will live long. Say hello to my author friend Tony Feldman—he's a real writer.

Yours truly,
SAM WHEELER,
Los Angeles, Calif.

The Big Nose Serrano Stories

Gangster Stories	Title	Words
1 1930 May	Serrano of the Stockyards	24,400
2 1930 October	The Gang Buster	27,200
3 1931 February	The Gunless Gunman	23,500
4 1931 June	Dames, Dice and the Devil	27,500
5 1931 October	Horses, Hoboes and Heroes	28,700
6 1932 February	Hell-Bent for Election	23,100
7 1932 March	The Crime Crusade	30,000
8 1932 July	Hangman's Holiday	21,500
1932 November (duplicated issue)	Hangman's Holiday	
Greater Gangster Stories		
9 1933 September	The Return of Serrano	24,600
10 1933 December	N.R.A.—No Rats Allowed	15,200
11 1934 April	Hell's Gangster	22,100
The Gang Magazine		
12 1935 May	Lead and Lyrics	11,000
Total		280,000

OFF-TRAIL PUBLICATIONS
Specializing in the era of American pulp fiction

THE WEIRD DETECTIVE ADVENTURES OF WADE HAMMOND
By Paul Chadwick
Volume 1: 10 stories, 180 pages, $18
Volume 2: 10 stories, 172 pages, $18
Volume 3: 10 stories, 202 pages, $18
Volume 4: 9 stories, 232 pages, $18

> *The Wade Hammond stories complete in four volumes. In these chilling adventures, all from the classic 1930's pulps,* Detective-Dragnet *and* Ten Detective Aces, *freelance investigator Wade Hammond battles a series of weird enemies. Some of the best of 1930's pulp fiction.*

DOCTOR COFFIN: THE LIVING DEAD MAN
By Perley Poore Sheehan • Introduction by John Wooley
8 novelettes, 178 pages, $16

> *Weird stories from* Thrilling Detective, *1932-33. A former character actor who faked his own death, Doctor Coffin runs a string of mortuaries by night and fights crime at night. One of the strangest detective series.*

SUPER-DETECTIVE FLIP BOOK: TWO COMPLETE NOVELS
From the pulp *Super-Detective*:
"Legion of Robots" (November 1940) by Victor Rousseau • Introduction by John McMahan •• "Murder's Migrants" (March 1943) by Robert Leslie Bellem and W.T. Ballard • Introduction by John Wooley
2 short novels, 174 pages, $18

> Super-Detective *started as a Doc Savage-like adventure pulp, then changed format to hardboiled detective. The* Flip Book *features a novel from each of the two phases with intros exploring the historical background. Exciting!*

PULPWOOD DAYS: VOL 1: EDITORS YOU WANT TO KNOW
Edited by John Locke • 180 pages, $16

Numerous articles from the writers' magazines by and about pulp editors, with ample biographical profiles. Editors include: Frank E. Blackwell (Detective Story, Western Story), Ray Palmer (Amazing Stories, Fantastic Adventures), Robert A.W. Lowndes (Columbia Publications), Edwin Baird (Weird Tales, Detective Tales), and many more.

GANG PULP
Edited by John Locke • 19 stories, 294 pages, $24

Hardboiled stories of the criminal underworld from the first year (1929-30) of the gang pulps: Gangster Stories, Racketeer Stories, etc. These violent tales came under immediate censorship pressure; the history is explored in an in-depth essay. "A remarkable work of popular-culture scholarship"—Mystery Scene, Fall 2008.

THE GANGLAND SAGAS OF BIG NOSE SERRANO
Volume 1: DAMES, DICE AND THE DEVIL
Volume 2: HORSES, HOBOES AND HEROES
By Anatole Feldman • Introductions by Will Murray
Each: 4 novels, 266 pages, $20

The first two volumes (of three) of the Big Nose Serrano novels from Gangster Stories, 1930-32. Feldman was the best of the gang pulp authors, and Big Nose was his most inspired creation, the berserking king of Chicago gangsters.

THE CITY OF BAAL

By Charles Beadle • Introduction by John Locke
7 stories, 240 pages, $20

> *Authentic stories of African adventure from an author who had traveled the lands he wrote about. Lost cities, strange tribes, jungle magic. Six stories from* Adventure *(1918-22) and one from* The Frontier *(1925).*

CULT OF THE CORPSES

By Maxwell Hawkins • Introduction by John Locke
2 novelettes, 150 pages, $13.95

> *Two weird detective stories from* Detective-Dragnet *(1931) by a forgotten master. Introduction discusses the weird-detective trend of the early '30s, and the career of Maxwell Hawkins.*

THE OCEAN: 100TH ANNIVERSARY COLLECTION

Edited by John Locke
20 stories, 234 pages, $18

> *Munsey's* The Ocean *(1907-08) was one of the first specialized pulps, a sea-story magazine. The best adventure stories are included here, along with 30+ pages of nonfiction material: a history of the pulp, and extensive author profiles.*

FROM GHOULS TO GANGSTERS
THE CAREER OF ARTHUR B. REEVE

Edited by John Locke

Vol 1 (fiction): 21 stories, 264 pages, $20 • **Vol 2 (nonfic)**: 260 pages, $20

> *Reeve was the leading American detective-story writer of the early 20th Century, with his scientific detective, Craig Kennedy. The astonishing breadth of his career is explored for the first time here. Vol 1 includes a cross-sction of fiction from all phases of career, including many never-before-reprinted pulp stories. Vol 2 provides a 40-page biography; an extensive Art Gallery of cover repros, interior illos, ads, etc; a 75-page guide to Reeve's work in all media; and more. An "excellent piece of scholarship"—*MYSTERY SCENE, *Spring 2008.*

AMAZON STORIES
Volume 1: PEDRO & LOURENÇO
Volume 2: PEDRO & LOURENÇO
By Arthur O. Friel • Introductions by John Locke
Vol 1: 10 stories, 222 pages, $18 • **Vol 2**: 10, stories, 286 pages, $20
   Collects Friel's first twenty stories from Adventure *(1919-21), following
   the strange experiences of two Amazon Basin rubber workers as they
   explore the jungle. The best of pulp adventure fiction.*

Shipping: $3.00 media mail; $6.00 priority
Check or MO to:
Off-Trail Publications
2036 Elkhorn Road, Castroville, CA 95012
Paypal: offtrail@redshift.com

www.ingramcontent.com/pod-product-compliance
Lightning Source LLC
Chambersburg PA
CBHW030331030726
47499CB00003B/724